A Broken Clock Never Boils

C.J. Weiss

ISBN: 979-8-9864877-0-0 (paperback)
ISBN: 979-8-9864877-1-7 (ebook)

Inquiries may be sent via email to business@cjweiss.com.

To my parents, for always supporting me and letting me find my
own path.
To my siblings and extended family, for a home everlasting.
To my friends, for providing sanity in a mad world.
And to my wife, for redefining the meaning of love.

CHAPTER 1

Depression and loneliness fed off one another, a snake eating its tail in an endless loop of misery. Dr. Claire Rossi wanted nothing more than to yank that scaly tail from her patient's mouth. She wanted to cure Diane Shapiro's woes with a snap of her fingers. Unfortunately, she could only wait. Ms. Shapiro needed to understand her condition herself before making further progress. Claire's frustration, stirred by not knowing a faster treatment, itched at her forefinger. She dug her nail into the armrest of her contemporary chair and released. Quick, sudden, over in an instant.

Ms. Shapiro hadn't seen. She was absorbed in her own thoughts. Slumped shoulders. A crestfallen stare. Limp arms in her lap. Amid the silent interlude, Claire brainstormed how to speed things along. Research topics entered and fled her mind. She played out both sides of multiple conversations. Then her mom interrupted with her personal brand of wisdom. *Patience comes to those who wait.* Claire suppressed making a fist. Her patient was only a little younger than her mom would have been.

Should have been.

Ms. Shapiro looked up, rescuing Claire from her rising bitterness. "Why do I feel this way, Dr. Rossi?"

Claire smiled, mirroring the broad expression by which she chose to remember her mother. "Breaking the cycle of depression takes time to retrain your brain. I'm confident that together we'll find the right approach to help you. Last week, you said you work remotely?"

"That's right. To save money, a couple of years ago they closed my office and moved everyone they didn't lay off to work from home. I was just happy they kept me on the team." Ms. Shapiro grabbed a fresh water bottle from the end table. She snapped its seal, settling back into her choice of two sage-colored patient seats. Short brown hair paved the way for thick glasses which overwhelmed her face. Long shirt sleeves crept over her wrists.

"Do you see anyone during the day?" Claire smoothed stray dirty blonde hairs behind her ear, brushing the top of a modest dress on the way to the legal pad in her lap. *Rationalizing Isolation* topped today's session notes.

"Not since Abby moved away," Ms. Shapiro mumbled, her head sinking. She spent most of last session discussing her former neighbor, perhaps her only true friend.

"That's understandable." Claire motioned for her patient to straighten herself—the confidence cheat they added last week—and waited until she did so. "Do you keep in touch with your coworkers?"

Ms. Shapiro, reluctant to answer, choked, "Not since the layoffs. I miss them too."

Bingo. Now she needed a push to connect the dots.

Claire leaned in, hands clasped together. She hung over the plain rug that created an intimate space within the larger room. "Have you considered reaching out to them?"

"A few times, but it gets harder whenever I think about it. Two of them lost their jobs, poor things. I didn't want to rub it in their faces that I kept mine." She shook her head, started slouching then righted herself. "And when I met Abby I sort of forgot about them. Does that make me a bad person?"

Guilt joined the ever-expanding notes.

"You're not a bad person, Diane. It's difficult to maintain friendships when a common interest such as work disappears. Nobody is to blame." Gestures complemented her reassurances. Aiding Ms. Shapiro wasn't particularly challenging, but it improved the world by the measure of one more person. "We can feel a loss of control when we lose something precious, such as co-workers or a friend who moved. This can compound and create distress, but your feelings are natural. If you distilled your negative emotions into one root cause, what would it be?"

Ms. Shapiro hunkered into her seat like a turtle retreating into her shell. Her fingers fidgeted with her sleeves. Melancholy thoughts painted her expression. She bottled her emotions, acting contrary to her interests. As Claire backtracked to where she went wrong, Ms. Shapiro woke from her introspection with a snivel. Watered eyes spilled onto her cheeks.

"I'm alone." She reached for the tissue box and dabbed at the tears.

Good. Loneliness was healthy. Loneliness was normal. Loneliness could be cured with tangible remedies, cracked and torn asunder. Or at least splintered enough to shine a light on her depression. One step closer to a solution, Claire sat back confident, ready to proceed as planned.

"I guess I'm not completely alone though," sniffed Ms. Shapiro. "Thomas helped me with the groceries last week."

Claire tapped the tip of her pen, failing to recall any prior mention. "Thomas?" she stressed, tongue braced against her bottom teeth.

"Nice young man. Tall. Closer to your age than mine. He must have circulation problems. He wore jeans and a heavy sweater in our August heat. Can you believe that? I wish I knew how to knit so I could make him something. Anyway, he kept me company while I unloaded the groceries. He even offered to help, but I said no, I could handle it myself. He disappeared by the time I went to close my trunk."

"Have you seen Thomas before? Around the neighborhood maybe?"

"No, but I saw him yesterday after another grocery trip."

Claire added the improbable coincidence to her notes. "Go on."

Ms. Shapiro plucked at the water bottle's label. "This time he didn't act as nice. We unloaded a few groceries. I even let him carry some to the door, though somehow it didn't seem to speed anything up. Once we finished, he started getting personal, but I wouldn't tell him anything." She hesitated. Claire beckoned her to continue. Ms. Shapiro sipped her water. "He didn't like that. He grabbed my wrist, hard enough to leave a bruise. He apologized, said if he really wanted to hurt me, he'd do it with three little words. Then he vanished before I could ask what words." She rolled up her sleeve to inspect her right wrist and shrugged. "I guess he didn't mark me up as bad as I thought."

The session's sudden shift absorbed Claire like a Mensa puzzle that mattered. Psychosis brought on by severe depression was rare but possible. The faintest chance of a hallucination was enough to investigate. Her mother's own ailment had started just as innocuously. "Do you mind if I take a look?"

"Of course not, Dr. Rossi. That's why you're the doctor!"

An oddly upbeat response mere seconds removed from recalling physical abuse. Claire set her notepad on the end table and ambled on black heels toward her patient. Not finding bruises, she pressed on potentially tender spots. "Does any of this hurt?"

Open-eyed winces spoke before Ms. Shapiro. "A little. Not too bad."

Broad musings occupied Claire's return to her seat. Had Ms. Shapiro manifested the injury herself, either through stress or a willfully forgotten accident? Was her depression the symptom of a worse illness? First things first: Ms. Shapiro's immediate safety.

"When Thomas first helped you, did he show any aggression? Not necessarily physical or even directed at you. It could be something as small as a snide comment about your kitchen or wallpaper." Claire motioned around the room's cream-colored walls, potted plants, and landscape paintings to broaden her patient's thoughts.

Ms. Shapiro's toes and heels rocked back and forth in her sneakers. "He said something about how much dirtier my sofa was compared to my shrink's. How did you know?"

Claire's brows lifted of their own accord. There wasn't a sofa anywhere in the office, including the private discussion room she shared with her colleague. First things *really* first: her own safety. "Did he mention me by name?"

"No, but he talked about wanting to see a doctor. Maybe he meant you?"

Claire's back stiffened. Why her specifically? "Did you discuss our sessions with him?"

Ms. Shapiro played with the remnants of a torn water label. "Not that I remember, but I must have let something slip."

Perhaps shame over seeking psychiatric treatment explained the sequence. That Ms. Shapiro exhibited no signs of aggression tempered Claire's concern. "Do you think you let something slip?"

"How else would he know? It's not like he can read my mind." Ms. Shapiro's brow furrowed, tilting her glasses frames. "Or can he? Am I imagining Thomas? Is he in my head?"

"What do you believe?"

"I don't know." Ms. Shapiro sat defeated and emptied, but the forward willingness to entertain the idea boded well if Thomas was indeed a construct. For most, acceptance was as difficult as treatment.

"Even in the healthiest of people, stress or loneliness can manifest in imagining someone that pokes at latent insecurities. Thomas might be real, he might not, but together we'll get to the bottom of it." Claire stuck her arms to the chair's, denying herself the desire to twist her hair. She focused on her patient, who suddenly seesawed between a standard case and a concerning one. "I want you to try something if you see him again. Is that okay with you?"

Ms. Shapiro corrected her glasses, her index finger on the bridge until she answered. "Whatever you say, Dr. Rossi."

"Great. To start, do you have a favorite song? Something that inspires particular joy or delight?"

"Oh, sure. 'Don't You Forget About Me' is what I listen to the most, but it's 'Just Can't Get Enough' that gets me dancing." She laughed, dispersing session-long tension. "Can you imagine me dancing?"

"Dancing is healthy for anyone," Claire reassured with a smile.

"Is that where you get your nice arms from?"

She chuckled, "No. And thank you." She glanced at her dress's short sleeves. "Rock climbing, actually." Among other outdoor excursions. No reason to share more than necessary though. "Now, the next time you see Thomas, go inside. Your car or your house, whichever is closer. Then ignore him. Close your eyes, silently count out two breaths, and hum 'Just Can't Get Enough'. Will you do that?"

Ms. Shapiro leaned forward, voice lowered as if Thomas was eavesdropping. "What if he thinks I'm crazy?"

"This is about *you*, not him or anyone else. *You* can only control how *you* feel, and that's our goal." Claire's hand sliced through the air alongside each instance of *you*.

"Then yes, I can do that. How long do you want me to hum for?"

"Try to last through the first chorus. Then open your eyes and look for any changes."

"What if he's still there?"

Claire's hand settled into a calming gesture. "Keep your distance. Make an excuse to get inside your home if you're not already. Ask him to leave and don't let him in. Call 9-1-1 if he persists." This plan should curb both a suspected hallucination and a genuine human, allowing time to uncover the threat's severity. And whether it involved her. "Humming your song should feel second nature, so let's practice. When you're ready, close your eyes."

Ms. Shapiro's eyelids shuttered tight.

"Concentrate on your breathing." *One, two*, she counted to herself. "Hum your song."

Upbeat tunes ricocheted off the contours of her patient's mouth. Rhythmic side-to-side head bobs visibly led to eased tensions.

Melodies converted to a familiar synth inside Claire's head. "How do you feel?"

"Better. I didn't know this would be so easy." Her mood improved faster than expected. Maybe she didn't feel as threatened as Claire believed. Another piece of the puzzle.

"Sometimes it is, sometimes it's not. The important thing is you focus on yourself." Nagging desire to identify the singer, and a near end to their session, prompted Claire to ask, "By the way, who sings 'Just Can't Get Enough'?"

"My, you are young, Dr. Rossi," said Ms. Shapiro, laughing and riding high on the therapeutic aid. "It's Depeche Mode. That was the first song my parents let me listen to on the radio." As in, shortly before Claire was born thirty-four years ago.

"Oh, right. Great band." Not the first time she had feigned interest in a patient's passion. She considered listening to Adele later to wash off the white lie. "This is a good place for us to stop. I look forward to your progress next session." Claire rose and moved toward the exit.

"Thank you, Dr. Rossi. Today felt good." Ms. Shapiro followed behind.

"I'm also going to prescribe two additions to your daily routine. Janice will call in the first to your pharmacy, a medication called risperidone. It's considered an antipsychotic, but I don't want that to alarm you. It's low dose and interacts positively with your antidepressant. That should alleviate more of your negative feelings, as well as assist you if you are indeed imagining any of your interactions with Thomas." Her peers might consider the treatment aggressive, but the planned dosage carried less risk than upping or altering her current antidepressant. "Take it at the same time as your current medication. Consistency is key.

"The second addition is to spend thirty minutes at your neighborhood park. Sit at a bench or table, whatever is convenient and feels comfortable. It can be morning, afternoon, or early evening, as long as the sun is out. I want you to smile at anybody that walks nearby. Greet them if they reciprocate. You don't have to continue talking past that if you don't want to. Spending time outside and engaged with people will help balance out working from home."

Ms. Shapiro petted her arm, her downcast stare not inspiring confidence. "Okay, I think I can do that." Her head bobbed to the same rhythm as her humming moments ago, before she looked up and beamed. That song held a lot of positive energy. "Thanks, again."

"You're welcome, Diane." *Though with today's turn,* she thought, *I might start treating you for free.* Enigmas like these taught her how to handle similar cases, a positive loop which ensured she never failed the desperate. "Remember what to do if you see Thomas again."

"That I can handle. Don't you fret," reassured Ms. Shapiro, wiggling her finger. Anyone spying her carefree grin would've never believed her a crying mess fifteen minutes ago. "Have a great day."

"You too." Claire opened the door to direct Ms. Shapiro to her secretary and spied a lobby of empty leather chairs. Her next patient was late. She frowned and shut the door, returning to her chair to flesh out Ms. Shapiro's notes.

Hallucinations. Depeche Mode—Happier Childhood? flowed from pen to page. She stared at the lines, flipped the pad to a fresh sheet, lingered, then turned back. Her lips curled around her teeth as she penned one last addendum: *Latent therapist obsession?* Did those words belong? Challenging patients satisfied like a technical climb, a problem with many solutions but often a single best. Where psychiatry differed was the lack of a safety rope. This Thomas, real or not, hadn't mentioned Claire by name, but that could sour quickly. She let the entry remain, forced to heed her mother's aptly timed advice. *Patience comes to those who wait.* She tapped the notepad, a literary reminder to remain cautious, and flipped to the next page in case her scheduled patient showed.

As if on cue, a knock at the door preceded her secretary walking in without waiting for a response. Janice moved with a gusto that belied her age. Wearing khakis as usual, a teal cardigan brightened her ensemble. "Mr. Abrams canceled. He'll call back later to reschedule."

"So I'm done for the day?"

Janice nodded. She held two thin envelopes and a glossy postcard.

"And I suppose I have mail?"

"Right again, Dr. Rossi. Thought you might like to read it in here."

Not particularly. She preferred the space she shared with her colleague for that. Crass paperwork like bills dampened the simple elegance of this room, but when Janice handed her a single envelope, she shrugged and split it open with her finger. Inside, a masterful stroke of penmanship said, *Enjoy your gifts.* Claire turned the note over, found nothing. She folded the message back in and called out to Janice before she retreated from the room. "Did this come with anything else?"

She scratched her gray curls. "No, the mailman came after lunch. I guess Jack is sick because I didn't recognize him. I'll try to catch his name next time. He was very handsome."

Her hinting smile ricocheted off of Claire's dead stare. Janice's nosiness knew no bounds.

"Anyway," she continued, without a lick of shame. "He set down the mail, said have a nice day, and left. The rest is for Dr. Wilson, so I'm sure that was it. Is something wrong?"

"An odd letter is all. Thank you." Claire examined the front of the envelope, barely registering the door closing. She didn't recognize the letter's sender, an *Imogene Aire* from *Fredonia, ND* at *19 Memory Lane*. Wherever that town lay, it was far from Denver. If it was real at all; the address sounded fake. She wrinkled her forehead, rolling the words, *Enjoy your gifts*, along her tongue. What kind of gifts? Physical? Metaphorical? Something to do with her patients? She crinkled the envelope as a detail from today's session struck her.

Three little words to hurt you with. Thomas's threat after his assault. Was he delivering a message through her patient? If Ms. Shapiro hallucinated him, how did that explain the letter?

She took a breath, counted out her inhale, then her exhale. Indulging wild curiosities led down a dark path; her mother wrote the blueprint for that. This was just a letter and Diane Shapiro was just a patient who needed help. Claire would find the truth. She always did.

CHAPTER 2

WWarm pajamas and the sofa wrapped Claire in their collective cocoon, beseeched her to return to slumber. She had worked into the wee hours of Sunday, until exhaustion laid her to rest on her lily-white couch. As it had off and on throughout the weekend, the strange letter's coincidences distracted her from more pressing matters. This time, from much-needed sleep. Now she was sitting up, arms crossed in thought, forcing her mind to more productive pursuits.

Was she missing anything about Ms. Shapiro? Or Friday's new patient who also described a potential hallucination? Some link besides the obvious?

She shook her head. Let her arms fall. Her left struck a fifth edition of the Diagnostic and Statistical Manual of Mental Disorders she'd apparently slept with. Her fingers drummed the cover. Other than the fact that the two patients lived alone, they couldn't have differed more. Claire had to wait for their next sessions.

Her thoughts shifted to the patient she'd fallen asleep contemplating how to treat. Mr. Jefferies long suffered from delusions of individuals stalking him. He was improving bit by bit, enough that he'd stayed with her longer than his previous two psychiatrists combined. But she knew a solution existed besides simply tweaking his medication. Her drumming grew more furious. Frustration already stirring her awake like a cup of coffee, she shoved the textbook onto the charcoal vinyl floor. The ensuing thud jolted her with memories of a famous incident with parallels to Mr. Jefferies's symptoms. It was the spark needed to shape her patient's next breakthrough.

She reached toward her laptop on the glass pane of the coffee table, searched the Internet for *aaron alexis shooting*. Results led to the 2013 mass shooter's personal life, the Washington Navy Yard shooting forever linked to his name, details regarding his mental health, and conspiracy theories surrounding his death. Everything but the Wikipedia article appeared too general. A subsequent search for *aaron alexis delusions* offered enough reasons to start writing things down. She stood up and strode toward the desk resting against the wall of her garden home.

Then her damn stomach grumbled, broke her concentration, and forced a glance around enclosed stairs and into the kitchen. The microwave's LED read 10 a.m. With a huff, she grabbed a fresh spiral from the desk drawer, then marched through the rooms of her open floor plan straight to the refrigerator. She pulled out last night's leftovers and threw the plate in the microwave. She nodded impatiently and rolled her wrist as if doing so would speed up the reheating. Idle thoughts inspired her next query when she resumed her research: *microwave vibrations*. At last, the timer dinged. She rushed the piping hot plate to the cushion where her morning had begun.

Claire slid out the same clicky top pen she kept in every spiral. She balanced the notebook on one thigh while setting breakfast beside the open laptop. In between mouthfuls, she explored search results and transcribed details regarding Aaron Alexis's delusions from screen to paper. After an hour, she circled similarities between Mr. Jefferies's case and this one.

Microwave conspiracies

Control

Trazodone

Work dissatisfaction

Wall/ceiling voices

Bugged room

Gang stalking

Followed

Paranoia

Research into other gang-stalking-related mass shootings

matched every symptom and every keyword. Only the drugs differed, clearly prescribed by general physicians rather than psychiatrists. Insomnia medication became antidepressants became amphetamines. "Great, make the delusions even worse," Claire criticized as if speaking directly with their doctors. She twisted her hair, eyes glazing over the monitor's dull glow. When it came to proper treatment, knowing what to look for helped, what not to do imperative, and what approach to take essential.

Evidence pointed to Mr. Jefferies having fabricated his stalkers, but it struck her as odd that he reported a once-friendly relationship with them. It was the main argument against a gang-stalking diagnosis. She put a pin in the thought and reached for the DSM-5 textbook on the floor. From between its pages, she yanked out looseleaf papers she had scribbled notes onto last night. *Imagination?* came into focus, blurring the other words. She folded the pages and tucked them into the back of her spiral.

Claire cycled through browser tabs of yesterday's queries like *adult onset imaginary friend* and *hostile imaginary friend* with a fresh mind. One discovery proved worth her while. Chains of discussion tunneled her toward a schizophrenic coping mechanism called a tulpa, basically a proactively generated imaginary friend. Individuals utilized them to combat loneliness or create metaphysical fantasies.

How did the tulpa delusion calm these individuals? Did any science corroborate their beneficial effects? Most of the sources themselves needed professional help, but it granted insight into a lucid version of self-made illusions. In every relevant discussion, the imaginer understood the tulpa wasn't real. That served as a key difference in separating a coping mechanism from burgeoning madness. She might even find a way to apply this glimmer of insight to her two more recent cases. She tapped her lips.

On the other hand, what if a patient invented a tulpa without knowing its fictitious nature? What if they didn't know they could control it? Did failure on these fronts signify descent into psychosis? What if—

The doorbell rang.

What if the tulpa had taken over? Could a—

Three knocks rapped.

If expressions could burn holes, Claire's would have scorched her front door.

"Claire? Please open up. I need your help," the interloper pleaded from the porch.

The voice sounded familiar but not enough to place it with a face. Who was beating down her door on Sunday morning? She checked the kitchen clock; morning had lapsed into afternoon an hour ago.

"I already tried the Andersons. And the Scholzs. I hope you're awake. I need help."

Claire sighed, displeased after having deduced the speaker: Amy Alba, her new next-door neighbor. She solicited like a daddy's girl who had had everything handed to her but was ultimately an innocent. Maybe someone verged on kidnapping her. Claire swiped a light sweater draped over the couch's arm to avoid searching for a bra. She stalked toward the door, the allure of the couch beckoning behind her. She stole a glance back before she pulled down the sweater, flipped the deadbolt, and braced for her neighbor's emergency.

Amy's hair frizzed out of its usually perfect sandy blonde curls, but the willowy middle-aged woman had found time to apply makeup and iron her sunflower dress. She bounced to the cadence of every elucidating sentence as if she had solved a crime. "Oh, thank goodness. I know you're normally home on Sunday so I considered trying you first. The Andersons and Scholzs have kids though, so I thought they were a better pick, but I guess they're still at church. Thank you so much for answering, Claire." Without warning or need, Amy placed her hand on Claire's covered forearm.

Claire contemplated slamming the door and returning to her investigation. This wasn't a patient. This wasn't an emergency. This was Amy.

Still, her unkempt hair, spastic speech patterns, and confusion thinking that the Scholzs would attend church outside of Christmas or Easter indicated a high degree of stress-induced anxiety. Neither time nor desire existed for a new patient, but with her concentration already broken, perhaps a quick session would usher back in the right mindset.

"Do you want to come in and take a seat?"

"Oh, Claire. Thank you so much. You're a kind soul. I would love to chat, but I don't have time." Amy's head snapped back, scouting the porch for something invisible to Claire. Had she really foiled a kidnapping attempt? Of course not. An absurd thought brought on by extensive time researching Mr. Jefferies's case.

A scrawny kid with a round face and cropped blonde hair materialized from behind the corner wall. Amy touched the fabric below her collarbone and breathed in relief. She waved permission to the youth to continue inflicting his wanton activity upon Claire's property.

Oh, no.

If she had inherited anything from her estranged father, it was his aversion to parenting. Unlike him, she hadn't required a child out of wedlock to discover that.

Her neighbor turned back toward the open door, whispering. "Nathan was in an accident. I got a call from the hospital twenty minutes ago and need to drive over. The doctors say he'll be fine but—" She wavered and clutched Claire's hands for support.

Tensed fingers appeased a visceral desire to jerk out of Amy's grasp. This afternoon was flying off the rails fast.

Amy blubbered, "They say he sustained multiple injuries to his face and arms. I don't know how long he'll be in the hospital, and I don't want little Bradley to see his father like this. You know how fathers are with showing weakness around their boys." True— Claire intimately knew the money grown men spent in therapy over it. It didn't alter her antipathy toward the impending request.

"So I wondered if you could watch him for a few hours?" Amy asked.

There it was. Claire predicted this conversation's ending, but like hell she wouldn't go down without a fight.

"Don't you have a babysitter?"

"I do, but she's out of town this weekend."

"Isn't there a service for emergency child care?"

"There is, but what mother would subject her child to a stranger's care?"

What mother would subject her child to Claire's care? "I'm not good with kids." She pulled away, tried to pocket her fingers. Wrong pajamas. She crossed her arms in conciliation.

"That's okay. Bradley's no problem. He's a sweet boy. Give him a few toys and some floor space, and he'll spend hours creating stories. He won't even move. Well, except to use the little boy's room obviously." Amy giggled. As if assaulted by Claire's profession, she added, "He's not autistic."

"I'm actually in the middle of work."

"Like I said, he'll stay out of your way. You'll barely even hear him. Just a few helicopter noises every now and then. I bet you'll worry about him not breathing before you worry about him causing trouble. I know I do."

Claire's shoulders sank, her excuses depleted. At least Robert Scholz, her one close friend in the neighborhood, hadn't mentioned anything negative about the kid.

Obviously sensing an end to her prey's resistance, Amy caressed Claire's sunken shoulder to deliver the final blow. "I need to see Nathan. Please watch him, just for a few hours."

Leave me the hell alone, thought Claire. Had that one slipped? Clearly not. Should it slip? Not worth it. Nosiness and gossip ran hand in hand. Robert might be the only neighbor she'd call a friend, but she liked others well enough. The ensuing fallout struck a bold check in the action's cons column.

"Fine. Only a few hours. I have a date tonight, and as you can see I'll need some time to get ready." Claire rolled her eyes down the length of her own body. Naturally rosy cheeks sufficed for makeup, but little else said put together. Though Amy didn't strike her as one to stay separated from her child for long, it couldn't hurt to reinforce the importance of timeliness. Even if her date was as real as a hallucination.

"Thank you so much." Amy shifted her caress into a hug. One hand still resting on Claire's shoulder, she turned to the side of the porch. "Bradley, Ms. Rossi is going to watch you for a few hours."

The boy, pressed against the corner with toy figures in both hands, looked to his mom. The child scuffing Claire's house combined with her neighbor forgetting proper honorifics resulted in her loosing a "Hmph," apparently too quiet to notice.

"Come along, Bradley. Gather your toys and do exactly as she asks. I'll pick up ice cream on the way home if you're good."

"Strawberry?" he asked, inspecting what little of the house's interior he could see, as if measuring the risk to the reward of entering.

"Only if you're really, really good."

Bradley eased himself out from the corner. After releasing his grip on the wooden siding, he darted to the comfort of his mother's hips. He wrapped himself around her narrow waist. Amy crouched to his level and repositioned his arms over her shoulders.

"Will you be good?"

"Yes, ma'am." The child nodded with the same enthusiasm Claire had been enjoying until very recently.

"Promise?"

"Yes, ma'am."

Claire studied the child's manners in pursuit of containing the potential menace. Locked onto Amy's face, obedience replaced shyness. Similar to most children, he probably felt safer meeting adults at his height. The straight-faced, puppy-like focus indicated a desire to please, but she'd soon find out for certain.

Amy embraced her son, kissed his forehead, and whispered, "I love you."

"I love you," he parroted.

She stood back up on her heels and placed her hand on his back. "Okay sweetie, go with Ms. Rossi now. I'll get the rest of your toys."

Bradley put one foot forward, then presented a toy with an open palm like an offering. Dirt ran up to his forearm. Amy shrugged, indicating this was off her script.

Claire examined the toy. Plastic molded into a lab coat draped female, complete with a stethoscope over her shoulders. So they *knew* she was a doctor but Amy couldn't bother to call her as such. "Is this for me?"

He nodded again, more carefully this time, as if fearing his meager gift would incur God's wrath.

What else was there to do? Pinching the toy between two fingers, she accepted his present. *Beware of the gift that keeps on giving.* Claire's mother whispered the phrase upon institutionalization at St. Mary's Hospital for the Wayward. Claire blinked, knowing why the memory surfaced. In place of practical work, her brain subconsciously obsessed over her cryptic letter. *Enjoy your gifts, indeed.* Thankfully, her latest patient hadn't hinted anything about those three little words.

"Are you okay, Ms. Rossi?" asked Bradley.

With the toy held inches from her waist, Claire rubbed her forehead. "Yes. Thank you for this."

Bradley's demeanor shifted from sullen child to intrepid explorer, back straightened with steel in his spine. He pressed a finger to his lips, then expectantly held out his empty hand.

Hesitation struck Claire before she led him inside by his slightly cleaner wrist. She set the child beside the coffee table where she could attempt to resume working without losing sight of him.

Amy followed, holding military and superhero figures. She laid the toys down beside their play master. Hugs and kisses later, she said, "I'll see you soon."

Bradley waved to his mom as she deftly balanced reciprocating the gesture with backpedaling out of the door. Crossing its threshold, she faced Claire. "Thank you again."

"Fine. Close the door on your way out." Amy obliged and left, heels clacking at bristling speeds down the porch steps.

Eager to clean her hands and dispose of her gift, Claire waved the toy at the boy. "I'll put this in a special place for safekeeping."

Theoretical warmth from his innocent smile felt wasted. She wandered into the kitchen, opened the first countertop drawer, and tucked the toy beside nails, a hammer, and a blender manual. After washing at the sink, she returned to her old position on the couch and studied him watching her. Was he waiting for a command? "You can play," she trailed off.

His attention snapped to his toys, turning the floor into his fantasy battleground.

Magic words, it seemed.

Satisfied the army figures' marches weren't scuffing her floorboards, she seized the spiral to jog her memory, but inert words remained as such, failing to spark ideas. She tugged on her hair and gazed at the laptop, tulpa highlighted in various spots on the screen. Reading search snippets reignited her curiosity. What if a tulpa went rogue? *Could* that happen? She suspected someone could find themselves the victim of their own imagination, much how drugs controlled a junkie.

Mock explosions boomed from below.

"Bradley, could you be good and play without making noise?" Claire replicated Amy's usage of 'good' in an attempt to stimulate recall of his mother's instructions.

The boy looked up to repent. "Sorry, Ms. Rossi. I'll be quiet." Attention returned to his toys. Clashes of plastic persisted sans color commentary. Fine enough, but surely this wouldn't last? She watched the boy for a minute, studying his delicate control over the pretend battlefield. As he maintained his quiet, she resumed her research.

What caused one's own creation to turn against their master remained unclear. Few people reported instances of anything but a helpful tulpa, surprising given anyone could say anything online. Supposed doctors offered fantastical solutions as often as should-be patients requested sound advice. In all cases, discussions around tulpas centered on how to create them, their beneficial arrangements, and proper interactions. No consequences, no regrets, no horror stories. It begged the question of whether these people's delusions had advanced to where the make-believe persona had assumed control. In that case, were they still the same person? After all, they themselves had produced the new personality, the new identity.

She smacked her pen against the notepad. Philosophy shared a kinship with psychiatry, but she risked veering too far off base. She scanned the room for inspiration, allowing her subconscious to guide her. Her gaze fell to her desk, refinished from the time her mom had owned it. In the side drawer, she had tucked away the letter from Fredonia, North Dakota. Yesterday's research provided little insight. Fewer than a hundred people lived there, and neither the return address nor sender existed. She didn't realize how fiercely she'd been resisting the mystery she couldn't yet solve.

Claire forced herself to turn away. Bradley and his toy figures clicked into focus. Her chin nestled into her hand, propped up by an elbow on the sofa's arm. Just two friends having a conversation.

"Bradley, can I ask you a few questions?"

His attention turned upward in compliance. He held a red ninja with raccoon ears in one hand and a tank in the other. Logical foes for an imaginative kid. "Okay," he said.

"How old are you?"

"Seven." Not triumphant, not proud. Simply matter-of-fact.

"You seem pretty creative. Do your parents or teachers ever say anything about that?"

"Sometimes my mom does. My teacher last year liked the dinosaur drawing I gave her for Christmas."

I'm sure she tucked it safely into her creativity trash bin. Claire blinked away the harsh comment. He didn't deserve bitterness leftover from her encounter with his mother.

"Have you ever had imaginary friends?"

He sat still, face scrunching in weird patterns, oblivious to the display of thought which children didn't learn to hide until adolescence.

"Racinja and Tanky and Mr. Handy and Bazooka Steve are like my friends at school because we play together, but I don't think they're imaginary because they're on the TV."

"That's true. They aren't imaginary. What about speaking with someone else not on TV?"

"Do you mean like how my dad says it's weird when I talk to myself?"

Idiot father. Conversing with oneself facilitated increased problem solving. Claire pursed her thin lips, quieting the craving to transition into a therapeutic line of questioning. "Not exactly. More like a friend that only you can see and only you can talk to."

Bradley gasped.

"What is it?"

He released the breath, ruffling the pajama fabric around her knee. His hands absentmindedly forced a clash between toys. Presumably Racinja and Tanky. "I saw someone in my closet last week. I think he was trying to talk, but he sounded like a frog. I screamed and my parents came to look, but he was gone."

"That doesn't sound like a friend at all." But it did sound indicative of an overactive imagination, which might serve her. "Have you seen him before?"

"No. Dad called it a bad dream and that I needed to sleep extra hard to keep the monster away. That's what I did, and it worked pretty well."

If only adolescent sleep disorders were so easily cured. "So you don't have any imaginary friends. What about your classmates?"

Facial wheels cranked again. "I don't think so," he answered at last.

"Alright. Thanks for talking with me." She settled back into an upright position, this time with legs propped up and feet competing for table space with the computer.

"Did I answer your questions good, Ms. Rossi?"

Dr. Rossi, not Ms. Rossi. Whatever. It was fine. She had already let it slip once with him and twice with his mother. Except it wasn't fine, and Bradley could likely adopt the correct nomenclature faster than his mom. She hated to admit it, but he had impressed her. Mainly because he hadn't disappointed her, but his behavior still earned him an invisible gold star.

"You did. You answered the questions so well I was hoping I could call you Brad instead of Bradley. What do you think?"

Brad beamed. "That would be great! All of my friends at school call me Brad too."

So the kid *could* vocalize emotion. He stood a chance of reaching adulthood mostly sane. "Wonderful. So we can be friends?" asked Claire.

"Yes, please."

"That's great. All of my friends call me Dr. Rossi." She tapped her chest. "And they never talk to me more than once a week."

"Really? Only once a week? I talk to my friends as much as I can."

She bent to hover a foot from his face, an intimate distance perfect for friends. "That's so lucky. You can get all your talking out with them so we can be *quiet* friends." Juvenile wiggling of Brad's eyebrows forced Claire to embellish on the made-up term. "Quiet friends are very special, so you have to promise to get your talking out at home or school so we can be quiet *here*. We'll even give it a special name—friendship quiet time. What do you think?"

Brad focused on his play figures, divining an adequate answer. Then his neck snapped up like the beginning of Mr. Jefferies's psychotic episode on Monday, albeit with a more preferable follow-up. "I promise. Friendship quiet time sounds fun!"

Claire inched back. "Just what I wanted to hear. Now, let's return to playing separately and quietly so we can practice being such good friends." Her forefinger sealed her mouth shut.

He squirmed with brief excitement before resuming the tussle between his toys. Their fights and flights rumbled with a new level of energy. Clattering soon faded to background noise alongside outdoor car engines and lawnmowers. Unfortunately, she had hit the end of the road with her own activity. Her brain needed a fresh pursuit. She shrugged and rummaged between cushions. After a few deep dives, she exhumed her phone. May as well try to find that date.

CHAPTER 3

One good story about a patient," pleaded Robert Scholz. "That's all I'm asking. I don't need a name." He sat across from Jessica Diaz at an espresso-white dining table, his back facing Claire's living room. A work-sanctioned button-down shirt and slacks conformed to his lanky frame. Claire and Jess forced the apparel purchase after his wife's repeated complaints about baggy clothes went ignored. Following that *memorable* shopping trip, Samantha Scholz convinced him to shave his thinning hair bald. He made up for those minor defeats elsewhere.

Or at least, he tried.

"Would you disclose confidential details about your government contracts?" countered Claire, filling up a glass of water from the stainless steel refrigerator several steps away.

"No, but that's the government we're talking about. They're important."

"And my patients aren't?" Eyebrows raised, her grin invited a second attempt.

"Come on, Claire. As much as you help people, I know science is your passion. I'm not trying to make this personal."

"Yeah," drawled Claire until the topic died. He was getting rusty. "Do either of you want something else to drink?"

"I think we're solid." Jess raised her wine glass. A simple bun contained her dark hair. She had ditched her professorial jacket on the couch, leaving a pearl tank top to accentuate a healthy feminine physique and partially cover her olive skin. Jeans wrapped around full hips, a sight that often relieved Claire and her flowing dresses from undesired gazes.

Robert, his sullen face indicating more interest in goading Claire than in either lady's appearance, followed her lead and clinked his stemmed glass against the one in the air.

"Are we really playing Agricola again?" asked Jess. "On a Friday night? I'm never going to be able to bring anyone over." She set down the glass and rested her other hand on the closed board game box, clearly not too concerned.

"Date smarter guys," said Claire.

"No thanks. Leads to trouble."

"Well, we can't play Catan." Claire patted Robert's shoulder before taking the seat next to him. She set her water beside her wine, fully intending to balance their consumption. Her trying week would challenge that resolution. "Robert plus wine and that game is liable to wake the neighbors with shouts demanding wood for sheep."

"At 8 p.m.?" Jess sized up the half-empty wine bottle resting on a pewter coaster. "Is that a real risk?"

"The new neighbor has a kid." Claire shrugged. "Honestly, I'm not sure I could handle Robert's incessant dealmaking tonight."

"Sounds like you're making an excuse for being scared," Robert said.

Jess set her drink down to lock eyes with Claire in a special code that said, *Charge!*

Despite her fatigue, she couldn't turn down the request. Whereas black and white filled Robert's world like Claire's downstairs, the two psychiatrists lived in grayscale. Having an engineer as a close friend supplied more fun than was fair.

"Actually, excuses arise from a defensive mechanism used to protect one's ego from shame," said Jess in a whirlwind of ever-so-expressive hands.

He threw his arms in the air. "How is that different from fear?"

"Fear is related to the belief or prediction of something threatening to inflict peril or pain. Shame relates to a bygone event for which one experienced a worse result than one's expectations. One emotion perceives a future event and the other judges a past event."

"Can't you make an excuse out of fear of the unknown?" He

draped his arm over the chair's, leaning back in a premature victory pose. Claire could almost taste his misplaced confidence, its inviting sweetness pushing today's problems back into the recesses of her mind.

If Jess's first glance signaled, *Charge,* this next one commanded, *Flank.*

Burgundy liquid spun in Claire's hand, its viscous legs dribbling down the sides of her glass, ostensibly drawing her attention. "You could make an excuse out of shame for feeling fear but not exclusively due to the fear itself."

"Fine. So you're ashamed of your fear of losing in Catan." Robert smirked.

Black cherry, chocolate, and toasted oak swished in her mouth. "The thing about fear is your body needs a reason to trigger the response—something instinctual or learned. My body, on the other hand, has no instinctual or learned reason to fear playing you in any game, which includes Catan. Thus, I lack the fear required to seek avoidance which would support your shaming theory."

Jess opened up Agricola, the thud of the game box alerting the arguing pair to begin setup. "Carry on." Troves of labeled plastic bags dumped onto the table.

"You two and your circular logic," huffed Robert. "All I'm saying is nobody I know sleeps at 8 p.m." He distributed wooden pieces around while ogling Catan on the kitchen countertop bar.

"At least you aren't arguing against how loud you get." Claire shuffled and passed out cards. "And you do know them. The wife has been hard to avoid since they moved in."

Robert's finger rapped on the veneer of the dining room table. "Wait. Are you talking about the Albas? Amy Alba lives next door to you? How did I not realize that?"

"Because you are one of the least detail-oriented engineers I know."

"I focus on details that *matter.*" He waved away Claire's criticism. "Samantha, Matthew, and I met Amy for the first time at the park. After maybe ten minutes she was already discussing childcare rotations. No way I'd leave my son with a woman I'd just met. Plus, there's a reason we stopped at one kid."

"She apparently came by your place last Sunday." Mercifully, Claire hadn't seen the Albas this week, but she knew Brad would come to collect on his friendship quiet time this weekend. "The husband got in a wreck."

"Is he okay? And how did you know she came by?"

"As far as I know. Amy went to the hospital and wanted someone to watch her kid. And since no one was home to bail me out"— Claire tilted her head in Robert's direction—"she practically smashed down my door."

"Someone left their kid with you?" Robert laughed.

"I know. Decently behaved, though. Listens to me better than Matthew." *That* boy was his father's son.

Robert's eyes tracked up in thought until they fell back down with the etchings of a smile on his lips.

"I convinced him we could be friends if we didn't speak more than once a week."

"Of course you did."

Jess checked her phone and placed it back on the table. "If you want to talk family, do it in Agricola. I hear enough about kids from my mom."

The trio dug into analyzing their cards. Claire poured the remainder of the wine for herself.

"How about a fresh bottle?" Jess tapped her glass.

"You know where they are. Feel free to pick whatever you want."

"Even from the bottom?"

"Only for you two." Paper treasures glittered like gold. She had been dealt a *Lover* occupation card. May as well wrap up another victory for the Agricola Queen. She continued studying her other cards, stopping on *Puppeteer* as motion interrupted her analysis.

A shadow flickered across the kitchen window.

"Actually, I'll get it for you." Claire sprang from her chair, checking two head-height windows behind Jess before walking toward the sink.

"Already figured out how to crush us?" asked Jess.

"Just in the mood for something specific. You aren't as skilled at picking out wine as you are drinking it."

Jess swung her legs back under the table, spreading her arms in a flourish. "I'd say between those two skills, I've developed the better one."

The window locks were latched. Dim floodlights signaled inactive motion sensors. Something *had* moved though, and she could've sworn it had a head and shoulders. It must have been a small animal. A raccoon jumping off patio furniture? The light sensor caught birds as easily as it missed dogs, but it always responded to people. She looked to her right, through narrow windows built into the backyard door, finding the sight similarly unremarkable. Patients' problems crowded her mind—three suspected hallucinatory patients counting this afternoon's session, a number almost too high for coincidence.

Claire thought Jess's concerned voice called her name. Whatever owned the shadow had moved on. She twisted to her friends. "Sorry. Thought I saw something."

"Living alone will do that to you," said Jess, her hands empty and cards face down on the table.

"You live alone."

"Which is why I limit my time at home, staying busy thanks to my award-winning personality."

Robert snorted, continued inspecting his cards. "Claire, isn't there a name for that in your profession?"

"Delusions of grandeur?"

"That's the one."

Pilfering Robert's glass, Jess drained the remaining contents with a refreshing, "Aah."

"You'll pay for that." He held up a solitary card and slid the empty glass to his corner of the table.

Claire grinned, their familiar bickering relaxing her overworked brain. Fingering bottles from her built-in wine fridge, she picked out a Chilean Cabernet Sauvignon and rejoined the group.

"Chilean wine? Are you trying to make me feel more at home?" Jess imitated a Spanish accent. "An apology of sorts?"

"I'm trying to refine your palate. And you're not Chilean." Claire reclaimed her seat and scored the wine seal before removing the cork.

"You're barely even Hispanic," added Robert. Claire poured the bottle until her friends' glasses were half-full, then placed it on the coaster.

"More than you."

"Debatable." Robert tapped his index finger to his lips before pointing at Jess. "How do you say *I'm first player, I'll take my turn now* in Spanish?"

Jess bounced a wooden disc off Robert's chest. She grabbed another piece, threatening to strike again, but instead began the game in earnest. "I don't know. I traded my Spanish dictionary in for a medical dictionary a decade ago."

"As if you ever owned one to begin with."

"Hey, I get enough of this from my mom. Having grandchildren isn't the only thing she badgers me about. It's not as if learning a language will make me a better Mexican."

Claire and Robert's chuckles faded as the game absorbed them in thought.

Glances to the kitchen distracted Claire throughout the second turn. When she turned back, Jess's piece lay atop the space she wanted. Claire fell back into a safe option and claimed some food.

"Really? Fishing?" Robert hunched over the table to peruse her face-down cards before he placed his piece. "You must need this Occupation space." She didn't. Not yet, anyway.

"You just fell into her trap," said Jess.

"Must be a collaborative effort then." Robert fanned his hand across the face-up cards before him. "To trap me into building up my farming empire."

"You're letting the wine speak for you again."

Robert stared Jess down and answered with a generous pour into his glass.

Claire couldn't lose to these two. She needed to play that *Lover* card.

Darkness shrouded her backyard.

She needed to gather more resources.

Something had been out there.

Nothing's there. Concentrate on the game.

"Save some for me." Claire reached for the bottle's neck before its base landed.

Jess sipped at her wine and helped Robert reset the board for the next round. She puckered her lips. "Better than massage therapy."

"Better than any therapy," goaded Robert.

"Let's not get carried away," slurred Jess. "Speaking of therapy, how does it feel to lose to two girls in a board game designed in your home country?"

"Do you often ask patients to indulge in personal fantasies?"

Claire shuddered at the idea of Robert as a patient. She tapped her player board until her focus returned to the game at hand. Time to play her *Lover* card.

Robert banged knuckles against the table, shifting a few of the cardboard pieces. "Of course you have that. Good thing you didn't get it out earlier."

"Early enough."

While Jess considered her next move, a flicker of light danced off the wine bottle. Claire turned around and squinted toward the front of her house, past the oversized fireplace and modern couch. Nothing there—probably a car.

"What a gritch play," Jess called her back to the game, then groaned. "Have you ever had a patient rub off on you?"

Claire's heart skipped a beat. "How do you mean?"

"I don't treat many patients anymore with the university job, but there's this teen who uses gritch to describe something swank. Actually, he uses it to describe pretty much everything. I've almost said it half a dozen times tonight, and it finally slipped."

"Sounds like a crush to me," said Robert.

"All the more reason not to treat kids." Snark fled Claire's mouth without thinking, but it didn't still the intense desire to fluff out a dress that suddenly felt tight.

"Big help you two are." Jess tracked two fingers from her eyes to theirs in an *I'm watching you* motion.

Claire inhaled until her lungs bulged with air, then released. She examined her cards, flipping between them as the final rounds approached. She was playing her favorite game with her favorite people. Why couldn't she shake this nagging sensation? Sipping wine soured her stomach. She pushed the glass to arm's length and took her first drink of water. Jess and Robert continued taunting one another while she stalled her turn. As she leaned over the table, cycling attention between cards and the board's state for a tenth or twentieth time, a black silhouette emerged over her *Conjurer* card.

She whirled in her seat. A towering, short-haired man stared from the sidewalk. Claire jumped up and rushed to the front of the house, hands hovering near the window. Her head oscillated between empty streets and yards. The person or figment or *intruder* or WHATEVER had disappeared. She smacked her cheeks a few times, hands enveloping her neck after the last strike.

A caress fell over her shoulder. "Claire? Hey. Claire, what's up?" asked Jess.

The street light one house down should've provided enough light to see him. Could someone flee that fast? What if he hopped her fence?

Claire blew past Robert into the kitchen to inspect her backyard. Silent, still darkness revealed an ordinary scene. Dim floodlights insisted nobody had entered her backyard. She wracked her brain for familiar figures matching the man on the sidewalk. She came up with little to show for it, save dirty blonde strands twisted around her finger.

"Claire? What are you doing? Did you see something?"

She unfurled her hair and faced her best friend, who stood a measured distance away. Robert peered out of the other front window onto her porch, hands in his pockets.

"Earlier, I thought I saw someone in the backyard." Saliva choked down her throat. "Then there was this strange flicker of light, like someone walking by. When I turned around, a man with the same build as the one in the backyard was standing on the sidewalk. Just"—Claire curled and uncurled her fingers at her side—"staring at me."

Jess crept forward, lifting her hand as if approaching someone during a psychotic episode, then squeezed Claire's upper arm. "It's okay. We're here."

"You should call the police," said Robert.

What would she even tell them? Police could barely handle tangible threats. A shadow in the night? They would only ruin the rest of the evening. "I didn't see enough to report anything useful. Did either of you catch something?"

Her friends gazed at each other. Robert shook his head. Jess locked onto a kitchen tile at her feet and wrinkled her nose. Looking back up, she said, "No, sorry. Wish we could help."

Claire's mind worked in overdrive, playing tricks to cope with the uptick in serious patients. As taxing as board games could be, they utilized different thinking patterns, ones she hoped would steer her from stress-induced imaginations and allow some sleep tonight. "We should finish the game."

"Are you sure?"

A wide smile and exaggerated lift of her brows feigned confidence. "Absolutely. It's not like it's the one stalking me."

Jess looked ready to call out the insincere bravado before snickering. "Doctor knows best, right?" She tugged at Claire's hand, reminding her of them traipsing through downtown a couple of months ago. It comforted better than any vintage of wine. They finished the game with a gradual return to casual conversation. It ended with Jess edging Claire for the victory and Robert close behind her.

"Should've played Catan," said Robert. "Nothing bad happens in Catan."

"Are you blaming Agricola for all of this?" asked Jess.

"Sure, why not?" He leaned back, his arm balanced on the top of the chair.

"Because we may as well buy a Ouija board if it's the game's fault and really let the good times roll."

Jess and Robert's cheeks filled with air. Their necks trembled on the verge of laughter. Claire looked around, her quivering smirk keeping them in check until it burst like a balloon filled with mirth. The three wheezed until tensions subsided, Claire thankful for light-hearted company that poked fun at the elephant in the room rather than evading it in fear.

The remainder of the night passed without incident. They finished the second bottle of wine and veered away from discussing work. At the night's end, the trio moved to the front of the house, Robert resuming his watch over the patio.

"Are you sure you don't want me to stay?" asked Jess, touching Claire's upper arm once again.

Claire rubbed her eyes hard enough to paint purple and orange spots over her friend's face. "I'll be okay," she said, knowing that depended on whether or not tonight's research into neighborhood safety turned up clean.

"Alright. Let us know if you need anything."

"And I'm always down the street," said Robert.

"I appreciate it. I really do."

She closed the door behind them. As Claire set her phone alarm, her gaze wandered to her refinished work desk. Next to a stack of papers lay the mail from Fredonia, North Dakota. Between the strange letter, a hefty workload, a new neighbor, and the increased frequency of her mother's quips, who could say what was to blame? Best case scenario, tonight's visitor was the result of tangled wires in her brain.

But, she wondered, as two cars rolled away from her street. As she recalled visits to St. Mary's Hospital for the Wayward. Was that scenario really for the best?

It certainly hadn't been for her mom.

CHAPTER 4

Notes summarizing Diane Shapiro's case sat underneath the tip of Claire's pen, but she didn't need them to relay the highlights to her colleague. "This was Ms. Shapiro's fifth week of treatment. The third reporting interactions with Thomas. She avoided using his name in our most recent session, indicating compartmentalization of fear. Her visual and auditory hallucinations responded positively to humming. Medication coupled with therapy resulted in decreased franticness. I plan to maintain this approach while exploring behavior patterns to explain the oddly consistent nature of the hallucination." She twisted her pen in anticipation. "Any suggestions? Does any connection with the four other patients jump out at you?"

Dr. Eric Wilson stood up and circled a long desk that matched Claire's. He perched on its edge, his feet stretched out on the walnut floor of their shared office space. He rested his charcoal-suited forearms on his thighs. "No suggestions. The treatment is sound."

"Then why do I feel like I'm about to hear a lecture?" She laid her pen across Ms. Shapiro's notes.

Eric donned the same reassuring expression he'd used with patients countless times. "The likelihood of five hallucinatory patients in such a short span is unheard of outside of a psychiatric ward."

"Which is why I'm looking for a connection."

"I know, but who's looking out for you?"

Claire crossed her arms and leaned back in her chair. Her dress's long sleeves hung loosely from her wrists. From the time Eric had taken her under his wing, he indulged in the role of overprotective father. She naturally settled into playing the rebellious daughter, despite barely a decade separating them. "We review patients on Fridays, not each other."

His forefinger flitted between them. "We're a team. Assistance isn't limited to collaborating on patients." He glanced back at the silly cross he kept on the wall, seeming to draw strength from it. "Let me ask you something. How do you feel when you're treating these patients?"

Claire squeezed just above her elbow. Something deep within rejected the notion of discussing herself in the same conversation as her patients. "I don't want a therapy session. Say what's on your mind."

"That wasn't my intent, but very well. We aren't Hollywood actors treating one-in-a-million cases on a weekly basis. I'm concerned about the toll these patients may take on you. Have you experienced any acute symptoms similar to these women?"

"What kind of question is that?" The bizarre game night was a week behind her—with no new personal plights. The board game stalker was a one-time sighting, a fleeting stroke of her imagination. Her patient load had obviously overwhelmed her at first. She was fine now. *Then why are you acting so defensive?*

"You're more invested in these cases than usual," said Eric, "as if it was personal. You know as well as I do that can create complications."

"These are the types of cases to get invested in. Improperly treated psychosis can quickly manifest in actual dangers, for both myself and the patient." She wasn't a helpless damsel, and none of this brought her any closer to a solution. Focusing on her health stole attention from her patients. *There's the answer to your question.* The faster she treated them, the faster she helped herself. Not that she needed help.

"It's more than that," said Eric.

"In what way?"

"There's the patients." He counted on his fingers. "The cryptic letter you brought up last week. The improbable spiritual creature you suggested might explain one hallucination. A tulpa, I believe?

Finally, the fact that all of these patients are also women who live alone."

"Mrs. Cathell and Mrs. Keller are married," she countered. *If this was about expediency, I'd just cede his point.* Her heart beat a little faster. She argued because validating Eric's worry meant a problem existed worth worrying about.

"As I recall, one's husband travels frequently and the other is recently separated."

Claire's squeeze of her arm turned into gentle tapping as she studied Eric's familiar face. Coffee-brown combover. Wire frame glasses. Predictably clean-shaven. She waited to speak until he averted his gaze. "You're suggesting what? That I might subconsciously affect symptoms as a form of sympathy? That sounds closer to something you'd do."

Eric ceded the point with a tilt of his head. "Perhaps, and I hope that if that ever happens, you'll be as candid with me then as I am with you now. You're strong and can handle more than most, but eventually a snowflake becomes an avalanche."

"And eventually a platitude becomes a platypus."

Eric laughed into his chest like someone on the outside of an inside joke, his chin grazing the knot of a blue and white striped tie. "What does *that* mean?"

"You say something so many times, it becomes unrecognizable." At least that's how she interpreted it. Sofia Costas, her mother, had taught middle school for twenty years. She'd developed an eccentric style in that time, perhaps *because* she'd taught so long. Claire saw no need to mention the increased frequency of recalling her aphorisms. Just one more thing for Eric to harp about. She didn't need that. She was fine. A little stressed, at worst. "So in a very roundabout answer to my original question, you don't see any other connections?"

"No, and I don't think you'll find any today either. Be patient. It'll come to you. In the meantime, will you please consider transferring a patient if personal symptoms do arise?"

Fat chance of that. Treating similar patients with similar symptoms helped discern the minutiae between their problems, meaning better and faster treatment. Why argue such an unlikely hypothetical though? "I'll consider it. If that's all, I want to look at my notes once more before heading out." Claire slid the one-page summaries over, fanned them out in front of her, then briefly stood to move their accompanying folders within arm's reach. "Need to clear my head before the weekend, and I have to file this all before I leave."

"No problem." Eric popped off the desk and strolled behind it. He reached for his briefcase and hoisted its wide strap over his shoulder. "A date will be a nice distraction." He grinned wide with knowledge he hadn't legitimately earned.

Claire gritted her teeth. She'd told her secretary about the date in confidence, and clearly she'd leaked it. "Janice?"

"Janice," he affirmed. "Want any advice?"

"From the guy whose wife is mad at him for bringing work on a weekend retreat? No thanks." She glanced at her patient notes with longing.

"Annie will forgive me. She gets upset, but that's who I am. She's always known that. We've already lined up another vacation." He buttoned up his jacket and approached her desk. "Try not to treat him like a patient."

"That's what I'm good at," she joked, hoping to avoid another time-consuming lecture.

"I know. That's the problem." Lecture it was.

"Eric. Stop." For a psychiatrist who read body language for a living, he acted oblivious to hers, like so many would-be fathers. She held a flat hand up and scowled, like so many annoyed daughters. Every acknowledgment of solid advice—such as when he armed her with the right questions to avoid a disastrous first home purchase—flew out the window.

"Alright, alright. I'm gone." Eric stepped past the desk to the door behind her. The latch clicked open. "Stay safe, and enjoy your deserved break." He *had* to throw that in. He *had* to remind her of the hairline crack in her mental health, intentional or not. Before she could retort, the door whispered shut behind his steady hand.

Claire shifted in her chair, readjusting side to side in an attempt to expel irritated energy. Uncomfortable with any position, she stood up and pulled her phone from her purse, half searching for messages from her upcoming date (none), half wanting to know the time (5 p.m.). After pacing, pacing, and pacing around her desk, she slid back into her seat to examine the sheets spread before her: five patients with evidence of hallucinations, organized by initial dates of therapy. Below each patient's name, Friday's summaries captured overall highlights. The exercise condensed broad details into digestible slices, allowing Claire to see what bigger picture, if any, connected them.

She palmed the first paper in the row and pulled back as if burned. *Enjoy your gifts*, ravaged her thoughts. *Enjoy your gifts*, barked a gruff, anonymous speaker alongside recollection of the handwritten letter. *Enjoy your gifts*. Claire massaged her temples until the distraction fled. Patient history and therapies settled into focus once again, the pen in hand to underscore key points. She slid Diane Shapiro's notes closer, confirming she'd read them to Eric almost verbatim. She set the paper aside and moved on to the next sheet.

Gabrielle Capers: Three sessions. Lives alone. No siblings or kids. Affable personality and dates regularly. Second week hallucinating Ted, a long and lean middle-aged male. Hallucination is consistent with schizophrenia, but his playful personality is unusual for a psychotic disorder. Prescribed Xanax for panic attacks. Exploring further signs of depression, anxiety, and stress.

Nancy Cathell: Two sessions. First hallucinatory experience this week. Initial session tackled self-esteem issues stemming from husband's frequent work travel. Hallucinatory figment described as borderline malnourished. Could have resulted from severe depression. Patient exhibits no history or signs of an eating disorder to explain hallucination's characteristics. Initiated Cognitive Behavioral Therapy and prescribed low-dose Lexapro.

Kathy Keller: One session. Lives with husband. Signs of physical and verbal abuse, though denied when probed. She booked therapy after occurrence of unnamed hallucination inside house. Hallucinatory conversation waned between cordial and friendly. Patient admitted almost not booking therapy due to enjoying his company until a friend pushed her into it. Hallucination described as a tall, clean-cut guy. Inadvertent tulpa? No medication prescribed but must dive deeper into potential abuse once trust is established.

Alice Kavina: One session. Unmarried and lives alone. Hostility, mistrust, and aversion to discussing her past point to post-traumatic stress. Opened up when discussing job as a social worker, as if flipping a switch. Hallucination, described as a towering and grotesque figure, appeared inside apartment. Patient swears all windows and doors were locked. Manifested as a way to cope with PTSD? Why now? Has aversion to medication but is willing to take low-dose Seroquel for depression, despite acknowledging its use as an antipsychotic. Begin Prolonged Exposure therapy next week.

"Tall hallucinations for women who generally live alone," Claire concluded. Likely culprits for their manifestations differed, but the coincidence was as hard to ignore as Eric coddling her. Her colleague noticed the bit about living alone, but he focused too hard on protecting her to notice the pattern with the hallucinations themselves.

On each piece of paper, she jotted down future questions seeking to link each patient's problems to one another. After finishing Ms. Kavina's paper, Claire drummed the surface of her desk. The chance of every patient experiencing homogeneous hallucinations ran low. Worse, their vague descriptions matched Claire's perpetrator from last Friday's board game night. She'd managed to ignore that coincidence until now, but it proved impossible with the truth staring her in the face. If she discovered enough similarities to indicate their issues stemmed from the same source, what did that mean—for them and for her?

Goose bumps broke out on her arms.

Eric's wrong. You're fine, remember? She dismissed the budding fear in a wave and contemplated potential answers.

One conclusion, a stalker or group had begun preying on lonely women, the start of something tragic in Denver. However, wizard-like appearances and vanishings inside Mrs. Keller and Ms. Kavina's home didn't mesh well with the idea. Shared delusional disorder explained it but required a delusionary origin point to infect others. Age, economic class, and social status differences between patients suggested that didn't exist. Mass hysteria, stemming from cohesive groups, also showed little support, and Claire knew none of these women prior. Crossing off those ideas left what? Dietary-induced mass psychosis stemming from poisoning, mold, or faulty sanitation? Claire shook her head. As improbable as it was, schizophrenia fit many of their symptoms. While she'd seen that error play out before, she had to treat them for *something*.

Hopping out of her rabbit hole, her fingertips ached from the force of violent drumming. Her other palm cramped from its tight grip on the pen pointing its tip against Ms. Kavina's sheet. What had her hand been busy with?

She slipped her fist aside.

A rough sketch of her imagined-or-not stalker stared back.

Her hands flew open, flinging the pen across the room and slinging Ms. Shapiro's sheet off the desk. Then she bore back down to clutch the paper. She tore Ms. Kavina's notes in halves, then halves again, until the paper bulged into too thick of a mass, and she hurled its perfectly symmetrical scraps into the trash. Strands of her hair, twisted in fury, took the brunt of calming her. One cluster of plucked tresses later, she admitted *fine* no longer seemed the proper word to describe herself. As she recomposed Ms. Kavina's notes, her anxiety-riddled brain added another troublesome reminder: her upcoming date was quite tall and more lean than not.

CHAPTER 5

Clipping a plain barrette into the center of a half updo, Claire judged her hair finished and checked the time on her phone. Ahead of schedule, she freed her mind to wander during the rote process of applying makeup, dwelling on the counter-intuitive idea of her dating at all. Forays into the personal lives of strangers dominated her work, a job devoted to eventually ensuring no need for said strangers to see her again. Imagining that same agreement with the express purpose of deepening those bonds stirred an uneasy dance of knee bends and shoulder adjustments.

She stilled herself and twisted open a half-full bottle of concealer. Bags, pimples, and other blemishes which marred her face lined up in the magnified makeup mirror. Her first dab against them revived her internal analysis. Simple physiology explained the desire for dating. Humans, as predictable as any animal, sought romantic companionship in the face of fear and uncertainty. Knowing that didn't temper her childlike excitement. Her smart watch buzzed, flashing eighty-five next to a blinking heart and reminding her to remove it. She rejected its suggestion to start a workout and unlatched it from her wrist, setting it near the sink.

Rick Novak had passed all of the text-based tests she could muster over the past week. Open sincerity separated him from the assault of sexual innuendos prevalent online. His tall and lean build still gave her pause, but recalling the depth of their conversations assuaged her irrational concern.

Such reassurance failed to quell her obsession with the bigger problem at hand. After returning from today's climb with Jess, she had dug further into the Fredonia letter's sender. Public records for Imogene Aire were near non-existent, and neither she nor Eric had ever treated patients with the same last name. The 19 Memory Lane address taunted her, as if the phrase *Enjoy your gifts* should spark a revelation. A clue had to be hiding somewhere. The mirror showed a missed spot along her hairline. She dabbed at it with the wand more than necessary, poking at her skin as if using an electrode to jog her brain.

The phone rattled on the counter. Claire startled, making an errant mark she'd have to blend in later. She pulled the wand away and looked down. Jess's text glowed on the screen.

How's date night?

"Half a face away from finding out," she informed her mirror image. Memories of lunch following their morning climb brought a smile to her velvety glossed lips.

Still getting ready. Thinking of spelunking, Claire replied. The two had agreed to go underground for their next adventure.

The screen lit up.

I'll go TONIGHT if you rescue me from this guy. Asshole not worth the free sushi.

I thought you never let dates pay?

Never, but he won't shut up about how chivalrous he is. CAN'T ESCAPE.

Laughter tipped her focus back to the present. Just a bad date? Or a bad date compounded by bad sushi? Growing up in California had spoiled Jess, but her friend found positives as easily as unshaded plants found sunshine.

Claire craned toward the mirror to examine her cheeks. Her skin's warm natural color hued a few shades lighter than her lips. Preparation complete, she typed away on her digital keyboard. *On your own tonight. Actually want to see if mine's as good as he seems.* She hovered over send, thinking again of stalkers and hallucinations, and added, *Though I might've tried for a double date before reading your texts. Safety in numbers and all.*

Claire sucked in one deep breath and exhaled. The mirror reflected even makeup with subtle color above a billowy green blouse. Her top's wide V stopped short of her bustline. Clasping a turquoise pendant around her neck, her fingers remained to dig in and root out surface tension. Noting the need for a real massage, she twisted around to examine the contours of her mid-rise skinny blue jeans. Satisfied, she walked downstairs. The phone rumbled in her hand a few steps from the bottom. At the stairs' end, the desk called to her, its stacked papers and books reminding her of med school. She tapped on Jess's message.

Hey, it's just stress. You'll be fine. Join me for some Donna later. I'll be dying for quality company.

Claire arched her eyebrows, slipping on two-inch heels and grabbing her clutch while waiting for the inevitable correction text. It came as she opened the door to the garage.

Drinks. I don't even know a Donna.

Sounded great, assuming nerves or a mystery stalker didn't kill her beforehand.

"Healthy first date thoughts." Claire gave one last glance to the desk's edge before leaving. There sat the Fredonia letter, inches from anything else, like a quarantined virus.

CHAPTER 6

Well-dressed patrons, from couples to foursomes, filled nearly every seat of Maggio's small dining room. Distressed pine flooring added an elegant ambiance to the room, lit by candles and dim recessed lighting. Appetite-whetting food from nearby tables resembled their online counterparts as accurately as Rick Novak matched his profile pictures. Tall enough to afford her heels clearance, black pompadour hair, and the right amount of scruff that said he cared but not *too* much. His checkered blue and white button-down fit his athletic frame and tucked into black slacks, separated by a black leather belt.

If only he would stop asking so many questions.

"I thought psychiatrists treated patients who talked to themselves and saw demons in mirrors. Do you really not treat that many . . ." He pursed his lips, hesitant.

"Crazy people? It's okay to say, at least around me." Normally a bald-faced lie, but tests produced more accurate results when subjects believed themselves unwatched.

"Well, yeah." He rubbed his arm protectively to shield the blow of . . . what? An offended slap? The pair sat at a white linen-covered table large enough to allow for a dozen plates. She'd have to climb on top of it in her nice blouse to lay a hand on him.

"Why would saying crazy offend me, my patients, or anyone?" Claire caressed the stem base of her half-full wine glass, enjoying the flipped dynamic of the conversation.

"I don't know. Crazy potentially sounds politically incorrect, and as a rule I try to avoid offending my date." Agreeability and uncertainty danced on his hands. Claire adored their expressiveness. Easier to read. "The thing is, mentally ill doesn't quite fit either. It may or may not mean the same thing to you, but to a project manager they're pretty different."

"What do they mean to a project manager?" She tapped the edge of the table with the length of her finger.

Rick's head bobbed from side to side, chewing on his words before responding. "Crazy is trouble. Mentally ill is troubled. Besides, everyone has mental problems."

Fair assessment, but she couldn't help but latch onto the last sentence. "And everyone could use a therapist." That sounded too self-righteous. She honeyed up her voice to offset it. "You don't have any deep, dark problems to work out?"

"Not that I'd admit to on a first date." A shame—though not as much as how little the question fazed him. Rick spread butter on a pill-bottle-sized bread slice and split it with his teeth. He set the uneaten half on a small plate next to his pint of beer. His beverage choice would rankle Jess, but Claire cared more about the absence of crumbs.

She tiptoed around playing doctor dictionary and decided to throw Rick into the deep end. Best to weed out underwhelming cognitive ability early. "Mentally ill is a generalized term. It's like describing a bad employee as unsatisfactory. Does the employee not get along with coworkers? Is he lazy? Does he lack appropriate skills? Was he never taught those skills?"

"Makes sense. Have to find the root cause." His right hand fell on his chest. "If I wanted change, I'd approach a specific person with the problem."

"Exactly. Crazy means different things to different people." Claire settled into her take on the matter. "Typically, the term equates to aggression, an untreatable condition, or simply a difference of opinion. Meanwhile, mental illness corresponds to physical illness, excepting its focus on a specific organ. Despite that, society wants to corrupt that term too. The problem isn't the words we're using. It's the misnomer of healthy people, as if any of us are without flaws." Callbacks to when she had lost the interest of many a date flashed in her mind and fizzled from indifference. She had no intention of censoring herself. "When speaking personally, the term you use doesn't matter as much as what you mean. You're smart enough to understand mental health deserves no less attention than a bleeding wound. Thus, I don't get offended when hearing patients described as crazy in private, except under one condition."

"What's that?" Credit to Rick, his eyes never glazed over.

"When they themselves are too crazy to register one's mental illness is the byproduct of a closed-off mind." She sipped her Cabernet, enjoying chilled blackberry currant fading into an oak finish. Wine mollified most of her annoyance against those who, intentionally or not, subverted her profession with their ignorance. Rick's handsome stubble eased the rest.

"Do you treat people for that too?" There's that snark from the phone. He finished his slice of bread and reached for another.

This date is going oddly well. "The challenge with closed-minded individuals is they don't realize what others do—that there's a problem to begin with. After all, since when is it wrong to be right?" Too serious of an answer, but judging his response would have to wait. The waiter had returned, with a quick adjustment to the top of his black vest.

"I'm sorry to interrupt. Are you ready to order or would you like more time?" His smile looked forced, born of either fatigue or dissatisfaction.

Rick redirected the waiter to Claire. "What do you think?" he asked.

"Chicken Marsala, please." She handed the menu over.

"Would you like salad or soup with that?"

The old this or that sales tactic. Psychology was everywhere. "Neither. Thank you."

"And you sir?"

Rick scanned the menu with his finger until stopping in the middle to confirm his choice. "The lobster and prawn risotto, please."

The waiter repeated, "Would you like salad or soup with that?" A perfect duplication, down to the intonation.

Rick looked to Claire before answering. Whether for guidance, approval, or not wanting to stare at the waiter while thinking, she couldn't say. "I'm good. Thanks, Brett," he said and placed the menu in his expectant hand. She mentally commended Rick's genuine interactions with the waiter. Names always sailed through Claire's ears. She tracked enough of those at work.

Before Rick started again and stole control of the conversation, Claire asked, "Have you ever tried spelunking?"

"Like, running in caves?"

"Not a lot of running but yes."

"Spelunking," Rick enunciated slowly. His thumb drummed his forearm in consideration. "Is that what you meant by liking nature and the outdoors?"

"Some of it. Climbing and hiking are great too, but spelunking is something special."

His drumming thumb settled. "I jog on trails every once in a while. Stop in caves if it's convenient and take a look around. So technically, I guess so? Why?"

"Cave hiking's a start, but spelunking is a whole other beast. My plan is to walk, climb, and crawl through every big cavern around Denver before I turn thirty-five." Two years left and halfway there. She hadn't meant to talk about *herself* so much, but the way he listened . . .

"Sounds dark."

Claire loosed a one-note chuckle. "That's kind of the point. They're dark until somebody shines a light on it," faltering before she finished, "it's sitting there, waiting." The description unnerved her for the first time in her life, despite regularly using it to sell her hobby. Sunlight had still brightened the sky when she entered Maggio's, allowing her to forget evening darkness, but facing its existence here sapped her confidence.

"Like a shadow waiting outside," said Rick.

And with that, it drained completely. Invisible strings of self-protection pulled Claire back from the table. The oddly specific phrasing cast her thoughts toward the board game stalker. "What?" she asked, buying time to recover.

"There's a metaphysical theory about shadows lurking until someone shines a light on them. The light is metaphorical, but the shadows represent a sort of alter ego to the soul."

Claire tensed up, not at all comforted by the notion.

Rick must have mistaken her narrowed eyes for confusion. "Part of my philosophy major resurfacing. Glad I managed to build a career after that choice."

Shadows lurking about—the alter ego of the soul. Claire suppressed a shudder; she regretted bringing up spelunking. The discussion distracted her from tasting the final drops of her hastily consumed wine.

"Claire?"

Distracted her from more than that, apparently. "That's an interesting theory."

"It's good if you enjoy pondering pointless things. Spelunking kind of bridges the gap between the shadow theory and Plato's Cave." Rick's lips twitched to continue and Claire lifted her brows to ask for it, uncertain of how to direct the conversation elsewhere. "He talks about the perception of reality, using shadows to represent false projections. Even in discovering what casts those shadows, we'll step no closer to the truth. There's always more out there that we can't comprehend because of our education and limited senses." His arms and chest had opened up while talking, his comfort level growing while Claire's shrank like a frightened rabbit.

"Sounds similar to psychology," spoken to talk rather than make a point. "The more we understand of the human mind, the more we realize what we don't know." If her face or voice exuded split attention or concern, Rick didn't pick up on it.

"I should've studied psychology then."

Claire shrugged, using the opportunity to compose a neutral posture. "Depends. Can you handle someone imagining you're their dead sibling, coaxing them back into reality, then easing them out of their inevitable tantrum when they reject the notion entirely?"

"Is that normal for you?"

"Only on Thursdays," she said, not feeling humorous but seeking to amuse and procure precious moments to continue recuperating.

Rick laughed and downed his pint. He dabbed at the foam residue around his mouth with a linen napkin, dropped it into his lap, then seesawed his forearms on the table's edge.

Claire joined her hands under the table, squeezing tightly to drive away distress. Time to return to evaluating Rick, back to normal date topics, away from shadows and darkness. "How often do you work with people as a project manager?"

"Only as much as I have to. Most of my job is planning, resource allotment, and creating estimates. I use Excel more than any human should. Talking is reserved for updating figures, telling somebody they're slacking, or engaging higher-ups when necessary."

"Ever get any problem children?"

"Sometimes. Then I have to figure out if it's lack of training, laziness, or something else." Rick counted one, two, three on his fingers then waved it away. "Doesn't matter when I'm telling them to fix things. People don't react well to critical micromanagement."

"I could teach you a few things about that," Claire blurted. She didn't take it upon herself to flirt often, but anxiety, fear, and genuine interest drove the desire for companionship ever deeper.

"I bet you could." He stole a glance at her breasts, indulging in the innuendo. Reassuring to know her flirting didn't require much practice.

Their waiter walked to their table with a tray of food balanced at head height and a prop-up stand in the other hand. Within seconds, he served their respective meals. "The chicken Marsala for you. And the lobster and prawn risotto for you. I'll be back in a bit to check on your food and refill your water. In the meantime, would either of you like another drink?" The waiter cleared empty glasses while waiting for a response.

Denying the desire to succumb to anxiety and dread, Claire indulged in the opportunity to embrace pleasant and present company. Emphasis on *company*. "Yes. Another glass of the Cab, please."

The side of Rick's lip curled up, taking his sights off Claire long enough to tell the waiter, "I'll have another beer as well. Thanks." The waiter nodded as if hypnotized, devoid of emotion and full of mechanical response.

Claire studied Rick looking back at her. Hopefully he kept his expectations grounded. Despite a slow return to normalcy and an eagerness to enjoy his companionship, a relaxing dinner date was her limit for tonight. Both of them opened their mouths simultaneously, stumbling on their first syllables.

"Go ahead," Rick encouraged, emphasized by a gesture of his hand.

"I was going to suggest we eat our food before it gets cold."

He recovered from a disappointed expression. "Smart idea."

Dinner dates blossomed or withered in these moments. Despite a brief detour, the pair carried positive momentum into the meal proper, but how would they fare after food absorbed the alcohol? Booze-tinted glasses often showed the only good part of a date. Was that too cynical? Three bad first dates in the past year suggested otherwise. On the bright side, the warm chicken tasted a perfect blend of savory, earthy mushrooms and creamy Marsala sauce. The Internet delivered solid food recommendations, regardless of its dating successes.

Rick stared at his food as if questioning its very existence.

"Is something wrong?" asked Claire.

"It's missing something." Index finger pushed into his temple, like a child struggling to remember an answer for an exam. "Booze." He flipped his finger away and wagged it. "It's missing booze."

Claire snickered with her mouth closed, swallowing a bite of food before she agreed. "I'd drink to that. If I could." Inspecting a glass of melting ice before staring at the empty space her wine once occupied, she sighed.

"Life is a cruel mistress."

"We have to put up with a lot. The tragedy of eating at a two hundred dollar restaurant." She opened the door for a legitimate complaint while hoping to hear none of it.

"This restaurant is two hundred dollars? Hope you don't want dessert."

"You're off the hook. Girls don't eat dessert on the first date."

"Never?" Rick leaned in, feigning inability to comprehend what she had said.

Claire shrugged, donning an innocent face. "It's pretty rare." She substituted a spoonful of Marsala sauce in place of a proper drink to moisten the next bite of chicken.

Her date sat back, leaving his fork holding hand extended. "Just checking. Sometimes you have to make exceptions so you don't miss out on something special."

"Like a quality degree?" Reassuring and counseling patients all day instilled a desire to poke fun at any would-be companion, romantic or not. To her delight, Rick seemed game.

"Good enough to afford a two hundred dollar restaurant. Though try as we might, I think it'll hurt the pocketbook a little less than expected." He reached for his half-full water to lift it for a toast. She followed suit with her glass of slushed ice. "To the best people who have been to this table in the past two hours."

"We haven't been here *that* long. Wasn't someone sitting here before us?" She kept her glass raised.

"Yeah, but they looked like accountant types. I'll take us over them—or Brett. You have to make assumptions in my line of work."

Brett? Oh, right. She had already forgotten the waiter's name.

"Then cheers," she said.

"Cheers." Clink-clink went the tips of the glasses.

As if summoned by the gesture, the waiter returned with a fresh wine glass and beer pint, followed by a busboy carrying a silver pitcher. If he regretted forcing them into using water for a toast, he didn't show it. "How does everything taste?" His associate filled Claire's water just below the brim.

"Good."

"Great."

The waiter bowed his head. "Please let me know if you need

anything." He remained while the busboy topped off Rick's water, then walked two tables down.

Rick stabbed at one of the few prawns remaining and asked, "Do you ever use hypnosis for your patients?"

Interesting question. "Sometimes. Most psychiatrists abstain from it."

"Why?"

Because people are closed-minded. Biting the inside of her lip, she reeled in her bitterness in favor of objectivity. "Can't prove it works and professors shy away from teaching it. Medicine is about testing and results, but the effects of hypnotism are hard to isolate."

"What's so different about measuring hypnotism compared to conventional therapy?" Rick spliced in a sip of water between gulps of beer.

"The problem is they're difficult to separate. Hypnosis is used to dive into repressed memories or push patients past their conscious comforts. It's more a reframing of problems rather than a therapy itself. Patients under the effects of hypnosis are treated similarly as to when they're not, so proctors question how much improvement comes from hypnosis versus traditional therapy." Claire polished her fingers on the linen napkin in her lap. "Why do you ask? Are you interested in hypnotherapy?"

He peered at the ceiling before returning with a sheepish grin. "It sounds fun."

"Sure, until you remember the dark secret you stowed away twenty years ago as a survival mechanism in order to tackle adolescence with any semblance of normalcy."

"I guess that's why it's important to trust your therapist."

"And why it's important not to date your therapist," Claire added in case any ideas had bubbled to the top of his head. Dating a psychiatrist differed from dating a masseuse, where one could render services in a detached manner.

"I can see how that would get messy." His finger brushed against his cuff, revealing a fresh scrape veining from his wrist up into his forearm. He itched inside his sleeve and tugged the shirt back.

Claire's grip on her fork tightened, the last chunk of chicken breast waiting at the end of its prongs. Notions of her backyard bushes scraping the skin of a fleeing intruder fizzled as she realized he had intentionally called attention to his cut. "What happened there?"

"I was running on a hiking trail, and my mind got hung up on some philosophical nonsense." As Claire's eyebrows curled to question, he added, "I know most people prefer music, but I started running as a way to examine those thoughts without pacing a trench into my floor. I tend to get pretty wrapped up in it, but I pay attention to my surroundings. Well, these bikers zipped by out of nowhere, and they definitely didn't call out. I jumped into a treeline to avoid getting bowled over. This giant branch I leapt into did a number on my arm." Between his thumb and index finger, he marked out an area equal to half his forearm.

"Some people think the world revolves around them," said Claire. "But you know, there are no bikes in caves." She spun the remaining swig of wine, chancing talk of darkness thanks to her comfort with Rick and two glasses of liquid resolve.

"I'll keep that in mind. Though I admit it sounds more fun with a guide."

"It is." She blinked with an enticing allure that would've earned a high-five from Jess—and had it promptly rescinded when Claire said, "You can hire one for cheap online."

"Oh." Rick's wit dulled in disappointment. He poked at the spoonful of remaining risotto. "Not what I expected you to say there."

"Expectations blind us from the truth. It's better to keep them in check," she said, as much for her as for him, cognizant of the fact her flirting and flippant responses sent mixed signals. She rationalized it as playing hard to get, even if she knew the real reason behind it all.

"Does that fall more under the purvey of philosophy or psychiatry?"

"I think it falls under dating 101."

Rick wiped his face with his napkin and set it on the table. "Touché."

His depressing demeanor sparked an impetuous olive branch. "If you want to keep moving forward, remember to fill up your tank with gas."

"Are we going somewhere? Or is that more dating advice?"

"Something my mom used to say."

He nodded with a fake understanding. It helped a little. Maybe.

The waiter strode over with renewed vigor, presumably eager for closing time. "Would either of you like dessert, or would you prefer the check?"

Claire waved off dessert and shrugged at Rick.

"The check please," he said.

The waiter pulled the bill from his waist and set it on the table. "I'll be right back."

Rick tilted to the side to dig out a wallet from his pocket. Claire considered splitting the check, but forcing herself into his debt made her more likely to venture onto a second date. The pair meshed well and deserved it, especially further removed her stalking experience. Unfortunately, what she wanted mattered only so much. Rick slid his credit card into the plastic slip without making eye contact. Were her jabs too much?

"Thank you for dinner. I had a great time." She made an effort, satisfied in continued single status if he broke *that* easily.

"No, thank *you* for dinner." He beamed and broadened his chest. No expression burned brighter than one following the climb out of a pit of despondency. "Where to next? Coffee? Bar? There are a few places within walking distance from here." Good. His feelings weren't that hurt.

Claire stared at an empty wine glass, pining for more of its acidic sweetness. Sound reason nudged her away, reminding herself how poorly excessive alcohol paired with irrational worry. Coffee seemed an ideal suggestion, pulling double duty in pushing the date's expected end result away from drunken sex. "How about an espresso? You can regale me with your latest philosophical breakthroughs."

"Coffee sounds great." His eyes sparkled with renewed interest in Claire, an ocean absorbing the light of a lighthouse.

"How about I head to the ladies' room and meet you outside?" She didn't need to use the restroom, but a few minutes to compose herself would serve the rest of the date well.

"Sounds like a plan, assuming I'm not still here waiting on Brett to run my card."

"Good luck." Exchanging her napkin for her clutch on the table, she rose with a readjustment of her blouse. She walked past half-filled tables to the back of the restaurant. Through a long hallway and past the entry into a lounging room, she finally came to a door with a chrome W in its center.

Analysis of Rick unfurled into a list of pros and cons. He'd have a hell of a time in some of the cramped caves with his height, but they could make do. Climbing offered him a better starting point since long arms benefited in reaching distant handholds. He showed excellent taste in food, and he acted as though a thirty-dollar entree wouldn't dent his finances. Occasional board games could swing either way. Project management coincided with the right brainwaves to play well, but some preferred turning off critical thinking at night. Something to probe during coffee. Eventually, she'd want to measure his handle on free-reign alcohol. Quickly downing two pints of beer could be nothing, but online dating had provided a lifetime worth of mid-thirties boys mentally stuck in college. He'd likely pass her little test though. Rick measured well, even if the evening hadn't gone as planned. Handsome, responsible, fun, and quick-witted went a ways toward building excitement for her inevitable call with Jess. One smart carrot, as her mom would say.

Washing her hands, she checked her makeup in the mirror. Blush and concealer continued to highlight her natural rosiness. Satisfied, she pushed through the series of restroom doors and returned to the dining room to find their table cleared and empty.

Claire strolled with easy steps toward the exit, admiring the restaurant and grading it positively. As she prepared to open the first of two glass doors, she halted three steps from the handle. Her hand flew back to tug on her blow-dried hair.

Outside, a dim overhead light cast an all too familiar shadow.

Height, hair, and build silhouetted her backyard stalker. Her heart thumped. The figure bent down. Thump, thump. Shadows rose from cement. Skin under her blouse dampened. The shade turned, profile facing the length of the cement sidewalk. Wine in her stomach fermented from ambrosia to noxious fumes. She froze as the man stepped out from his shroud, holding something slender in his hand. Entering the light, he morphed from the vague tracing of her backyard stalker into Rick—taller, sturdier built, and with a head full of thick hair, but she couldn't shake what she had seen. The scent of everyone's food congealed into an off-putting musk that resembled soured meat. The clack of her heels boomed in her head for the final steps between her, the double doorways, and her date. Clean night air cleared the rancid smell but failed to alleviate her growing headache.

"I have the worst luck with dropping phones," said Rick, raising the slender device to his face, precariously balanced between fingers. "I swear when this one breaks, I'm buying heavy duty. Anyway, where to?"

Claire clung to her purse for stability. Whether her subconscious detected subtle miscues and warned her, or an overactive imagination festered within, their night out lost its appeal. She needed space to come to grips with the fact that Rick loosely shared physical qualities with her board game stalker. A fact that didn't make him the board game stalker.

"I'm actually not feeling well," said Claire. "Sorry." Guilt clamped around her heart as Rick donned his mask of confusion. A twinge of annoyance might have layered underneath. "Can we talk about date number two tomorrow?"

Color trickled back into his cheeks. "Sure. No problem. Are you okay to drive? I can call a cab or drive you home if you don't feel well enough."

"I'll be fine. And I really did enjoy myself." She forced herself onto her calves to kiss his bristled cheek, beating back the desire to flinch after making contact. Any annoyed tenseness fizzled from his face, loosening guilt's grip on her chest.

"Me too," he said. "Talk to you soon."

Not a total disaster then. Though she could've done without standing beside him while the valets retrieved their cars. The awkward silence as they waited stretched time itself.

CHAPTER 7

I thought hypnotism was for magic shows. What are the risks? Could I wake up not acting like myself? What are the benefits? Can this actually cure me?" Greg Hampson asked his last question as if cut off. Suffering from aboulomania, he lacked the ability to decide much of anything. The more he asked, the worse he felt, so Claire and he had agreed to a four-question limit on any topic.

"Greg, do you trust me?" After five weeks of treatment, she hoped she had built some rapport.

"I think I do. It's a little easier to work now I guess." The overweight man bounced in his cushioned sage chair with the energy of a nervous child. He had already drunk half of his water, but a second unopened bottle stood on the end table next to him.

Seated at the other end of the garnet rug, Claire leaned on her knees, using physical proximity to show concern. "Greg, I'll ask again. This time I want you to answer yes or no. Do you trust me?"

Mr. Hampson sucked on his lip and shook the floorboards like a minor earthquake. His blank stare struck Claire as ghostly. "Yes," he relented, squeezing his palms together.

"Great. Because you trust me, I'll walk you through exactly how hypnotism works."

"Umm . . . okay. Can I ask? Before we start? If it's okay?" Mr. Hampson counted three questions with head waggles before an invisible line pulled his neck taut, forcing him to address his concern. "Is this a common trea—" he stuttered. "Is this a common and normal treatment?"

Normal, yes. Common, no. Months had passed since she last used hypnosis; the subject coming up on her date made for an odd coincidence. Flashing back to dinner reminded her to return Rick's latest text message. Five nights after their first date, they had mostly recovered from her awkward exit.

She sat back, resuming her authoritative straight-backed posture. Guiding her patient through therapy restored a sense of control that had diminished in recent weeks. "Yes, this is a normal and safe treatment. It's ideal for circumstances such as ours. Hypnotism will help you relax. While you're under trance, I'll guide you with questions, but it will be your brain sorting everything on its own."

"Could something go wrong?" Mr. Hampson finished the first bottle of water. "What if my condition is protecting me from something darker? Can you force me to do something I'm not ready for? Can you change who I am?"

"Hypnotism isn't mind control. I can't force you to do anything you don't want to or don't believe in. My role is to make suggestions. The hypnotic state will allow your subconscious to answer without the surge of information which would normally overload you." Claire motioned with arms wide open. Exaggerated non-verbals drove key points home faster and further than words alone. "I won't proceed unless you want me to, but if you trust me, then this is the best course of action."

"Yes, alright, okay." Mr. Hampson's bouncing eased. "Let's do it. Umm . . . do I look at a clock or a watch or something?"

"Watches are great for hypnotism, but the tool is of minor importance. What matters most is concentrating your attention on *one thing*," her emphasis subtle. She slowed her tempo and continued in a submissive pitch. "In order to give way to your subconscious. Instead of a watch, I prefer this." Claire rested her hand on a double-balled pendulum. "This pendulum will serve as your focal point. Meanwhile, I'll speak to your subconscious and wake you when the session is over. From there, our conversation will slowly fill your conscious mind, like a faucet dripping into a sink."

While the average person fell under the sway of hypnosis within minutes, Mr. Hampson's fear of commitment unintentionally subverted the process. Her tonal transformation from authoritative presence to servile guide helped to lower these walls.

"Greg, stare at the pendulum and focus on its movement." Claire pulled on a single string and let it loose. "Follow the ball as it swings from end to center, as it clacks and carries its momentum to the other ball. Think of nothing but their motion through the air. Watch as the ball sways from end to the center, as the second moves from center to end, end to center. Center to end. End to center." His ghostly stare morphed into that of a vigilant guard. "You are in control. You are always in control. I am here to guide you to where you want to go. While you watch the ball move, breathe in a rhythm which comforts you. Focus only on the pendulum swinging from center to end, end to center."

Mr. Hampson patted his thighs in measured beat to the pendulum's clacks, indicating a distracted mindset and a hurdle for hypnotic trance.

"Feel the weight of your hands grow heavy."

Patting slowed but persisted.

"Heavier and heavier, until it feels like pillows weighted with lead still your hands. No matter how hard you push, no matter how hard you think you can push, you're unable to lift your hands any further. Heavier and heavier, you submit to the heavy load. As you submit the tension falls away; it seeps out of your hands and out of every limb. Everything you are focuses on the ball swinging from center to end. End to center."

Wrists twitched in resistance, eased in compliance. Stiff torso and shoulders loosened, billowing out his frame.

Content with Mr. Hampson's level of concentration, Claire again shifted her voice, dropping into an androgynous octave, pausing between each sentence. "You are no longer in an office. You are now in an empty hallway, standing still. You stand five steps from a closed door." No reaction—good. "Behind the closed door lies the ultimate answer to every question." The door always corresponded to the subject's deepest desire.

"You take your first step toward the door. You feel calmer, not knowing what lies behind the door but knowing that it exists to help you."

The ball of the pendulum continued to clack at regular intervals. Mr. Hampson exhibited a statue's stoicism.

"You take your second step toward the door. Comforted by the door, you allow your subconscious to take control."

Clack.

"You take your third step toward the door. You embrace the desires of self, what you seek most. You desire truth. You will discover truth."

Clack. His breathing slowed.

"You take your fourth step toward the door. You are almost there. You begin to imagine what lies behind the door."

Clack. Mouth opened in relaxation.

"You take your fifth step toward the door. You open it and are filled with the serenity of *knowing*. You feel confident. You grasp at your desires. You now hold them in your hand. What are they?"

Mr. Hampson looked beyond the swinging pendulum, eyes lost in a pool of self-reflection. Eyebrows pulsed as if a spring loading and unloading. "It's a crystal ball, holding all the right answers. I can sense their . . . accuracy."

"How does the crystal ball make you feel?"

"Confident." Mr. Hampson gripped armrests with deliberation, without any trembling uncertainty. "It's all so obvious. All the right answers are staring me in the face."

"What makes these answers right?"

"That's the way they are. They're right *because* they're right. They are truth. I see them so clearly."

"Then who decides the answers are right?" Claire imagined her voice floating on the wind to him. She lived within Mr. Hampson now, an echo chamber for his thoughts, the disembodied void of self.

"The ball. But not really. It's only partially the ball."

"Who else decides on these answers?"

"The crystal ball shows a picture of me." He squinted. "It's me." An uncommon sprinkle of pride dotted his discovery.

Embrace the sensation. "What happens if you release the ball?"

"I don't want to," he hesitated, his fall from pride abrupt and signifying fear.

"Why not?"

Mr. Hampson rocked as if listening to music on a park bench. "I'll lose all the answers. I'll choose the wrong responses."

"What happens if you don't choose *a* right response?" A right response—not the right response. Mr. Hampson searched for catchall answers like a knight searching for the Holy Grail, with as much success. His framework required a shift to realize multiple answers could satisfy most questions.

"Disaster. No friends. Lose my career. Bad romance. Everything turns upside down."

It doesn't take a wrong response to turn everything upside down, Claire rebuked in silence. Her questions fired off as reflexively as Mr. Hampson's responses. It afforded moments of mental wandering, for better or worse. "Is that what the crystal ball says?"

Mr. Hampson struggled, "No. I don't see anything bad there. I only see myself, making the right choices. The ball only shows positive results. Positive results. It must be lying, but I can't let go. I don't understand."

He sounded as mad as her mother during an episode, peaking a few months into her institutionalization. *A broken clock never boils,* she barked over and over, the memory's voice once again distinctively *hers.* Heat flushed Claire's forehead. Thoughts of, *Why am I hearing . . .* faded into commands of, *Focus.* In the decade since that episode, she had learned to read and respond to cognitive wrestling such as Mr. Hampson's in a way she never could with her mother.

"You said the crystal ball shows you the truth. If it shows you the truth, can it lie?"

"No, that wouldn't make sense. So I have to keep it safe. Forever in my hands, I'll always have the answers." Words gradually softened from psychotic rant to calm resignation.

"Do you still see yourself in the crystal?"

"Yes, it's always me. I'm always there. Choosing the right

answers." He could have commanded an army with the intensity of his focus.

"If the crystal ball shows you the truth and shows you making the right answers, what does that mean?" *What does it mean, Mom?* Claire recalled asking many times. She had studied her mother, looking for consistency in thought which had accompanied her earlier in life. Toward the end, she failed to comprehend anything more than the ramblings of a mad woman.

"It must mean that *I* have the right answers." Perfect.

A yearning to scratch her calf stirred. She dug a fingernail into her palm to distract herself, not wanting the motion to wake him early. "If *you* have the right answers, can you put the crystal ball away?"

"I don't know. No. Wait. Why?" Attention remained transfixed on the invisible globe.

"You can always bring it back out. It's your crystal ball. Yours. But for now, why don't you put it away to see what happens? Don't you want to learn what happens without the crystal ball?"

Mr. Hampson sat silently, giving no indication of delivering a response. He stared below where the pendulum continued to clack and sway, assessing something Claire could only guess at. After completing his deliberation, his hands twitched inward.

"I put it away. It's gone for now."

"Do you still know the right answers?"

"I think so. I'm not sure. It's hard to say if they're right without it. I'll get the ball out again." His hands twitched in the opposite direction. His head bobbled in a circle. "Yes, it's all the same."

"Does the ball show you what you already know?" she asked, leading him.

"The ball shows what I already know."

"Do you feel comfortable putting the ball away again?"

"I do." Mr. Hampson's breaths deepened. Gasps now captured all the air the world could offer. While more therapy, and perhaps hypnosis, lay before the finish line, they were on track.

Idle curiosities turned to whether hypnosis could have staved off her mom's commitment. *Of course not,* she answered. *Psychosis and aboulomania differ as much as fire and ice.* Early signs of talking to walls at home persisted during her mother's stay at St. Mary's Hospital of the Wayward. Guiding Mr. Hampson through his mental corridors congealed with memories of long walks down bleach-white hallways with her mom. Most of the time Sofia Costas acted normally, showing concern over routine things like her daughter's college schoolwork, stirring wishful thoughts. Pleading and sometimes frightened conversations with unknown entities dashed those hopes. At the end of such episodes, she rambled phrases that she presented as more important than any school lesson. She would chant, *A broken clock never boils,* followed by incessant declarations of, *If you cast a long shadow, you're bound to get burnt,* until Claire said 'okay' a sufficient number of times. By comparison, Mr. Hampson's problems seemed opaque.

"Know that any time you need to confirm the truth, you can always bring out the crystal ball. Use it whenever you feel necessary."

"I can always bring out the crystal ball." Confident. Assured.

"Now I want you to look ahead. You face the same door again, the one you walked through earlier. Once again, you are five steps from the door in an empty hallway."

"I see it."

"You take your first step. You feel excitement building as you prepare to reenter the world with your newfound gift."

Without guidance, Mr. Hampson would eventually stumble out of his semi-catatonic state, deprived of the session's gains. Bits and pieces may accompany a gradual awakening, assuming one had several hours of quiet. More likely, a sudden sound would wrench the hypnotized subject into awareness. Premature waking severed any lessons the subconscious sought to impart on the conscious mind, erasing the incident completely.

"You take your second step. You walk beside yourself, two halves of a whole coming together in realization of truths learned."

If you cast a long shadow, you're bound to get burnt, echoed internally. After again hearing Sofia Costas's familiar whisper, a deluge of memories flooded Claire. One year of institutionalization ended when a heart attack terminated her mother's insanity as suddenly as it had begun. Self-inflicted bruises on her chest showcased a futile attempt to ward off her impending doom. Her coherency at the bitter end led Claire to question everything for a time, until time came to grow up and start med school. Only one of her middle school students showed at her funeral. He cried with a fury at the world, lamenting Ms. Costas as the best playmate he'd ever had. Other parents weren't willing to entertain the notion of their children mourning a mad woman. Which circled Claire back to square one.

Had she spent all that time, then and now, deciphering the mutterings of a mad woman? The persistence of these memories signaled deep-seated fragmentation at best. At worst, the crazy gene had finally flipped on. Uncertainty left her one way forward, a path she traversed while speaking words that guided herself as much as Mr. Hampson.

"You," she started, quivering from the amalgamation of anger, fear, and grief. She cleared her throat. Bolstered it for her patient and herself. "You take your third step . . ."

CHAPTER 8

H ow does this look?" Claire gazed over her shoulder, examining the above-knee dress in the mirror. Halter straps exposing the pale pink skin of her toned back and arms captivated her.

"Like if you don't buy it, I'm finding one in my size," said Jess. "Been a while since I've seen you wear something like that."

"You'd probably pull it off better."

"I can pull off a lot of dresses better. You know why?"

The pair stood near the curtained dressing room of the afternoon's third clothing store. Claire faced her friend, her hand patting the bare skin between her shoulder blades. Comfortable jeans called from the nearby display table. "Why's that?"

"Practice! It's not just about what you wear, but *how* you wear it. Plus, you can't compete with this complexion." Jess brushed the back of her fingers against her tanned forearms. "But practice helps."

Claire rolled her eyes. Two weeks had passed since board games ended with her tossing and turning in bed. Stressors in the form of her mom's voice and patient load had threatened to derail her further, but a *normal* second date with Rick provided a compelling respite. Last night's outing had sent her spirits high enough to agree to a rigid day of shopping, but she fast approached needing a break.

"I think I'll make this work. Let me change, and we can get out of here." Claire snuck behind the dressing room curtain and slid it shut.

"Make it work? You rocked it! I've never seen you show that much skin outside of a swimming pool. Must be falling pretty hard for him." Jess mocked Claire with kissing sounds.

"Falling might be a strong word." Claire shimmied out of the dress and reached for the comfort of her blue jeans.

"Is it? You're pretty consistent with three strikes and you're out."

"He hasn't had any strikes." None that she could hold against him. She pulled down a striped sleeveless shirt.

"That's my point. You're usually so eager to dish out strikes that every dinner date is over before dessert hits the table. You're the definition of picky. Ergo, since this guy has made it this far, you must be falling for him. Especially to buy a dress too risque to wear to work."

Claire draped the outfit over her arm and smoothed out its folds. She stroked its hem, not too short but riding two inches higher than anything in her closet. Reveling in jumping out of her comfort zone, energy flowed through her as if someone spiked her morning coffee with Adderall. That damn *whoever* or *whatever* wasn't going to ruin her life. The time had come to build her new routine. She pulled back on the curtain and feigned her best secret-spilling face. "You know. The truth is . . ."

Jess took the bait. "What's that?" She crowded Claire's space with equal parts concern and excitement.

"I've been spending way too much time with you," teased Claire.

"Yeah, yeah. You're welcome for having someone around to liven up your life." Jess led them toward the cashier. "Now pay for that dress so we can head to Niko's." She hadn't missed an annual sale at her favorite store in years. Their clothes molded to her full hips and curves as if the designers fashioned them specifically for her. While the store's merchandise didn't mesh with Claire's build or style, the timing offered a nice break to recuperate and send a playful message to Rick, assuming Jess didn't guilt her too hard.

An empty line made for a fast transaction at the sales counter. The teenage clerk put Claire's new dress in an *Out and Out* paper bag and handed it over with a youthful smile and a reminder about an upcoming sale. Jess and Claire thanked her with as much enthusiasm as they could muster and left the store, entering the vast open air of the Cherry Creek Shopping Center.

"Isn't there a smoothie place near Niko's?" asked Claire.

"Yeah, a few doors over. It's one of those where they add sugar to everything. But if you drink a smoothie"—Jess wagged her finger—"I'm not letting you off the hook for dinner. I haven't seen you in two weeks."

Two weeks, and they had only discussed what happened over a series of drawn-out text messages. Jess's psychological tricks proved as useful as Robert's attempts to swipe away emotions with rigorous logical analysis. They weren't equipped to solve Claire's problems any more than she. Only diligent research into her and her patients' problems kept her head above water. Jess swaying back from overly concerned mother to snarky best friend helped too.

Mostly.

Despite a high that coursed through her with drug-like effects, it failed to wipe out the image of a stranger under the cover of darkness, staring at her from the sidewalk.

Jess slid her arm around Claire's and pulled her close with the crook of her elbow, snapping her out of her musings and starting their march toward Niko's. "Don't let your mind wander. I need you sharp and tuned in on fashion."

"Sorry." She squeezed her friend's arm. "I was thinking about that guy at my house."

"I know. That's why I'm keeping you close. I'm a good luck charm, you know? In all of my life, I've never once been in the vicinity of someone who's been kidnapped."

"You make it sound as though I've won a carnival prize." A breeze carried the scent of roasted coffee beans from a nearby cafe. Nutty, smoky scents beckoned, drawing both ladies' attention for a moment.

"Me? A carnival prize? I think winning the lottery is a more apt comparison."

Claire chuckled, her final fits of laughter ending with closed eyes. Squeezing the narrow bone of her nose bridge between her fingers, she trusted Jess not to walk her into a tree or a bench. "I'm not worried, believe it or not. I just don't get it. Nothing fits."

Snapped fingers startled Claire into dropping the thinking pose. They passed the coffee roaster, a cookie cake store, and two shoe stores, all lined up side by side.

"Quick. Someone comes to you, recounting seeing a stranger in their yard late at night. What do you do?"

Claire saw through Jess's motives, but she indulged the make-shift game, and the answers came with ease. "Probe for signs of trauma. Recommend general counseling to determine if long-term therapy is necessary. Suggest they call the police, and tell them to make an appointment if it happens again."

Jess's finger drilled through Claire's dirty blonde hair, into her scalp. "So call Dr. Rossi if something happens again. Then call Dr. Diaz if you need a second opinion. And maybe, just maybe, call the police. Even two weeks late, it's smart to have it on record."

"Okay, *Dr. Diaz*. If it happens again, I'll call the police and invite you over for the Q&A. That way you can psychoanalyze my re-sponses to relay their meaning to me later." Her friend loved play-ing the psychiatrist card, irritating Claire even when right. She con-sidered divulging the Fredonia letter, its message, or her patients' hallucinations, without getting too specific. But in the face of Jess's haughtiness, she craved empowerment. That meant turning the conversation back around.

"You know, Dr. Rossi came up with some fresh advice." Claire pointed at the same spot Jess had poked. "She recommended I in-dulge in this fresh air until a blissful calm comes over me. It takes time she says, so it's best to set up shop outside the smoothie place while you're shopping at Niko's."

Jess scoffed. "You do know the whole helping each other shop thing doesn't work if *you* don't help *me*?"

"When have I ever gone into there?" Her mom had frequently shopped at the store that once occupied the same location, and Niko's hadn't renovated enough to dull the somber vibes.

"I don't know." She fell into a Mexican accent when annoyed. "Back when you were a good friend? Been so long I can't remem-ber."

Claire tugged on Jess's hooked arm, unbalancing her friend. "Here's an idea. How about I talk to Rick and let you live vicariously through our relationship. As my best friend, you'll be privy to juicy details I wouldn't share with anyone else." Which meant little, but baiting Jess with romantic gossip made a better pitch than re-explaining her aversion to Niko's.

"Fine, have your flirty boy fun. I'll go shopping *all by myself* and find a gorgeous dress *all by myself*." A smile cracked behind her accented assault. "Then I'm calling Karen and Frances for a pre-dinner warmup." A dinner Claire now remembered was planned for four tonight. Queen Socialite couldn't function without her subjects.

"Are those the woo twins?"

Jess mimicked the sound of a sizzling pan, "No. It's the two we grouped with for that scavenger hunt a few months ago."

An inward sigh pushed down rising anxiety that threatened to taint her Adderall-esque high. "I want to be sure of what I'm getting myself into tonight."

"Oh, Claire. That's the fun of it. Nobody knows." Jess unhooked from Claire and patted her forearm three patronizing times. "Now drum up some excitement to inspire me." Her friend shooed her away, Jess's walk morphing from casual stroll into confident strut.

Claire veered toward Smoothie Squared, targeting one of several empty round tables. Trees centered in individual gravel plots offered shade from the setting sun. "Send me a picture of anything that looks good," she called out.

Jess's fingertips brushed below her collarbone. "*On me?* I don't want to send you everything in the store. You'll never get anywhere with your boyfriend, and you promised me something juicy." She laughed, flipping back gold-streaked black hair. She waved as she sashayed away. "I'll be fine, as long as you don't run off anywhere."

Claire smirked. After examining table seats for stains, smoothie or otherwise, she took the cleanest one. She opened the inside zipper of her leather purse, pulled out a phone protected by textured plastic. Its white glow mesmerized her, conjuring messages to send to Rick. She hmmed in consideration.

You should feel special, she sent him, tapping the cased electronic in her palm while waiting for a response. Several tables inside and out remained empty. Out of pity, she considered walking inside to buy something, added sugar or no. Her phone's ding put the idea to rest.

Why's that?

I went shopping. Bought something for our next date. She grinned at the possibilities of what her vague message put in his head, until an odd concern vexed her. What if he preferred the jeans look? If any pictures in her dating profile showed legs, it was her hiking in workout shorts. She reserved skirts and dresses for work.

But this dress looked so damn beautiful. If he didn't appreciate it, they would have to part ways. Good taste was good taste—no exceptions.

Her phone rumbled. *Guess I'll have to do the same.*

Hard to believe. He seemed as attached to button-downs and slacks as a monk to robes, but after buying a backless dress, she admitted the possibility of anything. She pictured him in a dress of his own, laughing at first then peering upward to better imagine his long, lean legs. Clouds held their place in the sky despite a ground-level breeze sifting through her hair.

The same wind carried the sound of gravel crunching a few feet away. She looked down, ignoring the noise and intending to write Rick, but shot back up as crushed rock ground louder. The figure responsible ducked underneath a tree branch, then rested long-armed hands on the seat opposite her.

"Hello, Claire." A man in a cream trench coat loomed, his face and hands so pale the jacket almost camouflaged them. Jeans distressed from overuse and faux leather boots covered his lower half. Even his ears were hidden by the wide brim of a hat. Given today's warm weather, the attire did little to ease her suspicion. Claire pulled up Jess's phone number, leaving the digital *Call* button one click away and plainly visible on the edge of the table.

"Can I help you?" Careful articulation blended annoyance with reservation.

"That's exactly why I'm here."

She tried to place the backyard stalker's frame and face over the interloper's. Conservative clothes rendered any matching impossible. "What do you mean?"

"To thank you. For helping me," he said with manicured glee.

Hold strong. Don't look away. "I don't know who you are, but could you please leave me alone?"

"I can't do that. We're friends now." Off-white teeth flashed behind lips stretching into cheekbones. Blue eyes better suited to a doll unnerved Claire, distorting the world around her.

"We're not anything," Claire said, flat to filter out emotions she couldn't control. Frost spread through her veins, freezing limbs in place. Breath shallowed as if airlifted to the Rocky Mountain peaks.

"Close to what we'll be."

"What?" she snapped. He'd sound insane to an amateur. To Claire, the esoteric drivel hinted at a calculated agenda. Despite the warning signs, she dove deeper into his trap. Risk carried its own rewards.

"We're not anything close to what we will be." He grinned again, stretching it as if to test how wide he could spread his lips. "Relationships take time to flourish. Let's make sure we take it slow as we get to know each other. You don't want to rush into anything you might regret." Body language indicated he intended to intimidate rather than harm, at least out in public.

Stop talking and start questioning.

"How do you know me?" Her thumb tapped the phone screen, its dim light threatening to snooze.

"We go way back. Think of me as a family friend."

Claire scoured his face, making note of an inch-long birthmark on his left cheekbone. Sternness juxtaposed the levity with which he spoke. "A family friend? Who? What's your name?"

"Those are great questions. How about calling me Ryan?" An elongated neck cast an air of condescension. "If you need to know more, I'm sure you'll figure something out. You always find the right answers for other people."

Despite focusing on gathering details, base instincts demanded she bolt. Toes tapped at the edge of wedge heels that Jess demanded she wear for dinner. Running wouldn't take her anywhere fast. She resolved to do what she did best and kept him talking.

"Ryan, do you want to hurt me?"

"I couldn't hurt you. We still have so much to learn about one another."

"What does that mean?" Claire stammered. Not the right question, not at all. Her free hand rose to the table, relieving the other's phone duty.

"That you'll be seeing more and more of me over the next few weeks."

A tightened grip on her phone steeled her resolve. "What makes you think I want to see you?"

"Your eyes perceive what your mind wills."

"Whose mind are you talking about?"

"Whose do you think?"

The ongoing assault of cryptic messages persisted with no end in sight. For the first time, she allowed her greatest concern to bubble up: was she imagining the whole thing, as she suspected of her patients? If this encounter lived in her head then . . . well, she'd examine the underlying problem later, but the idea presented a solution to the problem at hand. Claire closed her eyes. She trusted in training to determine that if 'Ryan' was real, he intended no harm. Burying her face in her hands, she hummed the chorus of Adele's "Rumor Has It". Claire visualized herself sitting at the Smoothie Squared table—alone, happy, and undisturbed. Her throat vibrated with echoes of Adele's lyrics, casting aside reality to delve into her mental sanctuary.

Four fingers laid themselves on her shoulder. Claire reeled, grasping the edge of the table to pull herself up and run despite her footwear. Her eyelids flickered open to the sound of Jess repeating her name.

Claire scanned the outdoor mall in every direction, like a woman tracking a fly buzzing around her head. No sign of the stranger anywhere in sight.

"It looked like you were talking on speaker phone, but then you stopped and closed your eyes. Did something happen with Rick?"

Talking on the phone? If only. Her left hand cramped. She let the phone tumble onto the table, Jess's number still on screen from frequent taps to keep it awake. "Did you see anybody near me?"

As if expecting a trap, Jess drawled, "No. Just you sitting in that chair."

One thought repeatedly resurfaced, no matter how hard Claire flung it into the recesses of her mind.

Was this how it started for my mom?

CHAPTER 9

Max Childress towered over Claire when they stood side by side. Anyone glancing at the ex-college linebacker wouldn't have guessed how badly anxiety stifled his life. After four months of treatment, she finally felt ready to ask, "Would you like to move our sessions to every other week?"

"We've been making good progress. I feel so much better than when I first came to see you. I don't want to relapse. Do you—" he stopped himself, engaging in a mental tussle with the rug's carpet fibers before looking back up. "Okay. Two weeks from now. If I can't take it though, I can come in earlier, right? I don't want to lock myself into every other week, you know?"

Claire squeezed the top of Mr. Childress's arm. She didn't want to stop treating him. Conditions as simple as his, with appointments as regular, helped stabilize her amid an increasingly complex patient load. But it wasn't fair to him, wasn't the proper solution. "When you need me, I'll be here. You're free to schedule as you deem fit."

"Thanks, Dr. Rossi." Mr. Childress pounded a fist into his palm. "I'll keep plugging away at this."

"You're doing great. Remember: one day, one moment, one step at a time." Words she spoke effortlessly and often. She recalled researching and crafting the mantra to provide a mindful focal point to anxious and depressed patients. The repetition of 'one' intended to enhance its memorability and direct the patients' attention toward their inner feelings. Something she herself could use during the upcoming hour.

"One day, one moment, one step at a time," he repeated.

Claire followed Mr. Childress out of the private therapy room, handed him off to Janice for payment and scheduling, then ducked into her shared office space. Eric looked up from a stack of organized papers, the point of his pen still pressed against the top page. She chewed the inside of her lip to still herself from reaching for her hair and betraying her annoyance. She had intentionally left the hour open. Working on her and her patients' problems pushed down the fear that Ryan was watching her, even in a room without windows.

"When's your next patient?" he asked.

"Four o'clock. Yours?"

Eric picked up on masked annoyance better than anyone, probably because he set it off more. He didn't show anything though, which meant she had either improved at hiding her emotions or more probable, some patient's affliction preoccupied him. "Same. Had a cancellation. Guess we're getting a sneak peek of Friday."

Talking in the open directly opposed looking inward for solutions. Claire waved him off. "Not so fast. Need to review notes for my next appointment. Tricky diagnosis." She eased into her seat and set Mr. Childress's notes aside.

"Shouldn't be that hard. Isn't everything delusional disorder, schizophrenia, or dementia with you nowadays?" he accused, laying his pen across the papers.

Pick that pen back up.

The urge to twist her hair manifested in a quick flex of her hand. "Why do you say that?"

"I'm a psychiatrist. I observe. Attracting as many psychotic patients as you have over the past three weeks is less likely than winning the lottery."

Not preoccupied by a patient's affliction. Preoccupied by hers. "And yet people win the lottery every week." If she managed to hide her irritation before, her crossed arms and raised shoulders gave it away now. Her frayed nerves found respite in the act, easing off of torturing her insides.

"That doesn't invalidate the need to investigate something out of the ordinary." Eric twisted his wedding ring, his clearest sign of discomfort. Empathetic to a fault, at least he shared in this conversation's woes.

"What something are you investigating, exactly?"

"I feel that," he inhaled, puffing up his chest. "You may either be too hasty to assign such diagnoses or more concerning, that stress is tainting the analysis of your patients."

That killed any chance of confiding in him the mall man's ephemeral appearance. She didn't fully accept her diagnoses either, but only psychoses explained her patients' symptoms. *Then why doesn't it explain* yours? She rejected the idea that her own problems compromised her. Claire clapped her hands together, pointing them at Eric. "Or maybe there's a reason why so many of these patients are coming to see," then flipping them up at her chin, "*me.*"

"Interesting." Eric stopped rotating his ring, leaving a finger and thumb covering it, and leaned back. "Now, why would that be?"

"I don't know, but I have an idea." She had considered the question during stints of driving, showering, and cooking, always circling back to one inciting event. "Do you remember that letter from earlier this month? The one from Fredonia? Nothing attached, no mention of anything specific. All it said was, *Enjoy your gifts.*"

Eric studied her from across the room, his thick-framed glasses unable to hide narrowed eyes. "You're suggesting that somebody is finding these patients and referring them to you?"

Until last Saturday, she hadn't thought about the letter in over a week, not since her first date with Rick. The timing of everything now seemed less an errant mailing and more a purposeful taunt. "Not just somebody. The person who sent me that letter."

"Why do you think that?"

She'd play along with Eric's transition into psychiatric examiner. She lightly flicked her forehead to show the answer was obvious. "Logic?"

Playing along didn't necessitate flowery answers.

Her partner's ensuing sigh ruffled the sheets of paper below him. "There are a lot of leaps to cement that logic. That person would need to seek out or already have relationships with all of these patients." Fingers calmly counted each point into his other palm. "He or she would need a reason to send them to you. Finally, these patients would have to willingly schedule their appointments."

"Sounds right so far." She'd let him pass out from holding his breath before she admitted it sounded too outrageous.

"So your assessment is the logic I laid out is sound, thus the mailer is responsible for your increase in psychotic patients?"

"That's what I said a minute ago. The two are related."

"Do you have any evidence to back up that claim? How are your patients saying they found you?" Eric grilled. The impassive facade faded away. He wanted an explanation, which meant he wanted to believe.

"They aren't saying anything out of the ordinary. Finding an online ad or a compelling review. I've checked the referring doctors when available and didn't see any unknown names."

"Then discovering the origin of the letter is no easy task, *if* they're related," said Eric. He rose like Socrates from a stone bench. "Let's take a step back. Why would someone do all of this? You must have brainstormed to some degree."

Nothing in Claire's years of practice warranted psychotic and hallucinatory patients specifically seeking her out. Whoever led this charge did so with malicious intent, a belief reinforced by two antagonistic encounters. "I've been wracking my brain treating them and searching for an explanation." She stopped reigning in her attitude and let her hands run wild. "Since you're a psychiatrist too, and not directly involved, why don't you help and posit why someone might do that?"

Eric paced the width of the room, glancing at her and sidelining his first response with a head shake. "Someone suffering from delusions blaming you for a negative event which transpired. An unrequited lover seeking to win your attention and affection through sending extra business. You could even be the unlucky recipient of an elaborate prank. I'd surmise the most likely scenario is something in between. A person who respects you yet feels animosity toward you."

She had spent the last couple of nights mentally skewering acquaintances, past relationships, and former patients. Nobody jumped out as a suspect. Even if one did, that didn't explain the transient strangers at her home and the mall. She covered her lips, debating what to reveal.

Eric halted at the corner of his desk, bracing his heel against its leg. "I still want to hear your opinion. I know you've given the possibilities some thought, but it's important to consider the heavy toll these patients bring. Treatment of psychotic disorders is no easy task, both in terms of success rate and how it taxes the psychiatrist. Additionally, you've always liked treating diseases as much as, if not more than, the patients themselves. Without a deeper emotional connection, the technical aspect of treatment could spiral you into a series of adverse states."

Claire ogled the filing cabinet, eager to hunt through it in search of connections between her problems and her patients' but resigned herself to resolving her partner's concerns. Eric's compassion endeared at times. It fueled his talents as a great doctor and mentor, but it also interfered with what mattered: the truth. It cemented her decision to avoid discussing Saturday's encounter, but he deserved to know almost everything else—which might also salvage the remainder of the hour.

She stood up and joined him in the space between their desks, clamping her hands at her waist. Inadvertent Italian gesticulations threatened to distract from her words otherwise. "A couple of weeks ago, I caught someone staring at me from my front yard. I haven't seen him since, but it's possible someone is or was stalking me."

Eric's scrutinizing expression softened.

"You suggested," said Claire, "that a secret pursuer might try to win me over with new business. What if they know how much I love tackling challenging situations? I've swung back and forth with the who and the why and everything else, but I haven't progressed much further than your guesses. So what am I supposed to do?" She strode toward the door, letting the question linger before resuming her defense.

"Continue my job, that's what. You think the lack of an emotional connection hurts me, but it's *why* I can treat so many challenging patients without losing my mind. I don't know that the person I saw, the letter, or my patients relate to one another, but the alternative is that I'm misdiagnosing and mistreating while nothing suggests that's true." She about-faced two steps from the door. Drywall swallowed the sound of heels rapping against wood as she ambled back toward Eric.

"You are welcome to examine any of my patients for a second opinion if you fear I'm no longer meeting my obligations as their physician. Until then, I'll follow the course of action I find most logical for treating my patients. Hopefully, we'll discover there's no secret agenda and no one is out to get me." Claire added the last line to plant a seed that disagreement amounted to calling her crazy. Her points made, she situated herself on the edge of her desk.

The problem was, somebody was out to get her. While her words lingered in the air, her heartbeat quickened as visions of Saturday night's encounter with Ryan carved out a cave of fear in her amygdala. *I couldn't hurt you. We still have so much to learn about each other,* his voice reverberated. The tone indicated factual deference, as if obeying strict rules. What game did he play at? Were her patients linked to him? Was treating them the route to exposing Ryan?

Peripheral movement snapped her back to the present.

Eric bowed his head, showing strands of gray through his black hairline. He rolled back his shoulders before casting his hair toward the ceiling. "I had no idea about the person outside of your house. That's difficult to deal with, regardless of whether he comes back. If you want to talk about that—just that, no patients and no workload, then I'm here to listen." He lingered, resuming after Claire motioned for him to continue. "As for your patients, I don't need to examine any of them at this point. Just"—he extended his hand, palm up—"consider transferring any new ones with serious conditions into my care or turning them away. We know several psychiatrists to whom we could refer such troubled individuals."

Unacceptable. She needed their problems to shine insight into her own, to understand why they selected her out of hundreds of options in Denver, but her wishes might turn out irrelevant. The flood of hallucinatory patients had slowed to a trickle, with her only new patient this week describing symptoms of mild depression. Some of this might have come to a head. "I'll keep that in mind. Thank you."

"Will you tell me if you come across anything else? Seeing somebody outside your house again? Another follow-up letter? Whatever it is, keep me in the loop. An extra set of eyes better spots buried clues."

"Okay," Claire agreed, really meaning it, as long as the gain outweighed his overprotective backlash. She raised her hands in a peace offering. "If that's it, I'd like to start prepping for my next session."

"No problem. Sorry to take you from your work." It carried the tone of 'sorry, not sorry', but at least Eric might suspect less when she stayed late. Her colleague retreated behind his desk.

Claire roamed to the filing cabinet. "You know, I got used to it being the other way around. Me looking out for you overworking." The less he viewed her situation as abnormal, the less time she'd squander resorting to theatrics.

"It's appreciated." He wasn't buying it. Worth a shot.

She tugged at the top drawer to rifle through a new folder dedicated specifically to delusions, hallucinations, and reality distortions. After one of her hallucinating patients, Nancy Cathell, described a recent encounter as feeling like the beginning of the *Poltergeist* movie, she began copying similar events to a central location. She wished she had done so earlier, when time abounded. Three pages of notes weren't a lot to work with.

"That's a light folder. New patient?" His persistence proved inscrutable in the face of Claire offering a credible excuse to allow him to return to his work guilt-free.

"Recent notes on Mr. Jefferies. Progress had been slow until last week when we hit a huge milestone."

"He's your gang stalking patient?"

"Good memory."

"Anything I can help with?"

"Nothing that can't wait until Monday." She closed the drawer, relocating the folder to her desk. With half an hour remaining, she intended to salvage what she could. Frequent glances by Eric's puppy dog eyes dashed those hopes too. She swapped to Mr. Childress's notes, running through her regular post-session routine.

Within a minute, her shoulders relaxed, if only by a hair. Work was her sanctuary. Here, she was safe. Her hallucinating patients riveted her, but constant focus on them required an unsustainable degree of energy.

She hated to admit it, but Eric's meddling proved for the best. It forced some distance away from patients whose hallucinations were hellbent on infecting her too. And as Ryan tightened his hold over her, how many such breaks would his existence—or not—allow?

CHAPTER 10

Claire's head swirled with a fog of uncertainty, pressure pounding at the edge of her temples. She sat at her dining room table, facing the closed curtains of the front window. Above her, the chandelier's light stretched to the couch's back before segueing into dimness. At arm's reach, her phone sat silent near a steaming coffee cup. Heat dissipating from the ceramic mug emulated the sizzle of a Friday evening burning so hot, only to fizzle into the air.

While lost in aimless study of her living room's darkened corner, Claire pictured her jade dress stretched across her bed. A smile flickered as she recalled Rick's jaw dropping at the sight of the outfit, her prize from that tainted afternoon of shopping at Cherry Creek. She had wanted to believe her encounter with Ryan meant nothing, but this evening's events purged that wishful thinking. After showering to clean off as much of the psychological grime as possible, she now sat wearing a bulky cotton top and pajama pants. Clothes hung from her body as loosely as a woman who had won a dieting competition. Memories of a date cut short, presumably by burgeoning madness, played in her head like some horror-based streaming service.

Rick waited at the entrance to Dede's Tavern as a rideshare dropped Claire off at the front door. His eyes rolled up from heels to knees to chest to face. He plucked his hands from blue jean pockets and balanced them at his sides before dropping them at his waist. It didn't take long to vocalize what his straightened back already said. "You look fantastic. Jeans fit you so well, I didn't know what I was missing out on."

She smiled without thinking. Indulgence in the moment loosened instincts to test and assess her date. Her grip on her spruce leather clutch relaxed, not realizing how tightly she had been squeezing it in anticipation of his reaction. Five long strides brought Claire to Rick's side. She wrapped her free arm around his, tilting her head upward for a peck on the lips.

Accepting the invitation, Rick kissed her and wrapped his long arms across her bare back. "How was the ride?" he asked.

Claire shook her head. Rick had offered to pick her up, but the allure of a female driver proved too strong in the wake of strange happenings regarding tall men. An almost prophetic decision, given the events which unfolded. Her mind fast forwarded through the rest of Dede's Tavern.

A small forest's worth of wood surrounded them, better resembling a cabin than a restaurant. The pair had joked about bringing Castlewood Canyon to them, perhaps reaching too far with the idea, but jokes were made and they ordered drinks. Rick branched out into wine. He said it paired well with whatever he had ordered. Steak? Red meat? Definitely meat. Her grilled chicken tasted palatable from what she recalled. Happy events from the evening blurred together like a sponge smearing wet paint. She struggled to remember the hand holding, their inseparability after splitting the dinner tab, the flirtatious exchange of boisterous laughter and sly facial tells.

A shroud as black as her coffee obscured those images, letting in just enough light to make out the events' silhouettes. Claire sipped at her mug, shuddering as the shadow of the board game stalker emerged in her mind, an image that resembled Ryan more with every review. The inescapable image further dulled the best parts of Dede's Tavern until her mind shifted to destination number two: a jazz show at Leburton.

Anxiety stalled her initial entrance when silence greeted them at the club. Not complete silence, of course. Customers sat chattering amid a sea of circular tables, riled up by empty and soon-to-be empty drinks. But no music played. The band hid offstage. Speakers emitted a faint buzz. Blue and red lights shone down on the empty stage, tinting purple curtains that read Leburton sprawled in black across the fabric. Instead of amusement and class, it reminded Claire of a tyrant ruling his subjects from the hidden recesses of a shadowy throne room.

"Are you okay?" asked Rick. They had walked halfway to the hostess. A dark-haired woman around Claire's age stood with a face devoid of expectations.

Claire stared at the curtains, weighing the gloomy thought. A single waitress, taking orders, dashing from table to table, interrupted her scrutiny.

Had her subconscious laid out a warning, one quickly ignored in the pursuit of normalcy?

Instead, she replied, "I'm fine. Let's sit before the show starts." She caressed his arm as reassurance.

Rick confirmed their reservation with a credit card payment.

The hostess's face remained stiff as she walked them to an empty table in the middle front of the venue. Two cushioned chairs with backs that rose to shoulder height faced the stage. "Enjoy the show," she said flippantly, before resuming her post near the entrance.

After the pair sat, Rick said, "You'd think jazz would leave these employees a little happier."

Three weeks ago, Claire might have agreed. That night, something about the tenebrous room offset by the bright stage pushed her brain into overdrive.

"It's weird how quiet it is," she said.

"You think so? The piano could be a little louder, but it's not a rock concert. I do think that couple is trying to liven the place up though." Rick signaled behind Claire, who didn't need to follow to know who he meant. An East Coast accented man boasted about outrunning a bear so loud she could pick out every logical fallacy. The nasal woman with him responded with wheezed laughter. Muddled by their rambunctiousness, subtle piano emitted a classical composition over the speakers, and, as Claire suddenly realized, had been doing so since they entered.

Why hadn't she noticed the music?

"No, you're right. The piano is nice. I guess I couldn't hear it over the foolishness behind me."

"He's got a magic trick where the waitress leaves two whiskeys for each one she takes. Quite a show." Rick leaned in so Claire could see the start of two gray hairs spurting up in his beard. "Though not as impressive as the magic between us."

She kissed him and pressed him back into his seat, a playful smirk creasing her lips. Her sullen posture betrayed the flirtatious action, though Rick paid it no mind. Before anything happened, she already felt off. "That's sweet," she managed.

"Very sweet." He raised his hand. A waitress arrived with ice clinking in a highball glass. Rick ordered the house wine and some craft beer with a name that sounded closer to an exotic flower than a beverage. "Sorry, I would've asked what you wanted, but she seemed too busy to stick around. I can run after her if you want something else."

"House wine is fine." Claire scanned the room, examining patrons in the near-full establishment. Variations ranged from opera attire to Sunday school clothes. Everyone blended into the dark ambiance of Leburton, their conversations and words proving equally muddled, including those from her date. It was as though a thick fog concealed sight and sound from deeper inspection.

Rick was prattling on about something until he boomed like concert speakers. "And as good as we look in what we're wearing, I think we're going to look a lot better once we get around to wearing something more comfortable." He laid his hands on her bare shin, propped up by her other leg. He rubbed her lotioned skin with an intensity more friendly than romantic, then snatched it back as if from touching a hot stove. "Which I meant to mean hiking clothes and not, well, no clothes."

The stage, singing its siren call, stole her attention. Claire looked left of her date, who sat in a defeated, slouched pose, waiting for her to grant absolution. He faded back into the fog, her focus on the movement from the stage. Black curtains ruffled as tonight's headliner prepared to begin their show. The Jazzy Johnsons sounded like a joke, but reviews put them in the same company as Miles Davis. Despite this, the room's atmosphere stifled her with a vile thickness, as though the band's instruments had released toxic fumes. Sickness gurgled in her stomach, threatening to deliver an acidic protest to her chest if she chose not to flee.

Claire rested her hand on her stomach, her insides rumbling as the wretched feeling blurred the line between memory and reality. Her coffee mug sat three-quarters full, representing an unquenchable thirst compared to her wine consumption at Leburton. She should have given in to her instincts to leave, but cold logic rebuked her fears, demanding she see the show and pamper herself with classy entertainment.

Instead of suggesting they take the date elsewhere, a proposal he would have accepted without argument, *she told him, "We'll talk about clothes, or not, later. It'll be hard to focus on the show otherwise, don't you think?" She scooted her chair closer and slid her arms onto his lap.*

The lights dimmed before the stage curtain spread wide. The Jazzy Johnsons opened with a trumpet and trombone expelling brassy air to an upbeat tempo. The canorous rhythm set the audience's feet afire and tapping on the floor. The piano flared to life after a short instrumental intro. Hammers striking strings delivered a harmonious dichotomy, bridging the gap between a cadence of main-stay treble clef notes and ephemeral bass notes. The cellist joined the quartet, plucking deeper notes to reel the crowd back. Listeners ready to dance out of their seats fell back into jiving from the comfort of their chairs. Music flowed from song to song without any breaks, as if they intended to play a single, hour-long song before retiring for the night. The quartet worked the crowd, ebbing back and forth between jolly jaunts and peaceful serenity for twenty minutes before the sensation of something crawling on Claire's forearm jolted her attention to Rick. She pulled back to cover her torso, the psychology of fear demanding she protect vital organs.

Claire was biting her thumbnail. She *never* bit her nails. She forced her hand down onto her lap.

Rick slowly tapped his pint glass to the baseline beat of the trombone, while an invisible blood moon cast twilight over his body. Flecks of dirt dripped from his jaw as he turned toward her. "Are you okay?" he asked, the voice equal measures his and something foreign. White surrounding his irises turned midnight black. Shadows hovered over his head, but within the overwhelming darkness, a sympathetic face attempted calming reassurances.

He leaned in to assess. She recoiled. The shadow threatened to leap from his body to hers, teasing her, toying with its prey. He bit back, arms resting on his thighs, hands splayed out on his knees. At his fingertips, a gloom sucked the light from the surrounding space. A parasite had attached itself to Rick. Ignorance pleaded his innocence, but she couldn't risk catching it. Claire felt like a chemotherapy patient bullied by a lab full of bacteria. If that darkness touched her, she would . . . what? What would happen? Visions swirled of a complete and total loss of sanity, of self. Her body and mind entrapped by this parasitic phantom for eternity.

How could she have explained it? It barely made any sense to her, hours later. Part of Claire wanted to cleanse the memory with a bottle of cheap wine and whatever passed as junk food from her pantry. Anger boiled over at her weakness. She slapped the table, sending half-finished coffee to the mug's brim. Avoiding the problem, one her well-being depended on, solved nothing.

She pressed her fingers together into a stop sign. He swayed back, the shadows on his arms receding into a languid state. She checked his bottom half. Darkness wavered like flame licks from his shoes. Claire wrapped her feet around her chair's legs. A moment passed before she realized she needed to say something.

"This will sound weird no matter how I explain it, but I have this feeling I need to check on something."

Rick shrugged, his posture questioning the legitimacy of her concerns. "Sure, we can leave. I just need to close out."

"Sorry, I need to go now." Claire shot upward, right hand pressing her dress against her thigh. She only hoped he could distinguish between her fleeing him in emergency and fleeing him as the emergency.

He clasped his right hand over hers. Shadows woke from their dormancy, reaching out, sensing new territory to spread their domain. Beads of sweat formed under her palm as she forced herself not to tear away. "Didn't you take a rideshare?" he asked. "It'll be faster if I drive. I'm a little worried about you." The bleak void slid down the pocket of his thumb and onto her wrist. She had held on as long as she could.

Claire pulled back, exhaling as Rick let go. "I did, and she'll be outside in a second. Time to go. I'll text you later."

She faked a smile, soothing her guilt over leaving him in the dim lounge, despite melodious notes of brass and strings he could continue enjoying if he chose. Her feet loosened their coil on the chair leg and sprung up so quickly she almost fell onto the table. Claire balanced herself and marched away, wondering if Rick's frown followed her into the lobby. She pushed open the door with her forearm, her medical background instructing her not to touch the public door with a potentially infected hand. As the door shut behind her, she scanned for residue of the shadowy flickers. Seeing nothing, she shook out her hands for good measure.

Content enough, she unzipped her clutch and fished out her phone. She walked one block over and one block down until her thumb stopped shaking enough to press the "order" button. Claire backed into the door frame of a small hotel while waiting the three minutes for Anne, a driver with great conversational skills, to arrive. Hopefully those skills extended to knowing when to remain silent.

Passersby hustled, meandered, and ambled by her through the hotel doors. None paid her any mind save one man whose imaginary undressing of her sent her skin crawling in a less supernatural manner. The desire to hide and look away almost overrode her professional training. A stern glare pushed his attention back to his phone. Her jaw unclenched after he walked out of sight.

A black Subaru pulled up less than a minute later. After waiting for a wide berth between those walking by, Claire hustled into the backseat.

"How's your night?" bubbled twenty-something ponytailed Anne.

"Fine." Short. Curt. Cold.

The driver got the message.

Claire wrapped one arm around her waist and propped her other elbow on it to examine her hand, using it as a prop to assess her sanity. Peace washed over her, finally feeling some sense of safety in the backseat of Anne's crossover SUV, but the effort taxed her so much that thinking of anything substantive on the way home proved impossible. For the rest of the trip, she watched houses, trees, and streets pass by until the car stopped in front of her home.

An absentminded shower later and a cup of coffee in hand, she hunkered down at the dining table to relive the evening's events. Claire stood up to stretch and readjust baggy clothes bunched from leaning over for most of an hour. Kneading a tense neck muscle, she refilled her coffee then returned to her seat. She tucked her arm and raised her hand to her face, seeking answers in the creases of her palm. The only truth gleaned was the need for lotion. She shook her head. Between sips of coffee, she cycled through memories again, concentrating on minute details she might have missed.

Dinner at Dede's and the preshow at Leburton passed with similar recollections (or lack thereof). Nothing jumped out until Rick's hands reached to console her. Unable to look him straight in the eye, she instead focused on his ear. Past him, she saw a pallid man in a black suit, black pants, black tie, and black fedora sitting directly behind her date. His movements and facial expressions mirrored Rick's. She couldn't remember when the man had sat down, a near impossibility in her alert state. Where had he come from? Why did he resemble . . . *what? Rick's shadow? Facial features blurred save for sunken eyes and a clean-shaven face. While casting his manners upon Rick (or was it the other way around?), the shadow reminded her of Ryan.*

Feeling the need to move, a doe avoiding a nearby predator, Claire's feet propelled her from the table, knocking the chair against the wall. Cinching her pajama pants' strings, she paced the perimeter of her home, stopping near the front windows and hesitantly drawing back the curtains. Empty paved streets drank light like a black hole. Her hands hovered near the glass, shaking. She closed the curtains again, resuming her frantic walk around the first floor. She mulled over her options: texting Rick, calling Jess, or screaming out loud. Pacing and considerations crested into the calm of her trusty peacemaker: research.

She walked to her work desk and opened the right drawer. The first page from the notepad ripped easily, and she selected a pen at random from those adjacent. With a direction to entertain, her shaking subsided as she returned to the dining table. At the top of the paper, she wrote *Gifts?* and drew three circles, aligned and partially overlapping in a Venn diagram. She filled each circle with notes regarding her major incidents: the board game stalker, Ryan at the mall, and tonight's *whatever* with Rick. Claire absentmindedly dotted the areas where pairs of circles met, until abruptly moving her pen to the center of all three to sum up the incidents' commonalities:

Incorporeal

Sight/sound only

Sudden onset

Evenings

SCZ symptoms: Positive, Negative, Cognitive

All of which added up to a few conclusions. Whatever she was seeing wasn't human (though that didn't preclude a human from causing her problems). Ryan and the other manifestations (or were they all *him* she wondered, picturing the man sitting behind Rick) existed in her mind. Hallucinatory ailments such as kidney disease, epilepsy, or narcolepsy didn't fit due to missing other symptoms. Despite her age, she admitted the possibility of a brain tumor and wrote *MRI?* to the side of the diagram.

As if feeling left out, her mom's voice chimed in, *Don't count your blessings before they hatch.* As was the case lately, her brain plucked the saying from 2009, Sofia Costas's one year of institutionalization, rather than from the trove available the nineteen years prior.

"Blessing, huh?" Claire ran through warning signs of burgeoning psychosis: self-neglect, social withdrawal, and apathy. Cleared herself in short order. Besides, she wouldn't trust anyone but herself for treatment after how her mother's doctors so utterly failed.

"Better a tumor than that." She rubbed the side buttons of her phone before returning her scrutiny to the Venn diagram. An evening of brain burning resulted in barely plausible scenarios to explain what she could only describe as hallucinations. Claire stared at papers stacked on her desk. The Fredonian letter provided her the only real clue, even if the sender didn't exist. So what connected the letter to everything else? Perhaps nothing. Its sending might have been a coincidence, like Eric suggested. Hell, maybe the ghost of a former patient haunted her, and the letter came from one of the family members, because at this point—why not?

She was contemplating burning the damned letter to feel some sense of accomplishment when a patter struck her front door. She startled, twisting as she shot up, her arms shielding her vitals. Then her lizard brain gave way to her mammal brain and she recognized the pattern. Brad Alba, up way past his bedtime.

CHAPTER 11

The patter tapped her door again. Claire was bringing her hands to her side and recovering her fright-stolen breath when the voice of a young boy called out.

"Ms. Rossi? I mean Dr. Rossi. Are you home?"

The clock read 9:12 p.m. What business did Amy Alba have allowing her child to traipse around at night?

More knocking. "Are you home? I have to go to bed this time if you don't answer, but it's hard to sleep."

"And I'm not sleeping until you leave me alone to sort this out," she muttered.

Brad squealed, "Oh, you're home! What did you say? I couldn't hear you. Can you open the door? I was so excited that I jumped up when your lights turned on." Wind slapped away another voice. "What Mom?"

Amy, presumably, lectured her kid.

"Oh, right. Sorry for looking into your house. I promise I wasn't spying. I was playing in my room and I saw the lights. Can we have friendship quiet time now?" A mix of urgency and trepidation coated his tongue. Similar sensations tickled underneath her skin. She regretted capping their encounters to once a week; it had instilled a sense of necessitating their meetings for the young boy. As is, she couldn't ignore him without creating problems for later.

Claire hesitated on her walk to the door, considering the frankly paranoid idea that her tormentor mimicked Brad's voice in an attempt to snatch her. His, or its, modus operandi thus far countered the concern enough to break her self-imposed bonds. She allowed herself one hair tug before opening the door, irritation erasing any propriety concerns over answering the door in pajamas. She interrupted the boy before he could finish curling back his lips to talk. "Brad, I need to sleep. We'll have to have friendship quiet time another day, okay?" Amy waved a friendly greeting from below the porch steps. Claire didn't reciprocate.

Flailing followed a frantic, "No, no, no!"

His mom rubbed her bony clavicle.

Claire wanted her neighbors gone so she could think while tonight's events remained fresh. The fastest way to accomplish that seemed to be hearing him out. She rested her hands on her hips. "Okay, Brad. Can you tell me why not?"

"Because I don't want you to forget about me," pleaded Brad. His scrawny limbs subsided.

She examined Amy, whose narrow nose pointed back at Claire. The expression said she had already heard whatever Brad prepared to say, listened to every excuse for his shirking bedtime. Only instead of playing the parent, the neighbor chose the role of friend and passed the problem onto Claire. She didn't blame the boy but couldn't hold back the entirety of the venom in her voice. "Why would I forget about you?"

He didn't notice, either due to his age or eagerness to explain, which he did in a rambling manner prone to children. "Everybody's forgetting something, that's why. First, Dad forgot when he and Mom got married. Ms. Tanner forgot the cake she promised for the classroom. Then Tony didn't remember his homework. He always remembers his homework! Even the monster in my closet forgot where he lives, but that one's okay I guess. And Ryan forgot to fix our house even though my dad says it's been a month. That's a really long time. Now we're going on a vacation because my dad feels better from his accident and he yelled at Ryan until he promised to fix our house while we were gone. I won't be here this weekend or next weekend. It's so long, and I don't want you to forget me."

For a while, Claire didn't respond, attention flipping back and forth between mother and son. Brad's spirited zeal subsided while Amy's neck rubbing bordered on choking herself. The mention of someone named Ryan piqued more interest than fear. On any other night, she'd chalk his mentioning up to coincidence, similar to Rick and Ryan both bearing four-letter names starting with R. But tonight?

"Who is Ryan?" Claire's tongue reeled back reflexively.

Amy seemed intent on allowing her child to drive the conversation. Tense silence heightened her stare's intensity, her non-interference feeling out of character.

Brad answered, "Oh, he's the man who told people how to make our house look nice after Mom and Dad bought it. He messes with my hair a lot, but he gives me toys so it's okay. My mom only gives me toys when I get good grades so I like it when he comes over. But since the people who fixed our kitchen are done working, I haven't seen him."

A gust chilled the September air, and Claire wanted to move past this absent prattle. "I'll make a deal with you. We can talk for five minutes inside but only if you promise to head home and sleep right after." *When needles prick, pick them up.* Mom's adage from her youth instructed to leave no clue unexplored. Presumably, at least. Either way, five minutes seemed a fair price to check out the lead.

Brad nodded so enthusiastically his blonde-haired head would have popped right off had he been one of his toys.

"I'll have him home soon, Amy," said Claire.

Her neighbor relaxed her grip over her throat, then smiled with a grateful head tilt. She wanted to get her boy into Claire's house. Perhaps to appease him, perhaps for something else. Which again, sounded paranoid.

"Is Nathan home?"

"Yes, he's back. Thanks so much, Claire." Amy retreated from the porch's base, flip-flops cracking at her heels like whips to drive her home. Something was definitely up, but she'd have to save investigating it for another night.

"Come in. Sit at the table, you know—the one where you were watching me." A dose of shame might prevent this from reoccurring. Though again, the timing of it all felt significant.

Eyes cast downward, Brad marched to the table, taking his seat with the rigidity of one awaiting punishment.

Claire refilled her coffee and reclaimed the chair across from him. She pushed the Venn diagram away, rendering it unreadable. "Can you describe Ryan for me?"

"He's tall like Dad. Wears nice clothes. Has black hair. I guess that's it?" Great. She had narrowed him down to a generic-looking general contractor.

Alabaster thoughts painted her mind. "What color is his skin?"

"I guess like yours or mine. Not too dark." Rose beige flesh stretched across their bones, a far cry from the porcelain tone of 'her' Ryan. Brad's call out to darker skin treated the comparison as too binary, signifying a need for specifics.

"Does his skin look more like this wall or this mug?" She pointed from the gallery white wall behind her to the tan coffee cup.

Brad shuffled his eyebrows, his mouth opened into an 'O'. After a short deliberation, he nodded with a pleased face. "More like the wall."

Her heart skipped a beat. *Don't get ahead of yourself.* "Did you notice anything on his cheek?" Claire rubbed her own to highlight where she meant.

Brad fell back into the same pensive pose. "Nope. His cheeks looked like cheeks!"

Claire slid her hands through the crease of the mug's handle, her thumb stroking out stress on its ceramic surface. Warmth radiated in her palm. Brad sat at attention, his chair shifting as he dangled his legs beneath the table.

"Have you ever seen him around my house?"

"I don't think so, Dr. Rossi. When he leaves our house, he gets in his car and drives away really fast. My parents call it a Beamer, but it doesn't look special. My dad's car is nicer." If memory served, Nathan Alba owned an Accord, roughly ten years old. "Do they call it a Beamer cause it's as fast as a laser beam?" Melancholy caught in the young boy's throat. "My parents always laugh when I ask." He looked betrayed when Claire smirked.

"No, it's a nickname for the company that makes the car."

The answer restored his enthusiastic composure as his head danced side to side.

The kid has some good in him, she admitted. Though Claire didn't mesh well with Amy, Brad had turned out well, with faults limited to those found in every youth. With the time remaining, he had earned the opportunity to talk about something fun. Simultaneously chasing a nagging sensation, she walked to her desk and asked, "Where are you vacationing?"

"New Mexico." He turned to watch her, staying in his seat with a grip around the back of the chair. "There's lots of sand and UFOs and parks and funny mud houses. It's going to be so much fun. My dad says I have to be ready bright and early tomorrow, so I got all packed up because I was waiting for you." Brad blushed, presumably with the realization of his earlier impropriety. How adult. "Sorry again about that."

"That's okay."

She picked up the Fredonia envelope laying on a stack of papers, half-examining it while Brad chattered, "My dad is driving us. He said we're going to make it all the way there in one day. My mom is worried about him driving because of his accident. They stopped talking after that, so I don't know where we'll stop first. Racinja, Tanky, Mr. Handy, and Bazooka Steve are all coming too, plus I have my iPad for movies so my mom said it's going to be fun no matter how long it takes."

The envelope crinkled in her hand. Claire hadn't thought until now to ask, "Don't you have school?"

Brad giggled with his chin upraised. "That's what I told my parents! But my teacher said I'm such a good student that it's okay since it's not safe to live in our house for a week."

What kind of repairs rendered a house unlivable for a week? Brad wouldn't know. She read the Fredonia sender line for the dozenth time. Slim chance he knew the answer to this question either, but she asked anyway. "Brad, did Ryan ever mention someone named Imogene?"

Brad spent a long time thinking over the question, longer than any previous response. While waiting, Claire scrutinized the name, sounding it out in her head. *Imogene Aire. Fredonia, North Dakota.* Repeated it, over and over. Read it as written. *Imogene Aire. Fredonia, ND.* The names rolled up and down the curves of her tongue with all manners of cadence, inflections, accents, and abbreviations, until it practically slapped her across the face.

"What the fuck?" she mouthed, still cognizant of the child sitting ten feet away.

She had been pronouncing Aire as *ay-er*, or *ay-reh* and Imogene with a hard O. Prying into Celtic and Spanish origins had yielded no results. The wrong approach, all along; it seemed so obvious now. She sounded out her discovery, testing it for a spin in reality. Pronouncing Imogene with a country twang, and slinging it together with Aire as *er-e* produced what sounded like *imaginary.* The first three letters of Fredonia combined with ND sounded like *friend. Imaginary friend,* altogether. The biggest clue to her nightmarish puzzle had lain in plain sight this whole time. While *Enjoy your gifts* held multiple interpretations, Imogene Aire—*imaginary friend*—offered only one. The chance of randomly stringing those words together into something relevant measured too slim to ignore. Amazing that the combination of a date gone awry, Brad's need to see her, and an absentminded mention of a contractor who happened to be named Ryan, led to a bigger breakthrough than any purposefully intentioned research.

"No," lamented Brad. "I don't think so. I tried really hard to remember for you."

Tensing up, Claire created a defensive shell out of her lean frame. Anxiety trickled to her hand. The paper envelope gave no resistance against bending it back and forth. She almost forgot she had asked Brad anything. "That's fine. Thanks for trying."

Someone did this to her. Created another person and stuck it in her mind.

Except, how did *that* not sound crazy?

How? How what? Silencing doubts of her sanity, she turned

toward the stairs where heels sat. *How* did it happen? Something she inhaled, something she touched, something she drank. Claire leered at her coffee, then at the letter in hand.

A text message rattled her phone on the table. Teeth sank into the underside of her lip. Her head swiveled. Brad glanced at the phone, then looked at Claire. The boy smiled with precocious signs of unease and nervously clapped his hands, making barely a sound.

"Brad, I think I need to get you home. It's late." And much remained to explore.

His eyes floated between the door and Claire. "Will you be okay, Dr. Rossi?"

"I'm fine. Let's get you home." Her hand ached from supporting what felt like a twenty-pound dumbbell. She dropped the metaphorical weight onto the table.

Still innocent of the fact that adults lied, he accepted her reassurance and popped out of his seat. "Alright, bedtime now, but only if you promise you won't forget about me. I'll be back soon." As if a demon feasted on Denver's ample supply of memories in their collective hippocampus. Amusing, naive even, except when put against the realization that someone hunted her in an equally improbable manner.

"I promise," she said with all of the sincerity he needed to hear. "Let me grab my phone first." Curiosity bubbled over the text's sender. She walked to the table and reached around Brad to read a message from Jess.

Haven't heard from you. The night must've been one to remember. Talk to you tomorrow.

Claire imagined recounting the evening to a disappointed Jess before realizing her deeper desires. She had hoped to hear from Rick, to earn absolution for her earlier behavior as she lacked time to start the conversation on her own. For now, a child waited for her to deliver him home in the darkness, forcing her to return alone with who knows what waiting where. She clenched her teeth at the prospect.

For all of the problems Amy had foisted upon her in a short

while, Claire deserved some recompense. She could guilt her neighbor into therapy, and truthfully, the whole Alba family probably needed it. The uncertain issue brewing at home would eventually affect Brad no matter how well the parents hid it. Regardless, she had done her duty and kept Brad occupied for well over five minutes, earning the privilege of Amy braving the darkness in her stead.

Claire bent down to the child's level. "I'm going to call your mom to come over and get you. That way we can spend a few more minutes together. What's her phone number?" She had it in an email somewhere, but she would have wagered her practice on Amy Alba never allowing her son out of the house without memorizing an emergency number.

She won the hypothetical bet, and the two settled on the couch for a brief spell while waiting for his mom. Steel resolve or no, she drew the line at dirtying her pajamas outside, which was how Claire knew madness hadn't consumed her.

Yet.

CHAPTER 12

Diane Shapiro pushed the bridge of her glasses back into place. Clearly neither liking nor understanding the question, her reaction forced Claire to break it down and repeat it.

"Diane, have you ever *sensed* Thomas without interacting with him? Knew he sat or stood close by but didn't speak? Thought you saw him in place of somebody else? Felt him in the background of your home or a coffee shop?" Claire sat up straight, portraying confidence that her thumping heart threatened to betray. "Does any of this sound familiar?"

Ms. Shapiro's hands slid down her frames until fingertips brushed against cheekbones, dragging the corners of her eyes down with them. She smeared blush which had grown thicker with every session. Claire suspected the bright, fleshy makeup and lime dress served as attempts to ward off Thomas. A minute passed before her patient answered in a shaky voice, her right arm quivering in her lap.

"All of it. I think . . . I think this all started before I even saw Thomas that first time."

Claire jotted down the horror-stricken tone underscoring his name. No matter how poor her sleep, sessions with her hallucinating patients revived her like a full night's rest.

Ms. Shapiro rocked back and forth. "I heard some noises at my house one night. I thought it was a raccoon or squirrel at first, but the more it rustled, the bigger it sounded. I saw an oval shadow around the fence line, but everything below was too dark to make out. I convinced myself the troublemaker was a raccoon but I didn't really believe it, and I kept thinking about it until it scared me so much I closed the blinds and ran to my bedroom. With everything else that's happened since, I've been thinking . . . maybe it was Thomas out there." Her rocking stopped. "Is that what you think? Is that why you're asking me?"

"Maybe. What about since then?" asked Claire, curious more about how their progression of symptoms aligned than Ms. Shapiro's astute realization.

"I hear noises outside every so often, but living by myself, I'm scared to do more than peek through the blinds. And a few times, it sounded as though it came from inside—things like curtains fluttering or an animal ramming the wall."

In other words, experiences more common to a haunted house than real life. Not too dissimilar from shadows infecting a romantic date. "How long do these inside occurrences last?"

"Not long, nothing as bad as the rustling that one night. Do you think it's Thomas? You said to ignore him so I try just not to think about it, but now that you're asking about . . . is ignoring him bad?" Frantic brushing of her thigh intensified as she awaited an answer.

Managing Ms. Shapiro's fear while unearthing necessary details would prove a tight balancing act. As it would with all five of Claire's problem patients. "No, you're doing exactly what you're supposed to. Continue the same approach, but call my emergency line if you even *feel* it might turn violent. And if for some reason you can't get through, call 9-1-1." Not that the police could help if Thomas stayed true to his apparition-like nature, but Claire had yet to rule out the possibility of an elaborate and aggressive prank. Still, she had prepped for this week's session with the theory that *imaginary friends* haunted her patients, rather than hallucinations. Where that differed past semantics she hadn't quite pieced together, so she focused on the hallucinations seemingly acting of their own volition. They *wanted* something. Unfortunately, the week started off rocky when Mrs. Cathell missed her appointment. Thinking about it disturbed a well of anxiety, driving her to flick her fingernail. Hopefully Ms. Shapiro didn't think much of it. "Do you believe Thomas wants anything from you?"

Ms. Shapiro's mouth swung open before she panic-covered her

lips. When her hand fell away, she spewed her answer like a volcano. "I don't know. I'm supposed to avoid him, right? You said I'm supposed to avoid him. I hum my song like you said, but he won't leave me alone." She bordered on shouting. "I don't know what he wants. I don't want to think about him anymore, Dr. Rossi."

Irritability signaled developing psychosis, but it also presented more commonly in ailments as mundane as stress. If her patients were the *gifts* causing Claire's problems, they did so with equal damage to themselves. She searched for the safest topic to calm her patient. "You're doing great, Diane. I know this is challenging, but we'll get through it. How have your experiences been with sitting at the park?"

"Oh, those. They've been great." Tension visibly lifted, though an underlying current of nervous rocking returned. "Do you remember Kim? I ran into her again this weekend. Well, she ran into me. She was finishing a big walk around the neighborhood and sat at the bench to take a break. She told me . . ."

Claire listened to the story for several minutes, primarily to let Ms. Shapiro soak in enough calm to put her rocking to ease, but also to uncover any clues regarding the primary issue at hand. Had Ms. Shapiro ever witnessed a darkness outlining her new friend? She wondered but dared not stifle her patient's recovering composure.

". . . I'm considering inviting her over for tea. Is that a smart idea? I don't know her well, but she seems nicer than Thomas, and maybe it'll keep me safe from him. Maybe he only comes around because I'm lonely, you know?"

The idea merited further scrutiny. Manifestations of everyone's hallucinations seemed to occur while alone or in small groups, and though the gloom at the jazz club was strange, Ryan never completely materialized. "Making new friends is always challenging. When it comes to things like that, you should trust your gut." Advice inappropriate for someone suffering from a psychotic disorder, but Claire hoped to prove that not the case. For either of them. "Have you been able to get in touch with any of your old work friends? Or with Abby?" Claire made it a point to ask about Ms. Shapiro's old neighborhood friend every session.

"I called Abby last weekend and left a voice message, but I don't think she checks those. I meant to ask you about that. When is it okay for me to call her again? I don't want to seem crazy."

Discussing social cues derailed them from the bigger picture, but the glint in Ms. Shapiro's eyes indicated the merits of indulging her. "I'd try calling her again. Don't worry about leaving a voicemail, just see if she picks up and then you can try again in a couple of days." Oddly topical, given Rick had yet to return yesterday's text messages. "She might still be settling into her new place. So, is Kim the only person you've talked to personally over the past week?"

"I guess so. Is that bad?"

"Not at all." She wanted to discuss the tenebrous outline around Rick, to see if Ms. Shapiro had experienced something similar, but she couldn't figure out how to broach the subject without pushing her patient past the point of breaking.

"Actually," excitement coated Ms. Shapiro's voice. "This man named George stopped at the park bench to tie his shoe. We talked for a few minutes. I hadn't seen him before, but he looked handsome and around my age. I'd like to see him again."

That was Claire's in. "Did he resemble Thomas in any fashion?" She spoke slowly so the idea didn't jar her patient too hard.

Once again, Ms. Shapiro wavered in her seat, as if succumbing to a Pavlovian response for any discussion regarding Thomas. "Why did you ask me that? I'll never want to talk to him again." She caught her breath and shook her head up toward the ceiling. "They're both taller than me, and their hairstyle is similar I guess, but that's all I can think of. Thomas is much younger and paler."

"Have you ever seen an aura around Thomas? Or around anyone else when you may have sensed him?"

"How do you mean?" Rocking in her chair. Brushing at her thighs.

"As if something cast an outline around his body." *Like a demon struggling against its bonds.* "Like moonlight."

"Oh." Her rocking slowed as she drew her limbs inward. "No,

I've never seen that. I've never sensed or seen him when I've been around anyone else either. That must be good, right?"

For Ms. Shapiro, maybe. For Claire? She stifled a shudder at the budding memory of shadows threatening to jump from Rick's body to hers. At Ryan saying he and Claire were closer than she knew, jabbing at her privacy amid an open-air shopping mall. And while Ms. Shapiro remained physically unharmed, Mrs. Cathell missing her appointment stirred an unease greater than any interaction with Claire's *imaginary friend*. Hopefully, Janice would provide an update on the missing patient this afternoon.

"Diane, your case is unusual, but as I grow more familiar with it, it's clear there is a singular underlying cause. To uncover it, I'll need you to do something."

"Yes?" Eagerness displayed hope Claire had uncovered a solution.

Hope she had to quash. "I want you to ask Thomas one question about himself. Whatever comes to mind."

Ms. Shapiro reared for another fidgeting escapade.

Claire's hand inclined, an authority figure demanding obedience. "Listen to the answer then shut down and ignore him as we've practiced. We'll talk about whatever he says next week."

"Is that," Ms. Shapiro ran her tongue around the cavity of her mouth. Her water bottle sat untouched, forgotten. "Safe?"

I have no idea. But doing otherwise might be more dangerous.

Riding on the coattails of her daughter's thoughts, Sofia Costas's voice proclaimed, *Your secret is safe for all the world to see,* excitement curling her lips in place of the usual weighty gloom.

I'll take that as your approval, Mom, Claire responded to the voice for the first time. She chewed the meat of her cheek.

"Diane," said Claire, buying time to organize her muddled thoughts. "You've come a long way these few weeks. It may not seem that way." Certainly not to Ms. Shapiro, given the mountain of blush hiding her face. "While this remains challenging, you're adapting to deal with it. The more we know, the better the chance of resolving it completely. You're prepared for this."

"I'll try." Ms. Shapiro's smile quivered. "I think I can do it."

"Good. In the meantime, I want you to see your primary physician and get a physical to rule out any physiological symptoms." Which meant Claire should do the same, whenever she found the time.

"Okay, Dr. Rossi. I'll call him as soon as I get home."

"I'll also send in a new order to your pharmacy. We'll try a different medication to see if it helps." Something less potent but still effective as an antipsychotic. Testing required she continue to rule out mental illness as the culprit. She spent a few minutes detailing the medicine, what she hoped it would accomplish, and potential side effects.

"Thank God. That other medicine made me so sleepy." Her positivity spread, bringing a flicker of a smile to Claire's face as her patient shifted from scared child to excited teen over a small piece of good news. "I couldn't stay up past 8 p.m. most nights. I'm so far behind on The Mary Tyler Moore Show I'll have to look for episodes online."

How backed up could one get on a show that ended before Claire's birth? It was so silly it was heartwarming and so heartwarming it was guilt-inducing. She treated Ms. Shapiro similar to a guinea pig, but she couldn't chance excluding a single patient from testing the delineations between hallucinations and *imaginary frie*—. Claire exhaled a deep breath to expel rising nausea. Regardless, she'd be a fool to squander her *gifts*, if that's what they were. The new drugs, especially at the prescribed dosage, allowed for greater awareness during Ms. Shapiro's encounters with her apparition. *Apparition! A perfect name. Wannabe ghosts that I'm gonna bust like Bill Murray. As soon as I figure out where they're coming from.*

The faint squeaking of a cushioned chair signaled she'd spent a little too long in her head. The room's analog clock read five minutes 'til the hour. "That's our time for today, Diane. Are you booking for next week?" She didn't normally ask, but Mrs. Cathell's missed appointment had spooked her. She had to make sure Janice knew the importance of getting a hold of her, even if it meant a stern talking down.

"Yes. I want to get this whole mess solved and put behind me as soon as possible."

"We'll get there. The problem with Thomas is more complex than it first seemed, but as I said, we're making progress." Progress built on the backbone of five patients and one doctor with eerily similar symptomatic trajectories. Progress that would continue as long as they could bear the load. Claire used the opportunity to remind herself she was drawing closer to solving this, even if it didn't feel like it.

"I hope we can figure it out soon. I'm just not sure what's real or not anymore."

"I know, but we're working toward the cause every session. I promise you I'll devote special attention to your case until it's resolved." As if she had a choice. Claire rose to guide Ms. Shapiro to the exit, posing her patient's question to herself. *What, or who, is real? Thomas? Ryan? . . . Rick? He talked to waiters and paid for dates, how could he not be?* A fascinating puzzle, if only she had a little more distance from it all.

CHAPTER 13

You want me for a double date with Rick? Count me in." Jess's excitement triggered Claire to lower her phone's volume. "Only I need you to push it to next week. Karen's throwing her sister a baby shower, and their mom is coming into town from Mexico. Going to be a whole weekend of baby-themed activities." She stretched out 'whole' to the length of its own sentence.

Better than pushing it earlier. The past couple of days whirled with strange emotions between her and Rick. He had responded a few hours after her session with Ms. Shapiro. He was reconsidering their relationship and needed time to think it all over. Last night, he emailed from a supposed personal account to say he was up for another date if she was, but the only other time they exchanged emails was through his work account. They'd also have to plan around him not having a cell phone. Apparently, he swam with friends yesterday at Boulder Reservoir and left his phone in his pocket. Water damage did it in, and as promised, he ordered a heavy-duty replacement—one that meant a wait of seven to ten business days before calls and texts came back on the menu. It made sense that he didn't want to talk personal matters on his work phone, but the circumstances left her incredibly suspicious, so she fired off a round of test questions to confirm his identity.

Then at today's rescheduled appointment, Mrs. Cathell described a violent verbal outburst from her version of Ryan. Between that, Rick's behavior, and her own ordeals, the sensation of impending defeat had overwhelmed her. Upon coming home, she collapsed onto the couch and called Jess to focus on something controllable. Almost instantly, her friend's enthusiasm flipped her disposition.

"How many baby questions are you expecting this weekend?" Claire teased, fidgeting with the hem of her long dress.

"A couple dozen minimum. After I tell her I'm fine without kids or a family, Mrs. Gutierrez will offer to fly me to her hometown and set me up with a nice young bachelor. She knows everyone mind you, and plenty of men will be," Jess imitated a grandmotherly Mexican accent, "eager to marry a Stanford-educated woman who is as beautiful as you."

"Ever going to take her up on the offer?"

"What do you think? I'm not trusting a woman whose sole goal in matchmaking is to find someone who wants to impregnate me. Even my mom's not that relentless."

Claire scoffed with a hint of laughter. "Good luck this weekend. I'll check with Rick and see if next weekend works."

"Sounds good. Are you inviting Robert too?"

"He said to figure out what you and Rick could do." She refreshed her inbox to find it still blank. "And then he'd talk to his wife about getting a babysitter."

"You think Samantha wants to spend one of their few nights out with us?"

"If she doesn't, it'll make finding a babysitter a lot easier for Robert."

Jess chuckled. "Always thinking ahead, Claire."

"Always." Claire hoped Robert could make it a triple date, but she'd be happy with Jess. The sooner any of her friends confirmed Rick's existence, the sooner she could separate clues from red herrings.

"I'm looking forward to it, and I'm free all next weekend so you won't hear any more trouble out of me. I can start shopping for a guy once we get off the phone. If I act fast, he can pull double duty to get me out of those awkward conversations with Mama Gutierrez."

Claire tugged on a clump of hair. "You're bringing someone new?"

"I'm trying the quantity over quality approach. Believe me, you want me to bring someone new."

Claire pulled the phone away from her face and glared at Jess's digital picture before returning it to her ear. "I trust you. Just a little wary of strangers right now."

"Are you still thinking about that creep from board game night?" She sounded sympathetic, but a hint of incredulity lined her voice. It had been four weeks since *that* evening. A long time for an issue to linger given Claire's propensity to self-treat—something Jess knew well.

"It's harder to deal with than you think," snapped Claire. She had yet to divulge the truth about Ryan's appearance at Cherry Creek. As far as Jess knew, she had been talking to herself, a secret she planned to keep until finding a passable explanation. If fate reversed their roles, would her friend open up?

"You're right. I'm sorry. And if you want to talk to me, I'm always happy to listen. Or I can refer you to someone else." Jess left a short window for Claire to speak up, which she did not. "Either way, I'll err on the side of boring and safe for our double-triple date extravaganza. I might not pick the perfect guy, but I can handle that much." Her genuine empathy flattened Claire's irritation.

"Thanks. I'll call Rick and see what he says." Or she would if she could. Another refresh, still no email. She concealed her disappointment with overzealous enthusiasm. "Talk to you later."

"Adios."

Claire shook her head at the laptop and wandered into the kitchen. She dropped her phone off on the counter before opening the fridge in search of a French pinot noir opened days ago. She sniffed at the bottle's contents. A faint scent of vinegar trickled into the back of her throat, but vanilla and raspberry dominated the wine's profile. Still good. She took an empty wine glass from the cupboard and quarter-filled it, finishing the bottle and returning to her living room. The cushions of the white couch silently dispersed for her careful landing.

Remnants of her dinner, an extra-large smoothie, sat mostly full on a coaster atop the center glass surface of her coffee table. In the compartment below, she spotted a Colorado hiking guide and a copy of *Wild: From Lost to Found on the Pacific Crest Trail* by Cheryl Strayed. Two books she had only inched through in the past month. She sipped on her wine and shifted the coaster to hide the sight of the novel. Any activities besides company with her friends and working cases led to Ryan worming his way back into her thoughts. He was out there, somewhere. Whether in her mind or out of it, she wanted him gone.

Her laptop's white screen beckoned from the coffee table. Leaning over, she swapped from her email to her browser and began flipping through so many tabs, they resembled ants at the top of the window. She had increasingly turned to the internet in search of symptoms matching hers and her patients. Anonymous sources suggested everything from the supernatural, to clandestine cults, to a terrorist attack. Ideas filled her head, but nothing concrete transpired. Holes pierced every theory, with most threads ending with advice to seek a doctor. She slammed her laptop shut and fell back, raking fingernails through her hair.

These conditions weren't meant for online diagnosis, but where else could she turn for something so bizarre? Where else could she turn for how to save her life? How to save her patients? She loved her human puzzles, but the stakes had never risen so high. Dwelling on a suite of dead ends, she leaned over and rubbed the shell of her laptop as if expecting a genie to appear. The answers lay somewhere. Claire drew the wine glass to her lips to cleanse the bitter taste of uncertainty. She flooded her mouth with oaked berries and cloves, letting the glass linger on her lips and savoring the residue. Footsteps from the corner of her front porch shattered the indulgence. Claire slid her glass onto the table. Wine crested to a wave, barely avoiding a spill.

"Hello?" Claire asked at the front door.

Wood creaked from the porch's opposite corner. Claire crept toward the original footsteps, instinctively glancing at the Fredonia letter on her downstairs desk. She inched open the blinds, spying only night air hanging over an empty porch. Two more steps. From her bedroom. No, louder.

Stomps.

Claire turned, running her eyes up and down the stairs. Silence settled over her home. What had she heard? Calm weather contributed little more than the occasional breeze, and her house lacked the age for decrepit sounds. *It's Ryan, who else could it be? It's the next step.* Then why hadn't her patients reported incorporeal auditory hallucinations? *You're further along than the rest. He'll get* you *first.* Bullshit. Shapiro, Capers, and Cathell all detailed apparitions prior to Claire's board game stalking. *Not before you received the letter.* Shapiro had been coming in for two weeks by then. *For anxiety and depression, not for this.*

Between wine and budding fear, the back of her throat burned like she'd swallowed sand. She coughed, trying to push some moisture into her mouth. The front door stood only a few steps away. Could she outrace him in a work dress? Claire paced to the kitchen and back, wiggling as if bugs crawled all over. She had to stay inside. Home provided sanctuary. Her patients' hallucinations never entered their homes unless invited. *They've never turned anyone's place into a haunted house either.*

Whistling called her attention outside, freezing her in place. Nobody out there. *Then why are the bushes rustling?* As Claire argued with her toes to uncurl in order to investigate, the noise cut.

Frightful quiet seized the moment, stretching time by orders of magnitude. The air felt alive, stuck in a shape not of its choosing. It scratched and clawed until it exploded into a cacophony of sound, a gang of misfits recording band practice with whatever makeshift instruments they found upstairs. The first drummed her master bath's marble counter. The second squeaked bed springs with the cadence of a child jumping. The third splintered beams in her attic. As more added to the mix, their sounds merged into chaos indistinguishable from an earthquake.

This wasn't happening. These weren't the rules. This wasn't right.

Claire glared at her laptop, the good-for-nothing waste of time. She stormed over to it, readying to throw it at the first thing she saw. She squeezed the sides, loosing an overflow of volcanic frustration that almost heaved it across the room.

Knocking rapped at her kitchen window. For an instant, she spotted a pale man reflecting moonlight. Or thought she did, until he vanished into the night. She released the laptop and lurched forward to investigate, then stiffened, clenching the couch's back so tight she cut blood flow to her fingertips.

Thumps struck the ceiling loud enough she expected to see a gorilla barreling through, but the plaster above remained motionless.

Phantom musicians resumed practice on the second floor with intensified efforts.

Each strike pushed Claire closer to the floor until she knelt, their harshness daring her to sink lower, to bury herself under the earth to escape. She slid her legs under the width of the coffee table until her head rested against the couch, and she made earmuffs of her hands.

Ignore it. Hum something until it goes the fuck away like at the mall. She tried, before an outdoor squeal broke her concentration. She frantically looked around, wishing she cleaned her home a little less so she might find an impromptu weapon lying around. Closing her eyes, she studied the memory of her home in search of her phone. Its image materialized atop the kitchen counter. She raced toward it, yelping as her knee struck the coffee table's corner in her attempt to escape. Out of options, she took the advice she had given Diane Shapiro and dialed 9-1-1.

Claire yelled over the symphony of madness when someone answered.

"What's your emergency?" asked a Southern-accented female.

"There's someone in my house." The sandy feeling in her throat made it painful to talk. "I need the police."

"Ma'am, I hear you loud and clear."

Despite the implication, Claire continued shouting, trying to make herself heard over the barrage of rustlings, thuds, slams, and bangs. She responded to the dispatcher's calm line of questioning, supplying her address and describing the sanest possible account of the situation.

"Do you have a safe place to hide?"

"I think . . ."

"Go there. I'll stay on the line until the police arrive."

Scanning her house for movements that should logically accompany the chaotic sounds, she limp-hopped to the restroom tucked underneath the stairs. She almost closed the door before realizing the foolishness of blocking her only escape. Her bladder, already shrunken by fear, yearned for relief as she settled into the room. She clutched her dress with her free hand and rocked back and forth, finding some peace in the repetitive motion.

Until she heard *his* voice.

"Are we having fun, yet?" he called from the backyard. No, the roof. She couldn't place the *where*, but she had no problem identifying the *who*.

Ryan.

Two scenarios sprung to mind. The first, with her asking the dispatcher to talk and talk until her mind couldn't process the madness of Ryan's disembodied voice. The second, where she imagined herself as one of her patients, relying on their trusted doctor's guidance, guidance which requested they ask one question and report back next week. She muffled the phone against her chest, and asked aloud, "What do you want?"

"For you to let me in!"

She bared her teeth. Winced as she swallowed. Turned on the faucet for a hand-cup of water. If she wet herself a little at this point, she doubted it would form a memory in her hippocampus. She giggled at the notion, a giggle that grew into laughter and harmonized with Ryan's concerto of discord. *Hippocampus.* What a delightful word.

A car horn blared, off-balancing Claire, vacuuming the air of her false merriment. It cut through the symphony, making a hollow mockery of the clacking, clanking, and clanging surrounding her. She grabbed the door frame for support. The crescendo rebounded, cascading into a tinny screech that coalesced into a simple rapping at her door, silencing the rest.

"Claire, it's Rick." Three more knocks. Urgent, yet gentler than the noises before. "It's Rick. What's happening in there?"

What's he doing here? What if it was a mimicry of Rick's voice? *This has to be a trick.* Another auditory illusion?

"Are you in there?" he shouted. "Are you okay?"

Vaguely aware of the dispatcher saying something, she ran to the front window and yanked the blinds' cord. Rick stood there, smiling, hand over his heart. He signaled at the door.

Claire eagerly found solace in objectivity: the sound stopped when Rick had knocked. She sidestepped and flung open the door. She flew into his arms without thinking, then stiffened. Half of her cursed her foolishness, rushing into the arms of one whose presence she couldn't explain. The other half indulged in the warm respite of his body in the cool evening air. Her tension subsided when at last he spoke, and the worry of him physically hurting her passed.

"What's going on here?" he asked. She felt his shoulders shifting as he scanned the scene behind her. She stepped back and examined him. He looked different somehow. More . . . docile? She wiped her face, wiped away the thought. More important matters lay at stake. Urgent dispatcher cries yelled from her hand.

"I'm still here. My boyfriend"—Claire blinked. Was he?—"Rick Novak, just got here. I think he scared off the intruder."

They walked inside, Claire closing the door behind them. Rick moved to explore the grounds, but she snatched his wrist where his checkered sleeves stopped. He didn't resist, continuing to investigate the interior from his stationary position.

"The police will be there in thirty seconds. Can you give me a description of your boyfriend?"

Claire complied. Sirens blared down the street.

"Are you able to open the front door?"

"Yes. I'm walking to it right now."

"Go ahead and open it."

She did so. A breeze replied, its chill heightening the need to urinate. Claire drew her legs together and rubbed her arms.

"I'm going to take a look around," said Rick. "I loved playing hide and seek as a kid. Maybe I can find something."

Before Claire could reprimand him for exploring unarmed when the police would arrive shortly, he sailed through the kitchen and out into the backyard. She had a laundry list of questions to ask, but she'd have to wait until after the police finished. Two cruisers sped into parking spots in front of her house. Four officers slammed their doors shut, gazes scouring her home. Two remained outside, bookending her property line while the other pair approached with hands hovering over their holsters. How would they react when they inevitably found no sign of an intruder? At least she could use the opportunity as a roundabout way to assess Rick's reality status.

The officer's deep voice sliced through her musings.

"Claire Rossi?" A black-skinned, clean-shaven police officer climbed the stairs ahead of a chubby female with skin paler than Claire's.

"Yes. That's me." Claire spoke slowly to counter an emotional unsteadiness.

"I'm Officer David Johnson. This is Officer Shelly Gagnon." Claire stood with arms huddled for warmth. Neither officer motioned for a handshake. "We had a call about a home invasion. Are you okay?"

"I'm unhurt." No one would be *okay* hearing the sounds she had heard.

"Good. Can we come in?"

"Sure." Claire stepped aside to allow them entry. "Do you mind if I close the door? It's kind of cold." She did so following their approval.

They scanned the first floor with the scrutiny of cleaners inspecting for dirt while inquiring about her home's layout, pets, and other people present. She waved to the backyard to indicate Rick's whereabouts. They set about exploring the house, first upstairs, then downstairs, then the backyard. Claire zombie-walked to the couch, letting cushions consume her. Emotionally, intellectually, and physically drained, attempts to squeeze insight into this quiet window proved unproductive. For the entirety of their search, she shook her head in spurts, incredulous at the disaster that had consumed her life. Hand on her soon-to-bruise knee, she forced herself to rise when the officers returned.

"We didn't see any signs of a break-in. Can you tell us what happened?" Johnson asked. Gagnon pulled out a notebook to transcribe Claire's responses, like a challenge to assert which profession could better enter someone's head.

She kept it brief. "I was sitting on the couch, working on my laptop. I heard some banging outside and then upstairs a minute later. That's when I called 9-1-1."

"Did you see the intruder?"

She didn't have to in order to describe him and offered up a vague account of Ryan. "Yes, out in the backyard. Pale. Tall. Light clothing." It couldn't hurt to have presumably spotted him outside. It's not as if the police devoted many resources to a mystery man glimpsed in a fearful craze.

"Have you ever seen this man before?"

Her lips twitched. Breath caught in her throat. Gagnon noted it down or had exceptional timing. *Had she ever seen him before?* she repeated to herself. Was it so obvious? Between unwanted visits and patients that reminded her of Ryan with every session, she could hardly avoid him. Exhaling with an even slowness, she said, "I think so. A few weeks ago. It was dark outside then too, but everything I saw matched tonight's intruder."

"Why didn't you report it?" In another life, Johnson's neutral inflections would've made for a great psychiatrist.

"I had a split second sighting in the backyard and a glimpse at him in the front yard. I had two friends over, and neither saw anything so I chalked it up to a trick of street lamps and moonlight." Training should have told officers to take eyewitness accounts with a grain of salt, but Gagnon wrote it down with genuine interest.

"I see." Johnson glanced at his partner, who responded with two taps of her pen. "That's all we have. If you see anything, let us know as soon as possible."

Claire nodded her assent. "Did you see Rick?"

Johnson raised his eyebrows.

"My boyfriend? In the backyard?"

"Nope. Nobody there." His stare indicated he wanted to ask a follow-up question before his brows settled. "Can you sign this report?"

An absent-minded scribble of her name later, she was guiding the police to the front door.

"We'll hang around in our cars for a little bit. Do you have anybody who can stay over tonight? Or somewhere you can go? It can be hard to sleep after a break-in. Might help."

Claire almost laughed. What would any of that matter against someone only she could see? Then again, Rick and the police's appearance had effectively cast Ryan away. She'd call Jess or Robert if the apparition drummed up an encore. "I'll figure something out. Thanks."

After letting the police out, Claire crept back the other way for a backyard perusal. She hovered over the grass, steeling herself to walk the perimeter, for once seeking refuge in her mother's malapropos metaphors, her malaphors. Caution rooted her as the voice remained silent. She kept contact with the door frame, calling out Rick's name a couple of times until outdoor silence mirrored her mind's. He had left as little of a trace as Ryan. The observation lingered until it willed her body into action.

Teeth clamped on her lip. Feet skipped back into the kitchen. Hands slammed the door shut. After double checking the deadbolt, she raced to the bathroom. During her run to empty her ballooned bladder, four questions blurred together.

Why had Rick shown up when he did? If he *was* real, how had he left without anyone noticing? If he *wasn't* real, what did that mean for his relation to Ryan? Most importantly, none of her patients reported multiple unique hallucinations, so what did it all mean for *her* sanity? A fifth and sixth question trailed: for what reasons did her mind find fit to fill her head with her mother's twisted malaphors? And for what reasons did Sofia Costas decide when to remain silent?

A night felt insufficient to resolve these queries. Perhaps not even a lifetime. She was as lost as a bat flying in daylight. On top of that, she had missed an easy opportunity to schedule her double date.

And so, Claire sat down, relieving herself without feeling any relief.

CHAPTER 14

Anxiety and a fourth cup of coffee propelled Claire up and down the middle of the office she shared with Eric. Wedged heels clacked and tapped to the rhythm of a clock ticking as she awaited an answer. In the time between explaining her patients' situations and waiting for Eric's response, highlights from Rick's morning email poked at her like the little brother she never had. He opened with answers to Claire's test questions to confirm his identity. He followed with explanations to unasked curiosities she had obsessed over since Ryan's phantom symphony yesterday.

Why was Rick there? He had planned to surprise her with takeout but didn't know what she ate besides Italian, so he came over early. *Why had he left suddenly?* His boss called him in via his work phone, and he didn't want to interrupt her dialogue with the police. *How did he know where she lived?* She had left her address in an email. He apologized if using it creeped her out. *How had he left without anyone, including the two officers outside, noticing?* No mention of that, though it would've been an eerie inclusion.

The email struck her as supplicating, written specifically to satiate her concerns. Brief consideration of him as a tulpa arose until she nullified the theory. Research indicated people brought tulpas to life deliberately, which she played no part in. Rick sent emails and texts autonomously, providing physical and shareable evidence of his existence. Most importantly, a scenario in which he existed solely in her mind lent credence to imagining *everything*—a conclusion she deemed unacceptable. Which brought her back to the present, admitting the possibility of seeking problems where none existed and opening up to Eric for insight and direction. Debating doing so had consumed her during her previous session, making for a rather unproductive hour. However, given that her patient's bipolar condition wouldn't kill him in the next week, she deemed his sacrifice justified.

These thoughts passed in seconds, before Eric showed interest in aiding Claire as expected, though with an extra dose of smugness. "Claire Rossi is asking for my help? Color me confused." Eric pushed away from his desk and crossed one pant leg over the other.

"Don't take this the wrong way." She halted pacing to face her colleague. "I'm not seeking your medical opinion on their condition. I'm seeking your educated guess on their conditions' cause. I want to know what you think led to this suite of problems, not what medical diagnosis to attribute to them." Claire trod carefully. She hadn't revealed last night's incident, nor the one at Cherry Creek. As far as he knew, the problems she detailed applied to five people, not six. Even Jess didn't know about the haunted house. The thought of her best friend questioning her sanity threatened to officially drive her insane.

"If we don't precisely understand the condition that's afflicting them, how can we understand the root cause? Treating a psychotic patient with grandiose delusions involves assessing cognitive function, determining drug history, and studying family history. One shift of an answer points away from say, chemical imbalance, and leads to a CT scan in search of a brain tumor."

Everything in his approach mirrored how Claire would handle the situation normally, but the circumstances surrounding these apparitions were anything but. She needed Eric honed in on external factors. Hopefully, the right framing would push him there. "Every single one of these women suffers from the same problems. What's stranger is that each one's symptomatic trajectory also follows the same path." Except for her. Mulling over yesterday's events, the idea struck her that Ryan posed less of an immediate threat and more of one built for death by a thousand cuts, culminating in another motherly resonance. *Whatever doesn't kill you, will try, try again,* the voice tried to pull her from the present, but the present pulled back. She pinched her lips. "I can practically predict a session by what the group's last patient told me."

"Quite a coincidence. Perhaps it's some sort of a prank. Do you believe each of their claims?" He stared at her desk, scattered with pages of notes regarding the patients at hand.

"Yes!" Claire stomped her foot, drawing his attention back to her. She hadn't intended that, but stress had eroded her emotional control. "Them telling the truth is the one thing I'm certain of. The rest, I don't know." She stuck her arms to her sides, stifling the urge to tug on her hair. "I hate that I can't figure this out. Five patients, five weeks, and I'm at a loss of direction. If these were simple cases, I would have solved them by now. They're not, and I'm sure they're all tied together."

Eric looked at a framed picture of his family on the corner of his desk, his typical catalyst for rumination. What should Claire pitch first? A cult? The ratio of six women to zero men implied a human factor, perpetrated by some sort of misguided vengeance. The perpetrator or perpetrators wanted their victims to suffer. Her haunted house left little doubt.

Stretching his suit sleeves to his wrists, Eric asked, "All of your patients suffering from these supposed non-psychotic hallucinations are women, correct?" He practically read her mind. Earning his buy-in might prove easier than expected.

"That's right." Claire crossed her arms over her chest, puffing up the high neckline of her maroon dress.

"Are they related in any way, outside of being your patients?"

"Other than effectively living alone, not really." Hardly an easy thing to investigate without violating someone's privacy. Though at this point, she wasn't above snooping if she'd learn something valuable. "They live in different parts of Denver. Their ages range from a year younger than me to their mid-fifties. They all work in different industries."

"Isolation could be responsible. What's their social status outside of home?"

"Again, it varies. Some go out. Some stay in. All have grown more reclusive as the symptoms have worsened." Herself included. She hadn't been hiking or climbing in weeks, and the quality of her sleep suffered for it.

"Do you continue to encourage human interaction?"

"Of course." She pulled up her hand into a stop sign, then laid it back on her forearm. "Let's assume I'm doing everything right." The more attention Eric pointed at her, personally or professionally, the bigger chance he'd discover her place in the group. She admitted that knowledge might help, but he was liable to start from square one. And with Claire's family history, the possibility he'd inspect her findings with tainted lenses risked too much. "Let's focus on the victimized patients."

He looked embarrassed in nodding his agreement. Appealing to his sympathy for human suffering worked so predictably well. Best not to overuse it. "No problem," he said. "Are they depressed? You mentioned that for some of these patients."

More common in women, but *come on. Get more creative,* she thought. *If I'm the only one thinking cults or biological warfare, this really might exist all in my head.* "Not clinically speaking. Two of them suffer from bouts of depression, but this group's symptoms are more," she paused, "antagonistic than that."

He leaned forward, elbow on his thigh. "Antagonistic how?"

"The hallucinations, or whatever they are, exhibit behavior resembling a stalker. They act as if they know their victims."

"Unusual. Is it possible that your patients manifested these fantasies to fulfill a lack of outside attention?"

"Absolutely not," Claire defended, as if he directed the insinuation at her. "The victims harbor no delusion that their manifestations exist to provide anything positive."

"Speaking of which, some of your patients must present delusions in association with their hallucinations."

"No. Not at all."

"That's almost impossible." Calm, level-headed Eric lived up to his standards in the face of incredulity.

"Like lightning striking the same place five times." Claire mimed casting a bolt from the heavens. "I know."

Eric glanced back at the photo of his family. "They don't know each other. They're not faking it. They all came to you for help within three weeks of one another. You may have won the psychiatric lottery."

"Or been cursed by it." What gypsy had she pissed off to incur such a sentencing? She might've laughed if it didn't seem somewhat viable.

"I'm surprised that you, of all people, don't appreciate this opportunity. You always go the extra mile to solve the hardest cases."

Claire's cases never involved her on such a personal level before. She clasped her hands together in a pleading manner and directed them at her co-worker. "I'm asking for your advice. I can't go many extra miles than that."

Eric wore the congenial smile of a father proud of his daughter's maturation. "What did that letter you receive say again? Enjoy your gifts? It almost sounds like a practical joke."

"Or a veiled threat." Claire rolled her shoulders back a couple of times, exuding relief from the pores of her skin. She had purposefully avoided mentioning the letter today. Tainting Eric's answers with her own suppositions invalidated any unbiased insights. She sprung the last piece of information she was willing to share. "I looked at the sender again and noticed something. Imogene Aire. Fredonia. N. D. Say it together fast, and drop everything after the first syllable in Fredonia." She pronounced Aire like *er-e*, as she had when Brad visited late last Friday. Was he enjoying his trip to New Mexico? And why did she care?

Eric's response stopped her from dwelling on it too long. He stared up at the ceiling, mouthing words like a fish. "Interesting," he said, looking back at her. "Imaginary friend. But that's a stretch, isn't it?"

"That's right, and it's not a stretch. What do you make of it?" Muscles in her face and back relaxed with the weight of a burden unloaded. She had finally told someone.

"You said earlier that your patients' hallucinations behave similarly to a stalker. You experienced someone snooping around your house a few weeks ago. Do you think these occurrences are related?"

Claire rubbed the back of her neck. She had expected this question, rehearsed half a dozen answers, but still had no idea how she'd respond until asked. "My gut says yes, but how can I reconcile personal incidents alongside psychological symptoms in others?"

"I don't know." Not illuminating, but better than accusing her of something worse. Eric raised a sympathetic hand but didn't appear alarmed enough to uncross his legs. "I'd say if this was a horror movie, you should see a priest."

"Why?" Walking so that she stood over Eric's desk, she sprinkled it with imaginary holy water. "So they can wave around a globe of water and speak nonsense in Latin?" He'd hate the mocking of his religion, but he deserved it if his best advice amounted to reading the Bible. Then again, she *had* described last night as a haunted house and considered the possibility of a gypsy curse moments ago.

Regardless, he acted as if he hadn't heard her. "Actually, a Dr. Ingetti gave a guest sermon about identifying and resisting demons at my church last week. He's ordained to conduct rites of exorcism. I think he's in town for the rest of September. He won't help your patients, but you—"

"Me?" Claire hoped her stunned response came off as flabbergasted rather than frightened. Churches spouted nonsense to anyone who listened, but once considered, the idea of a true haunting sprouted quickly, infesting her from within, widening the pit which formed in her stomach. Preferable to madness, wasn't it?

Was it?

Eric slapped his shoe and chuckled. Relief found Claire before annoyance settled in. He wouldn't have laughed if he had properly read her anxiety. "Don't worry. You don't need to join a church," he snorted before recapturing his serious demeanor. "Possessions and hauntings exhibit similar symptoms to psychosis. That's why most exorcism calls result in a referral to a doctor. Obviously, I don't think your patients are haunted by their hallucinations, but he might give you some ideas. Dr. Ingetti has certainly seen enough strange things to consider consulting him. Plus, it might instill some empathy by taking a step back to assess the patients from a less psychological perspective."

"I'm empathetic," she said. Eric's blank stare challenged the veracity of her statement. "When needed." Her co-worker's demeanor remained stoic. Sure, she strayed from picking up her patients' emotional burdens. They interfered with solving their problems, the real reason for seeing her, and . . . her empathy didn't matter. Was he serious about contacting a priest? This Dr. Ingetti, a doctor, presumably of theology. *Ordained to conduct exorcisms.* Her stomach spasmed and knees weakened, forcing her to return to her desk. "I guess it's an idea."

Eric gave a half-shrug. "I won't come up with an answer that's better than a guess. We're psychiatrists, Claire. We're trained to diagnose and treat mental illnesses. I'm happy to offer a second opinion if you and your patients feel comfortable with the idea. Otherwise, if you're convinced these hallucinations originated from somewhere outside of your patients' heads then you should call the police. That's their job. Whether it's related or not, that letter sounds more ominous than I first gave it credit for. And that's something else *the police* can help with."

Stuck between a priest and the police, Claire began regretting this conversation. The police scoured her home and found no sign of an intruder. What use were they? She could show them the letter, she supposed. They could run it for prints, but unless the sender had built a record that wouldn't help. Worst-case scenario, she'd lose the only physical evidence she owned in this whole charade. Except that wasn't true—the worst-case scenario meant turning the police against her, establishing an identity as one of the crazies.

Memories surfaced of her mom's struggle with the police after escaping from St. Mary's Hospital of the Wayward. Sofia Costas left to warn Claire of something, but only days of repeated, *Boys in blue won't help you, unless you help the boys in blue*, remained in her mind. Thankfully, her mom avoided any serious injury from the incident, but it left Claire with a sour taste which she treated by minimizing her contact with law enforcement. She'd rather see a neurologist for a brain scan or hell, even a priest.

"Whatever you choose to do," said Eric, "please keep me in the loop. I'm worried about the patients, and I'm worried about you." Before Claire could open her mouth, he added, "Don't get defensive. You're a great doctor, but this is a Herculean task for anyone."

"Fine. When I know more, you'll know more." Which didn't mean telling him the whole truth, but opening up *had* imparted some relief despite triggering mild nausea. Acknowledging she required support to solve her and her patients' problems created another predicament: who should she talk to and what should she tell them? Possibilities from priests to police to friends abounded, leading to a Friday meeting as productive as her session with her bipolar patient. All she could think, as she and Eric discussed their remaining patients, was that hopefully she'd figure out something before Ryan came back to try, try again.

CHAPTER 15

The doorway into Dr. Samuel Ingetti's office revealed a small room with a smaller desk. Three parallel paper stacks, each a half-inch high, decorated its rustic finish. On the shelf behind, books huddled against each other in perfect alignment. In between the furniture sat the man himself. Short salt-and-pepper hair swept to the side matched a thick mustache beneath. His attire resembled a department store clerk: plain black jacket and a collared white shirt stained with the purity of conservatism. He looked a robust sixty, but research had informed Claire he was forty-five.

That research began with a deep dive into hauntings, demons, and spirits—topics barely given notice except to drive them from a patient's mind. *Demonic symptoms*, she had ridiculed with her first query. Symptoms! As if the right prescription could cure her woes. Ridicule turned to interest as encounters by supposed haunting victims drew parallels to her own experiences. Whereas psychosis, madness, and external factors like cults failed to adequately explain her situation, spiritual forces handled it with convenient grace. As she dove into solutions that promised an end to her suffering, she turned from ardent denier to zealous hopeful, lured by a framework that offered *answers*. A framework, she reminded herself, that drove people toward the misguided path of religion.

Internal dialogue waged war among hope, desire, and disbelief, cracking the foundation of her remaining sanity. On the brink of breaking Saturday night, she followed Eric's halfhearted advice. After researching Dr. Ingetti's credentials, which passed well enough for a man of faith, she called Heavenly Benediction Catholic Church. She expected to leave the priest a voicemail and fret over it until next week. Within an hour she had scheduled a visit for Sunday evening in his office.

Driving to the church tonight, Claire found herself hating what she might learn. Hating the idea of problems imperceptible by modern means of science. Hating how the apparition of hers and five others had reduced her to seeking a priest for help. Hating how anxiety compelled her to rush through the quiet church halls. By the time she entered his office, she had built up a mountain of scorn, which she attempted to pacify with a playful bite, "I'm surprised you're working today. I thought you rested on Sunday."

"I'll rest when the devil rests," Dr. Ingetti said. His lips offered no hint of anger or joy. He leaned in, hands clasped on the desk's edge, without succumbing to the hunching endemic to most people. "You must be Claire Rossi. Sit and explain everything."

No greetings. No pleasantries. Down to business. "Did some specific haunting draw you to the Denver area?" *Small talk, the solace of the nervous,* Claire shamed herself over not reciprocating his brevity. "This office doesn't befit someone with your experience." *Small jabs, the armor of the weary.* Her stiff chair gave her as little as she gave the priest.

He took no offense or simply didn't care. "The Vatican assigns me to places for any number of reasons. As a form of community building, I work out of local churches. They provide whatever space is available. In return, I meet with members of their congregation."

"I'm not part of the congregation."

"That's obvious. Can we begin?" Dr. Ingetti said with the tone of a father coaxing the truth out of his child.

"As a priest, are you obligated to keep our conversation confidential?" she asked, masking the real question nagging at her.

"Yes, yes, yes." His chin lifted higher with each usage of the word. "As long as you're not an immediate threat to yourself or others, I won't say a thing. That's not enough to stop wasting my time though, is it? What else?"

"Does it matter if I don't believe in God or the devil or any of this?" The aha moment: the reason for her contempt and her stalling. Claire unfolded her arms toward the ceiling like a flower blooming.

"Maybe so, maybe not. I don't care. If you're going to sit in that chair, you're going to tell me your story, or you can leave." She reconsidered her position. Dr. Ingetti deserved contempt, just not for his beliefs. He may not have been the quack she expected, but her feet itched to walk out all the same. On their brief phone call, he had said little between hello, goodbye, and a time to come in, but she never imagined such shit manners from a person who lived off of *donations*. She rubbed her thumb over her forefinger, staying a fist that itched to tug on her hair. *It's not worth it,* she told herself. *Just get to the point and move on. You're not here to argue etiquette.*

She loosed some anxiety with a stroke of her hair and then told her story, sparing no details in her string of tribulations. Over a half-hour, she detailed the Fredonian letter, the board game stalker, Ryan's mall conversation, Rick and his two incidents, the haunted house symphony, and finally the similarity in symptoms between her and her patients. She relayed this exactly how she preferred her patients to, not waiting for validation or judgment. In return, Dr. Samuel Ingetti listened in stoic silence, moving once to straighten his posture.

"It doesn't make sense, Dr. Ingetti." She threw in his honorific, appealing to his obvious arrogance. "Whatever it is shows up briefly to remind me it's still around then disappears without causing any physical harm, if it's even capable of that. I don't know if experiencing this nightmare alongside my patients makes it easier or harder to decipher. I'm treating them as if they're suffering from a psychotic disorder producing hallucinations, but I don't believe it."

"Because you don't want to admit you might be suffering from it too?" His question came as an accusation.

"Because it doesn't fit and there are too many coincidences," she countered. "We're suffering from threats that seem imaginary, but they all started after I received a very real letter."

"Remind me, Claire." She wrinkled her nose at his not returning the respect of her title. "What do you expect out of this conversation?"

"I want answers, whether they're mental, physiological, or . . . spiritual." Desire for insight tangled with her distrust of religion. "If nothing else, ruling out one solution brings me closer to the truth."

"Do you believe you're haunted by a spirit?"

"No," Claire said, her fist exploding into an open palm beside her face. "But that's not my area of expertise."

"Good, because you're not. Not haunted. Not possessed. Not anything requiring a blessing from God."

"How could you know that?" Enough playing nice. "Don't you go and throw holy water on things to see if they fizzle first?"

"Hauntings, as you think of them, latch onto individuals or places and not groups." Dr. Ingetti scratched above his eyebrow, with a grin hinting at his superiority. "Put into terms you might understand—they're not an infection. They're parasites feeding off of their host. Parasites don't move on until their work is complete. In the case of a demon, it means total possession. In the case of a ghost, it means accomplishing some feat left undone in life. Nothing you've described warrants ecclesiastical consideration."

"But—"

"I'm not going to comment on mental illness because you're more skilled in that department. Please extend the same courtesy to me with otherworldly entities. This is my area of expertise."

She stared at him, chewing on her lip. "That's not good enough."

"Why are you arguing this, *Claire*? You don't believe in any of this, remember?" He mimed her earlier arms flowering. "Now you're free to seek answers elsewhere."

Her shoulders tensed, readying for a verbal altercation. He must've noticed how much it bothered her when a stranger addressed her by her first name. *As if I were some child to ignore.* He wanted her gone but couldn't remove her over a simple disagreement, not from this charitable house of God, so he prodded her vanity, insulting her pride and intellect, mocking her until she stormed out in a tiff.

Like hell she'd make it so easy on him.

"Because I work in a complicated field where trained profession-als"—Claire's hand emphasized her points—"informed by decades of research and billions of dollars, require hours of therapy to properly diagnose and treat their patients. All of it is more tangible than your spirits, holy or otherwise. For your work to offer any va-lidity it would require intense scrutiny on an individual basis. It's impossible for you to deny, with absolute certainty, that this is a church matter in the span of a lunch break."

Dr. Ingetti rolled his neck, stopped, and rolled it the other way. "Perhaps I wasn't clear before. I can't help you."

Bullshit. Maybe nothing haunted her. She could accept that, wanted to accept it even, but he'd hardly tried. Where did he get off dismissing her? If she treated her patients the same way, she'd be out on the streets. *If your patients acted like you, where would they end up?* she countered. *Referred to Eric Wilson.* Not exactly the streets, but the brief introspection pushed her to change tactics. Dr. Ingetti's cre-dentials came with a wealth of knowledge which, like it or not, Claire had to put every effort into tapping.

"I'm sorry, Dr. Ingetti. You're the expert here. I'm not haunted, but isn't there more to it?" He looked unimpressed. She needed something to bring him to her side. If sympathy worked on church-going Eric, it stood a chance against a priest, no matter their grump-iness. "Do you think I'm imagining all of this?"

Behind sealed lips, a tongue poked at his cheeks while he con-sidered her. "No, I don't think you're imagining anything."

"So what is it?" *Get him started.* "What about a cult?" She felt foolish suggesting it aloud.

"Unlikely. They focus inward on controlling their members ra-ther than interacting with those on the outside."

"Satanic cults?"

"As a subset of cults, my earlier statement applies."

Insufferable, but the shell started to crack. "In your expert opin-ion, what is most likely causing the disturbances that my patients and I are experiencing?"

Dr. Ingetti tugged on mustache hairs, his first motion which resembled genuine reflection. He inched his hand away, leaving it within easy reach of his facial hair. "Your patients are real, correct? As in, they're corroborated by a third party?"

"Yes," she enunciated to cool budding rage. "The patients are real." *You pompous ass.* Was that a real question or another gibe?

"Are you certain their experiences are incorporeal?" No hint of ridicule. They were getting somewhere.

"Yes. Absolutely sure. Their behaviors and recounts are consistent with imagined or hallucinated entities."

"You saw your first patient with these symptoms and experienced them yourself *after* you received that letter?"

"That's correct." The priest had listened more than he'd let on.

"You mentioned the sender's phonetic contraction forming the phrase imaginary friend. Tell me the sender's address."

Claire had seen the letter so many times it took a single blink to visualize the answer. "19 Memory Lane. 58440 zip code. Fredonia, North Dakota."

"Does that location exist?"

"No."

Fiddling with his mustache for inspiration, Dr. Ingetti pulled out a whisker with a yank. "Assuming no environmental factors such as a carbon monoxide leak, and that you're not mentally indisposed yourself, my hypothesis is you and your patients are cursed. Possibly originating from that letter or its contents, though the curser would have needed your patients to interact with it in some way. Then again," he trailed off, drumming his fingers on his facial hair.

"What?" Claire asked after a few seconds.

"You mentioned you and your patients are victims to different apparitions, as you call them. It's not a singular curse then. How did your patients find you?"

A minute ago it was one curse, now it was six? She needed to reign him in before he said her presence put every patient in her practice at risk. "Unique apparitions, yes, but similar physically and in mannerisms. That must mean something."

"How did your patients find you?" he drawled, as if she hadn't understood the question the first time around.

"Normal channels," she responded behind clenched teeth. Sighing, she added, "Primary physician recommendations, online reviews, word of mouth. Nothing unusual." *Curses? Six of them? Impossible.*

"Have your patients received similarly strange letters?"

"Not that I'm aware of." Weeks had passed since Janice had first handed her the Fredonian envelope. Could a few pieces of paper really doom her and her patients? What a ridiculous notion. *More ridiculous than a cult poisoning your water?*

"You should ask them. You should have asked them as soon as you noticed a correlation of symptoms. Your decades of professional research must come attached with horse blinders."

And like that, he was attempting to run her off again. *What a complete—* she started, before hurt pride mollified her anger. Dr. Ingetti was right. Her obsession with the letter should've called into question whether her patients had received one too. But were they really discussing curses? Claire ran her hand over the smooth surface of his desk, clipping a stack of papers and drawing a fiery glare. "Fine, but can we back up? Explain the difference between a curse and haunting."

"Hauntings are born of spirits," he noted, as if angrily reading from an encyclopedia. "They have purpose but harbor no personal agenda. To a spirit or demon, one victim serves as well as the next. Curses are born of people, their victims specifically targeted. It manifests like a targeted trap in whatever object they imbue. While another will encounter their own perils holding onto such an object, the full brunt of its effect only triggers upon reaching its intended recipient. There is a ramp-up period, as the curse comes to life, so to speak. The progenitor must expel a great deal of energy to enact their curse. It speaks to a personal grudge to sacrifice what is necessary for such a feat, and if one individual is responsible for six curses, they are quite driven. Talented too—with years of experience, a strong teacher, or both."

Specifics became generalities as Claire summarized the priest's words with no insult intended. "We're basically talking about magic."

"No. We're talking about curses. Use your academic brain and absorb what I'm telling you."

"Semantics. If—" Claire dropped it. Dr. Ingetti verged on shutting down completely. "Never mind. Assuming they exist, do you think the odds of a curse outweigh say, I don't know, a biological attack? Like someone sprinkled something more mundane on the letter, and it infected me?"

"Have you seen a doctor?"

"Not until next week."

"They'll give you the all clear. Deaths are how terrorists measure success. Sending six people to a psych ward doesn't move the needle."

"Even if they're all women? Could be religious. No offense."

Dr. Ingetti huffed with the annoyance of a teacher taking a question from a student who missed most of the semester. "Religion isn't misogynistic. People are, and they use religion as one of many vehicles to justify those beliefs. If anything, the fact that it's you and five other women further points to a curse. Homogeneous groups are easier to hex en masse. I'd speculate that all of your problem patients are also white, with an age spread of twenty years."

Twenty-two years from Claire's memory, but close enough to break her barrier of incredulity. Eric had been onto something when he had inquired about patient demographics, but neither could have foreseen so broad a similarity playing a significant role. "Fine. Let's say I'm cursed. What do I do next? Can you bless me and cast it away?" An image popped into her head of a tornado carrying Ryan into the sky, followed by winds sweeping up Rick. If her safety demanded that sacrifice, so be it. Whether good or ill, she wanted *all* pseudo-hallucinations driven away.

"I can bless you, but it won't help. Blessings ward against Satanic influence, which I doubt is the case here, and require faith in God to work, which you clearly won't believe in anytime soon. Even if you did believe and discovered Satan's taint behind this all, the effects are temporary. It would prove as useful as mowing a weed instead of digging out its root. You must destroy the curse's source."

Claire's eyes narrowed. "You want me to find the person who cursed me and . . . ?" She didn't want to voice the thought of killing someone, even her tormentor. Lock them up for the rest of their life, sure. But killing?

Condescension dripped from Dr. Ingetti's tilted head. "Is everything in psychology so grandiose a gesture? Just burn the letter. If that doesn't work, look for anything else new in your or your patient's lives. And so that you don't develop any other foolish ideas, this applies strictly to inanimate objects. Curses require a non-sentient intermediary to transfer between people. Burn the letter, Claire." Commanding more than suggesting.

"It's evidence though. What if someone can use it? What if I discover another clue? If I don't find the curser, won't he or she just do it again? Will burning a letter really make this horror show stop?"

"Burn the letter. If it works, even if temporarily, you'll know it's a curse. It'll assist in solving your mystery in a more permanent fashion. And if you see a positive impact, it's imperative you gather the remaining cursed objects to burn simultaneously." The priest's halting hand silenced Claire as she opened her mouth.

"Cursed objects can be linked to one another. In such cases, burning one will only infuse its energy onto the others, empowering the remaining apparitions. One or two out of six is acceptable. More than half is perilous." His halting hand signal swung down, pointing at her. "Finally, because it's probably crossed your mind, don't think to take a picture of the letter before burning it. You'd ruin your life sending it up to the cloud." He waved up to the ceiling. "Go home, burn the letter, and be done with it."

Caught between wanting to ask more, to drain this aged fruit of his wisdom, and wanting to argue the impossibility of it all, she froze. As the priest's mouth opened to no doubt pave the way for a tongue lashing, her phone rang its generic tune from the confines of her purse. She pulled it out, relieved for a reprieve from a disconcerting world filled with magical curses. Identification marked the caller as Aurora Medical Center.

"I'm sorry. It's the hospital," said Claire, holding up her index finger.

Annoyance flashed across Dr. Ingetti's face before he settled into a position of interest.

Over the next few minutes, a nurse detailed Gabrielle Capers's admittance into their psychiatry wing. After responding to a frenzied emergency call, paramedics transported her to the hospital. Though seriously injured, she avoided necessitating critical care. Lacerations covered her upper body with wounds appearing self-inflicted. The nurse informed Claire that the attending physician would respond to her follow-up questions as time allowed.

Or I can drive there now, she thought.

"I need to leave." She was already digging out car keys. Were the threats against the quintet, the *cursed* quintet, growing more deadly? Or had Ms. Capers's imaginary friend driven her mad? Short-lived guilt overcame Claire following silent thanks for sparing her such calamity, until she realized the invisible clock ticking over her head. If the apparitions had turned physical, only time separated Ryan from assaulting her too. Perhaps worse, the logic which dictated the order of 'what happened to who and when' had broken down. Diane Shapiro or Claire should've been the first on the list for this. It added another wrinkle to the problem at hand.

"That was one of your cursed patients," said Dr. Ingetti, not asking but knowing.

Claire stood up, finger through her key ring. "I can't say, but thank you for speaking with me." The chair slid an inch as she bumped into it on her about-turn.

"Burn the letter," he shouted as she fled his office. "Burn it!"

CHAPTER 16

W ho are you?" demanded an overweight nurse, obviously not enjoying her evening shift.

"Dr. Claire Rossi, Gabrielle Capers's psychiatrist. I'm here to speak with her."

The nurse typed on the keyboard. "Don't see your name on her file. Visits are family only." She leaned back as if that concluded their business.

Claire grabbed the counter, tensing up to her neck. "A nurse literally just called me about her admittance. I'm clearly on file somewhere so look again or call somebody else."

"That's not how family only works, ma'am. Can't help you."

"Do you want to be the nurse that stopped a psychotic woman from speaking with her psychiatrist right before she stabbed someone? Is your job security that strong?" Claire doubted Ms. Capers capable of such aggression, despite whatever had happened, but this nurse didn't know that. Or much of anything it seemed.

The nurse folded her arms and rocked her head from side to side, either considering Claire's argument or sizing her up for a tussle.

"I'll take care of this," said a deep voice from behind.

Claire's heart raced, signaling her legs to follow suit. She clutched the counter edge for support.

Two feet away, standing as tall as Ryan or Rick, stood a clean-shaven man wearing a white coat over scrubs. He looked a few years younger than Eric. "You must be Ms. Capers's psychiatrist. I'm Dr. John McGee, her attending." Claire accepted his handshake after a brief hesitation. "I'm surprised you came down. Nurse Espinosa called you as a courtesy. She's doing alright, but I'm happy to show you to her room."

He bore enough resemblance to Ryan that she considered inventing an excuse and taking her chances with the desk nurse, which led to the realization she had remained quiet since Dr. McGee entered the scene. Assuming every tall, white male existed as a figment of her imagination would drive her mad if the . . . curse . . . didn't first. A forced smile cleared her mind. "I'd appreciate that."

"It's nice to meet you." The pair walked in silence until clearing earshot of the nurse station. "Sorry about earlier. That nurse would stop a surgeon from using a scalpel if the hospital had a rule against sharp objects on the floor."

"Sounds great for a people-facing role."

Dr. McGee chuckled. "I don't get it either, but I'm not in charge of staffing. Not that I'd want to be." He paused. "So I take it by your rushing over that self-harm is a risk. Should we transfer Ms. Capers to a full-time psychiatric center? We're not equipped for long-term patient care, and I wouldn't want anything to happen." His genuine concern reminded her of Eric.

"I'm not sure yet." Her heartbeat slowed to normal. "I'm here because breakthroughs for patients come in the strangest places. It's possible that between whatever happened and a new setting, we stand to make significant progress. I don't want to miss that opportunity."

"You're very dedicated to your patients."

Some more than others. Claire followed Dr. McGee around the hallway corner and channeled Eric to hide her vested interest in Ms. Capers's condition. "How bad are her injuries? Is she stable?" She then asked one question for herself. "Can I talk to her?"

"She's doing fine, and you can. She's in a private room for at least the night. However, she's not completely cleared. Her nurse and I are keeping a close eye on her condition, so if you want guaranteed privacy you'll have to wait a couple of hours. Even then, one of her friends has called twice to see when she can visit."

Claire doubled down on her facade. "Could you give me twenty uninterrupted minutes? I'd rather not lose a potentially key moment in assisting with her recuperation from the mental trauma suffered tonight. I'd be in the room the whole time."

"Sorry, but no. Despite my earlier comments, I do believe some rules are worth following. My responsibility is ensuring she's not a threat to herself or others, and that she'll remain stable through the night." Dr. McGee pushed open double doors that led them further down the wing.

"I understand." What more could she say? "Is there anything else you can tell me? Has she spoken with the police? Why did Nurse," she paused, unable to remember the name he had just said, "the nurse on the phone said the wounds might have been self-inflicted?"

"She called 9-1-1 herself. EMS drove her here before the police had a chance to ask any questions. Not sure if they found anything at her home. You'll have to ask her for the rest of the details." The attending pointed at an open door two rooms down and brought his voice to a whisper. "I'll enter first and let her know you're here. The sedation should be wearing off."

"Sedation?" Claire raised her eyebrows.

"She was rather hysterical when the ambulance found her."

"I imagine so, given the extent of her injuries," Claire scoffed. Emulating Eric had apparently left her defensive about her patient. Or she realized it could have as easily been her.

He curled his lip, chewing on a response before settling on a curt nod. Pale linoleum floors guided the attending to Ms. Capers. Claire stepped into the room behind him and waited. What had her patient seen? How much could she afford to ask? Stepping out of her head, she caught the tail end of her introduction.

"I'll leave you in Dr. Rossi's hands for now," said Dr. McGee, "but Nurse Espinosa or I will be back to check on you soon." He exited the room, gesturing from Claire to Ms. Capers and starting the invisible timer until his return. The door clicked shut.

"How are you feeling?" Claire's patient looked like her parents had died. Mascara streaked down her cheeks into smeared blush. Blotched skin surrounded inflamed eyes. Only a bruise on her left arm showed any injury though. Her torso must have borne the brunt of the lacerations.

"I'm . . ." Ms. Capers trailed off. Claire waited for her patient's vacant stare to fill. "Here."

"*Here* is how you get to *there*, Gabby." Ms. Capers began every session with a plea to call her Gabby until it stuck. It fit her affable personality, a disposition all but drained and in need of a pick-me-up, no matter how small. "I'm going to ask you a few questions. Please tell me if you ever feel uncomfortable."

Ms. Capers's defensive body language indicated to expect that sooner than later. She scooted herself up another inch but said nothing.

Claire walked to the other side of the bed, pulling forward the room's only chair. Her hand hovered over Ms. Capers's, wondering if her touch would come across as reassuring or terrifying, and she lacked time for the latter. "Who attacked you?"

"Ted." She struggled to swallow. "He's real, Dr. Rossi."

"I believe you." *Hold her hand. Either it helps or you put off talking to her 'til tomorrow.* But I need information now. *This isn't just about you.* Ugh—she had let in too much of Eric. She slid her palm into Ms. Capers's hand, encountering as little interest as she did resistance. "Are you able to explain what happened?"

Ms. Capers stared at the white tiled ceiling until her eyes welled, and her grip tightened. "I had gone out on a disaster of a date. A total disaster. The guy was as bad as they come, and I let him pick me up because of . . . all of this." She choked on a wet cough, covering her mouth until settling. "Thirty minutes after he dropped me off, I heard a window shatter and assumed it was my date, angry I didn't invite him in or something. I walked into my bedroom expecting to find a brick on the floor and instead found Ted, sitting on my bed, wearing that sadistic grin I told you about." Ms. Capers rattled off her tale faster and faster. "I tried the usual tactics: rationalization, humming a song, exuding control, leaving the room. Ted seemed amused by it all."

"He told me the time had come, that he was strong now,

stronger than that slob of a date. If I hummed louder or walked further away, his voice boomed to compensate. I retreated into the corner of the kitchen, as far from my bedroom as I could get. I should've ran outside or screamed or called someone, but instead I cornered myself. In the blink of an eye, he appeared near the counter and yanked the biggest blade out of the knife block."

Ms. Capers pulled away from Claire and crossed her arms in an X over her torso, wincing between breaths as she spoke. "He slashed me twice across the chest, then held me down, knife dripping my own blood on my face while he laughed to the heavens. Then he darted out of the room with his arms held high as if running a victory lap. I feared I'd die if I didn't get to a hospital, but I keep my phone near the front door, and I thought that's where Ted might've gone. So I froze again like an idiot until his laughing faded away. I finally stood, slowly enough that I thought to take a knife with me. I made it out and called 9-1-1. But Dr. Rossi"—she snapped to face Claire so fast her neck popped—"after the call, I noticed I had grabbed the *same* knife he attacked me with, the one he left the room with. How could two weapons be in the same—"

The door clicked open. Doctor and patient's attention darted to the newcomer, a woman with black curly hair that fell on lilac scrubs.

"I'm Nurse Espinosa. Looks like I'm interrupting something." Without waiting for a response, she walked toward Ms. Capers. "I'm just here to check your bandages. I'll be done in a minute. Could you uncross your arms, Gabrielle?"

Espinosa waited with the patience of a saint for compliance. She lifted the gown to one side so Claire couldn't see anything. Pleased with her quick inspection and palpation over Ms. Capers's right breast and stomach, the nurse gave her an all clear. "I'll let you two get back to it."

"Is that it for the night?" Claire asked.

"Oh, no. Gabrielle will have another few visits from me or the doctor, probably even after you leave. But if either of you needs something sooner, go ahead and press that button." Espinosa pointed to a remote stationed on the side of the bed, then waved herself out of the room.

In a normal therapy session, Claire would ask for the patient's interpretation of the duplicate knife's meaning. Due to Ms. Capers's horror over initially mentioning it, she transitioned to less traumatic topics to avoid a potential shutdown. "I'm so sorry about what happened to you, but I promise we'll fix this. Together."

Ms. Capers turned back toward Claire. She snatched a pained breath from the air and laid her arms to her side. "Thank you, Dr. Rossi. You're such a good listener."

"You're welcome." Claire tilted her head, letting Eric and Dr. Ingetti feed her their suggestions. "This may be an odd question, but do you remember how you found me initially?"

"Hmm. A day or two after Ted . . ." Ms. Capers squeezed her eyes shut. Once his name dissipated from the air, she continued, "showed up for the first time, I got one of your advertising flyers in the mail. You had a friendly but professional face, and I loved the dress you were wearing so I decided to give you a try."

Claire frowned. She and Eric didn't send flyers. They didn't advertise at all. "Why didn't you include that in your admission paperwork?"

"I don't think you had a box for it."

A costly oversight. "Do you still have the advertisement?"

"At home, I think."

Another interruption halted their conversation. Dr. McGee returned to the room, striding to where the nurse had stood some minutes earlier with a clipboard in hand. "Sorry to intrude. Just a quick update: there were no traces of any toxins or drugs outside of what I assume your psychiatrist prescribed." The attending looked to Claire as if to confirm but turned his attention to Ms. Capers before allowing a response. "We ruled out your date drugging you and most environmental factors. At this point, we'll continue to monitor you and your wounds, searching for any discrepancies those may provide."

"Discrepancies?" Ms. Capers's fist pounded on the mattress, causing a wince. "I was attacked. The police should be looking into this, not you. Hallucinations don't attack people. Tell him, Dr. Rossi." The doctor had to know his statement would ruffle her. What was the point of this? Claire studied the clipboard in his hands.

"The police searched your house for clues and are searching for the man you described," said Dr. McGee. The chance he knew the extent of their investigation seemed dubious, but it calmed Ms. Capers all the same. "Ms. Capers, I'd like to talk to Dr. Rossi about the attack in relation to your history with her. See if we can figure out something together we may have missed separately. I have release forms to allow us to share information, from your treatment here to your therapy with her. This may clue us in to details currently lacking to solve your problem. Would you feel comfortable signing them?"

Ms. Capers turned to Claire. "What do you think, Dr. Rossi?"

Under normal circumstances, Claire would have protested her patient too unwell to consent. Sharing treatment left too much out of her control. In this case, the insight of another physician—one she didn't work with daily—could serve as validation for separating physical realities from mental fictions. For her *and* Ms. Capers. "I think it's fine," she answered. "But it's your decision."

Ms. Capers meekly held up her arms to accept the paperwork. After a few signatures, the attending thanked her. "That's all I need for now. The nurse or I will be back in a little bit to check on you."

Claire waited a few seconds after the door shut. "Gabby?"

Ms. Capers slid her hand back into Claire's and squeezed. "Thank you for coming so quickly."

Claire smiled at her patient's improved demeanor. Despite everything, this makeshift session had progressed better than she could have hoped. Time to indulge her hunch. "Gabby, I want you to think back to when you received that flyer. Did you also receive any strange mail?"

"Strange how?"

Claire tiptoed around it, "Anything out of the ordinary. Postmarked from a distant location. Obscure contents. Different envelope shape." Her heart sank when Ms. Capers shook her head. Out of all of her patients, Ms. Capers's penchant for socialization made her the best candidate for not trashing mail from an unknown sender.

"Sorry, Dr. Rossi. I don't remember anything."

"That's okay. Does Fredonia, North Dakota ring a bell?" So much for not leading her.

"Actually . . . yes. Let me think." Ms. Capers grimaced as she adjusted in bed. Claire waited through a series of scrunched eyelids. "Yes, but I can't remember who sent it. It's weird because I completely forgot about it until now, but I remember the note inside. It didn't have much to say. Something like a mom . . . mom who loves them all? You know how I want to be a mom one day. I guess that's why I kept it. Even if I received it by mistake, it gave me hope of fulfilling that dream."

Anxiety blended with excitement in an overflow of adrenaline. "Why didn't you tell me about it in one of our sessions?"

"You never asked about it, and I didn't see what the hallucinations—or what I thought were hallucinations—had to do with the letter. But they're not really hallucinations," she said with the curl of a question. When Claire didn't respond, Ms. Capers looked down. "Not really hallucinations." Another silent moment passed, fermenting brief confidence into trembling fright. "The letter must have been a warning."

"Perhaps. Do you remember if you received it before or after Ted showed up?"

Her gaze fixed on her gown, peering through it at her wounds. Answers came half at attention, half involved elsewhere. "Before. There was that date with Sean, and the letter had me thinking how bad of a father he'd make. Ted appeared for the first time the next day. We talked about that in our first session."

"Right," Claire said with the confidence of a master liar, disguising how few particulars she remembered without her notes. What did 'Mom who loves them all' have in common with 'Enjoy your gifts'? Were the patients meant to represent Claire's children? Was Ms. Capers's letter one of Claire's gifts? She lacked data, but if one patient had received a cryptic message, it stood to reason the others had as well.

Ms. Capers piped up. "I liked it better when we were worried about stress causing my hallucinations. That was safe and comfortable. But now . . . it's so funny." She forced a chuckle. "My school voted me Prom Queen, and two decades later I've held onto that, thinking myself special and that special people don't go crazy. I never told you because I guess I felt embarrassed having such an egotistical and innocent belief. But I want my innocence back. Because the more I think about what happened, the more I . . ." Her breathing speed doubled. "What's to stop him from returning? He got in *so* easily last time."

Before answering, Claire paused to consider how to address her patient. Did she need a therapist or a friend? Which would better maintain her sanity? Better open her up to answers? Gabrielle Capers lived a vibrant social life compared to the others; she had friends to carry the social burden, to support her emotionally. Claire opted for distant professionalism.

"Ms. Capers," she said at last, withdrawing her hand. The resulting look of betrayal begged her to reconsider, but she continued, confident in the best course of action for herself and her patient. "What will stop him is figuring out why it's happening. You know that him appearing out of nowhere doesn't make sense with the reality of the world, which is good. You're thinking clearly in spite of all that's happened to you, and it makes me confident we'll discover the root cause. We're getting there. While you're resting, I want you to think about any other strange gifts you may have received. Focusing on known facts will prevent the unknown from consuming you."

Ms. Capers nodded here and there, the actions of one digesting words at a measured pace and assigning them her own interpretations. As she did, tonight's latest leads cycled through Claire's head: Ted using a blade never physically removed from its block, Ms. Capers receiving an equally cryptic letter from Fredonia, and the existence of a flyer advertising a business that had no knowledge of it.

Lifting her hand to her neck, she dug into knots borne of these revelations. She wished she had something to write on. It all sounded so fantastical stuck in her head, lending undesirable validity to the notion of Dr. Ingetti's curse.

When the door opened again, it sounded a mile away. She waited for the nurse or doctor or whoever to finish their work so she could wrap up in private.

"What a dull response for an old friend."

The entrant's voice yanked Claire from her thoughts; she jumped out of the chair, slamming her heel into its metal leg.

Ryan, dressed in jeans and a long sweater, assessed Ms. Capers. "My brother did his work well."

Ms. Capers, medication or fatigue slowing her, turned toward Claire. "Dr. Rossi?" she asked. Great, she couldn't hear Ryan either, despite the bastard talking about Ted like family.

Ryan's focus vacillated between Claire and her patient with the even tempo of a metronome. Shifting facial expressions seeded uneasiness as he morphed a clownish wide grin for Ms. Capers into a narrow sneer for Claire.

Claire pointed across the room, struggling to hide her panic. "Do you see anybody over there?"

"No, why?"

Guttural laughter taunted her from the room's exit. Claire plotted and rejected a half-dozen escape plans. Knowing the capability of these apparitions, she couldn't stand by. She scanned the room, steadying her gaze on the other side of the bed, to the remote Nurse Espinosa had pointed out. What if instead of getting out, she brought others in? There must be a reason why apparitions never fully formed in public.

"I have a bad feeling," said Claire, attempting to avoid alarming an already high-strung patient. "Can you call in a nurse?"

The two responded simultaneously. Ryan said, "That's so rude. I'm enjoying the view. Whetting my appetite if you will," as Ms. Capers said, "What? You know, I do see something. Like a hazy . . . darkness."

Claire filtered their separate conversations.

Ryan strolled forward, turning five long strides into twenty steps.

Panic infected Ms. Capers. "Claire, what's happening? The darkness is moving."

"Press the button. Now."

"The shadow. It's walking. It's coming." Ms. Capers broke into hysterics, shrinking into bed. "It's coming!"

"I wanted to savor this, but I guess I'll have to make it quick." He leapt at Claire, only leaving her enough time to brace for impact. Her back struck the chair's as she crashed onto the floor, her head landing inches from the wall. Ms. Capers's cries escalated to screaming fits.

Claire kneed him in the ass and writhed in an attempt to buck him. He absorbed the blow like a brick house. Hands cut through open space to seize her throat. Her airways tightened, letting in fragments of the breaths needed to survive. His guttural laugh returned, a triplet of chuckles huffed onto her face.

"Poor Claire. Poor Claire. Is this how it ends?" Ryan singsonged.

Wiggling, scrapping for air, she found it impossible to break free. She tugged at his grip, unable to dislodge hands rooted to her throat. *It's real. It's all real.* She scrunched her eyes to still the sensation of them bulging out of their sockets, to pretend this body was not her own. Pain shocked and shook, jumbling a sudden interest in the afterlife with mundane thoughts of leftovers in the fridge. And then she realized, *If he's real, I can hurt him.* She snapped her eyes open and drilled unusually long fingernails into his wrists. Ryan flashed a masochistic wince-smile then steadied himself with fully extended arms. Claire placed her forearms between his elbows and struck them from the inside, forcing a bend to maintain his stranglehold. As his face fell, she sliced her nails across his cheek's birthmark.

Ryan flailed as if stung by a bee. The sudden rush of available air overloaded Claire. She coughed and sat up, using his weight on her thighs as a fulcrum. Before she could maneuver for further freedoms, he tore back down, chaining Claire's wrists to the cold linoleum floor. Dull awareness caught Ms. Capers screaming at the top of her lungs. Even if she hadn't pressed the button, her shouts would do the job. Claire needed only to buy time, but how? Attention darted around the room as her arms and legs struggled.

"Look at me!" yelled Ryan, calling her focus back to her attacker.

Frost-colored eyes watched her study him. His careful consideration appeared entirely human. *Curses are born of people*, she remembered.

"What do you want?" Her throat stung as she spoke.

"I want to kill you." Ryan laughed as if it was a stupid question. "I'm kidding. It's all a game. Well-behaved boys appreciate their toys."

The door handle crashed into the wall. A security guard and two nurses hustled into the room. Ryan *disappeared*, releasing her. Shrill shrieks assaulted her from the bed.

Claire scurried to sit, pressing her back flush to the wall. She covered her ears, closed her eyes, smelled an aroma of perspiration, and swallowed what felt like lava. Inner dialogue zoomed through her mind. Anger rose and fled, the desire to destroy her attacker stilled by wonder at how to fight one who had appeared and vanished at a whim. *Cursed*, she thought. *Cursed. Is that better or worse than mad? Does it mean I'm not mad? It must. Capers saw him too. Was attacked too. How can a letter hold such power? How can a letter create such pain? How did it start? Why was I chosen? What does it matter? It doesn't. It just has to end.*

A small hand fell on her shoulder. Claire buried a reflex to lash out and simply breathed, parting her hands from her head to see a hawkish-nosed nurse crouched at her side.

"Are you okay?" the nurse asked.

Claire stared until the woman departed with a promise to retrieve some water. Images of fire consuming paper replaced her sight, creating a film that dulled the scene's aftermath. As people checked on her and left in the same breath, she imagined how her stare must appear to them: the glazed look of a zombie, its mind replaced by a singular craving.

CHAPTER 17

Standing in an open patient room sterilized of emotion, two police officers droned their questions at Claire. Unknown to them, she had slipped from the interview before it began. In her place, a stranger inhabited her body as it sat on the edge of the bed.

The stranger responded plainly to their queries, offering a mix of generalities and specifics seemingly intended to limit follow-up questions. She didn't remember the words but later recalled judging the replies as adequate. As the proceedings carried on with her disembodied husk, she contented herself by watching medical staff walk the halls in slow motion and counting dull colors found on furniture and walls. Words funneled back and forth through the air, obscuring her visual fascinations. She could almost reach out and touch them, if not for their forms crumbling upon her turning her attention to them.

When the officers' interests turned to elements where honesty called into doubt her sanity, the stranger feigned memory loss or answered vaguely. Unable to comprehend the words themselves, Claire assessed their transmission from one mouth to the next, accepting the results as facts without understanding what made them so, like a young student believing in physics before learning the math behind it. Incorporeal examination of the interviewers revealed they accepted these replies without suspicion. Meanwhile, the stranger controlling her body looked past them into a void. Its blank stare persisted until the police informed it that the cameras showed no sign of her attacker. The officers, fixated on her bruised neck, requested the stranger describe Ryan to a sketch artist. She shuddered from the final rendition, which had captured his essence down to his fiendish grin. The stranger remained as a block of ice, and what the police made of this response, they did not indicate.

The interview concluded shortly thereafter. She snuck back into her body, taking a moment to subdue the sickness and suffering she had briefly left behind. The police remained while she recovered enough to pose a question of her own. Revealing the Fredonian letter, and claiming uncertainty of its location, she asked what they would do with it if she found it.

Run it for prints and store it in a locker.

Away from purifying flames.

And so she said no more, opting to leave once doctors cleared her of a concussion and internal injuries. From the instant she started her car and began driving, a focus foisted itself upon her, as if she were a bee taking orders from her queen. Cars blurred into the background. Stop signs and people shared silhouettes. Murkiness darkened otherwise bright stars. Her concentration broke only once, when a long red light and a series of gulps seared into reality reminders of the evening's attack. Her windpipe closed as she relived the strangling, suffocating her, driving her to seek an outlet for relief. She messaged Jess and Robert, *Can't talk. Need you at my home ASAP,* then the phone slipped onto the floorboard, and she wondered if she should be driving at all. As the light turned green, the hive queen resumed its hold, dulling pain and fear until reaching home.

Robert, living only two minutes away, arrived first and waited on the porch. Jess knocked on the door fifteen minutes later. Both wore bedtime attire. No longer strengthened by adrenaline, Claire's simple greeting summoned painful tears. She communicated via laptop from then on, disclosing the attack and her intentions to burn the Fredonian letter. They attempted to comfort her for the former and asked why for the latter. Therapeutic catharsis she answered. The letter had arrived just before the first stalking incident, and it was something she could do. Other questions and comments came few and far between. She never mentioned the curse.

Claire's quiet rubbed off. The trio allowed the flames to mesmerize them until the night turned old, until black ashes powdered ceramic logs, dusting them with the remains of the envelope and its contents. Cinders and soot piled themselves in a small mound at the center of the oversized fireplace, its finish as dark as its contents. Doubt that this would change anything persisted throughout the flame's dying breaths, doubt that her horrors had originated from paper, but tonight, doubt held little sway. She leaned back on the kitchen counter, studying the embers in meditative examination and catching worried glances between her friends in her periphery.

At some point, Jess decreed her intention to stay for a few days, which gave Robert the confidence to return home. They all hugged and the two women returned inside. Absent-minded shrugs and head gestures met her friend's questions and attempts at consolation. The pull of the fireplace and its contents proved too strong. When Claire acknowledged the consoling touch on her back, they retired for the night, sharing her bed like a middle school sleepover.

Over a flavorless cup of coffee the next morning, Jess voiced her displeasure at Claire's intention to work. Robert's disapproval came in the form of a coddling text message. Their arguments fell on deaf ears and blind eyes. Then came Eric.

They met at work an hour before their regular starting time. Claire expected a barrage of questions; Eric shot only one. Why was she wearing a scarf in mid-September? She loosened the fabric to show the damage. From then on, he badgered her to return home and rest. Anger rose within her, an emotion that, like the others, now felt numbed and diminished. He finally relented after her scribbling, *Would you do the same?* and countering every refute by striking her pen against the written question.

The ensuing debate determined the specifics of their arrangement moving forward. Claire opened by pointing out the relative safety their office provided. She added a desire to occupy her mind with work, with perhaps an all too apparent obsession with the cursed quintet. Eric countered that her recovery trumped all else. He left unsaid his obvious desire to meet the rare patients which had come to Claire in droves. Walls began to break when she admitted her co-worker's intimate style of therapy might reveal something she had missed.

Her final capitulation came at the realization of having turned to a priest for solutions and the lack of energy necessary for a full schedule. Eric's occurred following her stonewall stare when he pushed for full bed rest. Urgent cancellations and reschedules followed, without them fully looping in Janice for concern over what she might reveal to the patients. With a work schedule reduced to the easiest cases, Claire whizzed by off her years of experience. Patients hardly minded the text-to-voice app she purchased ten minutes before her first appointment. In between sessions, during suddenly open time slots, she studied her notes on the cursed quintet, but the words read like a foreign language.

Drives to and from work resembled her auto-piloting home following the attack, with the queen bee's commands replaced by memories of flickering flames. At Claire's home, Jess balanced reading books and her phone screen alongside checking in on her.

Monday differed from Tuesday only in attempts to feed her. Neither fast food's guilty pleasures nor unseasoned chicken and vegetables drew more than nibbles. Remnants of Sunday's burn session occupied her being, inspiring her to periodically poke the ashes in search of feeling something. Her fiftieth attempt left her as unsatisfied as the first, stirring her to explore her home, to see if time spent pecking at food, lying in bed, and breathing fresh air through temporarily cracked windows imparted a change within her.

It wasn't until the fifty-first, or perhaps thousandth, prodding of the remains when Claire found serenity, when she saw the ashes for what they were: granules of hope.

CHAPTER 18

"Hey, get off the computer. I didn't take the day off just to watch over you." Jess scooted down the couch and squeezed Claire's jean-covered knee. Gently, as if it might shatter.

Claire side-eyed her friend and tapped the laptop, her inbox a click away. "You kind of did though." Talking no longer hurt, but she rasped like she smoked a pack of cigarettes a day.

"Fine, but I'd rather watch you *outside* of the house." She tilted her head toward the front windows, unsuccessfully drawing Claire's attention away from her computer.

Rick had emailed overnight, his first communication since last Friday. Convinced an empty house awaited her, she managed to stave off her morning curiosity. She hadn't factored in her friend's selfless, albeit currently annoying, gift. "Let me read this email, then you've got me all to yourself. And after you tell me what you've got planned"—Claire drew an invisible line up and down Jess's casual sports attire—"you can fill me in on how you knew I only had morning patients."

"No chance of that. Secrets keep a lady young. That said, I didn't think about lunch, so you're on your own there. Can't have you expecting home cooking while I'm staying over."

"I would never ask that. I've been through enough as it is."

Jess slid her hand off of Claire's knee and raised it, fingers splayed, as she walked away. "Yeah, yeah. I'll be upstairs for a minute."

Alone at last, perspiration built in anticipation of Rick's post-letter-burning correspondence.

Claire,

Sorry I haven't written. Work has been slamming me and doesn't look to let up until the weekend. It's probably the same for you, huh? Anyway, I used some of the psychology you taught me. Got an engineer to work on something he should've done weeks ago, so thanks for that. I'll have to pick up a gift the next time I see you. Speaking of which, are you free on Saturday?

- Rick

Claire expected more, but her half-dozen rereads found it rather mundane. No subliminal clues, nothing out of the ordinary. *Slamming* evoked memories of Ryan slamming *her* to the ground, each time eliciting a twitch between her head and hand, but she chalked the word usage up to coincidence. On the bright side, her companion of three dates, and savior against one cursed home invasion, had made an innocuous request for something she meant to inquire about last week.

Not only am I free, but I hoped to introduce you to a couple of my friends. What do you think about a triple date Saturday? Nothing too fancy. How about Caprice downtown?

- Claire

Satisfied enough to hit send, she shut the laptop and sank into the couch, resting until startled by trampling down the stairs.

"Sorry." Jess lifted an apologetic hand.

"It's fine. Getting back to normal will take some time."

"So who emailed you? Rick?"

Anxiety whispered that her friend verged on discovering the truth of her malediction. "How'd you know?"

"You don't have the obligatory bearing for work or that anxious anticipation when expecting something serious. You looked personally interested in whatever the email had to say, and not many people arouse such interest from you. I haven't sent you anything, and Robert's emails include too many dad jokes for you to rush to read, so that left your boy toy."

Claire clapped her hands in mock celebration. Underneath, an uneasiness settled in. She couldn't hide the truth for long. Her friend knew her too well and read people with equal talent. She considered coming clean.

"Have you told him about the attack?" Jess asked.

"Not yet. I've been preoccupied."

Jess's head cocked to the side, asking for an explanation.

"And we're only communicating over email."

She shrugged, seeking more.

"He lost his phone."

Eyebrows asked *really?*

"It's relatively normal compared to everything else in the past few weeks."

Jess's silent interrogation ended with raised arms saying, *whatever.*

Claire's gaze settled on the fireplace, on her granules of hope. "I think this whole stalker thing is past. I don't know for sure, but I have a feeling if I can make it through the week without seeing that asshole again then Sunday was the last of him. You're still free this weekend, right? I'd love to celebrate putting this behind me with you and Robert meeting Rick on Saturday. See if he's the guy that I think he is." *See if he's real.*

"I hope it's over too, but the stalker's been to your house. He's been—" she cut herself short. "Why do you think you've seen the last of him?"

Because a priest told her so. Because she hoped the fires which burned the Fredonian letter destroyed Ryan with it. If indeed they had then why bother coming clean? No matter what Jess hypothesized, she needed Claire to confirm it.

But what if it wasn't over?

"I feel you're holding something back. You've been staring at me with a 'that outfit is too racy' look."

"And *you* never answered about the date this weekend."

Jess pursed her lips and drew closer. "I wouldn't say this to anyone else, but is this how you want us to meet Rick?"

"What do you mean?"

"Ol' Robert and I are too worried about you to care about first impressions. There's a reason you haven't told Rick about your attack, and the abrasions on your neck won't fade by Saturday. Plus it looks like that cabrón bruised your right cheek, no matter how well you hide it with makeup." Taking a seat, Jess pressed her knuckles to the side of Claire's cheek. "I do want to meet him. It's just that we can schedule for another night, you know?"

"You're right."

"That was too easy." Jess folded her arms. "You are hiding something."

"Secrets keep a lady young." Her friend's unamused grin restored another speck of normalcy. "Didn't you say something about getting out of the house? I'm in for whatever," quickly adding, "as long we're in the car before dark." If Ryan returned, would her reaction seem more or less insane than if she revealed the truth here and now? "Where were you thinking?"

Jess's face painted a picture of mistrust. "I'll let you off for now." She poked Claire's nose, then plucked her phone from the corner of the coffee table. "I was looking at this hiking trail outside of Denver. It's not our usual scale of difficulty, but it looks worth the drive. Plus, there's a little cavern off the main path we can scope for later. Let me find the name."

The front door, a focal point for the uncertainty within Claire, entranced her. She patted her lower thighs without any specific tempo. She could tell Jess, right? *Should* tell her. That's what best friends were for. But would the friend or psychiatrist respond, and which did Claire want? Even if Ryan had perished as a result of burning the letter, it didn't mean the trauma he caused left alongside him. More immediately, opening up to Jess went a long way toward explaining why she needed this date.

"Claire?" Jess asked, with the tone of a third or fourth try. "I'd question if you've been before, but I don't think that's why you're ignoring me."

Claire burrowed her head in her hands, her messy mane hanging near her shins. She squeezed and released scalp hair like a stress ball. A growing pit in her stomach pushed nausea upward, a precursor to droplets of bile following close behind.

"I have something to tell you." The sickness subsided, buried beneath her heart racing. She emerged from her cave of hair and stood up. She walked to the fireplace, where the letter's ashes lay.

Her hand slid behind her neck to massage a knot, the movement of skin irritating the bruises on her throat.

"Yes?"

Claire lifted her hand from her neck to tug on her hair.

"Sorry."

Bile returned, coercing her mouth to open. "It's fine." She gradually met Jess's gaze. "For the past few weeks, I've been wondering if I was hallucinating." Recollections of events poured out from there.

She spared no details, allowing her emotions to show through and holding back tears with bated breath. She opened with her first encounter with Ryan at the Cherry Creek Shopping Center and ended with Sunday night's letter burning. In the middle came the priest and his curse theory, alongside the telling of five patients who remained nameless, with symptoms mirroring her own. Increasingly frantic reveals and harrowing accounts unsteadied her legs and forced her back to her cushioned seat.

Jess rested her head on a fist propped up on the couch's back as she listened. At the conclusion of it all, she continued staring, as if waiting for part two to begin after a brief intermission. She covered Claire's forearm with her free hand.

Claire turned her attention to charcoal floorboards to allow her tale proper digestion. She hadn't eaten, but a stomach full of nastiness dulled her hunger. Shedding her secret sickened as much as it relieved. When enough time had passed, she said, "This is why it's important I see Rick."

"What? Why?" Jess's tongue tripped over itself.

"We started dating around Ryan's initial stalking. For a while, I wondered if they were connected. They're about the same height with similar profiles, and after what happened at Leburton"—memories of crawling darkness shot a shiver down her spine—"it was hard to imagine one without the other."

"But you said Ryan never fully appeared there. You only saw shadows at Leburton right? Maybe a trick of the light?"

Was Jess already deconstructing her story? Start with one hole and poke it until the whole structure crumbled? "I don't think so. I think it has something to do with other people, as though he's weaker in big groups so he waits until I'm alone . . . or mostly alone . . ." To which fear returned to claim her steady hands and legs.

Jess read the signs and scooted in, offering faint physical touch from one knee to another. "I don't want to say I don't believe you—"

"So don't."

A shake of her head reminded Claire that wasn't her style. "It's hard to swallow something like this. All of it, except for the attack, can be explained with psychology. Even then, transposing one body onto another isn't unheard of. The two things keeping me afloat are how hard you avoid supernatural explanations for anything. That, and the focus in your eyes."

"That's why I need you to see Rick." Claire grasped Jess's hand. "I need to know he's real. Even if he's no villain, he may exist solely in my head. It's possible that during our dates what I took as Rick speaking was actually me projecting, holding two sides of a conversation. While I never caught any weird looks, brains can filter that out too, begging the ultimate question: am I crazy *and* cursed?"

Hell hath no fury like a stone unturned, a voice whispered.

Not more of that. Not more of her mother's malaphors.

But.

The voice had passed on from spooking.

To soothing.

Claire buried inner turmoil behind the chewing of a nail.

Jess withdrew her hand and straightened her elastic shorts. "Claire, I don't know. Talking curses and imagining people out of thin air isn't encouraging, but I'll reserve judgment for now because I've devised the perfect solution."

"What's that?" Claire pictured Ghostbusters and their spirit-detecting devices.

"It's pretty simple," Jess deadpanned. "I stick around, and if I see something throw you to the ground, it's safe to assume it's not in your head. You're not particularly clumsy after all. Besides, as movies are wont to point out, the ones who are mad never think they are." She ended her speech practically pulling in Claire for a hug.

Claire squeezed her friend, reciprocating the embrace. "Thanks, Jess." The two curled in each other's arms until a sudden interest in the fireplace pulled her away. Its midnight finish seemed to drain the surrounding light. "I hope this is over. I need this to be over."

"Me too. I can't believe you've been hiding all of this from me. Robert, I get. Anything not rigorously tested with science is automatically false. But me? I'm always on your side, even if curses are a little outside of my wheelhouse." Jess tilted her head away. "Maybe it explains why you were sleepwalking."

Claire's attention broke from the fireplace. "Sleepwalking?"

"I wasn't planning to mention it, thinking it a temporary byproduct of your attack. Your reveal changes things." She pulled her legs up onto the couch, curling them under her waist. "I came downstairs around three last night for water. You were up typing on your laptop. When I asked you about it this morning, you didn't remember. I know you haven't been sleeping well, but you acted more like someone possessed than an insomniac."

"Possessed?"

"You didn't respond to anything I said. Simply went on with your computer for a few more minutes, closed it before I could decide whether to take a look, and went back to bed like nothing happened."

"I wonder if it's related to Rick. Or Ryan. Or both."

"It's probably stress."

"Probably." She had been waking up off and on, tossing and turning at night. Even when she blacked out sleeping, she rarely felt rested. Sleepwalking explained that. But what explained sleepwalking? Stress seemed too convenient. Claire palmed Jess's upper arm. "Please tell me you'll go out on Saturday. I need to know what you see."

"Of course. For the record, I think Rick is real, and I think it's better to rest, but it would drive me crazy not knowing. I mean I'm going stir crazy as is, sitting inside this much." Jess frowned. "Sorry, I've got to stop saying crazy. What about that park? Flat walking so we won't overstrain you, and we can still get through one of the shorter trails before dark."

About as good of an answer as Claire could hope for. She tried to respond and winced from the dry strain on her throat. She pointed from her bruise to the kitchen and jogged over to fill a glass with water. After a sip, she said, "Let's do it." And try as she might to dwell on sleepwalking, her hunger had overcome her nausea and grumbled for its due. "Can we pick up something at Peach Tree Cafe on the way?"

"As long as you hurry up with that water and go get changed. Your clothes are laid out in the bed."

"That was presumptuous."

"I know my friend." Jess stared at the fireplace. "Though not as well as I thought. I'm sorry you've been dealing with this all on your own."

"It's fine. Nothing you could've done." Claire tapped the countertop bar on her way by. "I'm going to check the mail first."

"No way. Let's get moving. It's gorgeous outside."

"I'll be quick. It's been a few days, and I'd feel better getting back to normalcy with bills to pay, an envelope meant for my neighbor, and a couple of fast food coupons to recycle."

"Good luck on your mundane treasure trove," Jess scoffed as Claire closed the front door behind her.

The weather really was fantastic. Cool air sailed through her hair. Clouds dotted the sky, enough to cover the sun without clogging the scene. Serenity radiated from neighborhood yards in the quaintness of a weekday afternoon. But as she walked toward her block's mailbox, her throat cracked in dry anticipation of what lurked within.

Bundled papers piled atop each other with enough mail for two weeks. She sifted through the contents one by one, her empty stomach tense the whole time. Claire trudged back into the house, discovering nothing of note.

"Well?" asked Jess, lacing up her hiking boots.

Seeking fingers stopped on an ivory envelope hand-addressed to her. A single name occupied the sender line: Ryan. She threw the remaining bundle down, scattering mail to the coffee table's edges and onto the floor. She tore open the envelope, holding it in one hand while the other squeezed the corner of its contents.

"What is it?"

Claire read and reread the note. Her throat constricted as if reliving Sunday night's attack. Her heart beat faster than it would have on any hike.

"Did you not enjoy your gifts?" Claire read aloud. The tension in her stomach had clamped into a vice.

"What does it mean?" Jess inched forward.

"It's not over." Attempts to calm herself only worsened her hyperventilation. "It's not over."

CHAPTER 19

Claire Rossi, please," said a baritone voice.

"Speaking. Who is this?" Though Claire felt certain she recognized the voice.

"Dr. Ingetti, returning your call. What did you want?"

Claire shot out of her dining room chair, initiating a coffee-fueled pacing through her downstairs. "Where have you been? I've been trying to reach you all day, and your secretary could only tell me you were out with no return time."

"First, the church receptionist is not my secretary. Second, my primary purpose is, as always, to investigate possessions and hauntings. It is not to wait for you. It's not even to talk to you, so tell me your *urgent* news. Urgently."

"Fine. I burned the letter and guess what, Samuel? It's not over." If he wouldn't honor her title, she wouldn't honor his. "I got another letter from the same fucking creep. I've been taunted, tormented, and attacked by this curse, and your little tip didn't do a damn thing to resolve it."

"So, you believe now?"

"Believe in what, Samuel?" Claire squeezed her cheek. She was acting like a child.

He gave a thundering grunt. "Curses. What you described as magic days ago."

"Sure, I believe. Enough to set fire to a piece of paper and think it would solve my problems. Does it matter? It didn't work."

Jess walked by. Her fingers imitated walking legs over her palm, then she pointed toward the door with a quizzical shrug. Claire waved her out. Her friend had already spent the day sitting around in boots and exercise shorts instead of hiking as planned. Taking a break would do her some good. The locking of the door pushed her attention to the dining room where two half-full wine glasses sat in stasis next to a Pandemic board game.

"It matters," he said. "As does addressing me as Dr. Ingetti if you wish for my continued aid."

"Of course, Dr. Ingetti." She scraped her tongue against the top of her teeth.

He continued as if she hadn't spoken. "Receiving a new piece of mail so quickly significantly upgrades the likelihood of a curse. On the other hand, it's improbable the new letter is cursed. You should remember me telling you in our first meeting that it requires substantial willpower to generate a curse."

"So what is it?" snapped Claire.

"I'm getting there. Good things come to those who wait. So wait." His delay seemed intended to annoy her. "If the curser felt the link break or weaken, the correspondence may be a taunt to keep your fear alive. As I told you when we first met, it's possible to disseminate multiple curses from a single object. More advanced and more powerful is individually imbuing an item for each curse. Given your escalation of symptoms, I'm certain the person responsible has done as such."

Ms. Capers's equally cryptic message came to mind. "You mean like my patients receiving their own personalized letters?"

"Perhaps. In any case, that further increases the complexities for the curser. It cements that the person responsible didn't learn this talent specifically for you. They would require years of practice, beginning as early as a preadolescent."

"Could multiple people be responsible?"

"Perhaps, but as you might suspect as a psychiatrist, these individuals are not prone to groups."

Claire realized she had picked up her keys and gripped them so tight they threatened to draw blood. She studied the indentation of the keys' teeth before tossing them onto the coffee table. "What do I do?"

"Find the curser."

She rolled her eyes. "How?"

"I don't know. I'm not a detective. I didn't study psychology. And I don't have what probably amounts to a dozen clues lying around my home and office."

"This thing is going to kill me. Here you are, a supposed man of God, telling me to basically fuck off and—"

"I won't be in town much longer. If you have something concrete to tell me, you can call my cell phone, but I am going to stress this right now." His voice grew from apathetic to callous. "If you call me for any other reason, I will block your number. Immediately. Remember that curses are born of people, not the devil. You must find its source. I suggest you get on that."

"But I don't know where to start," pleaded Claire.

A dial tone answered.

"Bastard." She dropped the phone on the couch.

Where was she supposed to unearth this all-important lead? From the movies she had seen, she assumed that if curses existed so too did the specialists meant to dispose of them. Dr. Samuel Ingetti suggested otherwise, stranding Claire in a pit of despair. She breathed air meant to calm, but the inhale twisted and transformed into a savage intoxicant, fueling a spontaneous blow against the couch's back cushion. The visceral outlash empowered her, building righteous fury to strike the white pillow again and again, flattening it by half, until the front door clicked open and her assault ended with a grunt.

Jess strolled back in. "Love your neighborhood. How did it go? Learn anything?"

"Settle down. One question at a time."

"Okay," Jess trailed off until repeating, "How did it go?"

"Basically said good luck and try to find this asshole before he kills me." Claire's palm slid behind her skull to grip a small strand of hair. "So it went great. Fantastic even."

"Do you want me to kick his ass? I'm itching for some exercise, and that at least feels productive." Jess took hold of Claire's raised hand. "Better yet, do you want me to assemble a team to kick his ass? I bet I could find a willing few before midnight."

The distraction intoxicated Claire enough to embrace the fantasy. She withdrew from Jess's grip to fold her arms. "Would you really?"

Jess rested her hands on her hips and curled her eyebrow. "Do you have access to one of those lawyers who gets people off for murder?"

"I do not."

"Then it might be more of a verbal lashing laced with serious intimidation, but I guarantee you'll feel better, and I bet I will too. It's been a while since I've torn into someone. Even that crappy guy I went out with during your first date with Rick wasn't worth the effort."

And like that, the reality of the situation again consumed Claire.

"Sorry. Mentioning Rick probably didn't help," Jess said. "What's the chance you know the person behind all of this?"

"Curses supposedly require a significant expenditure of time, willpower, and effort. Seems reasonable that I know them given that. And that they hate me for some reason."

"Right. The curse. I'm still wrapping my head around what you told me." Jess drummed her fingers along her jawline. "If the letter cursed you and it's now roasted and toasted, doesn't it mean you aren't cursed anymore?"

"I don't know."

"Is it possible the new letter is a coincidence?"

"I don't know." What was the point of this Q and A session?

"What do you think abo—" Jess stopped mid-sentence.

Whether she halted due to Claire's twitching eyes, stiff limbs, flared nostrils, or another body part reacting reflexively with annoyance, she couldn't say, leaving only the fact that her fear had manifested into anger which scared her friend without any intention to do so. She heaved the kind of sigh which started sobs and hung loosely over the couch like a powered-down robot.

A hand pressed gently against her back, garnering no reaction. A moment ago she would have swatted it aside. Now her mind drifted from the incandescent glow of the fireplace's granules of hope to their remains fading into darkened shadows. A knock at the door tore her from this bleakness into something bleaker still: reality. "Who the hell is that?"

Jess crept toward the entryway, her palm held back at arm's length. "I'll get it. I bet it's your neighbors. They pulled up right before I walked in. I know their boy has a crush on you. He probably wants to check in," she said the last half with enough of a pause to suggest she had considered holding back on the joke.

To her credit, Claire didn't blow up.

The door opening revealed Jess's hunch had been correct. That boy needed a lesson in keeping his distance before he started dating. Brad, decked out in a wrinkled shirt and shorts, sputtered out, "You're not Ms. Rossi—I mean Dr. Rossi." He peeked around Jess without any concern for not knowing her. "There you are!" Brad waved at Claire, to which she responded by digging nails into the cushion she had just finished beating. "Who are you?" asked Brad to Jess.

"I'm Dr. Rossi's friend. I'm helping her with a problem." Jess peeked back at Claire, catching her plucking at seams. She switched to a teacher-esque tone. "It's like a homework assignment, and we need to think really hard. What if we come to your house when we're done? Before you answer, I want to warn you, it might not be until tomorrow." Claire's icy stare met her friend's follow-up glance. "Or Friday. But then you can play with both of us."

"No, that's okay. I just want to talk to Dr. Rossi. Is she doing alright? She looks sicker than last time."

Suspicion masked Jess's face as she swapped looks between adult and child. "She looks fine to me."

"Come in, Brad," said Claire. Could this be relevant? A little serendipity went a long way right now, and she cared a lot more about a potential clue than her appearance. On top of that, his last visit had coincided with her discovering Imogene Aire's true meaning. "What do you mean I look sick?"

Brad brushed past Jess, registering her leg solely as an obstacle.

She chuckled with ambivalence then waved outside, presumably to Amy, before locking the door.

"It's not normal sick," he explained. "Ummm . . ." He looked at the wall bordering the Alba house, twiddling his thumbs at his waist. "It's like a few hours after my dad drinks a lot of his adult juice. He's not really sick, but he acts different and talks different."

Translating the comparison stunned Claire into silence. She looked drunk? Jess's face said, *Whatever you're thinking, you're obligated to ask about this first.* Obviously, Brad's safety took precedence, but to what extent when her life was on the line? "Different how?"

Jess folded her arms. The forward tilt of her head indicated she expected more, but she remained silent and watched the child from behind, resembling Amy Alba in her overprotective stance.

"Well." Brad looked up, his eyes glazed over in imagination. "First he's really happy, then he talks louder, sometimes so loud he yells at Mom if I'm not near and I can hear whatever he's saying, but by then he doesn't sound happy. After a while he starts to look like you look now, with a face that's sort of the same as the ones from the bad guys Bazooka Steve and Racinja fight. He goes to the bathroom next to get rid of the bad guy sickness. Then he's back to normal the next day."

So it was an issue of potential marital strife between the Albas. Nothing obligated her to delve in further. However, her looking as if at the tail end of a bender or as Brad called it, like a bad guy, intrigued her. She would have never equated the face of drunken sickness to villainy, but it seemed plausible for a child. Was there something to the idea of children seeing supernatural elements hidden to adults? Claire's expression asked Jess if moving forward would earn her an earful later.

She gave her blessing to proceed.

Claire leaned on the couch. "You said I looked sicker than before? When did you see me first looking sick, like your dad with too much adult juice?" She carefully recycled his words.

"I guess the second time I came over. You were drinking adult juice the same color as Mom's." Brad bounced and pointed at the two wine glasses next to the abandoned board game. "It looked like that! You must have been really thirsty."

"Why's that?"

"You had a lot of juice that day."

Jess smirked then shook her head in disapproval. For what? Drinking around a child? Claire's steel gaze pushed her friend into signaling surrender with her arms in the air, but she widened her grin in consolation.

"So I didn't look sick when we first met?" Claire said, returning her attention to the child, "but I've looked sick every time after that?"

"I don't remember how you looked the first time so well, except you wore the same thing as right now." Sweater and pajamas, in other words. What an uncanny timing of visits. "So I guess I kind of remember, but I don't think you looked sick. You did look sick the other times, but now you look even sicker."

"How much sicker?"

"Worse than right before my dad goes to the bathroom to spit it all out."

Had he picked up on her stress? She rarely relaxed completely around him, always opting to work when he came over, talking only when he did or said something of particular note. She could have been nauseated those days, as she had been earlier this afternoon. Coincidences were bound to appear when grasping at straws, but dismissing the purity of his insight seemed foolish. She opted to question his thought process before considering anything further. "Do you know what a doctor is?"

"Sure. It's a person who cures other people."

"So if I was sick, wouldn't *I* know it?"

"I don't think so." He smiled as if he had wormed out of a trick question. "You cure other people, not yourself. Maybe the sickness got into your head, and you need to spit it up. I watched my dad do it once, so I can show you how, but it looked yucky so probably only enough to get you started then I'd go home. Sorry."

"I appreciate the offer." Childlike intellect which continued to impress, coupled with his recall of her clothing and drink from a month ago, cemented her confidence in his claimed evolution of her 'sickness'. She had met Brad after receiving the Fredonian letter. It implied that if he saw her curse as an illness, that something transpired in the week between their first two meetings. Which again, could be stress, the residue of nausea, or a combination of both. But what if it wasn't? Meeting Rick coincided with that time frame, but the possibilities from that hypothesis overloaded her, so she took this gift at face value: a child who measured her like a Geiger Counter for curses. Given Dr. Ingetti's reputation and the ephemeral nature of Ryan, it lent further credence to the curse theory.

"Dr. Rossi, is everything okay?" Brad asked.

"You haven't seen her this way before?" answered Jess, spoken like someone who didn't care which shelf her wine came from.

"I'm fine. I was sorting my thoughts." Claire walked to Brad and placed her hand on his shoulder. She crouched to eye level and mimicked his mother's honey-sweet voice. "I'm glad you stopped by. I want to hear about your trip, but since I'm sick I need to rest. Plus, my friend and I need to solve that problem she mentioned when you walked in." While Brad kept his attention forward, behind him Jess mimed drinking a glass of wine and gave an exaggerated look to the dining table. Given the positive turn to the day's events, the suggestion stood a good chance of coming to fruition. "Is it okay if I call your house when I'm better? We can talk about your trip all you want then."

"I thought we could only talk during friendship quiet time?"

"For very special occasions, we can make an exception." He had earned it, after all. "Me feeling better and you having been on a trip sounds very special to me. Sound good?"

"That sounds great!"

Claire let the ear-piercing shriek fade without reprimand. "Come on. I'll walk you back home." She rose and waited for him to take her hand. He filled the small gap almost instantly. "Is it okay if my friend tags along so I have someone to walk back with?"

"Whatever you want Dr. Rossi." Claire bet he would've agreed to anything from his lofty perch on cloud nine.

As Jess fell in line, Claire studied the granules of hope resting in her fireplace. She imagined them as the embers they once were, for they would soon reignite. She had already resolved to burn the new letter unless Dr. Ingetti specifically told her not to, and the plan formed from there. She would watch the renewed blaze in the company of her best friend, then tomorrow offer Brad a bonus friendship session to determine if she appeared any healthier.

But she was getting ahead of herself, and Brad's questioning look informed her she had lost herself in rumination again. Optimistic planning, rather than anxiety and distress, proved too alluring of a distraction. As she walked her neighbor home, she realized she owed this change of perspective largely to him and felt what she could only describe as affection for the youth.

Which surprised her almost as much as the idea someone had cursed her.

CHAPTER 20

It's been a few years since I've been here." Eric scanned the downstairs interior of Claire's home. He sat in a chair adjacent to the coffee table, still wearing his work clothes.

Claire pushed herself to the couch's edge, propping her elbow up on the narrow armrest. She had changed into leggings, her new go-to for loungewear. Two steaming cups of tea sat on the table between them. "I haven't seen your place recently either."

"Not for want of invitation. You missed Josh's fourth birthday in July."

"Don't do that. I haven't been to a fourth birthday in twenty-nine years." Claire pined for Jess's company. Between university midterms and skipping work yesterday for a hike that never happened, her friend needed time to prepare her lessons. Eric's substitution was proving less than ideal.

The evening worsened further when he crossed his ankle over his knee, as if beginning a therapeutic session. "It's topical. This may sound pedantic, but I'm worried you may not be forming new bonds. When did you last make a connection with someone outside of the office?"

The implication punched her in the gut. She buried herself in the couch, crossing her arms. She rolled her neck until she felt calm enough to answer in a level voice. "Screw you. I didn't invite you over to judge my social life."

He bowed his head. "I'm sorry, Claire. That wasn't my intent. I'm simply worried. Your treatments aren't adding up. The diagnoses you've assigned your patients range from delusionary illnesses to full-on schizophrenia. From my examinations, their symptoms present as something physical rather than mental. I'm concerned there's a stalker, possibly multiple, taking advantage of these women's fragile and lonely states. They may be imitating hallucinations well enough to deceive your patients, and thus you. On some level, their troubles might even resonate with you personally."

If only you knew. Thankfully, you don't. An aroma of chamomile and peppermint wafted from Claire's mug, still too hot to drink. She picked it up anyway to give her something else to squeeze instead of her arms. It calmed her enough to prevent a shutdown, but she hoped Eric had something more illuminating to reveal. Preferably without making it about her.

Her co-worker read her well. "We'll come back to that, but keep it in mind. While I treated your patients in line with your approach as best I could, I made a few deviations which produced some interesting findings."

Now he was getting somewhere. She leaned in, interested in his discoveries only slightly more than seeing how the great Dr. Eric Wilson treated *curses* with therapy. "What did you do?"

"I delved deeper into their backgrounds. Your work covered everything regarding their hallucinations, so I didn't think I'd find anything there. Unfortunately, Janice and I couldn't convince Ms. Capers to let me see her at the hospital's psychiatric unit."

Claire turned her palm up in question.

"Ah, yes. She stayed at the hospital following your . . . attack." Eric's lips turned up as if he tasted something bitter. "Not that her physician offered her much of a choice. After her traumatic attack, followed by witnessing yours, he wanted to keep an eye on her. I gather she hasn't been receptive to others trying to fill your role. I did learn she slightly changed her story to say that whoever assaulted her resembled *your* assailant." He seemed satisfied with Claire's mock surprise. "As for the other patients, most opened up to my prodding. It took some coaxing to breach Ms. Kavina's distrust and defensiveness, but the others were all forthright with their hobbies and past. Even Mrs. Cathell, surprisingly so given her missed appointment." He gripped his shin and pulled himself forward. "It turns out they all are or were involved with the same non-profit."

What a detail to miss. But was it? She didn't delve into personal histories unless a specific mention in therapy warranted it.

"Before driving to your house, I decided to stop by. It's called Den of Help. Just outside of Sun Valley. They initially weren't receptive to my coming by. Their group assists lower-income individuals and families, who seem to get unfairly targeted as criminal suspects. It's possible—"

Claire rapped her fingernails on the side of her mug.

"I'll assume you're telling me to get to the point." Eric rubbed his day-old stubble. "Once I told the non-profit I was a psychiatrist, they opened up. It turns out you treated one of their volunteers a few years ago."

If Eric mentioned this in relation to the cursed quintet, that didn't bode well for the mystery woman. Claire chanced a sip of her tea, finding its heat tolerable and its taste menthol-like. "Is she ali—" She cleared her through. "Okay?"

He fiddled with his glasses until they hung evenly. "She's at St. Mary's Hospital for the Wayward."

Autumn chill consumed her, freezing every limb in place.

St. Mary's.

The final place Sofia Costas had drawn breath.

Claire's fingers thawed first. Rubbing the mug for warmth, her mind soon followed. She rummaged through it for a name. Instead, an image appeared of a narrow-faced, tall woman with black unkempt hair. Despite attempts to convince her otherwise, she had been intent on seeking treatment at St. Mary's. What was her name? Claire closed her eyes to concentrate, massaging her left temple.

"Emelia Nelson," Eric read from his phone.

Memories flooded Claire, the name opening a lock to the past. Her eyelids snapped open. "That's right. Dangerous hallucinations followed her. She wanted someone to keep watch over her, and St. Mary's has a strict surveillance program. At least now," she added. Before her heart attack, Sofia Costas had attempted suicide once during her stay. The sloppy attempt and glint in her eyes had led Claire to suspect she did so just to tell her, *Time is the root of all evil.*

Repeating the mangled idiom as though a mantra all but confirmed her suspicion.

"I'm surprised you remember a patient in such detail."

Time is the root of all evil.

"It's where. My mom. Was," speaking as if overcoming a stutter. How had the hospital changed since Sofia Costas's death? "I'll. Go. Tomorrow. And," she blinked. *Stop seeking insight from a dead person.* "Visit Ms. Nelson," she said, speech returning to normal.

"Are you alright?"

"I'm fine. Been a while since I've thought about the place."

Eric tilted his head.

She tilted back, mocking, spurring him to move on.

"Regardless, tomorrow isn't an option. She's on an extended field trip with other non-violent patients. They wouldn't tell me any more than that. I also want to come along with you. Between the both of us, we can uncover what's afoot with your patients."

"I can handle it on my own."

"We need to do more than handle it. I already scheduled a visitation for two this Sunday. It was the earliest time we could see her."

"You're missing church?"

Eric tapped his shin. "Not technically. St. Mary's is funded by the Catholic Church. Besides, I think this is a very Christian endeavor, and reading between the lines, I got the impression she's only lucid for a particular window each day."

Claire rubbed her eyebrows. This meeting threatened to expose Eric to more than she wished. Worse, she'd reached the point of sourcing clues from an overmedicated ex-patient. Before chancing any revealing questions in his presence, she wanted to ensure his dedication. To her cause, if not to her. "I seem to remember some conjecture of yours claiming I projected my problems onto my patients. Something about my personal issues muddling their diagnoses?"

Eric uncrossed his legs to scoot the chair closer. He banged his knee against the coffee table for his efforts. Wincing, he said, "I don't know everything, but I know you're Claire Rossi, and that you won't rest until a problem is solved. I also know these patients are affecting you on a deeper level than you let on. You've got bags under your eyes the size I've never seen before, and the lack of attention to your bruised neck isn't consistent with someone who's just been attacked. It means there are more pressing matters and that you, like me, think this is bigger than it appears." Eric railroaded Claire's glare and donned a stern fatherly voice. "Stop that. Your pride is interfering with doing what's smart, which is letting me help you. Let's figure this out together and return some semblance of normalcy to our lives. I don't want you working full-time earlier than is healthy, but I don't think I can handle Ms. Kavina much longer."

"Was that a joke?"

"I thought you could use one." He smiled.

He wasn't wrong.

Claire relaxed her grip on her mug and gave a half-smile of her own. "Ms. Shapiro and Mrs. Cathell make up for it, don't they?"

"That might be true. I haven't had the time to assess their personalities." He rubbed his knee.

Claire sighed. Her co-worker had covered her cases without the hint of a complaint until now, if that even counted as complaining. He deserved to know more, at minimum about the tangible threats. "I received another letter in the mail. The from line read Ryan, the name of the guy who attacked me in the hospital. The same person who mailed me 'Enjoy your gifts' last month."

Eric hunched over, hands on his thighs. "How do you know it was the same person?"

"The isolated 'Did you not enjoy your gifts?' on an otherwise blank sheet of paper gave it away."

"Interesting. Did you inform the police?"

"I might, depending on what your Sunday appointment turns up." A lie, given that she had burned the letter last night —for all the good it did. Brad didn't detect any less 'sickness' on her. "What time did you say visitation started?"

"Claire, you should loop them in. That's their job."

"The time?"

Eric squeezed his thighs, lifted his hands up, then slapped them back down. "10 a.m."

"I'll meet you there."

He scanned her face, concealing his thoughts behind an undecipherable amalgamation of emotions. "Alright," he said at last.

Business concluded, Eric took the cup of tea Claire had offered when he first came in. He sipped at it for half an hour while the two bumbled around small talk. Every conversation circled back to therapy or Janice until he apologized for having to head home.

After letting him out, Claire returned to the couch. She flicked her palm, losing herself in her home's vinyl flooring. Three days separated her from a potential big break. It seemed an exorbitantly long wait, but she had survived six weeks since receiving that ominous letter. A few more days wouldn't kill her.

Right?

CHAPTER 21

Claire poked her head through the passenger side window. "Thanks for dropping me off."

Robert slid his hand back and forth over the steering wheel. "No problem. You sure you can find a ride home? I mean it when I say I'm stuck in meetings all day."

"What a fun-filled Friday for you."

"Says the person walking into a police station."

Claire looked behind her at the eleventh precinct. It better resembled a miniaturized city hall than a police station, but what did she know? She had never been in one before today. A smirk overcompensated for her budding apprehension. "I'll be fine. Talk to you later."

"Adios, amigo."

Claire chuckled, patting the door as she backed onto the sidewalk. "Don't let Jess hear you pronounce it that way."

Robert shrugged. "Math and English are the only languages I've ever claimed fluency in."

The two exchanged waves before he drove off in his late-model sedan. Claire approached the precinct's double glass doors. Cool air brushed against her face and bare forearms. Denver stood on the cusp of autumn as she stood on the cusp of a breakdown. Without her friend to occupy her mind, she yielded to the swirl of emotions within. Shock shielded her from succumbing to complete hysteria, but the detective's call left a mark which threatened to forever stain her psyche.

Her patient, Mrs. Cathell, had died.

Detective Kline called this morning to ask if she could come into the station. He mentioned three things: the death of her patient, evidence he wanted to show her, and a few questions he wanted to ask her in person about Nancy Cathell. It wasn't until after she messaged Jess and Robert to see if either would drive her that she considered the call on a more rational level. How did he know about the connection between her and her patient? She batted down gruesome images of her name spelled out in blood, settling on the more likely event of them having tracked down Mrs. Cathell's ever-traveling husband. But what did they want to ask *her?*

She opened the door to the lobby. The precinct possessed as much vitality as a classroom during nap time. She poked around her bare throat to check her bruising. It hurt less now, but the desk officer's lingering gaze revealed a still noticeable discoloration.

"Can I help you, ma'am?" asked the stocky policeman.

"I'm Dr. Claire Rossi. I'm here to see Detective Kline."

"I'll take you to him. Follow me, please."

They walked down the beige hall, turned two corners, and passed through a closed door into a space the size of her living room. Five faux-wood desks were spread throughout. The two men within turned around.

Her guide stopped at the setup closest to the entrance. "Dr. Claire Rossi here to see you, sir."

"Thanks," said a middle-aged black man in a well-fitted suit. Weathered eyes and shades of gray peppered his goatee, putting him at over a decade her senior. Below his bald scalp hung a navy necktie as classic and boring as something Eric would wear.

"I take it you're Detective Kline," said Claire. The young officer inspected her neck once more before heading back to the front.

"That's right." He reached out, shaking her hand after she paused to accept it. If he noticed or cared, his measured composure didn't say. The room's other detective returned to typing on his computer. "Why don't you sit down?" His tone mirrored the one she used with her patients: professional, authoritative, and somewhat but not altogether cold.

Claire pulled the cushioned wire chair away from the detective before sitting, distancing herself so as not to look up at him.

"Thanks for coming in. First, let me say again that I'm sorry about your patient."

"Thank you. I've never had anything like this happen." Claire brought her hands to her navel to straighten her shoulders. "How did you know I treated her?"

Kline maintained perfect posture while studying her. Not answering right away indicated he wanted to withhold that information, but eventually he relented, "Her husband told us."

"He was home? Did he find her?" Before discovering the curse, Claire suspected Mr. Cathell's frequent travel schedule created much of the distress responsible for his wife's mental state. Even if that were true, he didn't deserve to find her dead body.

"We spoke on the phone yesterday before he flew in. Talked again this morning and he signed this." He slid a piece of paper to the desk's corner. "It's a release allowing you to discuss Mrs. Cathell's patient history with us."

"I'll need a copy of this."

"Sure. I'll give you one on the way out."

"Now, please. Hopefully, you don't enter houses without a warrant in your possession. I don't break my patient's privacy without something similar."

He crossed his arms, his tongue poking at his cheeks behind closed lips. She could tell he wanted to shout something like, *She's dead. It doesn't matter, and there's a murderer on the loose*, but propriety held him in check.

"Even if . . . you know," Claire said, understanding the situation all too well. The gravity of Mrs. Cathell's death seeped past guarded barriers. That could've been her. Could still be her. Could be all the remaining members of the cursed quintet. Surrounding air took on a grave weight.

"Alright. I'll be right back," Detective Kline snatched the waiver by its top side and cracked open the room's entrance. He stuck his head and the paper out into the hallway, ordering a passerby to make a copy before he marched back to his seat.

"While we're waiting, you wanted to show me something?" asked Claire.

"Yes, but first I've got a question that doesn't require a waiver. On September 17, you called the police to investigate a break-in. On September 20, you were attacked at the hospital while visiting one of your other patients." Claire hoped she didn't sound as callous when listing the traumatic events of others. "In your statement, you mentioned a letter from Fredonia, North Dakota sent by an Imogene Aire. Did you ever find the physical copy?"

Scattered ashes filled Claire's mind. "No. I'm not sure where it went. Why?"

"Hmm." He pulled open the top drawer of his desk and withdrew a small envelope. He placed it midway between the two of them.

Claire almost lunged for it. Another letter! Near confirmation that each of her cursed patients had received something similar. She had to have it. "What's that?" Practiced patience took over.

"A letter from the same sender. Fake name, fake address, barely real town. Inside it was one line, similar to your message, but arguably more ominous. It reads, *My sisters fall.*" Kline tapped the closed envelope. "Does that mean anything to you?"

Like how all of the curse's victims were women? "Not any more than what you might conclude: that this is a deranged individual, and it may not stop with Mrs. Cathell."

"What's the chance that she was being stalked?"

"Since I'm waiting on that release copy, I can only speak to the cryptic letter, my own experiences, and generalities. Based on those, it's unlikely, at least in how we normally view the term. Stalkers tend to focus on one individual, and they're rarely so clean as to not leave a trail. You should have found something at the crime scene if that were the case. More probable is a targeted crime or some sort of serial stalker."

"The assaults against you and Gabrielle Capers up the odds of a serial stalker, doesn't it?"

"That's more your department."

The two stared at each other, Kline practically sizing her up while Claire considered and rejected notions to procure Mrs. Cathell's letter. Legally, in an ideal world. The swing of the door turned their attention to a chubby female officer walking into the room. Claire recognized her from her house call, but neither displayed signs of having met.

"Thanks." He slid the copy over to Claire. "Let's backtrack a minute, was—"

She glanced it over. "Do you mind signing off on it? I don't see any witnesses listed, and I certainly wasn't there watching Mr. Cathell agree."

"Fine," he grumbled. He leaned over to scribble his signature on the page. His cushion puffed as he plopped back onto it. "Now, was Mrs. Cathell suicidal?"

She examined the release form, shifting the paper from side to side on the slick desk. She had no further recourse to remain silent. "Nancy Cathell exhibited no signs of self-harm during our sessions, nor did she present any indication that she might start. Someone or something troubled Mrs. Cathell, but she had committed to the proper steps to resolve those issues. She wanted to get better, and she worked for it."

"A minute ago you blamed a serial criminal. Now you're saying someone or some*thing* troubled her." He pulled his notepad close and grabbed a pen. "What did you mean by that?"

Detective Kline was smart and attentive. With enough effort, perhaps she could sell him on a world where magic curses existed. As it stood, she lacked the time to try, and that letter provided a vital key, which meant enduring his questions until she concocted a reason to transfer its possession to her.

"When I first saw Mrs. Cathell, she displayed common signs of erotomanic delusionary hallucinations, indicating schizophrenia. Initial treatment lent further credence to that diagnosis." Claire readjusted to stretch her lower back. "She responded well to techniques meant for a schizophrenic or similarly troubled individual.

Only recently did I begin to suspect something more nefarious."

Kline wiggled his pen. The recording of their conversation made her feel as scrutinized as a patient during hospital rounds. "Elaborate on suspecting something more nefarious."

Thus began the ultimate balancing act, maintaining the possibility of hallucinations while pushing the detective toward a serial criminal, all so as not to call into question her psychiatric ability. To get that letter, she had to present herself as an integral part of this case past her role as a victim. "It's clear when someone is being stalked versus seeing hallucinations. The coping mechanisms and drugs prescribed had a positive impact on what threatened Mrs. Cathell, supporting schizophrenia as the root cause of her troubles. But as our talks evolved, the hallucination presented goals outside of the bounds of erotomanic delusions, indicating some real-world component. I wondered if her hallucination was warning her of something but"—she gestured toward the detective—"I never got to explore the idea."

"So you originally thought she heard voices? And what does erotomanic mean?"

"Schizophrenia and hearing voices is pop fiction. It happens, but like hallucinations, it's one side effect. All the diagnosis means is an abnormal perception of reality. Erotomania is the delusion of believing another is in love with them. Typically this targets a real individual, but in Mrs. Cathell's case, it seemed focused on a hallucination which manifested naturally." As a tulpa, she had once considered, but its mention didn't serve her purpose.

The detective scratched his wrinkled forehead, opting to write down far less than she said. "So in your professional opinion, is it more likely her death originated from a stalker, serial or not, rather than from a mental issue?"

"As I said, she wasn't suicidal. I don't understand the point of these questions. Isn't it the job of the coroner to determine how she died?"

"They concluded homicide based on the injuries, but those working the scene couldn't find evidence of anyone else in the house that night. It looked like she had gotten into a fight with herself."

Of course. It fit with Ms. Capers's illusory knife and the disembodied sounds in her own home.

"Let's assume Mrs. Cathell's hallucination was actually a stalker." Kline smoothed out his tie. "Did she describe him to you?"

"From what I remember, she described her *hallucination*," Claire said, trying to maintain the narrative of its existence coinciding with a stalker's, "as a tall, light-skinned male. No facial hair. Lanky I believe."

Detective Kline studied the bruising on her neck, slowly mapping out the pattern of discoloration. "Could she have died because of her connection to you?"

Her head reared back. "Excuse me?"

"One of your other patients was attacked less than a week ago, followed shortly by an attack on you. Could someone have a grudge against you or your practice?"

Plans weaved together in an attempt to procure Mrs. Cathell's letter. "Not that I know of, but I'm glad someone is thinking outside of the box. It could've been me whose murder you're investigating."

Kline responded with stoicism, a sign of rationalism in the face of rash emotion. That was Claire's in.

"We're discussing conjectures. At this point, I'm more concerned with definites, such as Mrs. Cathell's letter with the same sender as the one I received, bearing an equally cryptic message. Discussing that sounds infinitely more useful."

"What more is there to say? I told you its contents." He glanced at the envelope with the interest one might give an old carpet stain.

Claire stood up, partially to gain physical ground, ostensibly to underline the envelope's from line with her index finger. She gambled on him being the type to dig into any clue rather than dismiss it for sounding far-fetched. "Did you notice that Imogene Aire sounds like *imaginary* when spoken quickly? And if you mash Fredonia with the initials for North Dakota, you get *friend*. Imaginary Friend. Weird thing to send to a psychiatrist and her patients, isn't it?"

Kline leaned back in a relaxed pose, arms resting on the chair's.

"Could be nothing, but I noticed that too. It's part of why I asked you to come in. There are some strange coincidences in this case that, added up, feel a lot less like coincidences."

He noticed too? What else had he pieced together? Stunned, she took a moment to compose herself, ensuring she stayed on track for her primary goal. "Here's another coincidence," Claire said, chancing Gabrielle Capers would forgive her upcoming breach of confidentiality, if she even discovered it. "That patient in the hospital your officers interviewed—did you know someone sent her a letter too?"

His feet pushed against the floor, launching himself up and shooting his chair back. He stood several inches taller than Claire. She wished she had worn heels.

"What did it say?" Kline asked. The room's other detective turned to inspect the scene.

"I don't remember exactly. Something about a mom," she lied.

"Sisters and a mom. Is tormenting women a family business now?" Disgust dripped from his lips. Apparently, once his emotions turned on they went full speed.

Taking the opportunity from his rhetorical question to seal the deal, she opined, "Madness has hereditary ties, from nurture if not nature. I don't think so, but there may be a way to find out. My practice partner and I see hundreds of patients, but only a half-dozen exhibit problems remotely similar to Ms. Capers and Mrs. Cathell. I agree the circumstances leading to attacks on myself and two of my patients hardly seem coincidental. It's possible other patients of mine have received similar letters. I have a few in mind to ask, and I think I should be able to get a hold of them today or over the weekend. I'll let you know what I discover—as long as I don't have to divulge anything personal."

"Just give me the names, and I'll investigate it. Evidence procurement is my job, not yours, and I'll have follow-up questions."

Claire shook her head. "I can't give you a list of my patients without their consent."

"I could get a warrant." Kline crossed his arms.

"Do you want to risk a perpetrator's future conviction on the legality of a search warrant? I hope not, because as a victim I will be furious if something like that causes him to walk." Claire didn't know the law in Denver regarding warrants and evidence admission. She hoped the question vague enough to instill a concern Kline could conjure on his own.

"No risk if a judge grants the warrant. I'm only concerned about a murderer running loose in the time it takes to get one."

"Which I greatly appreciate considering that the next victim could be me." She pressed a loose fist against her chest. "But I'm not jeopardizing my practice on a hunch that *I* suggested."

The detective looked to the side, tapping his left bicep. His throat clearing resembled a tiny jet engine. "Fine. We'll do it your way, *if* you can provide some sort of lead by Monday evening."

"Then if we're doing it my way, I want to borrow Mrs. Cathell's letter. Envelope and note both."

"Why?"

"I'm asking patients to recall mail they received weeks, if not months ago. Some sort of physical reminder increases the chance of that recall."

"Alright. I can get you a copy. What else?"

She doubted burning a copy would have any effect. "I need the original. Little things such as smell or handwriting can trigger a memory, which may be all we're getting if others tossed their mail."

He stroked his smooth scalp. "I can't believe this." Desperation on no leads mixed with emotional concern and enough logic to fill his empty coffee mug was about to pay off. "I'll give you a one-week rental on the letter. If anything happens to it, I'm booking you on evidence tampering."

"Not a problem."

"Let me make a copy for our records." He snatched the closed envelope from the desk. "Larry, I'll be right back. Make sure she doesn't touch anything while I'm gone."

"You got it, Jalen." The other detective stared her down like a hawk.

Whatever made them feel better. She got what she wanted.

CHAPTER 22

D o you mind getting in the back?" Jess asked from the driver's seat. She gestured from the passenger window to down below. "All my stuff's in the front." Rush hour's precursor traffic muffled her voice. It took context clues of stacked papers held by giant rubber bands to understand what she said.

"Sure." Claire slid into the rear seat, pushing aside a pair of spare clothes. She melted into the padded leather. Her friend treated cars like a second suitcase but picked them with the scrutiny of purchasing a home. She couldn't remember a car which hadn't exuded comfort.

"How are you doing?" Jess turned around. She wore a blazer and suit slacks.

"As well as can be after two hours of a police interrogation about a murdered patient."

"I still can't believe it. Even after what happened to you at the hospital. How are you holding up?"

"Better than I should be. I'm so wrapped up in figuring this out, I haven't had time to process it." And before she started to, Claire withdrew Mrs. Cathell's envelope in a death grip from her purse. "I did get this. The police found a letter inside her house. Just like the one sent to me, only with a different cryptic message. I'm thinking if I can gather them all, that might be what it takes to end this."

"I'm surprised they gave it to you. You must have picked up some of my talents." Jess battered her lashes. Then her eyes grew large. "Wait. You're not planning to burn police evidence, are you?"

Claire mimed flicking a lighter underneath the paper and made a sizzling sound. "If that's what it takes. I'd rather hire a lawyer than fight that *thing* again." She tucked the envelope back into the edge of the purse. "Not many options when the only other ideas come from a priest more concerned with proper titles than saving my life."

"I thought Eric hit on something big?"

"That was before one of my patients was murdered. I'm not waiting when I can do something now."

A decrepit truck pulled in behind them, its driver blaring his horn. Claire and Jess looked at each other with confusion, expecting it to stop given the open lane beside them. Another long honk dismissed the fantasy.

"Vete a la mierda." Jess threw a dismissive wave, then put the car in gear. The old man shook his fist, following behind until a yellow traffic light separated them.

"Look at that. In a hurry to go nowhere," said Claire.

Jess muttered something under her breath then shook her head.

"Your Spanish vocab opens up a lot when you're angry."

"Emotions bring out the best and the worst in us," Jess snapped before huffing herself into a calm. "I'm just glad it's the weekend."

"I wish I could say the same. The days are blurring together."

"Even with our triple date night coming up tomorrow?"

"I'd forgotten about that," Claire said as they passed through another green light. "There's almost a sense of Rick not even existing unless he's on my mind."

"There's so much existentialism to unpack in that, I'd have to say—"

"Please don't."

Jess chuckled and turned on music loud enough to mask the road noise.

Claire slumped in the seat, leaning on her headrest. She closed her eyes and let the odd compilation of Shakira and Nirvana whisk her away. Harmonious minutes passed until a light brushing swept under her ear. She smoothed her hair from top to bottom to calm the troublesome strands and struck something solid.

A finger.

Instincts fired. She chopped outward at chest height, striking between two ribs. Her arms recoiled, eyes opened. Ryan sat directly behind the driver's seat. She slid her purse underneath her thigh.

"That's no way to greet an old friend." Ryan writhed with laughter, stomping the floor like a sprinter running in place. The remnants of her fingernails' deep scratch bordered his cheek's birthmark.

"What the hell are you doing?" she screamed.

Jess glanced in the rear-view mirror. "What's wrong?"

"I'm so glad she could be here for this. I've been trying to meet more of your friends, but something keeps stopping me. I guess that's less of a problem now. We're like one big, happy family all driving back home after church services." Ryan scooted to the middle seat. Claire tucked herself in the corner. "Did you find anything exciting in the police station? Did they fill you in on the gory details of Nancy's death?"

"Claire?" asked Jess, concern lengthening the question.

"It's Ryan. He's in the car. You can't hear him or see him can you?"

"No."

Ryan stroked his neck in the same place he had caressed Claire's a moment ago.

Her air supply thinned to Mount Everest levels.

"I'm pulling over," said Jess.

Claire forced herself to study Ryan, restraining ruptures of fear with deep massages of her palm. A long jacket and hat covered everything but the workings of a sniveling grin, which stretched his scar until it glistened with unexpected freshness. Sunlight glinted off an unused seat belt clip beside him, and the chaotic swirls of an idea coalesced in her mind. "No, keep driving. Take Zuni Street, but turn two streets early. Fast."

"Yeah, sure. Okay." Jess's hands shook on the wheel.

Ryan petted Claire's arm like a cat. Or a lamb before slaughter. "I've felt less connected to you the past few days, but I think I know why. You tried to sever our connection, didn't you? And on the same night in which we shared such an intimate moment no less."

Claire stiffened, fighting urges to lash out or jump out of the car. She didn't want to cause a wreck tangling with Ryan, especially not while her best friend drove on a busy street at a busy hour. Squeezing her legs together and hunching, she made herself small to buy time with subservience.

"You know what? I forgive you." Ryan tugged up on the skin of Claire's forearm as if expecting the elasticity of Play-Doh.

She yelped.

"Did you get to see any pictures of what my brother did to Mrs. Cathell's skin?"

Claire's butt braced against the door, unable to withdraw any further. Ryan's smile stretched to clownish proportions. She shook her head once.

"What a pity. I didn't either, yet I could feel him peeling away at her sweet softness. If it's any consolation, I don't think it lasted long before he grew bored and put an end to it all. All of my brothers tend to be hasty. When I think . . ."

"What's happening?" Jess asked.

"He's talking to me about my murdered patient. Just drive," Claire yelled over Ryan's continued monologue.

". . . it makes me wonder whether the greatest page of this story is reserved for us. I believe it is, don't you?"

Acceleration pushed Claire and Ryan back into their seats. Exactly what she hoped to see. Horns blared as Jess cut off two cars in quick succession.

Ryan swung his head left. "Your friend is such a shit driver. I wonder what it would take to"—he stroked his bottom lip—"interact with her."

Claire followed Ryan's sinister gaze. Was it possible to infect others with her curse? *You look sicker than last time,* she recalled Brad saying. Moisture fled from her mouth; she circled her tongue around inside of it, then scrambled for a way to occupy his attention. "Why are you doing all of this?"

His nose sniffed at Jess before resuming his caress of Claire. "That's what friends do, Claire. We're here for you even when you don't want us, don't need us. Can you imagine an imaginary friend who never comes out to play?" He drew close, combing through Claire's hair and massaging her scalp. "How do you keep it all in there? You have such a big brain it's amazing it doesn't . . . leak out. Maybe I should get in there and give it a good scrubbing."

"Jess," Claire said, holding onto the 's' in her name. "When you get a minute, look back." She cringed to limit her scalp space. "Tell me if you see him messing with my hair."

"Yeah." The road and her driving speed distracted her. "Okay."

"What are you expecting out of all of this, my dear?" asked Ryan. He pushed down with one finger. "I'm in your head." His finger relented only for another to press against her scalp. "But am I here?" Pressure shifted again. "Or here?" Then his hands played freely in her hair. "What does it matter? I'll be with you forever. Until your dying breath."

The car lurched left. They entered the opposite side of traffic. A few seconds after, Jess cut back into the proper lane. Someone screamed from the sidewalk and a horn honked, then road noise again filled the background.

"Sorry, had to get ahead of that guy for some space." Jess glimpsed Claire from head to waist before snapping her focus back to the road. "The only thing I see is frizzy hair, but you're sheet white. I should pull over."

"No, we're almost there. Go!" She would kill this fucker, then find the person responsible. She'd spend every waking minute searching. She'd survive on two hours of sleep a night. She'd make sure this never happened to anyone again.

"I can tell you're using that big brain of yours. And I do so want to get inside of there to take a look. Sadly, recovery is a hard process." His hands moved down to her thigh. "I suppose all good things are worth the wait." He massaged Claire from her knee to her groin without a hint of sexual desire. More like a butcher testing meat for tenderness.

The car's right turn catapulted Claire to within an inch of Ryan's face.

"We've had a breakthrough." Ryan chuckled, his eyes dead-locked with Claire's. "*You* finally came to *me*."

Claire sneered. "Get used to it. I'm not going to cower like this for long." She reeled back from his pale face and yellow teeth.

"You should. I won't play so nice the next time we meet."

Claire bit down on her lip and looked out the back window. Empty roads all the way to Zuni Street. No chance of a rear-end collision.

"But if there's one thing I can tell."

Claire glared at Ryan's scratch. "Jess, Stop. Break now!"

"It's when you want me gone."

The sedan skidded to a halt. Papers flew in the air. Clothes in the back slammed into the front seat and fell to the floor. Claire jetted forward until the seat belt caught.

"What was that about?" asked Jess. She breathed even heavier than Claire.

Claire covered her breastbone where the seat belt had almost certainly bruised her. With a grunt, she pulled on the seat in front of her. A mess of papers lay strewn about, but there was no sign of Ryan. "Fuck," she sighed and fell back, her focus drawn to the seams along the sunroof.

"Why the hell did I do that?" Her friend braced against the console to twist further back.

"Sorry. I scratched Ryan when he attacked me at the hospital, and the cut gave me an idea. If I could hurt him with an errant swipe then shooting him through a car window could do some real damage."

Two cars drove around them. One honked, to which Jess responded with a bleep of her own horn. "And?"

"It might've worked, but he caught on and vanished at the last second."

"So now what?"

She raced back through the one-sided conversation, stalling over Ryan's insinuation that he lived as a figment of her imagination before her bruised neck argued otherwise. Then something more positive came to mind. "Recovery is a hard process," she said, more to herself.

"What?"

Claire looked down, chewing on Ryan's words. She had affected him, and burning the letter must have been how. It had mattered, not enough, but it meant he had a weakness. It proved physical objects tethered him to this world.

"Now I stop thinking of ways to hurt him and find ways to kill him." Despite Claire's bravado, she shook in the back seat with nauseating fear.

CHAPTER 23

*T**he darkest horse rides before the dawn.* Sofia Costas's bloodshot eyes blazed in Claire's mind, casting equal parts hope and concern as they did thirteen years ago. At 11 a.m., Claire dialed Diane Shapiro again.

While the line rang, she studied the nearby countertop bar. Surrounding a coffee mug and a half-eaten pastry lay four envelopes, the results of obsessive calls to surviving members of the cursed quintet. She had set to work after arriving home yesterday, eating from then until now only when coaxed by Jess. It turned out all of her patients had kept their Fredonian letters readily accessible, explained by rationalizations that sounded eerily similar to compulsions. That evening, Jess chauffeured her to Kathy Keller and Alice Kavina's homes and to the hospital to borrow house keys from Gabrielle Capers. Confusion initially met her request for their mail, but trust in Claire's claim that it would solve their hallucinations eased their concerns. After failing to reach Ms. Shapiro last evening or this morning, Claire planned to dial the police if she again didn't answer.

But on the fifth ring, Ms. Shapiro's soft-spoken voice said, "Hello?" She sounded guarded.

"Diane. This is Dr. Rossi. Are you okay?"

"Dr. Rossi! No, no, no. I'm not okay at all. I can't believe I'm even talking to you. I thought I died. Ouch. That smarts."

"What was that? Is someone there with you? Is"—she briefly blanked on Ms. Shapiro's apparition's name—"Thomas there?"

"Just touched my head and oh, it hurts, Dr. Rossi. My arms too," she sobbed before sniffling loudly. "Thomas attacked me last night. He would've killed me if it wasn't for Kim."

Kim? Ms. Shapiro's neighborhood friend? "Are you safe right now?"

"I think it's all clear." Ms. Shapiro breathed painful pauses between syllables. "I woke up on the couch when you called."

Someone who started work at 8 a.m. *just* woke up? The letter could wait. "Tell me what happened last night."

"I had finished heating up dinner and was flipping through new movie releases. All of the sudden, Thomas was sitting in the chair next to me. I asked how he got in and what he was doing, but all I remember is his scary grin before he jumped me. Oh God, I fought with him, struggling to push him off. He was so strong, and I'm so little. I couldn't do anything."

"Remember to breathe, Diane."

Ms. Shapiro steadied herself before continuing, though it didn't last long. "He threw me around like I was a doll . . . did he break anything? Oh, it hurts too much to stand again. I'll have to check later. Where was I?" She continued before Claire responded. "He threw me so hard, Dr. Rossi. Everything hurts so much. He didn't even say anything. I don't know what happened. I think he's so bored of me he's ready to *kill* me."

Claire waited for Ms. Shapiro to swallow the gravity of the situation. Most patients required several sessions to recover from such attacks, and those were grounded in reality, though for her and the cursed quintet, she supposed this was reality.

"Then Kim *appeared*, like Thomas had, and the two were fighting each other. I watched them turn my house into a wrestling ring. Kim scratched and clawed at Thomas, who attacked with punches and kicks. I couldn't believe she fought him off, she's even smaller than me. But she did it and then . . . I don't remember. I started humming my favorite song like you told me to, but I don't remember stopping. I guess I blacked out and woke up when you called."

Kim fought off Thomas? How did another person, much less someone smaller than Diane Shapiro, fight off an apparition? Claire tapped the counter. She considered calling Samuel Ingetti later, countered by a fear of him cutting off contact for an unnecessary interruption. And then by worry he'd reveal that in addition to curses, guardian angels existed too. Tapping turned to drumming turned into a fist bouncing off the counter. *One day, one moment, one step at a time.*

"I'm glad you're safe. Kim sounds like a good person to keep around."

"She's great. I wish she had a phone so I could call her to say thanks. I haven't seen any sign of her since waking up."

Curiosity threatened to steer Claire away from her purpose, but she held strong. "Diane, this may seem a strange question, but did an Imogene Aire send you a letter from Fredonia, North Dakota? The street address would be on Memory Lane."

Ms. Shapiro grunted. "How funny—yes. I thought it was junk mail so I threw it away weeks ago."

"Oh." If the letters held the key to ending this curse, what effect would destroying *most* of them have?

"But then," said Ms. Shapiro, "it showed up in the next batch of mail. The exact same letter, open and everything. I thought I was imagining it. I tucked it in the guest room to not have to look at it. If you're asking me about the letter, does that mean it's real?"

Claire walked toward her downstairs desk to scoop up Jess's keys. "It's very real, Ms. Shapiro. Do you mind if I drive over and pick it up? There's a patient experiencing similar symptoms as you, and I devised a treatment plan using a personalized letter they had also received."

"You mean there are more of these? Is Thomas real too? Should I be talking to the police instead of you?"

"It's a complex issue, but we're nearing the end of it. What matters is you're safe and I get that letter." And that she burned it before Thomas came back to finish the job. "I also recommend you invite friends or family over for the weekend, or see if you can spend the night at someone else's house. Worst case, maximize your time in public."

"You're the doctor here, so I'll trust what you have to say. I'll call Abby and I guess my old work friends if she doesn't pick up." Ms. Shapiro gave a short, shaky hum. "It'll be nice to have your company for a bit. Maybe you'd want to stay and have some tea? We could . . ."

While Ms. Shapiro spoke, Claire walked to the couch. Jess was working on her laptop, headphones in her ears. Claire shook the keys until her friend looked up. She mimed driving a steering wheel, pointed at Jess then back at herself, and raised her shoulders in question.

Jess plucked the headphones out and said, "Sure," quiet enough to require reading her lips.

Claire mouthed, *Thank you.*

Ms. Shapiro continued, ". . . there is also—"

"I'll head over now. I can't stay for tea, but while I'm on the phone with you, is there anything else you wanted to talk about?"

Ms. Shapiro laughed awkwardly. "Oh, dear me. I'm so silly, you must be busy. Well, I will have that letter for you. I don't think I could lose it if I tried. And since you ask, will you be back in the office next week? The other doctor was nice, but I think he suspected me of hiding something. He asked a lot of personal questions."

Rising from the couch, Jess took the keyring from Claire and looped it around her finger. She looked ready to go whenever, picking up her phone from the coffee table and dancing her thumb around its screen.

"I'm planning on it, and yes, Dr. Wilson can have that effect, but he's a great doctor. He left me great notes, so between those, the letter I'm picking up, and having rested for the week, I'm confident we'll close in on the root of your problems."

"That sounds swell. I'll see you soon then?" The words briefly caught in her throat.

"See you soon." Claire gazed down, reassuring herself that burning the letters provided the best course of action. With a self-affirming nod, she pulled the phone from her ear and saw an email notification from Rick. She tapped to open it.

"Now what are you doing?" Jess asked.

Claire held up her finger while she read.

Can't believe it's been days since we last talked, even if it is only over email. I'd ask how you're doing, but I guess I'll find out tonight. I had a bad feeling that hit me out of the blue. I'll feel a lot better when I see your smile. Good news is that while I've spent the whole week slammed by work, I'm so far ahead now that if anyone even thinks to call me I'm hanging up immediately. You've got me all to yourself and your friends tonight. That said, I'm not sure I can manage a late night out, even if I preemptively drain a pot of coffee. What do you think about all of us cozying up around your fireplace?

- Rick

Her fireplace? A little too topical, but she rationalized it as an innocent ploy to sleep over. "That was Rick." She held her phone up. "Looks like we're set for tonight. You ready to roll?"

"Not yet, I messaged Robert while you finished up. He's meeting us here. I think that another analytical brain"—Jess sucked on her lip, cutting off something longer—"could help."

"Only one thing will help, but it's fine if he's already on the way." Claire walked to the front window, opening the blinds to watch for his car. "Also, can you not say anything about this curse business until after we get back? My patient is expecting us, and I don't want to delay."

"You're the boss." Jess's sullen tone prompted Claire to turn around. Her friend was flicking at the glass screen of her phone, her shoulders slumped.

"If that were true, I'd make you liven up."

"Kind of hard when my best friend is less than a week removed from a strangling. When she fights with an invisible man in my car. When she drinks more cups of coffee than sleeps hours in a night. When I'm driving her around for pieces of mail to burn while she starves herself." She shook her head at the counter, at the cursed letters and pastry, with the discontentment of a parent who said they weren't mad but disappointed. Then she took a seat on the couch, rubbing her cheek. "None of this is natural. Should you call the priest back before we do anything?"

"He practically said I'm on my own, but if this doesn't work I will," she said, mostly to appease Jess. "Come on, it's date night.

What better way is there to put all of this behind us?" She took the couch's middle cushion. A jolt of confidence electrified her, brought on by the prospect of destroying Ryan for good and soon learning whether Rick actually existed. She just wished her friend shared her enthusiasm. "I bet you've lined up a model to make me jealous."

"Honestly, Claire, I don't care. I asked Paul."

"From work? I didn't take you for the type."

"Paul's married." Jess sighed and ran her tongue between her teeth. "He's not a date. He's someone I know. Someone I trust. With everything that's happening, that's who I want around you."

"You don't need to worry. I've got this taken care of. Afterward, it's business as usual."

"I hope so."

Then the two sat in silence up until Robert's arrival, who took his damn sweet time in coming over.

CHAPTER 24

You think you're cursed and burning these letters is going to end it?" Robert dug his hands into his pants pockets.

"Exactly. Can you tick the fireplace up one level?" On the mantle, Claire arranged six letters atop their respective envelopes at even widths. Flames licked the edge of the fireplace. An evening heat wave, combined with the fire inside, created trickles of sweat across the trio's foreheads. Dampness slickened the skin under her arms and around the waist of her jeans.

"What? It's hot enough as is."

Seated on the couch's arm, Jess tapped her wedge heels on the floor. "Let's just get this over with."

"Why didn't you tell me about this earlier?" asked Robert.

"Because maybe I didn't want to talk about magic curses twenty-four seven." Claire spun around and poked his chest. Time had eroded both her bravado and her patience. "You've been working every angle to sow doubt since I told you about all this, and that was hours ago. There's no way I could've dealt with you acting this way for days on top of everything else." She lowered her finger as she raised her voice. "You're right. It doesn't make sense. I don't get it either. It is what is. The priest said to burn whatever tied the curse to me, and as far as I can tell it's these letters. Now if you come up with something new, please tell me. I want to know your thoughts, but I don't want to hear any more questions about how or why. I. Don't. Fucking. Know."

"That wasn't exactl—"

Claire lifted her hands near Robert's cheeks, ready to crush the skin and bones between.

Robert signaled his innocence. "Fine. Give me something I can work on. What do the letters say all together again?"

After arriving home and explaining everything from square one, the trio looked at ways to sort the envelopes, eventually deciding on address numbers as the only logical course. Starting with the contents of the letter marked 10 Memory Lane, Diane Shapiro's letter, to 19 Memory Lane, Claire's burnt letter, six cryptic lines formed a poem.

Claire raised her hand for silence and turned back to the mantle to read aloud the verses.

"One by one." Ms. Shapiro's letter. 10 Memory Lane.

"My sisters fall." Mrs. Cathell. 11 Memory Lane.

"Seizing love for a son." Mrs. Keller. 13 Memory Lane.

The next paper had folded back on itself. Claire huffed and straightened it out with her free hand.

"Who loved Mom most of all." Ms. Capers. 14 Memory Lane.

"So to you who caused our rift." Ms. Kavina. 16 Memory Lane.

"Enjoy your gifts," Claire recalled from memory. Her mail, now a pile of ash, was represented by its follow-up letter. 19 Memory Lane.

Her hand dropped to rest on the mantle's edge. Fire consumed her attention as she mentally repeated the poem, simultaneously looking for new insights as well as memorizing its lines in case she needed them after tonight.

"We agree on the first four lines," said Robert. "Someone killed or wanted to kill his sisters because of jealousy or something similar. The last two lines get confusing. What if this person blames you and your patients for something that went wrong with his plans?"

"What could I have done?" Claire fidgeted with the corner of Nancy Cathell's letter.

"You would know better than me."

"Is this something we need to figure out now?" asked Jess. "Let's burn them and be done with it."

Claire slapped the paper down and whirled around. "We will. I want to burn the damn things more than anything, want to send

Ryan back to the hell from which he came. As far as I know though, it won't do a damn thing against the *person* responsible. What if it gets worse after this? What if I think everything is fine, and this starts over in a year? Nancy Cathell and what happened to her," paused Claire. *Could* she have done something to prevent her patient's death? "Shows I'm up against a clock, but there are two problems here, and solving the first one means losing our biggest lead on the second. I want to make sure we haven't overlooked anything—the way the lines were written, a new system to arrange the letters, hell, even how the papers were folded. Once I'm content, we'll turn them to ash."

"Can't we take a picture?" asked Robert.

"No!" Claire screamed. Robert's eyes grew large. She balled her hand into a fist then flexed it open. "Sorry, no, because I don't know what will happen. Dr. Ingetti warned me against taking pictures. He suggested it would make the curse permanent. And copying it down seems too similar."

"What if somebody else already did?"

"Then I'm fucked. I don't know." Claire tugged on the back of her hair. "I can't help anything out of my control."

Jess folded her arms. "Robert, it's not helping."

Robert glanced between them. "Fine." Despite that, he looked ready to argue before a resigned sigh preceded his cupping of Claire's upper arms. "I'm sorry. You can do this. We're with you."

His encouragement sounded more calculated than heartfelt, but she didn't care as long as he focused, which all of them seemed to have trouble with. Flames continued drawing perspiration from her middle back. She vented the bottom of her shirt. Robert stepped toward the dining room and put a single hand back in his pocket. Jess resumed tapping her heel. They weren't getting anywhere.

Why choose these specific address numbers if the point was just to order the letters? Why not use one through six? Claire itched to fling the envelopes to their doom, but she sensed secrets unrevealed. Why couldn't she think of anything? She stepped around Robert for a dose of her coffee, hoping to spark an a-ha moment. Drinking only spread further warmth through her body, but she continued until the cup ran dry.

It was then that Jess broke the monotony of fire crackling, drink gulping, and her own foot tapping. "I've got an idea." The statement lifted Claire's spirits. "What if the numbers are a code? We could index them into people's names or addresses. Like use 19 Memory Lane to take the first and ninth letter from Claire Rossi and follow suit with everyone else."

"We can also index into the lines themselves," added Robert, tapping his chin with his index finger. "Do you have a pen and paper?"

"That's not it," said Claire. Her friends looked expectantly at her. "We're not dealing with a criminal mastermind. He's driven by emotion. He isn't leaving clues like he's playing a game with the police. It's something more obvious. He's either gloating or needs the numbers ordered for some reason. Maybe to work his curse?"

"Oh, of course." Robert snapped his fingers. "They're years."

Claire raised her eyebrows. "What? Why do you say that?"

"*You* said it. The poem is ordered. What's a more obvious ordering than chronological? It fits."

"But what's the significance of the years?" asked Claire, half to herself.

"It could be anything. My guess is meeting dates. Your envelope says 19 Memory Lane. Maybe you met this *son* in 2019? It gives some logic to the street name too."

Jess bounced up from the couch. "And doesn't he need a personal tether to enact his curses? The year he met each of you makes sense. How old are your patients?"

"They would have been in their twenties or thirties based on the dates." Hands hanging at her waist, Claire flicked her palm. Was it that simple? Even she had said it was, and Robert's theory made sense. Looking into her and Eric's patients from 2019 should produce a narrow list of suspects. Anger issues, family problems, and personal projections made for uncommon combinations, so silent irritation struck when her mind blanked searching for a lead. Still, that was a damn keen observation. "It's perfect. Great job." She drummed her thighs as caffeine stimulated and invigorated her. "That leaves the meaning of the poem itself. Either of you hiding another revelation?"

"I doubt there's more significance to it than a psychotic individual murdering his family, growing bored, and finding a new group to torment," said Robert.

By now, Claire had memorized the poem line by line. She assumed that her tormentor believed her responsible for breaking apart whatever relationship the son had foisted upon his mother. Hence the *gifts* for those who caused the *rift*. She just didn't know enough to piece together the puzzle, but with the poem memorized she felt satisfied by the answers gleaned.

"No, it's significant. I can't tell how yet, but I'm confident we've exhausted these letters' usefulness."

"So now what?" asked Jess.

"Now we burn them." Claire cracked a smile. This would end Ryan. It had to, what else could happen? Yet doubt lingered in her mind like the morning remnants of a nightmare.

Jess bounced off the couch as if she had taken three doses of Ritalin. "Operation mail torcher is live. Let's get this over with." Excitement replaced the lifeless gaze in her eyes. "I believe we've earned ourselves a triple date. Do you want help tossing everything into the fireplace?"

Claire waved her friend away. "I'll take care of it. Stand back a little bit and watch for anything strange. I doubt this will run quite according to plan." Something about the coincidences in these cases—especially her mom's twisted idioms and Eric's recent linking of an old patient to the place where she died—had layered a sense of foreboding. Her friends exchanged curious looks, but both did as asked. Feelings aside, the task before lay clear.

From the mantle, she picked up the first envelope and letter pairing in the row, the one addressed to Diane Shapiro. The name Imogene Aire entranced her. *Imaginary friend,* she thought. *This has been anything but imaginary. Is it really almost over?* She hovered the papers over the flames with ritualistic precision until the corners lit. The papers curled an inch before she tossed them in. They shrank into ash with complete normalcy, but the air felt different. Denser. The weight of a dozen bricks pressed on her shoulders. She looked back to inspect the scene behind her. The interior of the house hadn't changed, but her friends sensed the same thing. Or read her body language.

Jess itched the knuckles on her fist, but she smiled all the same.

Robert nodded once to Claire then continued scanning the living room like a security guard.

She grabbed the second mail pairing and added it to the fireplace as carefully as the first. Then the next, and the next. Whether from anxiety or her proximity to oxygen-hungry flames, her breaths grew more shallow as she reached for the fifth letter. Her hands convulsed, forcing her to use both of them to grip the papers. She held out the offering to the orange blaze until it singed her fingertips. Claire recoiled and grimaced at the pain. A distant voice called out. When nothing followed, she resumed her task.

The sixth and final pairing of papers, her second letter, succumbed to flames as easily as the other five, with as little fanfare. Claire rolled her shoulders, imitating a boxer preparing for a bout. She engaged in a staring match with the bright flames, listening to its flickers liven up the grave atmosphere.

After an uncertain length of time, Jess called her from her musings. "Is that it?"

Claire blinked moisture back into her eyes. "I don't really—"

"That was quite the experience!" shouted a fourth voice.

Ryan. As recognizable as a crash of thunder.

Claire spun to face him. Halfway between Jess and Robert, he stood wearing a white sweater and jeans without shoes. Seconds after locking on, her friends inspected the same area, occasionally casting glances between each other and Claire to see what they were missing, clearly not hearing or seeing the apparition.

"Very sad to see all of my friends pass into oblivion. Well, *feel* them pass. It's strange how connected to them I was, like pieces of clothing on my body. Now those clothes are shed, and you know what? I'm free, stripped of what weighed me down. I'm stronger than ever before, and I have you to thank for that." Ryan crouched as if preparing to jump for the ceiling.

"Let me show you." And he bounded into a sprint toward Claire.

CHAPTER 25

Claire sidestepped just in time to avoid Ryan tackling her into the fireplace. The adjustment sent them flying into the corner, him landing on top. With the agility of a gymnast, he planted himself over her waist. A refrigerator's weight immobilized her.

"No scratching me this time," he squealed, pinning her wrists to the ground. By then her friends had sprinted over.

She writhed against her imprisonment. "Get him off me!"

They crouched at her sides, Robert practically touching the wall, Jess with open space behind her. They drove their hands unwittingly into Ryan's arms, bouncing off as if striking a force field. He cackled at their failed efforts and tightened his grip. Claire's hands started to numb.

"We're trying," said Jess, her face partially obscured by Ryan's shoulder. "Something's in our way. It looked like a tornado scooped you up and threw you to the ground. Is it him?"

"What's happening?" Robert fumbled his way around Ryan's back and limbs.

Jess investigated similarly on her side.

"It's. Ryan," Claire growled.

"Your curse? Then why don't I give this a try . . ." Robert's hands outlined the apparition's side into a target. He reared back and slammed himself shoulder-first into Ryan's ribs. He shook off the failed attack and tried again, crashing into the same spot. A quizzical look fell over his face, the same expression as when calculating moves in a board game. "It's like ramming a mattress."

Ryan grunted. "What a rude intrusion against our precious alone time." He evaluated Jess head to toe, did the same with Robert.

Claire seized the moment to jerk to one side. She may as well have tried to bend steel. The apparition didn't even notice.

"I can actually *feel* them. Utter vermin. Rats scurrying over my body. Disgusting." Ryan ran his tongue along the front of his teeth, his eyebrows creased into sharp angles. "Once I've finished with you, I think I'll clean house with them."

"No, you won't!" shouted Claire. She shifted downward, putting all her weight behind her legs and driving them up. Ryan wobbled, then slid a tick and stabilized. She panted; each effort tired her as much as a hundred-meter dash.

"Is any of this helping?" asked Robert. He switched from slamming against Ryan to jabbing where a kidney would normally reside.

Claire continued struggling, her body sweating from head to toe. Fire raged near her feet, allying with physical exertion to drain her strength. She loosed her frustration in an unintelligible howl.

Robert threw another punch. "What'd you say?"

Claire lacked the energy to respond.

Jess yelled, "Stop hitting him and help me get her up!"

"How?"

"Her hands are pinned. Let's start there."

What could they do? Claire wanted to tell them to escape and save themselves, but fear and fatigue silenced her. Without help, Ryan would kill her. Burning the letters had only empowered him. What had he said about the other apparitions? They were weighing him down? Had the curser planned on her burning those letters? Her mind raced to make sense of it, until Ryan's fist plunged into her gut, and she cried out in pain.

"I'm losing you, Claire," he elongated each word more than the last. "Don't get lost in that pretty little head of yours without me." His ear-to-ear grin reminded her of the first time they met, when he wore that cream trench coat and towered over her. Now, up close in his thin sweater, he looked malnourished despite his impossible weightiness.

Her friends' hands found their way under Claire's. They plopped back-first onto the floor and shoved upward. The sudden resistance forced Ryan to reposition again and gave Claire an opening to strike his rear with her thighs.

Ryan lost his grip and fell forward, bracing against the floor with open palms.

Claire scampered out from under him and toward the open space behind Jess. Blood flowed back into her sleeping hands, pricking her with invisible daggers. Thumping sounded nearby, but disorientation made placing it impossible. Anything but crawling forward became superfluous. She made it halfway to the front door before Ryan seized her.

"He's got my leg." She kicked with her free foot until Ryan's vise grip clamped onto it too.

Jess wrapped her arms around Claire's waist and pulled. Little by little, she lost her hold, her arms sliding up Claire's torso and lifting her shirt.

Robert dashed straight into Ryan's back, rebounded, then swung wide around him. He grasped Claire's outstretched arms and planted his feet, bringing the tug-of-war to a near standstill.

"This is getting old." Ryan released his hold, sending the trio sprawling into a jumbled pile near the front door.

Claire looked up at the knob, then the deadbolt. If she could get out, she had a chance. She didn't need to outrun him forever. Only until he retreated into the ether. The more people she surrounded herself with, the harder it had been for Ryan to maintain his form.

Her arms pushed against the mess of bodies. Jess and Robert scooted away as she flailed to escape the pile. Her calves cramped, calling forth a grimace and groan. She blinked away a tear. Locked calves prevented her from standing. She boosted herself up with one hand and reached for the lock with the other.

"Help her open the door." Jess had retreated to the coffee table.

Before Claire reached her goal or Robert reacted, she was lifted up and thrown. She crashed past Jess, onto the far edge of the coffee table. The glass tabletop echoed a hollow sound but held solid, the side of her head and shoulder absorbing the impact. Momentum carried her back-first onto the floor beside the couch. She strained her neck protecting her head and lay with her legs toward the fireplace.

"What the fuck," cried Jess. "Claire." She crawled toward the landing zone.

Another series of thumps. Louder now. From the porch?

"What's happening in there?" panicked an outside voice.

Rick? Is that Rick? wondered Claire. *I must have a concussion.* She flexed muscles to inject some life into her limbs. She had to get out before Ryan inflicted more permanent damage.

The apparition sauntered in Claire's direction. His hate-filled stare marred an otherwise relaxed composure.

Knocking struck the door like a series of drum rolls, but it didn't shift the wooden slab an inch. "Let me in!" shouted . . . Rick. Definitely Rick. But how? They weren't supposed to meet for hours.

Jess fumbled over Claire, checking her forehead and shoulders with gentle touches. "Are you okay?"

Ryan continued creeping. He sidestepped the coffee table, approaching from the opposite side of Jess.

"Open the door," whispered Claire. She tried to steady herself and repeat it louder, but her body refused. Only the frailest of voices persisted. "Open the door." She breathed as rhythmically as possible, each inhale stabbing with her pain.

Jess leaned down, staring inquisitively at Claire until she mouthed the words once more.

"Robert, open the fucking door!" Jess shouted loud enough for neighbors across the street to hear. It gave Claire a headache, but maybe the bump on her head was catching up to her.

"Got you." Ryan clamped onto Claire's jean cuffs and dragged her away. She thrashed with her legs and healthy arm to no avail. Jess fell over trying to pull her back. Unimpeded, he pulled until the warmth of the fireplace embraced her from the knees down. "Play time's over," he said, straddling her stomach.

The door swung wide, crashing into the wall. Ryan paid it no mind. She cast the remainder of her strength into flailing and beating his lower back with her thighs.

"Stop that," said Ryan, slamming fists into her legs.

Charley horses rippled through both limbs, forcing their limp weights back to the ground. She shoved against his chest with her forearm. He swatted it away. His fingers reached down, poised to tighten around her throat. The fight in her faded.

"You've been nothing but a pest for our blessed reunion. Time to finish what I started in the hospital."

But before he touched her neck, Ryan went soaring into the dining room.

Rick stood over her prone body. "I'll handle this. Stay safe and out of the way." He marched toward the prone apparition.

Claire slid away from the impending fight. Jess grabbed under her arm but released at the ensuing yowl. If her shoulder wasn't broken, it was seriously contused.

"Sorry." Jess backed off to allow Claire to keep scooting. "We need to get you to a hospital."

"Not yet." She stopped shuffling and looked up. "I think my luck's about to change."

"What?" Jess clasped her hands on top of her head, rubbing them back and forth, frizzing her hair. "How?"

Chairs clacked against tables as Rick and Ryan jockeyed for position. Grappling with one another, they disappeared behind the couch. Grunts and groans came in waves measured by pops and thuds.

Robert jogged to her side. "The door's open like you asked. We making a break for it?"

"She said not yet. Why are we staying?" asked Jess.

"Rick. He's here," answered Claire.

Robert massaged his chin, his eyebrows searching to make sense of the scene. Then he dropped his hand and his face lit up. "She's got a concussion. Let's haul her out. I have my keys."

"I said no."

Jess raised obliging hands. "Okay, fine. We're not going anywhere. What do you want us to do?"

One of the combatants went flying over the kitchen counter. The other leapt over the bar to follow.

"Help me stand and get me to my desk. It's out of their way."

Jess and Robert pulled on her upper back until she sat upright. Her friends reached for her sides.

"Not my arms. Boost me from behind."

They crouched to comply. Two pairs of hands lifted from below, then shifted to support her lower back. She pushed off with her good arm and slowly gripped the floor with her feet. Sighing away a deep ache, she steadied herself to walk to the desk, her friends' hands assisting to prevent a fall. For the first time since Rick's entry, she saw more than glimpses of the fight. Both men were beaten bloody. Bruises blemished their faces. Ryan held a steak knife in his hand, but it didn't look like he had cut Rick with it. Rick backpedaled out of the kitchen and swatted at the advancing apparition, testing him. At last, she reached the chair. Sitting down sent a cascade of painful spasms through her torso. Jess was right about the hospital. Claire needed an x-ray, but if Rick had a chance to permanently end this she was sticking around to offer any help she might provide.

"Are Rick and him . . . fighting?" asked Jess.

Claire meekly waved her off. "Shh."

Jess made a confused face in Robert's direction and motioned for him to stay silent. With nothing else to do, she tried, and clearly failed, to watch the fight unfold as Claire saw it.

Several rounds of posturing led the opponents to in-between the couch and fireplace. Ryan swiped his knife at Rick, who danced back and landed a counter-jab. Ryan's head reeled back and snapped forward in equal measure. He thrust the blade at Rick's chest, who sidestepped the attack. The blade drove into the couch's arm, flinging cotton stuffing into the air.

Or not. The rules of the curse left in doubt such physical ramifications.

Rick grinned and took the opportunity from the overextended lunge to drive a fist into Ryan's backside.

Ryan growled and leered at Claire. She inched back as he yanked the knife out of the couch. "She's going to pay double for that."

The two circled around until Ryan again faced Claire with his back to the fireplace. Ryan swung the knife wildly, occasionally catching his opponent's shoulders or arms with glancing blows. Through it all, Rick remained unfazed. He drove the apparition back with jabs and crosses of his own. Ryan backed up to the edge of the yearning flames, his head practically touching the mantle. With nowhere else to retreat, Ryan hissed like a vampire and turned his swipes into a single thrust, piercing through Rick's stomach.

"No!" Claire squeezed Jess's hand with all of her might.

But instead of falling back, Rick shot forward, driving both him and Ryan into the fireplace. Two ceramic logs spun out onto the hearth. Flames wrapped around their bodies. Ryan writhed in agony, clawing at Rick's back in a desperate attempt to escape. Rick grappled with and punched Ryan as if the fire's licks were rain drops.

"Oh my god," she said, uttering a phrase long since struck from her vocabulary. Her heart prepared to beat itself out of her chest. She dug nails into Jess's hand, which her friend calmly peeled back out. Claire sat on the brink of bounding out of her seat, or at least attempting it. "Are you seeing any of this?"

"Any of what?" asked Jess.

"Nope," said Robert. "Just doing what I can to make sure you don't go flying again."

Uncertainty plagued Claire. Should she cut the fire? If Rick was real, there'd be no question, but he wasn't, and helping Rick get out of there meant giving Ryan another chance to escape, and this all looked so close to over.

Rick made the decision moot, jumping out of the fireplace and rolling on the ground. Fiery clothes morphed into smokey tatters. His arms, legs, and head were spread out in a star pattern. He held a steak knife in his limp hand.

Ryan's body lay draped over the remaining logs. Motionless.

"Rick," Claire called out to no response. She chanced hobbling to his prone body. Sore muscles begged her to halt. Her friends' steadying hands on her backside provided the confidence to push on. As she drew close, she smelled the scent of burnt clothes, flesh, and hair mixed into a sickening charcoal odor. "Rick," she cried again, groaning as she knelt by his side. She lowered her hands. One covered his chest, the other his punctured stomach.

"Rick? What happened?" Jess and Robert asked. Their confusion melded with the background.

"Where did you come from?" Shame inflamed her cheeks. Shouldn't his health concern her more? "Is there anything I can do?" She repressed the urge to dial 9-1-1. How would they help? Deep down she knew Rick wasn't a real, living human. That didn't change her debt to the man, or whatever he was, that had saved her.

"I came over early to surprise you," Rick coughed. Claire didn't buy it. He tried sitting up, winced, and laid back down. Squinched eyes illustrated pain with every sentence. "Then I heard all of the banging. I didn't know what was happening, but I knew I had to protect you. Knew that only I could protect you."

"I believe you. I don't know how all this works, I really don't, but I believe you. Thank you for saving me."

Standing behind her, Robert said, "Who are you—oof." Jess's shush followed.

"You'll figure this out," continued Rick. "Once you're not fighting for your life." Sweaty hair curled over his forehead as he smiled. "This is it for me though. For us. I'm sorry we couldn't spend more time together. But Claire—listen to me."

"Yes?"

"I don't think this is the end of Ryan." His concern mirrored Claire's latent fears, as if he had plucked the growing worry from her head. "Next time I won't be here to help."

"I know." She stared at the apparition's seemingly lifeless body slumped in the fireplace. *I burned every single letter,* she thought. *What more can I do?* She looked back at her champion. Helplessness and loss overwhelmed her, stirring a light sob.

Rick's final moments mixed a series of grins, grunts, and grimaces. Claire clasped his hands, then surrendered to a deep wail of lament. Tears dropped to his unmoving chest and rolled onto the floor. She hung loosely over his body, channeling sadness and pain into an egress of misery. When the load on her lightened enough to warrant standing, she blotted the wetness of her eyes with the back of her hand, halting mid-motion at an outside sound.

Someone was marching on her porch.

"This is Denver PD," boomed a deep voice. "Our guns are drawn, and we're coming in." The front door was still open. "Keep your hands where we can see them."

CHAPTER 26

I don't have anything to add." Claire adjusted the ice pack on her shoulder and pouted. Paramedics had come after the police, miraculously clearing her of any serious injuries. A minor fracture with no dislocation at worst. "We told all of this to your police friends an hour ago." *Her* friends sat beside her, letting her lead the interview with the detective as she had with the responding officers.

On the other side of the table, Kline crossed his arms and stared at each of them past the point of comfort. He nodded after his silent assessment and relaxed in his chair. "One more question then, and I'll get out of here."

Here it comes: where's the letter?

"Why's your fireplace on? It's almost eighty degrees outside." He vented the long sleeves of his shirt.

Claire looked at the hearth, restricting her shudder at the sight of Ryan's body draped over the logs. Scorch marks and a permanent sneer left him marginally less threatening than in 'life'. Flames seemed unable to degrade his body and cast a haunting glow. She tried to steady her gaze from dropping further, but curiosity overtook her. Rick lay sprawled in the same position in which he expired. The memory of spent tears threatened to call them to the present. She rubbed her eyes, half to temporarily blind herself, half to stall a bout of sobbing. "I was showing off how hot it could get. After he," Claire paused, "showed up again, I haven't had it in my head to turn it off."

Kline gave a sympathetic half-smile. "As long as you remember before bed."

"I can handle that." The thought of approaching the bodies chilled her spine enough to offset the fire's warmth. She'd have to ask someone else to kill the fire.

"I'll get out of here then. I know it's frustrating the officers weren't able to find anything, especially with the damage done." He pointed to the glass crack in the center of the coffee table, the only sign of Ryan's intrusion besides Claire's abrasions. "I want you to know we're doing everything we can do to find this guy. We've circulated his sketch to nearby precincts. I'm confident it'll turn up a lead soon."

This isn't the end of Ryan, remembered Claire. *If I don't figure out something, the next* lead *will be my dead body. For all I know, he'll be back tomorrow with warpaint made of soot.*

"Thank you," Jess filled the silence. "We feel a lot better knowing there's a competent detective on the case."

Her piping up snapped Claire out of despondency. She had to figure out something, perhaps after brainstorming with her friends. But first, she wanted Kline gone. "Yes, thank you. I'll let you out." She set down her ice pack and ambled to the front door.

With curt nods and a little too long of a glance at Jess, the detective made a straight shot for his car.

Claire stepped out behind him onto the porch. Alone for the first time in hours, she allowed her mind to wander. It betrayed her, replaying Rick's death throes in crystal clear detail. She bowed her head and crossed her arms with one hand covering her face. Tears welled up in the crook of her thumb and index finger. She took one deep breath and reminded herself that Jess and Robert didn't need to see this. They were helping enough without worrying about a total breakdown. *Too fragile for company, too scared to be alone,* she judged. She sniffled, dragging her fingers across closed eyelids to clear them, then stepped back inside. Before she could close the door, a familiar voice stayed her hand.

"Claire, are you alright? Bradley heard screaming. I thought he made it up, but then I went outside and heard the commotion, so I called the police." Of course, Amy was responsible.

Her hand fell from the door. She faced the sidewalk, watching the Albas approach. Amy wore a knee-length dress too bright for

Claire's mood. Brad's black patterned pajamas seemed more appropriate.

"I'm fine," said Claire, colder than Amy deserved for safeguarding a neighbor, but as nosy people tended to do, her interest complicated matters. In her case, with another police report.

Amy ignored Claire's reticent body language and climbed the front porch holding her son's hand, dropping it to embrace her.

Claire groaned and pushed her away with her uninjured arm. "My shoulder."

Amy reeled back. "I'm sorry." Her face flushed all over. She scanned Claire's arm, neck, and a particular spot on her face that had probably bruised. "I didn't even think about you getting hurt. You're always so strong. I bet that's why Nathan didn't want me coming over. He tried convincing me not to call the police, telling me to," her voice deepened in imitation of her husband, "mind my own damn business." Then she smiled. "I'm glad you're safe."

"I'm glad you're safe, too," repeated Brad. "Umm . . . I know Mom's hug hurt you, but do you think I can hug you if I'm really careful?"

Claire started to frown, then bit her lip. Brad hadn't done anything wrong, but she wanted the Albas gone too. "Sure, but then I need to rest, alright you two?"

Amy raised her hand as if taking an oath then backed off. She looked thinner than normal. Makeup and curled hair attempted to hide an exhausted face.

Brad wrapped his arms around Claire's lower back, seeming to test the waters, then squeezed when she offered no resistance. "I'm sorry, Dr. Rossi."

With her hurt arm held high above his head, Claire patted his back with her other hand. "It's fine. It's not your fault."

He squeezed harder, pushing his ear into Claire's navel. "I think it might be," he fretted. "You only looked sick after me."

"Bradley, that's ridiculous," scolded Amy. "I'm sorry, Claire. I just wanted to let you know we cared. We'll head home now." She didn't sound happy about the prospect but reached for her son anyway.

"He's fine." Claire motioned for Amy to stop. "Brad, I won't be mad with whatever you say, but would you please let go of me and tell me why you think it's your fault?"

A series of breaths reverberated through her thigh. With a final huff, Brad pulled away. He alternated glances between her and the wooden patio.

"Go on. I need to rest soon."

His gaze remained downcast. "I gave you a toy when we first met. I said it was mine, but it wasn't really. Someone told me to give it to you, and he said we wouldn't be friends if I told you where it came from."

"Who told you?" Claire and Amy said simultaneously.

"The man who helped Mom and Dad make the house pretty."

Something jammed Claire's airways.

Amy stammered, "The Realtor? That doesn't make any . . . wait, do you mean the remodeler? Ryan?" She knelt down and lifted Brad's chin. "Ryan did that? What else did he have you do? Bradley, you need to tell me right now!"

"That was it, I promise." Brad shook his hands in imitation of a frustrated adult. "I'm sorry for keeping secrets."

Your secret is safe for all the world to see.

Don't count your blessings before they hatch.

Beware of the gift that keeps on giving.

Her mother's malaphors flooded her mind. Had she been warning her the whole time? Claire's brain jumbled trying to rationalize the possibility in conjunction with Brad's revelation. As she wheezed her breathing back to normal, she crouched to the Albas' level and placed a staying hand on Amy's shoulder.

"Brad, are you talking about"—Claire coughed—"that doctor figure?"

"I'm sorry, Dr. Rossi." He looked to the floor again.

"Hold on a second." Her arm pressed to her chest, Claire jogged by a confused Robert and Jess and into the kitchen. She pulled open the junk drawer and found the toy tucked under her blender guide: a female doctor in a lab coat with a stethoscope around her neck. She hadn't noticed before how much it resembled her. She also hadn't looked at it since Brad gave it to her over a month ago. Claire slipped the toy figure into her back jean pocket. More fuel for the fire before giving it a rest for the night. But first, she had questions.

As she shifted back toward the door, a compulsion begged she check the fireplace; Rick and Ryan had vanished. *Why now?* she wondered. *Stop it, Claire. One step at a time.* She strode outside, where Amy quietly admonished Brad. They both looked up when she stopped at the threshold.

"Why don't you two come in?" Claire closed the door behind them, then gestured toward the couch. "Jess and Robert are my closest friends." She motioned beside her. "Amy and Brad are my neighbors."

The adults exchanged pleasantries while Brad added an enthusiastic, "Nice to meet you." He stared dumbfounded at Jess until recognition lit his face anew. "Oh, I remember you."

Jess smiled and waved.

Starting before Amy could dive into anything personal, Claire withdrew the doctor figure. "Brad, you said the man in charge of renovating your house gave you this, right?"

He barely glanced at it before his head slunk back toward the floor. "I'm sorry."

Enjoy your gifts.

All this time, Ryan the home contractor *was* related to cursed Ryan. It fit too well for a coincidence, and Claire no longer took such incidents for granted. If she had followed up when Brad first mentioned him, maybe Nancy Cathell would still be alive. But how was she supposed to know?

Maybe because your mom was warning you. What sane person would've interpreted those twisted idioms as warnings? She couldn't look for every needle in every haystack near every broad side of a barn. She could've tried a little harder though. *This isn't helping. Focus.*

"Don't apologize," said Claire. "I'm not mad. All I want you to do is answer honestly, got it?"

"Got it." Joviality returned to Brad's face.

"Great. Do I still look sick to you?"

Amy opened her mouth, then closed it after a firm look from Claire.

"Yeah, even sicker than last time," lamented Brad.

"Brad, I like you, but I don't like this doctor figure. Will you be sad if I put it in the fire?"

"I guess not. It wasn't really my gift. He said you would like me if I gave it to you and then we played that day, and it was so much fun. I didn't think—"

"I don't blame you for any of this," said Claire, cutting his explanation short. Truth aside, she didn't have time for his remorse.

"Okay." His tone said he didn't believe her. Then his emotions flipped like a switch and he jumped with excitement. "Is it okay if I watch?"

Claire laughed, finding strange joy in his excitement. Brad joined with a giggle of his own while the other adults tried to figure out what they missed. Mother and son followed her fireplace approach, with Amy positioning herself between Brad and the blaze.

She tossed the figure into the fire. As the plastic warped and began to melt, she mentally noted a need to replace the ceramic logs once the curse resolved. Which this would do, right? But what if it didn't? She gingerly stretched her back, expelling tension brought on by hypotheticals without moving her bad shoulder.

This is it, she reassured herself. *With this, the curse dies. And now I know who's responsible.* Maybe it *was* just a toy, just a coincidence? *Doubtful, but there's an easy way to find out. Once confirmed, I'll make the prick pay.* Amy had to have his phone number—she'd get that tonight. Budding plans invigorated her, but a sensation nagged the back of her head as molten plastic dripped on the synthetic logs. She ruffled Brad's hair. "One last question for you."

"What's that?"

"Do I look any healthier?"

Brad inspected from front and behind as if she were hiding something. "No," he trailed off before stammering, "Maybe you need some time."

Time is the root of all evil.

Sofia Costas's words played on repeat, until the doctor figure's head vanished into the flames. With it, one last phrase made a final encore.

A broken clock never boils. Claire massaged her palms in alternating fashion. *No,* she countered, *but hopefully a melted toy breaks curses.*

CHAPTER 27

Sleep came easier than expected.

Claire owed part of that to her friends' willingness not to postulate on who, or what, Rick was, and her ability to compartmentalize her own feelings and theories for later examination. The remainder she attributed to Robert crashing on the couch and Jess sharing her bed. They wouldn't be much help if Ryan rose again, but the safety of company and a little bit of wine lulled her into much-needed slumber.

She awoke steeled for her return to St. Mary's Hospital for the Wayward, but her morning took an early nosedive. Ryan Fretz, the Alba's general contractor, turned up with an out-of-service phone number and an address pointing to an empty warehouse. She responded by breaking a mug and breaking down upstairs, but as the clock ticked, resolve filled her once again. She readied herself to meet up with Eric, hiding bruises with a turtleneck, jeans, and concealer.

The one thing she couldn't mask was a nagging sense of foreboding.

Following their meeting at the hospital, and a short conversation with the St. Mary's front staff, they were on the way to see Ms. Nelson. No more than a few seconds had passed when Eric dropped behind the stocky male nurse leading them. "You seem distant," he whispered.

Claire lagged with him and stared where faded beige walls met the white ceiling, searching for new cracks in the plaster since her last visit. "I haven't been here for a decade. Not since my mom died." The excuse would satisfy yet she felt drawn to continue. "The hallways look the same. My mom saved her most lucid moments for our walks."

"How did that make you feel?"

"Really?" Claire cocked her head. Her shoulder strained, but painkillers dulled it to an ache.

He raised a defensive hand. "It's a question from your friend, not a psychiatrist."

Dubious of his ability to disconnect that part of his brain, Claire almost lashed out, but the toll of the weekend left her too drained for a prolonged argument. "My mom preferred speaking in private but said the walls were too thin for her room. Everyone could hear us in there, supposedly. So we'd walk these halls, catching up on generic family banter until she'd abruptly stop and whisper one of her muddled adages. It was like she waited for the exact place and time to say whatever she had to say."

"Mom knows best."

The ball is in your bandwagon. Déjà vu struck Claire as she passed an empty laundry room. Mirages of her younger self pleaded with her mom near the drier. "I'm not sure about that."

Rationalizing the malaphors—then or now—tried her patience, but this one gave rise to an odd sense of comfort. Sofia Costas knew of what she spoke, even if no one else did. What if she meant to imply Claire was in control, but bandwagon followers like Eric played a pivotal role? Or was Claire trying to convince herself there was a method to the madness?

Several steps later, the nurse dropped them off at a public room where Emelia Nelson sat alone. A half-dozen occupied tables surrounded them. The woman's alert gaze fit Claire's memory, but everything else seemed more composed. Straightened black-gray hair and clean pressed clothes stood in stark contrast to the disheveled woman she had treated three years ago.

"Dr. Rossi, it's been so long." Ms. Nelson fiddled with a topaz heart charm hanging from her neck. "How are you? And who is this handsome man?"

"Hello, Ms. Nelson. I'm Dr. Wilson. Please feel free to call me Eric." He shook her hand and Claire followed suit. Both doctors sat opposite Ms. Nelson. Her eyes darted between them.

"It seems you're doing well here. And you're not my patient anymore, so feel free to call me Claire." If Eric wanted to play it casual, she decided it best to join him. Maybe it would calm her former patient.

"Then you can both call me Emmy. You were always so formal during our sessions. I didn't realize how much hearing my last name bothered me until St. Mary's gave me time to rest and reflect. It reminds me too much of my kids." She puffed as if to psyche herself up, but her words came off as pleading. "Talking about them is painful for an old woman like me, especially now that it's not part of my ongoing treatment. Other than a few memories, I keep thoughts of them to a minimum."

Pushing aside the healthiness of such an attitude, Claire understood the sentiment. Emmy's daughters had all either committed suicide or been driven catatonic by a madness seemingly endemic to the family. "That's okay. We're not here to talk about them."

Relief washed over Emmy's face. She clasped her hands together. "So why are you here? Not that I'm not happy to see you. You're welcome anytime, my dear."

If not for some pointed questions at the front desk, it would have been hard to believe Emmy's medication schedule restricted her lucid moments. As is, her current level of awareness meant a limited window before her next dosage. Claire crossed her legs and set to work. "We wanted to ask if you knew some women in particular who volunteered at or were assisted by Den of Help. You helped several women there, correct?"

"I did. Do you remember how my husband and I had some . . . problems? After he left, and then my daughters . . ." Emmy glanced down before returning with a fake smile. "Den of Help helped me so much, I returned the favors as much as I could. It kept my mind off of everything, at least until it reached the point when I came and saw you. I stopped all my outside activity besides work by then."

"You told me you volunteered. I didn't know how integral they were to your life."

"They helped me survive long enough to get to you, and"—Emmy spun her hand in the air—"to get here."

"I'm thankful for that. Do you mind if I tell you some names to see if you remember them?"

"I'll do my best."

Claire proceeded to name and describe the cursed quintet. Eric's eyes bugged, presumably at disclosing her patients' identities without a formal release. She had wrestled with the breach of confidence in the car ride over. With Ryan Fretz's leads dried up, this was the only path left for answers—answers that ensured her and her patients' ongoing safety.

Emmy's face lit up. "I've been in here for three years, and it's been five since I've seen any of them, but I remember them all. Glad to know part of my brain still works."

"You seem rather coherent," said Eric. "Have you considered checking out of here under Claire's supervision?"

Emmy swallowed and squeezed her fingers together. "That's kind of you to say." Her earlier tenseness took hold. "I'd rather stay here though. St. Mary's has a lot to offer."

Claire glanced at Eric. She wanted to know if Emmy's phrasing sounded as odd to him as it did to her.

Eric smiled and said, "I understand."

Apparently not. Emmy was hiding something, and Claire bet it wasn't a coincidence. An ache throbbed at her temples. She blinked to refocus. "How well did you know each of them?"

"Pretty well. I met them during my volunteer phase and even ate lunch with them on occasion. They opened up to me about marital problems or general loneliness. We had a strong support system at Den of Help, and I was proud to be a part of it." Her cheeks drooped. "Did something happen to them?"

Emmy didn't pay attention to the news. Nancy Cathell's murder had headlined for two nights, but honesty might derail a conversation that could prevent five more deaths. "Nothing too bad. What's odd is that they share a problem. They're all haunted by similar hallucinations." The more she revealed about the cursed quintet, the greater the professional risk, but Emmy had once suffered from her own hallucinations. Claire targeted empathy to keep her talking.

Blood drained from the ex-patient's face. Her expression froze like a snowman devoid of holiday cheer. "Can you," her shoulders slumped, "describe the hallucinations?"

"Tall, pale white men. All of them with short hair, albeit different colors. Different ages but none looked older than forty. Most have some sort of distinguishing feature, but none of them share the same one." Claire's nose wrinkled at the memory of Ryan's birthmark.

"What about the clothes? Do they dress warmly?"

Images of trench coats and sweaters seized Claire's calm. How did Emmy know? The hallucinations she described as a patient had been as generic as they come. "Yes, they tend to dress warmly."

"How often do these hallucinations show up? Is it frequent?"

"It used to be every other week. Now it's every other day."

"Do they have names? What are their names?"

"Thomas, Ted, Ryan—"

"No!" Emmy buried her face in her hands. "Please, no." Her chest heaved as she began crying.

Claire's heart raced. Before she could follow up, a ponytailed nurse came around to check on the scene. After a short inspection, the woman leaned against a distant wall. She folded her arms, watching the three of them, and motioned to continue.

Best to calm Emmy first. "Do you remember what we say to stress?" No answer.

"One day," Claire drawled. "One moment. One . . ."

"One step at a time." Emmy's face remained buried, but her chest steadied. "Ryan . . ." She sat still for a few seconds, until she sniffed and wiped a trickle of tears from her downcast face.

Saying the wrong thing meant sending Emmy into a deeper spiral, resulting in her and Eric's almost certain expulsion from St. Mary's, so she rejected openly hazarding suspicions over Ryan's identity. She instead turned toward Eric and found him already looking her way. Brows raised, he pointed at her and mouthed, *Ryan?*

Assuming he wanted to reconfirm Ryan as the name of her attacker, she nodded.

Eric lost himself, with an extended thumb rubbing his chin. What was he thinking?

"Claire," said Emmy.

She'd have to clarify his thoughts later. "Yes?"

"There's something I never told you about my family."

After a long silence, Claire asked, "What's th—"

"Actually, there's a lot I never told you." Emmy looked up, her arms folded across her stomach as if cradling an invisible baby. "I remember our first session together. I picked you because the photo on your website reminded me so much of my middle daughter, Megan. I never told you that."

Claire would've pointed her to someone else if she had. She silently admonished herself for not catching it.

"It made the sessions a lot easier. When I first saw you, I hoped you could fix what was in my mind. The hallucinations never tortured me as bad as my daughters, but it was hard to have a life. I could only work part-time, so I had to rely on my son for extra income. He preferred working nights, but he ended up somewhere with flexible hours so he could sync his schedule with mine."

Previous theories burned away like cursed letters. "I don't remember you mentioning a son."

"I never did." She glanced at the ceiling and blinked, her voice shaky. "His name was," she caught herself, "is Ryan Nelson."

Saliva caught in Claire's throat, expanded, congealed. Consumed her from the neck up, casting her into a void of realization. Eric's sleuthing had uncovered the mother of her tormentor. *Had he, though?* she asked herself. Ryan was a common name. *But standing at the center of five women going insane* isn't *common.* The last bastion of coincidental buy-ins fell. *This* is *Ryan's mom.* The revelation stunned her into silence.

Speaking his name generated a similar effect for Emmy. She recomposed herself before continuing, granting Claire time to recover. "Even then I knew he was behind what was happening to me, what happened to my daughters. I don't know how he did it, but he was so controlling and so jealous, especially after his dad left." Emmy sounded scared, as if reliving a nightmare, but the words poured out. "He used to have a friend named Thomas, his only childhood friend. The boy acted so sweet. He complimented my cooking no matter how bad the meal turned out and told me how pretty I was in that innocent way young boys do. He even hit it off with Ryan's older sisters. One day, they stopped playing together, and when I asked Ryan he said he didn't know what happened to him." She paused. "I do wonder what became of him," she trailed off, her eyes glazing over until she shook herself back to the present, "You need to know this. Don't let me get distracted."

Startled by the outburst, it took Claire a moment to spit out, "Okay."

But Emmy was already speaking. "After Thomas stopped showing up and I gave birth to my youngest daughter, Ryan created a suite of imaginary friends. One for each of his sisters. He named them Thomas, Ted, Frank, Cameron, and Ben."

Vested in the story, the revelation of the names matching the apparitions registered as a mere blip for Claire.

"Brandon, my ex-husband, didn't like it. He told Ryan he was crazy, and he'd get in *adult* trouble if he continued. My ex didn't hit the children too hard. No worse than pops on the butt, but he screamed so fierce it scared everyone when anyone got in trouble. It didn't stop Ryan. I'd still catch him playing pretend. I never said anything because his happiest moments came with those boys, whether they were real or not, but when Brandon left, so too fled his imaginary friends. I don't know what Ryan last spoke about with his dad, but from then on he looked after me with religious conviction. Whenever I questioned him, he'd say he was doing what was best for us and not to worry. He wouldn't leave me, he said, not like Daddy."

"One by one, my daughters grew sick. Or worse." Emmy fidgeted, brimming on the edge of hyperventilation until she clasped her hands along with one giant breath. "You know that story. Den of Help supported me through it all. It became my sanctuary. I loved it so much that I volunteered, putting any free time I had into giving back. But at some point, I had to stop going. I noticed how he looked at the women there, with the same contempt he cast on his sisters. I couldn't risk anything happening, so I stopped volunteering. I lost a piece of myself after that, which is why I sought you out for therapy. I thought if you couldn't help me, then you could get me in somewhere like here.

"You were great. You're still such a lovely young woman. My Megan might've grown into someone like you if things had gone differently. But despite varying my appointments, Ryan learned about our sessions. The way the hallucinations talked, I got the feeling they were spying on me for him. One started showing up more than the others, like the spirit of my ex-husband returned, watching everything I did. He even called himself Brandon. After a while, it became too much. That was when you guided me toward long-term psychiatric care. I know you preferred I choose somewhere else, but this turned out for the best. They gave me enough drugs that weeks flew by as fast as hours. I didn't see the hallucinations anymore. After a year, they lowered my dosages. The staff told me my son had last visited three months before that. I assumed he had forgotten about me. That it was over."

Emmy leaned over, her expression as grim as the reaper's, and placed her palm on Claire's knee. "It's not over. It never will be until someone stops him. You have to find a way to stop my son. I don't know how he's doing"—she leaned back, shaking with exasperation—"what he's doing. I'm so content with life here I stopped thinking about it after the hallucinations ended."

"Your hallucinations," said Claire. "You didn't call any of them Brandon in therapy. You said one resembled your ex-husband, not that he looked similar or had the same name."

"I know. I'm sorry for keeping so much from you. I wanted to pretend I dreamed it all. The nightmare turned out to be real, didn't it? My son is a monster."

No argument here. Claire wanted to slap Emmy for hiding so many pertinent details, but would the reveal have changed anything? She never would have suspected a curse three years ago, and it wouldn't have prevented her from institutionalizing Emmy. "Do you know where he lives?"

"I don't," she hesitated. "Last I knew he lived in our old house. I can give you the address. When I think about those poor women suffering because of him, because of me, it sickens me. I won't be able to sleep for days after this."

"That wasn't our intent. We're sorry to have bothered you," said Eric. "We can leave if this is too upsetting."

Claire glared at Eric, but his focus on Emmy left her unnoticed.

"Thank you, but no. Somebody needs to know the truth, and I don't think I'll ever be strong enough to do this again. I confronted him after Tiffany, my oldest, went into shock. He fixated on her as he did with Nicole, the second oldest, before she committed . . ." Emmy cleared her throat. "He acted saintly when I asked him about it, offering unrelenting support. I believed him innocent because I wanted to, but he demanded all of my time and carried on when I paid attention to anyone else. And the more attention I devoted to my daughters, the sicker they grew. I had five other children." Shame tinged her tone. "It was impossible."

"How do you know it was Ryan?" asked Claire, seeking to assuage the piece of her still denying the truth.

"Mother's intuition, I guess? I can't prove it's him if that's what you're asking. I don't understand how he did it. Maybe he drugged their food. If so, the police never found evidence of that or other foul play."

"Did you tell the police your suspicions?"

"He was my son. I couldn't. When they found everything in order, I convinced myself I was making up stories to explain the tragedies. That is, until you got me into here." Emmy sighed. "Then I realized my last child died with Ashley."

"Do you think your son might target those women we discussed earlier?"

"I took him with me often enough that he would have known

each of them by name. If he could harm his own sisters, there's no telling where he'd stop for anyone he deemed to have stolen too much of my time. That's what it really came down to in the end."

And who served as a greater offender than the psychiatrist who admitted his mom into the hospital? Mental brush strokes painted an angry portrait of Ryan the apparition. The canvas went up in flames, and Claire's face hardened. "If he wanted you, why come after you with his cur—" She caught herself. "His attacks?"

"I was never as bad off as my daughters. I think he wanted me weak enough to leave me house-ridden, but I kept working as I could."

"That's certainly a string of strange occurrences," said Eric. "Did your daughters ever say anything negative about your son?"

"They didn't get along with him as well as they did with each other, but the only things they came to me with were handfuls of cryptic messages. Nothing I could make sense of."

Eric scratched his cheek. "I see." Which meant to Claire he certainly did not see. Without knowledge of the curse, how would he explain someone driving their whole family mad?

Her compassion eroded, and having learned what she needed, she chanced riskier questions. "Do you want to try talking to him?"

"No!" she barked, her whole body flinching. "I can't go. Can't leave. I'd rather die in here. It's safer than seeing that *man* again."

"Of course." Claire leaned back in the seat, giving Emmy more space. "One more thing. I know this is hard for you, but this is important." She stared at her former patient, who tilted her head in assent. "What years did your daughters pass or become catatonic?"

Emmy closed her eyes. They twitched until tears dropped from their corners. "Tiffany was in 2010. Nicole in 2011. Megan, 2013." She coughed. "Beth, 2014. Ashley in 2016. Ashley was such a fighter." Tears flowed freely down her cheeks as she sucked rapid inhales. "My sweet children, all gone. I'm sorry. I can't do this anymore."

"I understand. Thank you for speaking with us."

"We really appreciate this." Eric passed a judgmental glance at Claire. "I know the difficulty in opening old wounds. If you need somebody else to talk to, I'd be happy to make another visit, pro bono."

Couldn't let it go, could you? Claire ran her thumb along the meat of her palm, waiting for the scene to play out.

"Thank you, but as I said, I don't think I'll ever be able to talk about this again. Good luck. I hope this helps you save those women before anyone else gets hurt."

The psychiatrists rose from their chairs. Claire sought the pony-tailed nurse and motioned to indicate they were finished. The woman nodded but remained on her perch.

"Oh, you know what? Take this." Emmy unlatched her topaz charmed necklace and balled it up. "Ryan gave it to me as a gift after Ashley died. I could never destroy it, but I can't wear it anymore. I haven't been able to find someone to give to before now. Maybe it'll help you figure things out."

"We couldn't do that," said Claire, but Eric held out his hand to receive it. She snatched it from the air before it fell into his hands. She placed it back in Emmy's palm and curled her ex-patient's fingers around it. "It's best if you keep it. Use it as a reminder of the joy your daughters brought you. It may not seem like it, but happy memories are healthy memories. You'll feel better if you can turn that negative into a positive."

Emmy clasped the wrist of her balled hand. Her head wavered without conviction. Claire and Eric left her in her trance. On the way out, they passed a young nurse carrying medication in her direction.

"Why did you do that?" whispered Eric. "It's better for her to let go."

"It's not better for *us*."

"What do you mean?"

Claire pressed her tongue against the back of her lip. "Meet me at my house. I need to explain a few things." Perspiration wet her armpits. On the walk out, strategizing how to tell Eric the truth met ceaseless interruption over whether that last exchange had cursed her yet again.

CHAPTER 28

Eric walked back to the dining room table like a robot on auto-pilot. Next to him, Jess's downtrodden gaze cast concern at the fireplace. The two of them sat opposite Claire and Robert.

"Satisfied?" asked Claire.

"For now." Eric circled his finger on the wooden table. "It's a lot to take in, but I trust Jessica's expertise in the matter."

"You should." Robert folded his arms and leaned back as if annoyed to speak on the matter. "I don't believe in higher powers or life after death, but something inhuman attacked Claire. You don't need a professional opinion. You need eyewitness accounts, and what Jess and I saw barely makes any sense, even with Claire's explanation. It's as logical as saying bridges stay up via invisible giants."

"That's a terrible analogy," muttered Jess. She hadn't bothered to conceal the circles under her eyes.

"Whatever. You get what I mean."

"Analogies aside." Claire focused on her co-worker. "It's worth mentioning that everything I know about curses I learned from Samuel Ingetti."

"You spoke to him?"

"A few weeks ago. I worried I was hallucinating, but it didn't add up. As you pointed out some time ago, we aren't Hollywood actors treating one-in-a-million cases on a weekly basis. Dr. Ingetti gave me another avenue to pursue, even if he was an ass about it."

Eric smiled in commiseration. "He has that reputation."

"Great. We're in agreement. This is real, and it's absurd." Robert drummed his fingers on the table. "Now that we know who's behind it, what are we doing about it? I don't know how much more Claire or Jess can take."

"I'm fine." Jess tugged at the neck of her long-sleeved shirt. "Might be in a bit of shock, but what I've experienced is nothing in comparison." She pushed her lips to the side, stretching her cheek. Wide-open eyes pitied Claire.

I'm still alive, stewed Claire. *Ryan will pay for this.* She gripped a tuft of hair and tugged, considering the gamut of ways to end his terror spree.

"What are you thinking?" asked Jess, quickly adding, "We agree the police aren't much help, but that doesn't give you free rein on revenge. As much as I'm sure you'd like to, we can't kill him or anything."

She dropped her mess of hair and brushed the remaining strands behind her shoulder. "I wouldn't kill him, even if I could. It's too good for him."

Eric said, "Claire . . ."

"Don't scold me. I'll make sure he can't hurt anyone again, without putting myself or any of you in legal trouble."

Robert chuckled with an absent-minded expression.

"What's so funny?"

"If this were the seventeenth century, it wouldn't be hard to convince a village of puritans Ryan was a witch."

Claire palmed her forehead. "Really?"

"Parts of society were better back in the day."

Eric's gawking and upturned nose suggested he would've said something if he knew Robert better.

But Jess knew him plenty well. "Burning innocents as witches was part of a better society?"

"Until this weekend, I thought they were all nuts, but I'm betting they must've nabbed a few real ones."

"You're an idiot."

"This is asinine." Claire smacked the table. The reverberations ran up to her injured shoulder, drawing a wince. She was behind on her meds. "And not helpful."

Robert thumped his bicep across his folded arms. Jess massaged the back of her neck. Eric clutched his chin. Claire filled a glass of water and downed two pills from her purse.

"Can we get him to admit to killing his sisters?" asked Jess.

"That sounds good." Claire returned to her seat. "How do you propose we do that?"

"Go see him and record the conversation. Colorado is a one-party consent state. It would all be admissible."

"Wait." Eric shook his head as if he had been clocked across the face. "You want to send her into his house alone? Considering what he's done, you must realize how unsafe that is."

"Not really, but at least this way we can supply backup. If we don't come up with something, she'll try to do it on her own."

That's not a terrible idea, thought Claire, *especially compared to their earlier plans.* The problem with involving them, assuming she could even get Ryan to talk, was it carried the hazard of Eric and Jess reacting prematurely to any sign of trouble. Robert could stay level-headed to stall their panic, but she had one shot to end this. And the longer the idea lingered, the more she realized relying on a confession risked not truly ending this. She had to break him. Truthfully, she *wanted* to break him. "I've got an idea."

Jess pursed her lips. "I'm sure you do, as sure as I am it's a heroic solo effort."

"I know he's dangerous." Claire tapped her temple. "I'm not stupid."

"Then where do the three of us fit into this plan?"

"You'll be a safe distance away, in a car so he doesn't notice you. My backup, as you suggested." Claire *would* call if she needed help, but her friends hadn't suffered the curse directly. They hadn't treated her tormentor's mother for the same symptoms. Their involvement added a liability. While her patients now lived free of their curses, her slipping up could result in a whole new round. "I need to confront him by myself. He preys on the lonely, and those who aren't lonely he torments until they're withdrawn. He needs to feel in control."

"I can't believe you're considering seeing this dangerous individual alone," said Eric. "At best, he needs therapy to root out deep-seated attachment issues. At worst, he's a full-blown psychopath. That's assuming there isn't something more sinister at work."

Robert quipped, "Like Satan?"

The voice of Claire's mom whispered, *Better to be lucky than in hell in a handbasket.* She blinked herself back to the conversation.

"Perhaps. People aren't capable of creation and manifestation. That's the realm of God and angels."

"Seems like a humble home renovator proved that theory wrong."

"You're Claire's friend." Eric straightened his cuffs with a sharp pull. "Why are you joking about this? Ryan is a serious threat."

Robert put his elbows on the table. "He is a serious threat. Which is why if Claire is dead set on confronting him by herself, I want her prepared to face a demented waste of human life and not a biblical threat."

What a team Claire had assembled. While they bickered over the best way for her to confront Ryan, she schemed out a plan. At least enough of one to wing the rest. She was a psychiatrist—a job that opened people up to express their troubles. It served as the backbone of her plot, but her friends wouldn't accept the mere etchings of a plan without a reason.

Which led to Emelia Nelson's necklace. "I know how to handle Ryan. I don't want to say more in case another imaginary friend is brewing."

"Right. The necklace that should've been his." Robert nudged his chin in Eric's direction.

"Why not call Dr. Ingetti and ask?" suggested Eric, ignoring Robert's insinuation.

"It doesn't matter." Claire shrugged. "He won't definitively know one way or the other. He never does. It is or isn't, so I'll assume the worst case."

"Putting all your eggs into the basket of," Jess fumbled, "you'll call when something goes awry from the inside of a madman's home doesn't really . . . make sense."

"You suggested I visit him first."

"With the idea of stationing ourselves outside of his house, ideally with one of us coming inside with you. We don't know that these apparitions can communicate with him. Coordinating a plan *together* is worth the risk, isn't it?"

Claire's focus drifted to the fireplace. Jess meant the best and had been her lifeboat, but this was the home stretch. She owed it to her patients, and to Nancy Cathell, to take the necessary risks to put an end to this madness. It required lowering Ryan's guard, which meant acting alone. "You're right. We don't know, but does it matter? If we approach him together, what can we accomplish? In the unlikely scenario we force or trick him into confessing he killed his sisters, any competent lawyer will argue it was made under duress. We might even face trespassing charges."

"So then what are you going to do?" Jess threw her arms on the table. "Ask him to stop being such a bad guy? Convince him he's not acting in his best interests when he tortures people?"

"Isn't that our job? We've turned around dangerous individuals before."

"Sure, but those people *wanted* help. He's been trying to kill you for weeks."

Claire's faint shrug mirrored her brow raise. How could she convince her? Dr. Ingetti had made it clear that willpower fueled these psychotic attacks. It wasn't a weapon they could destroy through conventional means, even if they engineered jailing Ryan. She had to simultaneously shut him down at the source and drive him into a well-monitored institution.

"One of you two must have something to say." Jess turned to the guys. "Eric, you didn't even buy into this curse talk until half an hour ago. And Robert, you hate showing it, but you're almost as protective of Claire as you are of your son."

"I'm with you, Jessica," said Eric. "I think it's a terrible idea, but if she's set on something, we'll have to tie her up to keep her from it. I'll continue brainstorming. We all should." He toyed with his collar. "In the meantime, I'll remain optimistic. I've always respected Claire's talent. It's possible she gets through to him. I'm content in trusting her, as long as she promises to keep a phone handy."

Claire offered him a half-smile, to which he simply adjusted his glasses.

"I agree." Robert's scowl toward Eric turned into a grin at Claire. "This isn't my preference, but if we can call you, and you think you can get inside this guy's head, then go for it." He raised his index finger. "I will point out my son isn't nearly as willful as you. I can occasionally talk sense into him."

Claire chuckled, equally relieved for Robert's pausing his argument with Eric as for his support.

Jess threw up her hands and jumped out of her seat. Her mood darkened the white couch she paced around. After her third circling, she stormed back to the dining table and seized the top of the chair she had just stood from, pushing it halfway in. "Fine, you win. I think this is stupid though, so we're setting a deadline to send in the cavalry. Otherwise, I'm liable to buy a gun so I can shoot the bastard myself." If she had the strength, her grip would've torn the chair clean in two.

Claire rose and strode toward Jess. She peered into her friend's eyes and considered how these trials had eroded her high spirits. She opened her arms and hugged her.

Hands ran up Claire's back to return the embrace. "Be safe," whispered Jess.

"So now what?" asked Robert.

"Now," said Claire, slipping her hold to Jess's arm. "We all get some rest. Keep brainstorming, but the current plan is: come morning, I'm driving to his house. Anyone who wants to tail me better be ready."

"I'll call Janice," said Eric. "Tell her to inform the patients there's been an emergency. We'll figure out something." His head in the clouds indicated he was already working on that something.

"You don't have to do that."

"I do." He grounded himself with half-attention. "I entered medicine to help people, and I can think of no one I'd rather help tomorrow than you. Even if it's only in spirit."

"Thank you."

"Guess I'm calling in sick too," said Robert. "How do you know this guy will be home?"

"His mom said he worked nights, and old habits die hard." Old habits like driving people insane for two decades. The barrier of her friends overcome, a sudden anxiety fueled rapid heartbeats. Sheer exhaustion fogged her mind. Rest beckoned, but to get any sleep she needed to take her mind off the problem at hand.

"Eric, have you ever played Agricola?"

CHAPTER 29

Yes, yes, I got it. I'll call at the first sign of trouble." Claire hung up the Bluetooth call and turned at the stop sign. Phone GPS put her at ten minutes from Ryan Nelson's house. Without her friends' worries distracting her, she felt more jittery than as a college grad awaiting her MCAT results. Her foot bounced on the gas pedal, alternating between coasting and joyriding. Searching for something more concrete to focus on than her mother's malaphors and a dozen what-ifs, she focused on last night's preparations.

Insomnia had provided hours of insight into Ryan, whom she approached as if he were a patient on a return visit. She jotted down everything she knew about him: background information (his family, researched through online news articles), personality (presupposed based on his curse's alter ego and her talk with Emmy), and motivations (abandonment and complicated jealousy). She spent so long revising and staring at these notes, she could picture their penned words as clearly as if written on the windshield. The key to ending this saga permanently and non-violently lay somewhere between what she knew and what she would soon learn.

If it were even possible at all.

Did she really expect to reverse decades of deep-seated mental turmoil in an afternoon? Her plan to make a plan as she went was no plan at all. It was a fool's errand. She began drumming her fingers on her neck when a nearby voice croaked.

"Where am I?"

Claire snapped her head to the right, veering the car to within an inch of the curb. A pale, pock-marked man sat in her passenger seat, bent over at the waist; he could've been Ryan's older, gray-haired brother. She jerked her attention back to the road and straightened the car out. Her knuckles whitened on the steering wheel. She pushed the gas pedal to the floor. Five minutes to Ryan's.

"Where am I?" he asked again. He sounded lost.

This can't be happening, thought Claire. *Not again.* She ran a stop sign.

"I was at an old folks' home, sleeping peacefully. Now I'm in a car?" The man rocked up and down in his seat. "Where's Emelia? Where am I? Who are you?"

She blew through another intersection, then screeched the car to a halt. Her phone promised Ryan Nelson's house in two minutes, but . . . *Emelia? Who or what is this thing?*

"It was so nice," he said. "So peaceful. So nice. So peaceful."

Similarities between him and Ryan began and ended with their looks. This apparition better resembled a confused puppy than a homicidal maniac.

"What's," Claire started, already suspecting the answer, "your name?" She fiddled with her keys, unsure whether to run the rest of the way or finish the drive.

He chuckled as if he had heard the stupidest question ever. "Brandon," he choked through tremors of laughter.

That damn necklace.

Her dashboard registered an incoming call from Jess. Claire jammed the button to hang up.

Intense urges to throw a tantrum and pound the dashboard incited her into peeling out. Beside her, unceasing laughter provided the haunting music to which she sped. Her passenger's jovial episode subsided when she rolled to a stop in front of the Nelson house.

Gripping the car handle, body scooted to the edge of her seat, Claire suggested, "Why don't you rest here? I'll take you back to the old folks' home later."

He stared at the floor of the passenger seat, grunting to himself. Chuckling. Grunting. Chuckling. Grunting.

Leave. Get up. Go! But she remained still. If apparitions could pass through walls, what did it matter?

Brandon twisted his head in her direction, maliciousness poisoning his grin. "What if I don't want to go back?"

And he leapt at her.

Claire flung open the door, escaping just before he grabbed her. She slammed the door on his reaching arm, drawing a cry more angry than pained. She skirted around the car, watching him. He thrashed in his vehicular prison, but as she reached the sidewalk, Brandon's head slumped as if turned off. Still wary of his phasing through metal walls, she crept halfway to the house before turning her attention to it.

Cracks marred the cement leading to the front door. Small holes and animal damage defaced the single-story home's wood siding. Weeds sprouted amid patches of dirt and dead grass. Neighboring houses glittered like gold in comparison, all one story taller and two decades newer. This house bordered on condemnation.

Her phone vibrated in the pocket of her knee-length summer dress. She clicked it to silent and rubbed her forearms for warmth, regretting her clothing choice until she remembered why she picked it. Flowery patterns and big pockets hid the phone well, and the dress reflected feminine vulnerability in a way jeans couldn't. At least tights warmed her lower half.

When Claire reached the front of the house, she opened the screen and hesitated, her knuckles an inch from the door. *Are you sure about this?* Her hand answered, knocking twice.

No response.

Tires kicking up road debris came to a halt behind her. She glanced back, confirming it was Eric's Toyota Camry.

"Come on you piece of . . ." she whispered. She banged with her fist.

The door creaked open.

"Hello?"

No response.

Great—the horror cliche continued, and here she was doing her part to make it worse. She peered into the dim living room. Green carpet and a cracked leather couch reeked of the seventies. The interior looked as abandoned as the exterior.

This was so stupid of her.

She entered the house, venturing no further than her hold on the door allowed. Claire pushed it until the handle touched a closet, aiming to maximize interior visibility for her friends.

"Hello?"

The house smelled musty. The air felt heavy and warm, as if the threshold separated heaven from hell.

You should go. Run. Leave. Get out. Run away. Now. Go, yipped a voice in the back of her mind.

Claire shook her head and released the door to delve further into the house. Ryan lurked somewhere, setting her up for something. She knew she was wandering into a trap, but that's what she wanted, wasn't it? Appear weak and vulnerable to enact her plan. She only needed to survive his initial strike.

Only.

She searched the living room. Styrofoam containers and newspaper shreds littered a stained coffee table. Small piles of trash dotted the room. Open entryways offered two separate paths forward. In the kitchen to her left, plates, cups, and empty cans lay in random arrangements, filling up half of the counter space. A block of knives next to the sink drew her attention. Tempted, she ultimately rejected taking a pocket-sized blade, determining the potential legal trouble not worth it. She knew she couldn't trust herself not to use it once she saw him in the flesh.

Through the other entryway, a small room fed into a long hallway. She passed through, glancing left to find a mausoleum of a dining room. Plates and silverware lay set for two, but a blanket of dust encased them in time. A four-door hutch ran the length of the dining room wall, its windowed place settings barely visible. Even the floors showed little wear compared to the rest of the home.

He's been waiting. But for who?

She turned back to the hallway.

Four closed doors alternated sides down the corridor, ending with a fifth at the hall's end. Each felt miles apart. Claire crept on, opening the first door and confirming it didn't lock from the outside before proceeding in. Bunk beds hugged the wall. A dresser propped up pictures of the family, everyone's head blacked out except for Emelia's and presumably Ryan's at various stages of his life. His fair skin looked a shade darker than the alabaster-white tone of his cursed namesake. She checked the closet with one eye trained on the door behind her, finding only teenage girls' clothes and an assortment of high school textbooks. She left the bedroom, moving on to the next.

Between two twin beds ran a cramped, narrow space. Ryan must have shared this with one of his sisters. The comforter on the left-hand bed alternated black and crimson, a stark contrast to the other beds' lighter tones. It was also the only one unmade. Inside the closet, five toy princesses were lined up on a shelf. Claire reached for one then reeled back. Now was not the time to touch unknown objects. She retreated into the hallway.

"I know what's going on. I'm trying to help," Claire announced. She had to start building some form of trust. "Help both of us."

The halls remained silent.

Calming herself with a breath, Claire opened the next door to a narrow bathroom. She felt silly drawing the curtains to the shower. Ryan controlled the situation and knew it. She could probably sit in the living room and wait for him to make his entrance, but the motivation to press forward persisted, perhaps keeping her from fleeing the house altogether. Claire huffed. She wanted this over weeks ago.

Her pace quickened toward the fourth room: another bedroom with bunk beds. She tossed the comforters from the mattresses, blowing off steam and rationalizing that losing control would further lull him into a sense of security. The handle to the closet screeched as she turned it. Clothes hung from the closet rod. Sitting on the shelf above were bright-colored scrunchies, a pair of teal roller skates, and two small backpacks. Old versions of Monopoly and Trivial Pursuit lined the carpet floor beneath.

"I guess you're not quitting until you find me."

Claire whirled around to find Ryan aiming a handgun at her chest.

"Congrats. Your search is over."

He resembled his cursed apparition, or rather the apparition resembled *him*. He loomed a gangling half-foot above her and wore a long sweater. His haggard face looked twice the age she had estimated, hair thinned out like a chemotherapy patient. Pallid skin painted him as an anemic with a serious case of the flu.

She lifted her palms in defense. "I know what this is about and I can—"

"Shut up. You stole what was mine." Each word louder than the last. A faint scar lined his cheek.

Claire's heartbeat quickened. Her lungs sucked air to keep pace. He wouldn't shoot, would he? She leaned against the closet frame, scooting her feet close together.

Make yourself small and submissive.

She hunched her shoulders, portraying defeatism. Should she fold her arms too? No, he could interpret that as a defensive move preparing to fight. She left her torso exposed, both to Ryan and the firearm in his hand.

Ryan hobbled to the side of the room and waved his gun from Claire to the hallway.

"I've got a surprise for you. Walk on out and through the last door. I'll be *right* behind."

Despite his height, Claire could overpower him. Was his frailty the cost of creating these curses? She followed his orders, shuffling out of the room to maintain her meek facade. She intended to avoid a physical altercation, even if she could disarm him.

The once-closed door at the end of the hall opened into the master bedroom. The carpet had been ripped out, revealing a concrete floor. Black, foreign scribblings and symbols painted the ground. A queen-sized bed occupied half of the room. To her immediate right, a long black dresser with knick-knacks and accessories took up much of the remaining space. An open door near the bed led into the bathroom. The counter looked spotted with fresh blood.

"Keep walking," ordered Ryan.

Claire stepped over the threshold, onto the concrete floor. Unsure where to proceed, she continued toward the bathroom.

"Stop."

She obeyed, putting her in the center of a giant eye. She turned around, buckling her right knee intentionally. "Please don't hurt me."

Ryan chuckled. "I don't hurt people. They hurt themselves when their brains make them do crazy things. I'm merely an assistant."

What did that mean? How could she use it? He seemed more talkative, and she didn't know how many chances he would offer. "I think I can help."

"I don't need any help."

How was he not sweltering in this stifling room? Claire's thighs sweat from tights that barely provided enough warmth outside. "I talked to your mom. She told me about you. Said if I found a way to help, you could be together again."

Ryan peered at her, tapping the side of the gun with his finger. "I don't want to hear your psycho babble. That's what stole Mommy from me in the first place. Besides, that's all in the past." His nostrils flared. "What I want is for you to make amends."

"How?"

"I worked so hard on all of those gifts, gifts made specifically for you and the others. Gifts to enjoy until the day you all died. Except *you* were never going to die. I made sure you would wind up battered, bruised, and mentally shattered. I wanted you to follow Mommy's path into the hospital. Then you had to ruin it, you spoiled brat. All you ever do is take. Just like my sisters."

He's getting too worked up. "I know I'm selfish. My mom also left me for a hospital. The same one as your mom, in fact. That's why I wanted to help. I feel guilty."

"The same hospital, huh?" Ryan chuckled, shaking his head at the ground for a moment until it shot back up. "You know what? You can help. At first, I didn't comprehend my luck with you coming here. I considered escaping through the bathroom window while you snooped around, until I understood my fortune at your arrival. What better way to deliver your next gifts than in person? It's been. So long," he savored the words, "since I've witnessed. My creations at work."

"More gifts?" Claire's voice caught in her throat.

"That's right." He sidestepped his way along the empty nearby wall. "There's a watch and a glass turtle on the dresser. I'm *gifting* them to you."

Claire examined the objects on the wooden surface. An analog watch, inset into a stainless steel band, ticked with an occasional crackle. The hand-blown glass turtle beside it looked as if retrieved from a dumpster, smudges tarnishing its fine craftsmanship. Sorrow and darkness emanated from the relics, worming a sickness inside of her based on appearance alone. She didn't *have* to pick them up. He stood five feet away. She could dive for his legs, limiting the chance of his shooting vital organs. Then what? She couldn't shoot him inside of his hom—

"What's taking so long?" Ryan griped. "I tweaked those gifts to perfection. For you. We're linked now. Like me and Mommy once were. Think of yourself as her replacement. Though you'll never reach her greatness, I think we can find other areas for you to excel in."

His veiled threat reinforced his fragile mindset. Fighting back wasn't the answer. She had planned for another solution, and it had worked so far.

Mostly.

Fear still took its toll in the face of reason.

And she lacked the final piece of the puzzle she had pinned her hopes on finding.

"I'm sorry." She almost collapsed walking to the dresser, her once-feigned feebleness no longer enacted by her own volition. Doubt overwhelmed her mind as stress did her body. This plan was foolish, utter nonsense. Curses set out to haunt her once again, seemingly by twice the effect. How could this end with anything but her . . . ?

Wait. The watch was perfect.

Claire wrapped each hand around a *gift*. She picked them up and turned back toward Ryan. "Now what?"

"Now, we wait." He smiled like the devil striking a bargain.

CHAPTER 30

*L*ook *small. Look weak. Look helpless.* Her future depended on Ryan feeling in complete control. "What's going to happen? Claire asked.

"I think you've got an idea." Ryan rested the handgun's body against his stomach. "Either way, you won't have to wait long to find out."

"What do you mean?"

"You deserve something special." Her tormentor caressed the pistol's barrel. "That's what I've prepared."

"Why are you doing this?" Claire licked moisture onto her lips. She had him where she wanted him, overconfident and seemingly in charge, but anxiety festered over his implications, drying her mouth and eyes.

"All I wanted was my mommy to myself. I had that until you. You say you can bring her to me, but all your types ever do is lie and collect your money. People like you couldn't help my sisters. I gave them five tries. No one figured it out," he snorted. "They couldn't help them, and you won't be able to help yourself."

"But I did figure it out." She stated matter-of-factly, bereft of emotion which might sway his mood.

"Only because it was your life on the line. That's the only time it matters, isn't it?"

Claire looked at the floor, stooped in faux defeat. She had already chosen her words but gave him time to gloat. "You worked so hard on your gifts. You wanted me to find you, didn't you?"

Ryan's lips stretched into a broad grin. "I wanted to see if anyone could figure out how I brought my childhood friends to life. I'll give you half-credit."

"And you brought your father to life for your mom."

Ryan fingered the trigger. Claire's breath caught. His face twitched and twitched again before answering. "I brought him to life for *me*. To teach her a lesson. To show her how good she had it before she tried to hide from me in therapy."

"Did bringing your friends or your father to life tire you out more?"

He glanced toward the master bathroom. "Neither compared to what I made for you."

Claire's chest tightened. She reassured herself that his vengeance-fueled obsession gave her the upper hand. "And you used this old watch for it." She lifted it so it faced Ryan. Flared nostrils clued her in to its significance. "Was it exhausting finding a watch similar to your father's?"

"It's *his* watch," he snarled.

Better than expected. "Do you remember what time he left you?" Claire counted on firmly rooted anger and overconfidence to keep him talking.

He studied the watch. "2:35 p.m. He tried to hit the road before I got home from school, but my teacher had *mysteriously* fallen ill." He chuckled "They let us out of school early. She was such a fun playmate." A combination of a sneer mixed with lament stirred déjà vu, but he didn't leave Claire time to place it. "Dad sure was surprised to see me. I believed his lie when he said he'd be back later. He left me stranded with a few words of wisdom and a bunch of sisters who picked on me." He wrinkled his nose. "Do you treat people for being bitches?"

How could she keep his attention trained on the watch? "Time is important. What time did you get revenge on your sisters?"

"How should I remember? I didn't have time for the time," he cackled and lowered his chin. "I was too busy keeping my sisters in line. Even at twelve I did better than my dad. As if he ever cared about me or anyone besides himself. Mommy was the only one who mattered."

"Did you or your mom get him this watch?"

"Neither, you dumb bitch." Ryan wagged the gun at Claire. She winced, but he paid her no mind. "My uncle gave it to him as a gift when I was born. Apparently, Dad didn't want to keep anything from his past life. What do you make of that, doctor bitch?"

"He made the wrong decision, but maybe this watch is the secret to making amends."

"It sure is for you. Soon, you'll wish for death. Fate is tick-tock o'clock."

Fear relieved Claire of her wits. She gulped, but her mind recovered and clawed against defeat. "How much more time will it take?"

"Oh, I don't—"

"Tell me the time. How much more time?" She found no difficulty in sounding frantic.

Her plea drew his gaze back to the watch. While calculating in silence, a grin crept across his face. "No longer than a half-hour. We won't have to wait past noon."

"That's so soon. It must have tired you out creating such powerful gifts." She clenched her abs and locked her hips, apprehension budding as she prepared for the hardest part. "All that strenuous effort didn't seem to harm the watch. It looks as good as new."

Ryan grunted and extended his neck for a better vantage. "Sure does, except for that one scratch you're too blind to catch. I loved the idea of giving it back to my dad with a special surprise, but I'll gladly settle for giving it to you."

"Do you notice something off about the minute hand?"

His brows furrowed at its glass face.

"Can you see it? Maybe your muscles need rest. Your mom told me something at the hospital, but first, what time is it?"

"11:35. Not much longer. What did she say?" His head started to lift.

"Look at the watch. I need to know how much longer I have so I can tell you in time," said Claire, drawing a smirk from Ryan as his focus dropped back down. "Your mommy said time is important, it's all we have. Think about what she said. Imagine you're back together with her, here in your house."

"Back together with Mommy. Here in my house." Ryan's eyes glazed over.

"You have won. You've earned your revenge. You feel contented, able to rest easily."

Blissful reverie slackened his facial muscles. Arms hung limp at his side, the gun more an extension of his hand than a weapon. "I'm glad my dad left. I have Mommy all to myself."

"She's yours, in a room all alone. All you have to do is walk to her. She's only five steps away. Can I guide you to her?" He seemed as calm and relaxed as he would ever be, and not much time remained.

"Yeah, do that. She's the one that matters. I want her to give me a hug and say she's sorry."

"Listen carefully, my dear." Claire imitated Ms. Nelson's warm cadence, almost choking on its sweetness. "Five steps away is a closed door. Behind it sits your mom, waiting to show you her love. You take your first step toward her. You feel calmer, knowing what lies behind that door."

Tick-tock. Ryan's breathing slowed.

"You take your second step forward. Comforted by the door, you allow your subconscious to take control." Could she handle speaking to his subconscious? What if it wanted her dead instead of tortured? Would this charade end with a bullet in her head?

Tick-tock.

"You take your third step toward her. You embrace the desires of self, what you seek most from her. You desire love, and you will discover what love means."

Tick-tock. His brows evened and mouth opened in relaxation.

"You take your fourth step toward her. You're almost there. You begin to imagine the warmth of her touch."

Tick-tock. Fingers curled in and out of the palm of his free hand.

"You take your fifth step toward the door. You open it and are filled with the serenity of love. You feel the warmth of your mommy's embrace."

He looked in her direction but focused on something beyond

her. She tested him, swaying her head from side to side. Satisfied with his vacant stare, she led him deeper.

"Everything in the world disappears besides you and your mommy. Your mommy tells you to breathe deep. It's okay now. It's only a matter of time until you're with her forever."

Hypnagogic jerks indicated entry into a hypnotic state.

In response, Claire's back straightened. Muscles in her arm burned, fraying like a rope from steadying the watch. "Your thoughts pour out to your mom. She knows what you did, you did for love. She accepts you. Describe what you see."

"She's smiling. Sitting down and watching me like when I was a child playing with my friends."

"How does it make you feel?"

"Good. Great. At home."

"What about the homes on Memory Lane?"

"A fun diversion. Nothing compared to the real thing. It was so easy." Prideful bliss stretched across Ryan's lips. "Showing up after they moved in. Offering cheap services in the form of workers I had cured of demons that I created. Giving the kid the toy. My fake credentials, my fake name."

"It was so easy," Claire repeated for his subconscious to feel heard. "What do you remember about that family?"

"The dad wasn't sticking around. I've seen his type. The mom needed her boy, the boy needed his mom, so they were fine." Ryan growled.

"What's wrong?" Claire dragged her thumbnail over the ridges of the watch band, textured sounds to keep him entranced.

"I felt jealous of the boy having his mom look after him. It's not fair that *she* left me."

"What is fair? What do you deserve?"

"We deserve to be together," he fumed. Animalistic features overtook his face. "We're the only ones for each other. I'll kill any-one who comes between us, who thinks to take her away. She's mine. I'm the only one who's worthy enough. I won't be forgotten in a herd of women all vying for her attention. I won't walk home from school while my sisters get car rides after cheerleading practice. Band practice. Soccer practice. I won't be separated by them or by old hags crying about their failings. They all want to take my mommy, but I won't let them. I won't be alone, not ever again. With her, I have everything I need: my mommy and my friends, friends that I'll share with the world. I'll share them with those who need it most, the ones so lonely they think they can steal *her* away. They'll never be lonely again. Never. Not until they're dead, dead in the ground, and away from me and Mommy forever."

Repulsion sparked fires in Claire's chest and spread to her limbs. She stilled the desire to slap him across the face, worsening the stiffness between her biceps and forearms. "What does the glass turtle mean to you?" she asked.

"It's for Mommy." Ryan spoke calmly, insightfully. "She said she would always protect me."

"And what does the watch mean to you?"

"The last moment I was happy and safe, the time I want to return to. When my parents had time for me."

"You can take control of these things. You can return to the past. Do you want to know how?"

"Yes." Anger infected his voice.

"Hold out your hands." Claire raised the turtle up beside the watch. "I will give you the means."

"I shouldn't accept," he said, now serene. "They're not meant for me." He licked his lips. "They're meant for someone else."

Just fucking accept it, you brat. "This is why you must accept them. They're meant for someone else now, but to return to the moment you were happy and safe and your parents had time for you, you must take them for yourself. You must return to when they were yours."

"I want to accept. I want to accept." Ryan slid the handgun into his waistband. He lifted his hands, palms facing upward, and chanted, "But I shouldn't accept." Even in a trance, he knew their dangers. It signaled an inner discord threatening to break her hypnotic hold.

Claire deposited the watch and glass turtle in Ryan's hands, gauging his muted reaction before releasing them completely. "I give these gifts to you," she said, unsure if the words *give* and *gift* held some ritualistic power necessary to transfer the curse. She drew her head back, worried the objects would snap him into awareness.

The trinkets sat cradled in the valley of his palms. He stood like a statue. Sweat percolated under the seams of Claire's dress. At last, he curled his fingers around the objects. His right thumb stroked the smooth underbelly of the glass turtle, every caress widening the smile across his face.

"Do you still see your mommy?" asked Claire.

"She's right next to me. It's just us, like you said it would be. It's all I wanted."

"That's what she wanted too. Now you need to lock them away so you can stay with Mommy forever. Do you want to stay with her forever?"

Rage resurfaced. "Yes."

As the monosyllabic reply fell from the air, Claire noticed the defensiveness with which he spoke. Fear over losing his mother heated his vitriol. "It will be as you wish. Lead me to where you can keep these *gifts* safe," she said, finding confidence in her successful use of the term earlier.

Ryan continued rubbing the glass turtle as he rotated toward the bedroom's entrance. He exaggerated his first step over a squiggly sigil on the ground, landing with his heel on the master bedroom's threshold. His second step began his march down the hallway.

Claire followed his exact path. With his back turned, she snuck her phone from her dress. She held it near her chin, maintaining peripheral sight of Ryan while she texted Jess, *Need help. Call the police.* Her friends could use the heads-up to formulate a reason for camping outside of the house. She also needed a little more time and doubted she'd get another chance to safely use her phone. She pocketed the device as Ryan rounded the corner into the dining room.

He beelined it past the dusty table and its place settings, crouching at the hutch's bottom cabinetry. Claire slipped behind him to watch his subconscious work. Her hypnotized 'patient' looped the watch around his thumb, freeing his fingers to slide open the drawer. In it sat an unremarkable, small metal lockbox. Its key already pierced the lock, twisted open. He raised the lid. His hands hovered with the watch and turtle over a space filled with jewelry, dolls, and birthday cards. Claire's eyes grew wide.

Those must be . . . his sisters' . . .

"My safe space," he whispered, repeating the phrase over and over as he lowered the trinkets into the box. He positioned them in a seemingly intentional pattern that Claire couldn't understand. Then he closed the lid. "It's all safe. Now I can be with you forever, Mommy."

"That's right," Claire reassured. "Would you like to go to her bedroom where it's nice and comfortable?"

"I'd like to go back to her bedroom, where it's nice and comfortable." Ryan rose, leaving the cabinet drawer open, and walked back to the hallway foyer.

This time she didn't follow. She waited. Once his footsteps came to a halt, she bent down to the open drawer, locking the box and withdrawing the key. She considered moving the container, but the possibility of a half-dozen curses permeating its cheap metal cautioned her against it. Standing, Claire pushed the drawer closed with her foot and dropped the key in her pocket.

Then she walked to the living room to wait some more. She sat on the cleanest section of the couch. Images of *potential* futures flipped and flashed through her mind.

The police barging in. Ryan's screams echoing down the hall, signaling the maturation of his cursed progeny. The first step toward institutionalization.

His waking. Pressing the cold pistol tip against her skull. Pulling the trigger.

But the worst of the three made the most frequent appearance: a failed plan cursing her twice over, set to blow like a bomb at any moment.

CHAPTER 31

J ess drove Claire a half-mile outside of the neighborhood before breaking the silence. "Want to talk about what happened?"

Shrieks echoed in Claire's mind. Screams of fury and anguish. Halfway through replaying the police's confrontation with Ryan, she managed to clear her head. "Not right now. I'm going to call Dr. Ingetti and explain the past few days. One recollection is my limit for the day."

Jess nodded. She had driven Claire's car before, but never with the level of care she demonstrated today. Her turns edged the curb. She halted for every stop sign. The first instances bothered Claire, but as their taciturn journey continued, she appreciated the time for reflection.

Daydreams of Eric and Robert yelling at one another on their way home morphed into them celebrating her newfound safety. Filmlike visualizations of apparitions chasing her patients swirled into final sessions with them, proclaiming them cured. Ryan's spittles of rage and madness as the police dragged him out of his home . . . turned to blackness. Calming blackness, tuning out the world. Halfway home, she realized she sat where Brandon had manifested a few hours earlier and stiffened.

Jess noticed the unease with either a spying eye or a well-timed check-up. "Are you okay?" Fiddling with the gear stick, she glanced over three times before Claire answered.

"I'm fine. Stop looking at me like that."

"Like what?"

"You know what you're doing. You're as bad as Eric."

Jess looked offended. "Please tell me I haven't gotten that bad." Another triplet of glances. "Come on."

Claire's grin grew wider with every look. "I hate to say it, but there's no hope for you. You're doomed to a life of eternal vigilance and overreaction."

The slit of a smile curled on Jess's lip. "That's too bad for you."

"It really is. And I thought my life couldn't get any worse."

Both of them broke into fits of laughter, followed by an abrupt squeal of tires. Jess looked up in time to brake before hitting a car at a red light. She posed with her best oops face, and their uproarious merriment renewed, the triviality of a fender bender relieving them of the past few weeks' horrors. The moment passed, the light turned green, and the drive continued.

Memories of Emmy's apparition returned. Claire warded off ensuing anxiety by digging a thumbnail into her palm and tracing her lifelines. When she had built enough confidence, she told herself, *It's over. Brandon was a fluke. It's over.* The cycle of digging and encouragement continued until Jess again broached idle conversation.

"We should visit a winery this weekend."

Claire snapped to the present. Her hands dropped to her lap. "You want to visit a winery in the beer mecca that is Denver?" Rick's frothy grin came to mind, followed by her last session with Nancy Cathell, eliciting a window stare to avoid sharing unprocessed emotions.

"First, I want *us* to visit a winery. Second, *I* want to visit Sonoma, but we're off season. Third, wine is good in *any* city. Robert will be in. You should invite Eric too. He looks like he could use a vacation."

"Because he never takes one," Claire huffed. Neighborhood sidewalks passed by. Uncertain feelings were pushed down until a safe time came to indulge them.

"Then I think your best friend's provided another winning idea."

Claire nodded absentmindedly. Whether or not they'd go through with it, the suggestion to visit a winery settled her. Her future had felt so murky, so defined by momentary struggles, she hadn't planned for anything past survival. As a psychiatrist, she should have known better.

Bitter self-admonishment coated her tongue, but instead of indulging it, she swallowed. *It's over. Brandon was a fluke. It's over. That's all that matters.* With something to look forward to, with the belief she'd *live*, the reassurance finally took hold. Muscles eased, as much as her knots and aching shoulder allowed. Thoughts wandered to more personal interests. To the forefront came the mystery of Rick's existence. On a hunch, she did something she hadn't done for two weeks—she texted him.

And received an almost immediate reply.

I'm dating someone else now. Sorry. Please don't contact me again.

Claire's jaw dropped. Her mind went blank.

Jess again put her talent to task and peered over. "What's up?" Her careful driving made a lot more sense.

Considerations of teasing her for emulating Eric's protective nature came and passed. "I texted Rick. He texted back. I think he thinks I'm a lunatic, and I don't think the Rick who saved my life is the same Rick I just texted."

"That's a whole lot of Ricks." Jess shook off obvious confusion. "What does it mean?"

"I don't know." Claire tapped the phone into her palm. "But I'm about to talk to someone who might."

CHAPTER 32

R yan didn't cry out until police threw open the glass screen," Claire recounted this morning's finale to Dr. Ingetti. "The bang, the boots on the ground, and their shouting snapped him to awareness. I don't know if he cried out from anger at being tricked or the curse taking hold, but I think by the time they cuffed him, he knew what I had led him to do. Hypnotic suggestion normally takes days to recall when broken forcefully, but he looked at me with knowing hate when the police dragged him out."

Claire leaned back in her dining room chair, glancing at Jess playing with her phone on the couch. "In any case, his violent, visceral reaction gave the police all the reason they needed to take my side. With Ryan in custody, two responding officers sat me down, first scolding me for visiting my stalker's house alone, then asking questions to clarify my story. I told them all the truth they would believe, leaving out mentions of the cursed trinkets. I closed by suggesting someone perform a psychiatric evaluation before jailing him." She popped her lips. "That sums it up."

An awkward quiet tainted the line. He had yet to say anything since demanding to know why she had called. Was he even listening?

If so, he was less likely to ignore a direct question.

"What my friends and I want to know is—is it over?"

"It sounds like it," Dr. Ingetti sighed as if she kept him from more pressing matters.

This guy. "It sounds like it? What does that mean?"

"You found a way to spin the curse against him. Now he'll slowly devolve into insanity until it kills him. Highly professional."

His takeaway was that *she* was the bad guy? She grinned wide. He'd love this then. "I don't think that's true."

"How's that?"

"Remember his mother from the psychiatric hospital? She's healthy despite the curse remaining active, as evidenced by my touching her necklace and transferring it to me. Hopefully temporarily." Her not-so-subtle request for reassurance went unheeded. "Modern medicine continues to stymie the curse, limiting her periods of awareness but keeping her safe. It means the end Ryan meant for me doesn't have to happen to him either."

"Ah, yes—your brushing incident."

Claire massaged her temple, racking her brain for a memory of the term, finding none. "Brushing incident?"

Jess turned around, propping her head up on the back of the couch.

"It occurs when one touches a cursed object bound to another without taking ownership," Dr. Ingetti said, like a professor forced to teach kindergarten. "Depending on several factors, one can interact directly with another's curse."

Claire pulled the phone away from her head and mimed crushing it. Jess bit her lip; her cheeks puffed out and her chest rattled in silent laughter. The return of her friend's cheerfulness countered Claire's annoyance. "But it's not permanent?"

"Not if you didn't take her necklace. Then it would be called something besides brushing."

She shook her head, wondering whether to call him a bastard over the phone or merely continue thinking it.

"Now explain why this curser's manifestations won't kill him."

Claire's head tilted down, taken aback. She had captured his interest after all. "Administration of a heavy dosage of medication to Emelia Nelson has prevented her cursed apparition from fully taking form for three years. However, as we know from my *brushing* incident, the curse remains active. Ms. Nelson's initial sedation lasted one year. Doctors should have weaned her off prior to that. As she is still medicated, it's safe to assume recurrent episodes resulted from lowering her dosage past a certain point. This leads me to believe the curse exists in a manner akin to schizophrenic hallucinations, essentially residing in one's mind. Judging by Brandon's groggy state in my car, medicine affects the apparition as well, furthering my theory."

Jess covered her mouth. Facial muscles moved with an *oh my god* rhythm.

Claire had no idea what for, and the priest's prompt response didn't offer the opportunity to think about it.

"Brandon?"

"Emmy's apparition. The one who represents, and is named after, Ryan's father."

"Yes, of course," said Dr. Ingetti, as if he had been listening attentively the whole time and simply forgot. "So you're saying that the curse, if treated promptly, responds to sedatives?"

"Yes, those and antipsychotics. Perhaps something with an amnesiac effect such as lorazepam to dull the recurrent horrors. It's unclear whether the initial prescriptions proved unnecessarily strong or actually contributed to weakening the apparition, allowing current dosages to keep it at bay."

"Interesting. I'll make a note of that in my research." He sounded disappointingly unruffled, but his tone *did* soften. "How can you guarantee that he ends up in a hospital and not a jail?"

"I can't, but any competent lawyer will mount a not guilty by reason of insanity defense. It should help his case that as his victim, I'll press for his admittance into a state institution. They'll watch for sharp objects to prevent self-harm, which seemed part of his ritual. And they'll treat him for a psychotic breakdown as they did his mother, sedating him until they find the right mixture to allow some coherency. Either way, nurses would closely monitor him, which means the chances of creating new curses, *if* he can somehow overcome these, is near zero. If all goes well, he'll live out the remainder of his days, unable to hurt anyone ever again."

"At some point, Dr. Rossi, I have to wonder—is this a better life for him than letting the curses kill him?"

Stunned by the usage of her title, she stumbled over the rest of what she'd heard. "Is a priest asking me whether someone is better off dead or locked away? Isn't life sacred to you?"

"I'm not asking to suggest what's right. I'm asking for you. You're condemning him to a life of torment or near-comatose sedation. God's answer is clear, but do *you* feel you've chosen the ethical path?"

"I don't know." Poetic justice held a certain allure. Ryan had earned his torment and much more, but his life now served a simpler purpose: keeping her out of a murder investigation. "I can't decide. All I know is if he runs free, he poses an untraceable threat to the world. This was the best way I could think of to handle the situation."

"That is fair. Many in your shoes would disregard his life, but such views endanger both parties. It's good you've given it thought. I may consult with you on future curses if that's acceptable."

Claire stared at her phone like a slab of hieroglyphics. She toyed with spouting off a *fuck you*, but the consideration of helping someone against struggles all too familiar changed her mind. "That's fine."

"Good. I can't say I entirely approve of how you've handled everything. The course of action dictated by the church is to burn all such artifacts. Passing them onto others muddles morality, as you have discovered. While I may not approve, I understand the reasoning."

"Does that mean this all stays between us?"

"All of our conversations remain confidential, as long as I hear no signs of physical danger from you." An annoyed undertone resurfaced. "Are we done?"

Tired of his arrogant attitude, the word *yes* danced on her lips. In response, nagging repeats of Rick's text message played in her mind, dictated in his voice. The small key in her pocket grew to the weight of a brick. She rolled her eyes and spat it out. "I texted Rick before I called you, the first time since he told me his phone broke. He said he was dating someone else, sorry, and please don't contact him again. It doesn't make sense. The last time I saw him he dove into a fire to save me. He wasn't real. He couldn't have been. My friends were as blind to him as they had been to the apparition attacking me. Could I have dated a real person and then conjured an alternative version of them in my mind? If so, how did my *imagination* interact with the curse?"

"Never heard of that. It sounds more of a question for someone of your caliber. If you discover anything, please let me know."

Why did the supposed curse expert's lack of knowledge continue to surprise her? She rapped her fingernails on the dining table. "Fine. Final question. I took the key to the lockbox holding Ryan's cursed objects. Is that going to bite me in the ass?"

"Unlikely. I've never encountered a curse permeating and transferring through a container, much less through a key."

"Have you ever encountered someone who created a dozen curses?"

"No, but my point stands. I'd worry more about the police searching for evidence than yourself. A missing key won't stop them from breaking the box open."

She had thought about that. Detective Kline wanted to speak with her once she felt ready. She had considered excuses to ward him off the box's contents without sounding crazy but came up empty. Best case scenario, the district attorney agreed to Ryan pleading insanity. If they didn't need evidence, they wouldn't search his house. Given Ryan's affinity toward his creations, that might work in favor of convincing him to agree to—

"Is there anything else, Dr. Rossi?"

Rake the ashes 'til they're dust. The last words of maternal wisdom spoken a week before her mom's heart attack, delivered with measured finality, as if she knew the end was approaching. Despite the mixed metaphor, the interpretation seemed one of the clearer ones: look back once and move on. Easier said than done.

"No, I think that's it."

"Good. Congratulations on ridding yourself of the curse. Call again if you require my help."

Help? Don't flatter yourself. She sighed. He *had* pointed her on the right path. "Thanks," she said and hung up. She chucked the phone on the table and stared at it, clasping fingers behind her neck.

Jess interrupted the blissful silence. "You done?"

Claire filled her lungs with earned freedom, then looked up. She recalled her friend's animated expression from earlier. "Yep. What's up?"

"I know who Rick is. Or was." Jess bounced in her seat. "You told me so yourself. You basically told it to the priest."

Claire's grasp on her neck slipped to her cheeks. Blood vessels pounded against her skull. Her mind felt like a hollow mess. "I did?"

"You did. You created him," Jess paused, "and he protected you. It hit me when you told the priest about your ex-patient's apparition. The curse is mental, right? You effectively created a defense against it like an antibody, the foundations of which happened to have been based on an ex-date. Alongside a human version of Rick existed another, strictly within the confines of your mind."

After a long silence, Claire asked, "But how?"

Jess shrugged. "I'm a psychiatrist, not a wizard. Weren't you researching something along those lines when this first started? Now that you're not fighting for your life and scaring your friends in the process, you can set aside some time to figure it out."

Maybe, but not tonight. She buried the proliferation of ideas with thoughts of a pillow-soft bed. "About that." Claire yawned, covering her mouth. "Do you mind sleeping here for one more night?"

Her friend smiled. "Sure, on one condition."

Claire shrugged to say whatever she wanted was hers.

"We go to the store, and you buy me a comforter. I'm tired of you stealing the blankets."

Claire laughed until Jess had enough and raised her eyebrows.

"I'm serious."

Through breaths of a final few chuckles, Claire said, "You got it."

"Okay," Jess trailed off with an expression which either questioned Claire's sanity or suggested an overdue need for sleep.

Whatever the case, she knew she'd feel better in the morning.

CHAPTER 33

Amy Alba lacked a single planning bone in her body. She showed up an hour after Claire's first day back at work to ask for help with watching Brad. Not later this week, not tomorrow, not later this evening.

Now.

Detective Kline was scheduled to show up in the next hour and probably didn't want a child around to hear his questions. Amy pleaded—she and her husband were scheduled for after-hours marriage counseling and *needed* that appointment. She apparently had come over earlier to ask, but no one answered.

Because Claire was at work.

Skepticism questioned whether Amy had asked anyone else. Brad's eager expression supported the notion. She reflected that two months ago, she had fought with all of her strength to bar their entry into her home. Today, affinity for the child and a dose of sympathy tore down her guard. She let the boy in, designating his usual spot on the wooden floors near the couch to play with his toys.

Brad occupied himself for fifteen minutes, with occasional starry-eyed gazes, before he asked, "Dr. Rossi, you're going to be okay, right?" He settled on a downcast stare.

Claire leaned over to take a sip of her adult juice. Berries and oak folded around tannins on the meat of her tongue. "Why wouldn't I be?"

He shrugged. "I don't know." He played with his toys with the enthusiasm of doing his homework. "I made you sick."

"Hey."

After registering the message, Brad looked up.

"You didn't make me sick." Glass clinked against glass as Claire set her wine down on the coffee table. "Besides, do I look sick now?"

"No." Dejection hollowed Brad's response.

"Brad, I don't blame you for my getting sick. You're a good kid."

"Really?" The annoying twinkle in his eyes returned. Good kid but still a kid.

"Really."

"So," said Brad, kneeling and grasping at the cushions more than Claire preferred. At least his hands appeared clean. "What happened to your pretty friend and the one without any hair?"

The one without any hair? She laughed until she bordered on tears. "Dr. Diaz, the pretty one, is returning to work. She's a teacher."

"She must have a lot of homework to make up for her students."

"That she does." The time off would hurt her professionally. Claire owed her big, but Jess had yet to bring it up. Rejecting nights out on the town was a thing of the past. Maybe she could inspire a few more weekend wine getaways instead. "The one without any hair," Claire chuckled. "Mr. Scholz. He's back at work too. Has a boy about your age. His name is Matthew. You should play with him sometime." Robert would love that given his initial interaction with Amy.

"Do you think my mom will let me?"

"I do." If Amy wanted to continue using Claire as a last-minute babysitter, a few compromises were heading her way.

"If everybody is working, does that mean I won't see you as much?"

"For a little while." Claire looked away from Brad, grimacing at the crack on the coffee table. She'd have to replace it once work settled into its new normal. "My co-worker is taking a break starting tomorrow, so I'll be working extra."

"That sounds boring."

Claire smiled. "It can be, but I enjoy my job. It's very . . . routine."

"Why is he taking a break?"

"You know how you get summer vacation? Sometimes adults

need long breaks too." Hours equivalent to part-time work flew by for Eric in providing second opinions for Claire's cursed quintet. Those efforts turned into a second job following the hospital attack. Then, after her final ordeal with Ryan, he had insisted on covering her patients for a full week. The time away from his family coupled with his earlier failed vacation imploded his marriage. Its savior lay in a three-week getaway, *without* books or computers. She didn't know how he'd survive.

Brad's hands struggled to stay on the couch as he adjusted from kneeling to sitting cross-legged. "That makes sense. Summer can get boring though, and sometimes going to school is fun. I hope he doesn't get bored on his break."

"I can relate." Claire patted Brad's hand. Psychiatry had always intrigued her, but work had never sounded so blissful.

When the knock came at her door, she reeled. Memories of Mrs. Cathell's funeral and her own apparition's final assault over-whelmed her, freezing her lungs until reason thawed them into res-piration. Curses lacked the politeness to knock, and Kline had his appointment. Raps beat at the wood again, igniting a follow-up de-sire to yell, *come back later*. Talking to Brad about life settling into normalcy eased her tensions better than drinking wine. The detec-tive threatened to ruin that.

"Who's that?" asked Brad.

But the police wanted this over with as much as she did. Best not to delay the process. "I'll be right back." Claire motioned for Brad to stay put, then walked to the door, opening it before the detective knocked again. Cool air swept in, countering the hard work of her heater.

Detective Kline wore the same black suit as always, but today's purple tie added a regal quality that, when combined with his goatee, exemplified authority. Much better than his penchant for the stuffy navy material. The detective's grip ran down the length of his tie, straightening it out. "Hello, Dr. Rossi. Do you mind if I come in?"

Porch flooring creaked as Claire stepped outside. She tugged the door handle until its lock clicked shut. Her hands hung clasped at her waist. "Actually, is it possible to talk outside? I'm babysitting my neighbor's kid and would rather him not hear any of this."

"Sure, I understand." Kline pinched a notepad from the inside of his pocket, complete with a pen clipped to the first few pages. "Do you want to grab a coat first?"

"I'm fine." Alcohol and misplaced agitation warmed her well enough.

A suspicious stare challenged her candor. "Alright. I'll get this over with so you can go back inside. You told the officers who responded to the scene at the Nelson house that you suspected Ryan Nelson of stalking and assaulting you, correct?"

"That's right."

Kline pointed the clicky end of his pen at Claire. "Then why did you visit his house alone?"

"I told all of this to the officers."

"As I'm sure you're aware, live accounts and written accounts vary."

She didn't mind telling him so much as worry he might catch an omission. Annoyance crept into her voice until she smothered it with measured speech. "I didn't know what he looked like until I got there. Originally, I went to his house to investigate a coincidence discovered by talking to my patients." She had excluded Eric's name from the discovery to simplify the subject. "It turned out the coincidence was bigger than expected."

"What coincidence was that?"

"A group of patients suffering from similar afflictions spent time at a non-profit which coincided with another former patient of mine. My co-worker and I visited the woman last Sunday. The conversation indicated her son may have had something to do with the problems at hand. When he answered the door, I recognized him as the man stalking me."

"The mother being Emelia Nelson?"

Claire hoped she concealed her surprise. "How'd you know?"

"I'm a detective." While scrawling notes, Kline added, "Your coincidence was big enough that I would have investigated—had you called me."

Claire shrugged her shoulders with her hands wide, feigning ignorance without suggesting disinterest. "If I could do it all over again and not have had a gun pointed at my head, I would've."

"Fair enough. And the name of the non-profit?"

"Den of Help."

"Thanks." Kline tapped the notepad with his pen. "I'll follow up with you on that later. For now, I want to build up as much of a case as possible against Ryan Nelson. You said he may have been involved with your patients' problems. Do you think he stalked them as well?"

Concern for her patients stirred a defensive delay. The descriptions of their apparitions differed too much from Ryan's appearance. Calling them to testify in court threatened them in multiple ways. Their reliving of traumatic events weighed on her as heavily as attorneys poking holes in their accounts. Wouldn't her testimony suffice to put Ryan away?

Kline chuckled like a farmer watching city folk tending crops. "I've seen that look before." He was sharp. Only seconds of consideration lapsed before calling her out. "We can come back to this later. Stalking's not a big charge, but it'll help us build a case for the DA. Probably don't even need them to testify—just answer a few questions. Plus, we already have contact with Gabrielle Capers. Assault or attempted murder is more of what we're after."

"I'll get back to you after I've had time to examine my patients." The surviving members of the cursed quintet all had appointments coming up in the next week. Plenty of time to assess her feelings of guilt and discuss the matter with them personally. "So," she said, getting a word in before he could do likewise. "How is *he* doing?"

The glance away, coupled with scratching his eyebrow, implied Kline wasn't settled on whether to discuss the subject. He looked up after not too long, cleaning his teeth with his tongue before he opened his mouth. "From what I understand when the two officers arrived, he was screaming like a man who bet his house on red and lost. Not much has changed in the past week. He's still carrying on about a married couple harassing him. Really, it's gotten worse. He's got this three-parallel-line tattoo on his thigh. He keeps picking at it. Thrashing himself into bruises and flinging himself around. Saying it's *them* attacking him. We moved him around, but it didn't help."

Claire flung her arms in the air. "Wait. He's acting that recklessly and still in a jail cell? He needs psychiatric attention."

Hands held up from Kline asked her to calm down. "He's under sedation after the last episode. I haven't checked on him since, but he should be fine. The real issue is that this is going to improve the odds for an insanity deal."

Not an issue at all. Him in a supervised psychiatric ward benefited everyone. Assuming he survived that long. "What medicine did you give him?"

"Not my field."

"Whatever it is, let me know if it doesn't work. I have a regimen I can send over." It seemed reasonable what worked for Emmy Nelson would work for her son. In fact, she'd send it Kline's way regardless of whether he asked. Because he probably wouldn't.

"Sure." His dismissive tone all but confirmed her theory. "Back to his sanity. Was he off-kilter before the police arrived?"

"No. Other than pointing a gun at me, he seemed fine until the police entered the house." Before Kline flipped his notes to the next page, she added, "I don't mean he was mentally sound, just that he wasn't claiming anything was attacking him at the time. He acted on edge throughout our conversation. He sounded delusional when describing how I wronged him," she said, air quoting, "Like his sisters."

Kline tapped his chin with the butt of his pen. "I looked into his family tragedies. It's improbable he mentioned his sisters coincidentally, especially given the conversation you had with his mother." He flicked the pen in front of Claire's face like a tape recorder. "So he's a psychopath?"

"I don't believe so. Psychopaths rarely suffer from hallucinations and are generally grounded in reality. He could have killed me, or worse. Instead, he lectured me for a half-hour about his sisters stealing his mother until he ran into the other room. That's when I called the police."

"So he forced you into his house with a gun, ranted for a bit, then fled the room. He had to know you'd use your phone. Why, in your professional opinion, do you think he left you unsupervised?"

Hypnosis wasn't the answer he wanted to hear, if he even believed her. She barely did herself. Her ploy had worked, but she hadn't factored in a new batch of cursed trinkets. If not for Ryan's attachment to his father's watch, it might be her begging for death. More importantly, this opened the opportunity to steer the detective toward accepting Ryan's mental illness. "He has a fascination with his mother. The detailed symbology in the master bedroom speaks to a form of perceived intricate interactions with her. I imagine he felt called there, forgetting everything in the present. In short, compulsion drove him rather than rational thought." A partial truth.

"Interesting. Well, that fills in the missing details. Do you mind if I stop by again? I prefer talking in person. This will be a tricky case to work, and with his family history, I expect to unpack a lot of secrets."

He had no idea. "Sure, as long as you call ahead. I'm a little apprehensive about people suddenly showing up."

Kline nodded. "Right." He jotted down one last series of notes and opened his suit jacket to tuck the notepad away. "One last thing. Where's Mrs. Cathell's letter? I'll need it back with the suspect in custody."

Dropping ashes in his hand likely wouldn't help. Claire stuttered, "I don't know where it is." She looked down, half her face scrunched in pretending to recall its placement. She shook her head. "I'm sorry."

Breath funneled out of a slit in Kline's lips. "I don't believe you, but somehow your answer doesn't surprise me. There's something weird, something off about this case." He slapped the back of his hand into his palm. "But I don't need to know what it is, as long as Nelson ends up behind bars."

"Or an institution," suggested Claire.

Kline snorted. "That's a consolation prize."

"It's not." Claire crossed her arms. "He needs help. Possibly for the rest of his life. I think it's safer for him and everyone else that he gets professional support."

"We'll see about that, but if his lawyer gets him on the streets by the margin of a sheet of paper, our future conversations will be a lot less pleasant."

"We might disagree on his best method of sentencing, and you might not believe what happened with the letter, but . . ." Claire slipped out a crossed arm to reach behind her head. She tugged on long strands of hair and steadied her gaze. "Know that I want him put away more than you do."

The two of them engaged in a staring match like children discovering the contest for the first time. Kline blinked first, granting her an indifferent, "I'll bet. Let's assume it'll all work out for the best then." He opened his hand, proffering an invisible peace offering. "I'll let you know when the trial date's been set. We're still turning his house over for evidence."

Claire jabbed the floor of her mouth with her tongue. Guess they weren't waiting for formal charges. It was now or never then. "Did you happen to find a black lockbox?"

"There was something about one in the report. Why?"

"I believe it's mine. It has some family mementos in it. I thought I had misplaced it. When things calmed down I started searching for it without any luck. I'm wondering if when I heard Ryan," Claire paused to scrape the nastiness of his name off her tongue, "in my house, he snatched it."

Narrowed eyes threatened to resume their staring contest. After loosening tense facial muscles, he said, "Can you prove it's yours?"

"I've got the key. If it doesn't fit, then I guess it's not the same box. Assuming he didn't take anything out, I can tell you its contents including the model year of the watch inside." Or she could once she figured out Ryan's birth year.

"So you didn't report it as stolen initially, but instead waited until the week after visiting his house to say something. Is that right?"

Claire feigned insult. "I don't know what you're implying, but yeah, I've been a little busy. Trying to avoid getting killed by a lunatic while helping my patients avoid the same fate ate up most of my time."

"Here's what I'll do," Kline sighed. His hands pushed aside his suit jacket to rest on his hips. "You show me the key fits. If it does, we'll take a few pictures then lock it back up and keep it in my desk. Once the trial wraps up, and I know I won't need anything in there, you can have it."

The warning from Dr. Ingetti regarding digital photography entered her psyche. "Are those pictures uploaded anywhere? Or stored in a database?" Hearing her frazzled voice, she forced enunciation to slow her follow-up. "I have a thing about broadcasting my belongings."

"Why does that not surprise me?" Kline met her silence with a dose of his own, shaking his head when she proved unwilling to elaborate. "We store everything on a computer with some backups. No one's going to see a thing."

Claire started to counter and blinked, realizing she lacked a solid reason to convince him to do otherwise. *I've done what I can,* she told herself, almost content by the time Kline offered his own consolation.

"Regardless, it's not as if the box will do any good in that house."

"What do you mean?"

The smirk on his face irritated her as much as Amy's unannounced arrivals. "If he goes to jail or even an institution, you can bet the house won't stick around. It's in his mom's name. The state will sell it and put it toward her care at St. Mary's. And when houses in that neighborhood get sold, buyers demolish and rebuild."

"I see. Well, as long as nobody touches anything in the box, your plan sounds fine. I wasn't doing anything with the trinkets inside except appeasing my mom's memory by keeping them around. I don't know how else to prove to you what's mine."

"I don't need you to do anything else. I'm only keeping it in case my gut about you is wrong, so that I'm not giving up more evidence that'll disappear. As long as we lock away a dangerous man, whatever you're hiding from me can stay hidden. Maybe you even have a legitimate reason for it."

Claire kneaded above her shoulder blade. "Is that all? I do have an unattended child inside."

"That's all." He smirked. "Have a nice evening, Dr. Rossi." He waved, and without waiting for a response, strolled to his car.

When Claire opened the front door, Brad was whirring and blasting to the motions of toys colliding with one another. He dropped them when she entered, bouncing plastic off the floor. Hopefully not denting the floorboards.

"Sorry, Dr. Rossi. Was I being too loud?" Brad asked.

"A little, but that's okay this time. Why don't you tell me about what's happening with all of . . ." Claire circled her finger at the pile of figures on her floor. "This."

Absurd tales of heroism and villainy rolled off Brad's tongue like water down a cliff. They were the kinds of tales that only a child concocted. It held little interest for Claire, but it made Brad smile and provided a distraction from the gnawing sensation in her gut. Would Ryan weasel his way out of the charges? Would Kline turn on her? Until a jury announced its verdict, she had no choice but to wait and see.

EPILOGUE

Four months later, one nagging sensation persisted in causing Claire periodic consternation. She couldn't place its source amid the positive resolutions which concluded her twisted fairy tale.

A judge had committed Ryan Nelson to the Colorado State Mental Health Center. Sedation and crazed antics left his testimony too unreliable to use during trial. His public defender had no problem bypassing the courtroom and getting him committed. To Claire's knowledge, they were still tinkering with his medication to allow some level of coherence but had yet to find any success. Detective Kline handed over the lockbox shortly after the committal. He opted against charging her with obstruction of evidence. Once confident no one would come asking for them, she carefully transferred the Nelson sisters' trinkets to a small winter bonfire. Every few weeks, she checked on the two still living but comatose sisters to see if the action had had any impact, without any success.

Brad celebrated his eighth birthday amid Amy Alba and her husband's trial separation. It meant Claire saw him more frequently, hitting her limits at times but redeemed by his budding interest in board games. His visits fulfilled any latent desire for motherhood, which made the email she received today even more bizarre.

After rushing home from a lunch with Jess and Robert at Quixotic Biscuits, Claire's shaking hands impeded her entry home. Keys jingled to the ground in her first attempt to open the lock. Three stabs later, she found her mark. She scanned the clean and organized living room, complete with a new solid oak coffee table. The laptop sat by itself on her desk, once the housing place for research into curses and tulpas. She had reopened her inquiries into the nature of tulpas after Jess offered her theory on Rick Novak's existence, but research turned up little more than what she already knew. The email from the evanescent man himself offered to change that.

Fingertips tapped the glass screen of her phone while she waited for the two-factor authorization code to arrive, one of her new security-inclined habits. She typed the code with one hand while transporting the laptop to her couch. Cushions sank at the corners as she nestled in to read the email, the computer's warmth heating her lap.

Sender: Rick Novak (richardalexnovak@gmail.com)

Subject: Like Mother, Like Daughter

Body: Hi Claire,

I'm not sure how long it's been since we've exchanged emails, but if you're receiving this it means it's been a while. I've updated this message a handful of times—mainly coming back to reschedule the send date. I've known for a couple of weeks that my time was limited. Sometimes what one says in the moment, is not meant for that moment.

Today is September 25, 2022. Your reading this suggests you've survived the ordeal which created me. I realized I existed as part of you before you did, despite my ephemeral nature. Though I'm gone, I like to think a piece of me will always live on with you. I always felt so connected to you when sending these emails. It was the only time you let me fully inhabit your body. It's funny thinking these daytime emails were composed in the dead of night, when you sleepwalked and dreamed of fictional events. I can't fathom anything more real. I imagine if you desired, you could bring me back, but I believe it would cause both of us pain. Sometimes words transcend time, and those are enough.

I also met your mom. Your version of her anyway. You're so very alike, in more ways than you imagine. Sometimes the subconscious knows what the conscious does not, but perhaps these are little details best left buried.

Goodbye,

Rick Novak

P.S. - If you want to keep moving forward, remember to fill up your tank with gas.

Whatever Rick was, his email and her lack of shock confirmed he and she were one. It seemed the sleepwalking which Jess had accused her of had turned out true. Claire must have corresponded with herself via email. Her mind inadvertently created a person to defend herself against Ryan's curse. Maybe she had picked something up from researching online, but maybe . . .

She stroked the meat of her thumb with the tip of her forefinger. Ideas swirled over the meaning of her mom's collective words of wisdom. Her voice had gone dormant following Ryan's sentencing, and Claire struggled to recall it once again. If she understood Rick's email—no, *her* email—then her mom had meant those malaphors for adult Claire, not college Claire. Clearly the intention was a guiding light, but how could her mom have known about the curse? Was the P.S. line another clue, or simply Rick reinforcing a tie between his ephemeral existence and Claire's mother?

The tangled weight of analysis muddled her brain. She shut her eyes to pick a starting point from which to unravel the chaos and opened them just as quickly.

"I'm not getting into that," muttered Claire. If she had learned anything from her experience, it was that the truth was never as clean as she once believed. She was missing something. She tried imagining the possibilities, but relaxation held a strong allure. For many, that meant giving in to the desire to rest. For Claire, it meant pulling up a list of America's top caverns for spelunking. She fired off a text to Jess with her top three choices, and only then did she sink into her blissful couch.

She didn't care which Jess picked. Didn't care whether she countered with suggestions of her own. Exploring tangible earth wherever it was—balancing her hands, feet, limbs, and body on physical rocky crags—meant an engagement with perceptible reality that she sorely missed.

Her imagination could wait.

ACKNOWLEDGMENTS

I want to thank everyone who finished reading this book in its early stages. You will likely have no idea who these people are, but without them, the book would have come out in far worse shape. So thank you to Rachel, Mike, Kevin, Mark, Paul, Lisa, Sara, Maddy, and Katie.

Additional thanks go out to numerous individuals throughout various friend circles and the Internet. These great folks provided feedback on individual chapters to shore up various scenes. They are too numerous (and in some cases, too anonymous) to list, but they all played a key role.

Last, but most certainly not least, thank *you* for supporting a debut author. This book has consumed a large portion of my life, and to experience that with you (however distant we may be) is pretty amazing. Bonus thanks to anyone who supports me through word of mouth, online reviews, or interacting with me via social media and my website.

As a proactive gift to show my appreciation, I will share my amazingly healthy and delicious breakfast that I eat every morning: ½ cup of oatmeal, 1 ½ cups of frozen berries (defrosted), 1 tablespoon of peanut butter (natural – oil separation is normal!), and some arbitrary amount of chocolate protein powder and cinnamon.

ABOUT THE AUTHOR

C.J. Weiss is a debut author from Austin, TX. Aside from reading and writing, he loves hiking, video games, traveling, and peanut butter. He's willing to try anything once—even writing an awkward "ABOUT THE AUTHOR" section. If you'd like to read more by him, you can get a free copy of his short story anthology *Control* by signing up for his newsletter at his website below.

cjweiss.com
twitter.com/_cjweiss
facebook.com/cjweisswrites